Dear Reader,

I can't believe that it has been thirty years since my first Long, Tall Texans book, *Calhoun*, debuted! The series was suggested by my former editor Tara Gavin, who asked if I might like to set stories in a fictional town of my own design. Would I! And the rest is history.

As the years went by, I found more and more sexy ranchers and cowboys to add to the collection. My readers (especially Amy!) found time to gift me with a notebook listing every single one of them, wives and kids and connections to other families in my own Texas town of Jacobsville. Eventually the town got a little too big for me, so I added another smaller town called Comanche Wells and began to fill it up, too.

You can't imagine how much pleasure this series has given me. I continue to add to the population of Jacobs County, Texas, and I have no plans to stop. Ever.

I hope all of you enjoy reading the Long, Tall Texans as much as I enjoy writing them. Thank you all for your kindness and loyalty and friendship. I am your biggest fan!

Love,

Diana Palmer

NEW YORK TIMES BESTSELLING AUTHOR

DIANA PALMER

LONG, TALL TEXANS:
Gabriel
Coltrain

Previously published as
Texas Born and *Coltrain's Proposal*

HARLEQUIN® SPECIAL RELEASE

ISBN-13: 978-1-335-00708-7

Long, Tall Texans: Gabriel/Coltrain

Copyright © 2019 by Harlequin Books S.A.

First published as Texas Born by Harlequin Books in 2014 and Coltrain's Proposal by Harlequin Books in 1995.

The publisher acknowledges the copyright holder of the individual works as follows:

Texas Born
Copyright © 2014 by Diana Palmer

Coltrain's Proposal
Copyright © 1995 by Diana Palmer

Recycling programs for this product may not exist in your area.

Printed in U.S.A.

www.Harlequin.com

CONTENTS

A prolific author of more than one hundred books, **Diana Palmer** got her start as a newspaper reporter. A *New York Times* bestselling author and voted one of the top ten romance writers in America, she has a gift for telling the most sensual tales with charm and humor. Diana lives with her family in Cornelia, Georgia. Visit her website at dianapalmer.com.

Books by Diana Palmer

Long, Tall Texans

Fearless

Heartless

Dangerous

Merciless

Courageous

Protector

Invincible

Untamed

Defender

Undaunted

The Wyoming Men

Wyoming Tough

Wyoming Fierce

Wyoming Bold

Wyoming Strong

Wyoming Rugged

Wyoming Brave

Morcai Battalion

The Morcai Battalion

The Morcai Battalion: The Recruit

The Morcai Battalion: Invictus

The Morcai Battalion: The Rescue

Visit the Author Profile page at Harlequin.com for more titles.

GABRIEL

For our friends Cynthia Burton and Terry Sosebee

CHAPTER ONE

MICHELLE GODFREY FELT the dust of the unpaved road all over her jeans. She couldn't really see her pants. Her eyes were full of hot tears. It was just one more argument, one more heartache.

Her stepmother, Roberta, was determined to sell off everything her father had owned. He'd only been dead for three weeks. Roberta had wanted to bury him in a plain pine box with no flowers, not even a church service. Michelle had dared her stepmother's hot temper and appealed to the funeral director.

The kindly man, a friend of her father's, had pointed out to Roberta that Comanche Wells, Texas, was a very small community. It would not sit well with the locals if Roberta, whom most considered an outsider, was disrespectful of the late Alan Godfrey's wishes that he be buried in the Methodist church cemetery beside his first wife. The funeral director was soft-spoken but eloquent. He also pointed out that the money Roberta would save with her so-called economy plans, would be a very small amount compared to the outrage she would provoke. If she planned to continue living in Jacobs County, many doors would close to her.

Roberta was irritated at the comment, but she had a shrewd mind. It wouldn't do to make people mad when she had many things to dispose of on the local

market, including some cattle that had belonged to her
late husband.

She gave in, with ill grace, and left the arrangements
to Michelle. But she got even. After the funeral, she
gathered up Alan's personal items while Michelle was
at school and sent them all to the landfill, including his
clothes and any jewelry that wasn't marketable.

Michelle had collapsed in tears. That is, until she
saw her stepmother's wicked smile. At that point, she
dried her eyes. It was too late to do anything. But one
day, she promised herself, when she was grown and no
longer under the woman's guardianship, there would
be a reckoning.

Two weeks after the funeral, Roberta came under
fire from Michelle's soft-spoken minister. He drove up
in front of the house in a flashy red older convertible,
an odd choice of car for a man of the cloth, Michelle
thought. But then, Reverend Blair was a different sort
of preacher.

She'd let him in, offered him coffee, which he refused politely. Roberta, curious because they never had
visitors, came out of her room and stopped short when
she saw Jake Blair.

He greeted her. He even smiled. They'd missed
Michelle at services for the past two weeks. He just
wanted to make sure everything was all right. Michelle didn't reply. Roberta looked guilty. There was
this strange rumor he'd heard, he continued, that Roberta was preventing her stepdaughter from attending
church services. He smiled when he said it, but there
was something about him that was strangely chilling
for a religious man. His eyes, ice-blue, had a look that
Roberta recognized from her own youth, spent follow-

ing her father around the casinos in Las Vegas, where he made his living. Some of the patrons had that same penetrating gaze. It was dangerous.

"But of course, we didn't think the rumor was true," Jake Blair continued with that smile that accompanied the unblinking blue stare. "It isn't, is it?"

Roberta forced a smile. "Um, of course not." She faltered, with a nervous little laugh. "She can go whenever she likes."

"You might consider coming with her," Jake commented. "We welcome new members in our congregation."

"Me, in a church?" She burst out laughing, until she saw the two bland faces watching her. She sounded defensive when she added, "I don't go to church. I don't believe in all that stuff."

Jake raised an eyebrow. He smiled to himself, as if at some private joke. "At some point in your life, I assure you, your beliefs may change."

"Unlikely," she said stiffly.

He sighed. "As you wish. Then you won't mind if my daughter, Carlie, comes by to pick Michelle up for services on Sunday, I take it?"

Roberta ground her teeth together. Obviously the minister knew that since Michelle couldn't drive, Roberta had been refusing to get up and drive her to church. She almost refused. Then she realized that it would mean she could have Bert over without having to watch for her stepdaughter every second. She pursed her lips. "Of course not," she assured him. "I don't mind at all."

"Wonderful. I'll have Carlie fetch you in time for

Sunday school each week and bring you home after church, Michelle. Will that work for you?"

Michelle's sad face lit up. Her gray eyes were large and beautiful. She had pale blond hair and a flawless, lovely complexion. She was as fair as Roberta was dark. Jake got to his feet. He smiled down at Michelle.

"Thanks, Reverend Blair," she said in her soft, husky voice, and smiled at him with genuine affection.

"You're quite welcome."

She walked him out. Roberta didn't offer.

He turned at the steps and lowered his voice. "If you ever need help, you know where we are," he said, and he wasn't smiling.

She sighed. "It's just until graduation. Only a few more months," she said quietly. "I'll work hard to get a scholarship so I can go to college. I have one picked out in San Antonio."

He cocked his head. "What do you want to do?"

Her face brightened. "I want to write. I want to be a reporter."

He laughed. "Not much money in that, you know. Of course, you could go and talk to Minette Carson. She runs the local newspaper."

She flushed. "Yes, sir," she said politely, "I already did. She was the one who recommended that I go to college and major in journalism. She said working for a magazine, even a digital one, was the way to go. She's very kind."

"She is. And so is her husband," he added, referring to Jacobs County sheriff Hayes Carson.

"I don't really know him. Except he brought his iguana to school a few years ago. That was really fascinating." She laughed.

Jake just nodded. "Well, I'll get back. Let me know if you need anything."

"I will. Thank you."

"Your father was a good man," he added. "It hurt all of us to lose him. He was one of the best emergency-room doctors we ever had in Jacobs County, even though he was only able to work for a few months before his illness forced him to quit."

She smiled sadly. "It was a hard way to go, for a doctor," she replied. "He knew all about his prognosis and he explained to me how things would be. He said if he hadn't been so stubborn, if he'd had the tests sooner, they might have caught the cancer in time."

"Young lady," Jake said softly, "things happen the way they're meant to. There's a plan to everything that happens in life, even if we don't see it."

"That's what I think, too. Thank you for talking to her," she added hesitantly. "She wouldn't let me learn how to drive, and Dad was too sick to teach me. I don't really think she'd let me borrow the car, even if I could drive. She wouldn't get up early for anything, especially on a Sunday. So I had no way to get to church. I've missed it."

"I wish you'd talked to me sooner," he said, and smiled. "Never mind. Things happen in their own time."

She looked up into his blue eyes. "Does it…get better? Life, I mean?" she asked with the misery of someone who'd landed in a hard place and saw no way out.

He drew in a long breath. "You'll soon have more control over the things that happen to you," he replied. "Life is a test, Michelle. We walk through fire. But there are rewards. Every pain brings a pleasure."

"Thanks."

He chuckled. "Don't let her get you down."

"I'm trying."

"And if you need help, don't hold back." His eyes narrowed and there was something a little chilling in them. "I have yet to meet a person who frightens me."

She burst out laughing. "I noticed. She's a horror, but she was really nice to you!"

"Sensible people are." He smiled like an angel. "See you."

He went down the steps two at a time. He was a tall man, very fit, and he walked with a very odd gait, light and almost soundless, as he went to his car. The vehicle wasn't new, but it had some kind of big engine in it. He started it and wheeled out into the road with a skill and smoothness that she envied. She wondered if she'd ever learn to drive.

She went back into the house, resigned to several minutes of absolute misery.

"You set that man on me!" Roberta raged. "You went over my head when I told you I didn't want you to bother with that stupid church stuff!"

"I like going to church. Why should you mind? It isn't hurting you…"

"Dinner was always late when you went, when your father was alive," the brunette said angrily. "I had to take care of him. So messy." She made a face. In fact, Roberta had never done a thing for her husband. She left it all to Michelle. "And I had to try to cook. I hate cooking. I'm not doing it. That's your job. So you'll make dinner before you go to church and you can eat when you get home, but I'm not waiting an extra hour to sit down to a meal!"

"I'll do it," Michelle said, averting her eyes.

"See that you do! And the house had better be spotless, or I won't let you go!"

She was bluffing. Michelle knew it. She was unsettled by the Reverend Blair. That amused Michelle, but she didn't dare let it show.

"Can I go to my room now?" she asked quietly.

Roberta made a face. "Do what you please." She primped at the hall mirror. "I'm going out. Bert's taking me to dinner up in San Antonio. I'll be very late," she added. She gave Michelle a worldly, patronizing laugh. "You wouldn't know what to do with a man, you little prude."

Michelle stiffened. It was the same old song and dance. Roberta thought Michelle was backward and stupid.

"Oh, go on to your room," she muttered. That wide-eyed, resigned look was irritating.

Michelle went without another word.

She sat up late, studying. She had to make the best grades she could, so that she could get a scholarship. Her father had left her a little money, but her stepmother had control of it until she was of legal age. Probably by then there wouldn't be a penny left.

Her father hadn't been lucid at the end because of the massive doses of painkillers he had to take for his condition. Roberta had influenced the way he set up his will, and it had been her own personal attorney who'd drawn it up for her father's signature. Michelle was certain that he hadn't meant to leave her so little. But she couldn't contest it. She wasn't even out of high school.

It was hard, she thought, to be under someone's thumb and unable to do anything you wanted to do. Roberta was always after her about something. She made fun of her, ridiculed her conservative clothes, made her life a daily misery But the reverend was right. One day, she'd be out of this. She'd have her own place, and she wouldn't have to ask Roberta even for lunch money, which was demeaning enough.

She heard a truck go along the road, and glanced out to see a big black pickup truck pass by. So he was back. Their closest neighbor was Gabriel Brandon. Michelle knew who he was.

She'd seen him for the first time two years ago, the last summer she'd spent with her grandfather and grandmother before their deaths. They'd lived in this very house, the one her father had inherited. She'd gone to town with her grandfather to get medicine for a sick calf. The owner of the store had been talking to a man, a very handsome man who'd just moved down the road from them.

He was very tall, muscular, without it being obvious, and he had the most beautiful liquid black eyes she'd ever seen. He was built like a rodeo cowboy. He had thick, jet-black hair and a face off of a movie poster. He was the most gorgeous man she'd ever seen in her life.

He'd caught her staring at him and he'd laughed. She'd never forgotten how that transformed his hard face. It had melted her. She'd flushed and averted her eyes and almost run out of the store afterward. She'd embarrassed herself by staring. But he was very good-looking, after all—he must be used to women staring at him.

She'd asked her grandfather about him. He hadn't said much, only that the man was working for Eb Scott, who owned a ranch near Jacobsville. Brandon was rather mysterious, too, her grandfather had mused, and people were curious about him. He wasn't married. He had a sister who visited him from time to time.

Michelle's grandfather had chided her for her interest. At fifteen, he'd reminded her, she was much too young to be interested in men. She'd agreed out loud. But privately she thought that Mr. Brandon was absolutely gorgeous, and most girls would have stared at him.

By comparison, Roberta's friend, Bert, always looked greasy, as if he never washed his hair. Michelle couldn't stand him. He looked at her in a way that made her skin crawl and he was always trying to touch her. She'd jerked away from him once, when he'd tried to ruffle her hair, and he made a big joke of it. But his eyes weren't laughing.

He made her uncomfortable, and she tried to stay out of his way. It would have been all right if he and Roberta didn't flaunt their affair. Michelle came home from school one Monday to find them on the sofa together, half-dressed and sweaty. Roberta had almost doubled up with laughter at the look she got from her stepdaughter as she lay half across Bert, wearing nothing but a lacy black slip.

"And what are you staring at, you little prude?" Roberta had demanded. "Did you think I'd put on black clothes and abandon men for life because your father died?"

"He's only been dead two weeks," Michelle had pointed out with choking pride.

"So what? He wasn't even that good in bed before he got sick," she scoffed. "We lived in San Antonio and he had a wonderful practice, he was making loads of money as a cardiologist. Then he gets diagnosed with terminal cancer and decides overnight to pull up stakes and move to this flea-bitten wreck of a town where he sets up a free clinic on weekends and lives on his pension and his investments! Which evaporated in less than a year, thanks to his medical bills," she added haughtily. "I thought he was rich...!"

"Yes, that's why you married him," Michelle said under her breath.

"That's the only reason I did marry him," she muttered, sitting up to light a cigarette and blow smoke in Michelle's direction.

She coughed. "Daddy wouldn't let you smoke in the house," she said accusingly.

"Well, Daddy's dead, isn't he?" Roberta said pointedly, and she smiled.

"We could make it a threesome, if you like," Bert offered, sitting up with his shirt half-off.

Michelle's expression was eloquent. "If I speak to my minister..."

"Shut up, Bert!" Roberta said shortly, and her eyes dared him to say another word. She looked back at Michelle with cold eyes and got to her feet. "Come on, Bert, let's go to your place." She grabbed him by the hand and had led him to the bedroom. Apparently their clothes were in there.

Disgusted beyond measure, Michelle went into her room and locked the door.

She could hear them arguing. A few minutes later they came back out.

"I won't be here for dinner," Roberta said.

Michelle didn't reply.

"Little torment," Roberta grumbled. "She's always

watching, always so pure and unblemished," she added harshly.

"I could take care of that," Bert said.

"Shut up!" Roberta said again. "Come on, Bert!"

Michelle could feel herself flushing with anger as she heard them go out the door. Roberta slammed it behind her.

Michelle had peeked out the curtains and watched them climb into Bert's low-slung car. He pulled out into the road.

She closed the curtains with a sigh of pure relief. Nobody knew what a hell those two made of her life. She had no peace. Apparently Roberta had been seeing Bert for some time, because they were obviously obsessed with each other. But it had come as a shock to walk in the door and find them kissing the day after Michelle's father was buried, to say nothing of what she'd just seen.

THE DAYS SINCE then had been tense and uncomfortable. The two of them made fun of Michelle, ridiculed the way she dressed, the way she thought. And Roberta was full of petty comments about Michelle's father and the illness that had killed him. Roberta had never even gone to the hospital. It had been Michelle who'd sat with him until he slipped away, peacefully, in his sleep.

She lay on her back and looked at the ceiling. It was only a few months until graduation. She made very good grades. She hoped Marist College in San Antonio would take her. She'd already applied. She was sweating out the admissions, because she'd have to have a scholarship or she couldn't afford to go. Not only that, she'd have to have a job.

She'd worked part-time at a mechanic's shop while

her father was alive. He'd drop her off after school and pick her up when she finished work. But his illness had come on quickly and she'd lost the job. Roberta wasn't about to provide transportation.

She rolled over restlessly. Maybe there would be something she could get in San Antonio, perhaps in a convenience store if all else failed. She didn't mind hard work. She was used to it. Since her father had married Roberta, Michelle had done all the cooking and cleaning and laundry. She even mowed the lawn.

Her father had seemed to realize his mistake toward the end. He'd apologized for bringing Roberta into their lives. He'd been lonely since her mother died, and Roberta had flattered him and made him feel good. She'd been fun to be around during the courtship—even Michelle had thought so. Roberta went shopping with the girl, praised her cooking, acted like a really nice person. It wasn't until after the wedding that she'd shown her true colors.

Michelle had always thought it was the alcohol that had made her change so suddenly for the worse. It wasn't discussed in front of her, but Michelle knew that Roberta had been missing for a few weeks, just before her father was diagnosed with cancer. And there was gossip that the doctor had sent his young wife off to a rehabilitation center because of a drinking problem. Afterward, Roberta hadn't been quite so hard to live with. Until they'd moved to Comanche Wells, at least.

Dr. Godfrey had patted Michelle on the shoulder only days before the cancer had taken a sudden turn for the worse and he was bedridden. He'd smiled ruefully.

"I'm very sorry, sweetheart," he'd told her. "If I could go back and change things…"

"I know, Daddy. It's all right."

He'd pulled her close and kissed her forehead. "You're like your mother. She took things to heart, too. You have to learn how to deal with unpleasant people. You have to learn not to take life so seriously…"

"Alan, are you ever coming inside?" Roberta had interrupted petulantly. She hated seeing her husband and her stepdaughter together. She made every effort to keep them apart. "What are you doing, anyway, looking at those stupid smelly cattle?"

"I'll be there in a moment, Roberta," he called back.

"The dishes haven't been washed," she told Michelle with a cold smile. "Your job, not mine."

She'd gone back inside and slammed the screen.

Michelle winced.

So did her father. He drew in a deep breath. "Well, we'll get through this," he said absently. He'd winced again, holding his stomach.

"You should see Dr. Coltrain," she remarked. Dr. Copper Coltrain was one of their local physicians. "You keep putting it off. It's worse, isn't it?"

He sighed. "I guess it is. Okay. I'll see him tomorrow, worrywart."

She grinned. "Okay."

TOMORROW HAD ENDED with a battery of tests and a sad prognosis. They'd sent him back home with more medicine and no hope. He'd lasted a few weeks past the diagnosis.

Michelle's eyes filled with tears. The loss was still new, raw. She missed her father. She hated being at the mercy of her stepmother, who wanted nothing more than to sell the house and land right out from under Michelle. In fact, she'd already said that as soon as the will went through probate, she was going to do exactly that.

Michelle had protested. She had several months of school to go. Where would she live?

That, Roberta had said icily, was no concern of hers. She didn't care what happened to her stepdaughter. Roberta was young and had a life of her own, and she wasn't going to spend it smelling cattle and manure. She was going to move in with Bert. He was in between jobs, but the sale of the house and land would keep them for a while. Then they'd go to Las Vegas where she knew people and could make their fortune in the casino.

Michelle had cocked her head and just stared at her stepmother with a patronizing smile. "Nobody beats the house in Las Vegas," she said in a soft voice.

"I'll beat it," Roberta snapped. "You don't know anything about gambling."

"I know that sane people avoid it," she returned.

Roberta shrugged.

THERE WAS ONLY one real-estate agent in Comanche Wells. Michelle called her, nervous and obviously upset.

"Roberta says she's selling the house," she began.

"Relax." Betty Mathers laughed. "She has to get the will through probate, and then she has to list the property. The housing market is in the basement right now, sweetie. She'd have to give it away to sell it."

"Thanks," Michelle said huskily. "You don't know how worried I was…" Her voice broke, and she stopped.

"There's no reason to worry," Betty assured her. "Even if she does leave, you have friends here. Somebody will take the property and make sure you have a place to stay. I'll do it myself if I have to."

Michelle was really crying now. "That's so kind…!"

"Michelle, you've been a fixture around Jacobs County since you were old enough to walk. You spent summers with your grandparents here and you were always doing things to help them, and other people. You spent the night in the hospital with the Harrises' little boy when he had to have that emergency appendectomy and wouldn't let them give you a dime. You baked cakes for the sale that helped Rob Meiner when his house burned. You're always doing for other people. Don't think it doesn't get noticed." Her voice hardened. "And don't think we aren't aware of what your stepmother is up to. She has no friends here, I promise you."

Michelle drew in a breath and wiped her eyes. "She thought Daddy was rich."

"I see," came the reply.

"She hated moving down here. I was never so happy," she added. "I love Comanche Wells."

Betty laughed. "So do I. I moved here from New York City. I like hearing crickets instead of sirens at night."

"Me, too."

"You stop worrying, okay?" she added. "Everything's going to be all right."

"I will. And thanks."

"No thanks necessary."

MICHELLE WAS TO remember that conversation the very next day. She got home from school that afternoon and her father's prized stamp collection was sitting on the coffee table. A tall, distinguished man was handing Roberta a check.

"It's a marvelous collection," the man said.

"What are you doing?" Michelle exclaimed, dropping her books onto the sofa, as she stared at the man with horror. "You can't sell Daddy's stamps! You can't! It's the only thing of his I have left that we both shared! I helped him put in those stamps, from the time I was in grammar school!"

Roberta looked embarrassed. "Now, Michelle, we've already discussed this…"

"We haven't discussed anything!" she raged, red-faced and weeping. "My father has only been dead three weeks and you've already thrown away every single thing he had, even his clothes! You've talked about selling the house… I'm still in school—I won't even have a place to live. And now this! You…you…mercenary gold digger!"

Roberta tried to smile at the shocked man. "I do apologize for my daughter…"

"I'm not her daughter! She married my father two years ago. She's got a boyfriend. She was with him while my father was dying in the hospital!"

The man stared at Michelle for a long moment, turned to Roberta, snapped the check out of her hands and tore it into shreds.

"But…we had a deal," Roberta stammered.

The man gave her a look that made her move back a step. "Madam, if you were kin to me, I would disown you," he said harshly. "I have no wish to purchase a collection stolen from a child."

"I'll sue you!" Roberta raged.

"By all means. Attempt it."

He turned to Michelle. "I am very sorry," he said gently. "For your loss and for the situation in which you find yourself." He turned to Roberta. "Good day."

He walked out.

Roberta gave him just enough time to get to his car. Then she turned to Michelle and slapped her so hard that her teeth felt as if they'd come loose on that side of her face.

"You little brat!" she yelled. "He was going to give me five thousand dollars for that stamp collection! It took me weeks to find a buyer!"

Michelle just stared at her, cold pride crackling around her. She lifted her chin. "Go ahead. Hit me again. And see what happens."

Roberta drew back her hand. She meant to do it. The child was a horror. She hated her! But she kept remembering the look that minister had given her. She put her hand down and grabbed her purse.

"I'm going to see Bert," she said icily. "And you'll get no lunch money from me from now on. You can mop floors for your food, for all I care!"

She stormed out the door, got into her car and roared away.

Michelle picked up the precious stamp collection and took it into her room. She had a hiding place that, hopefully, Roberta wouldn't be able to find. There was a loose baseboard in her closet. She pulled it out, slid the stamp book inside and pushed it back into the wall.

She went to the mirror. Her face looked almost blistered where Roberta had hit her. She didn't care. She had the stamp collection. It was a memento of happy times when she'd sat on her father's lap and carefully tucked stamps into place while he taught her about them. If Roberta killed her, she wasn't giving the stamps up.

But she was in a hard place, with no real way out. The months until graduation seemed like years. Roberta would make her life a living hell from now on because she'd opposed her. She was so tired of it. Tired of Roberta. Tired of Bert and his innuendoes. Tired of having to be a slave to her stepmother. It seemed so hopeless.

She thought of her father and started bawling. He was gone. He'd never come back. Roberta would torment her to death. There was nothing left.

She walked out the front door like a sleepwalker, out to the dirt road that led past the house. And she sat down in the middle of it—heartbroken and dusty with tears running down her cheeks.

CHAPTER TWO

MICHELLE FELT THE vibration of the vehicle before she smelled the dust that came up around it. Her back was to the direction it was coming from. Desperation had blinded her to the hope of better days. She was sick of life. Sick of everything.

She put her hands on her knees, brought her elbows in, closed her eyes, and waited for the collision. It would probably hurt. Hopefully, it would be quick…

There was a squealing of tires and a metallic jerk. She didn't feel the impact. Was she dead?

Long, muscular legs in faded blue denim came into view above big black hand-tooled leather boots.

"Would you care to explain what the hell you're doing sitting in the middle of a road?" a deep, angry voice demanded.

She looked up into chilling liquid black eyes and grimaced. "Trying to get hit by a car?"

"I drive a truck," he pointed out.

"Trying to get hit by a truck," she amended in a matter-of-fact tone.

"Care to elaborate?"

She shrugged. "My stepmother will probably beat me when she gets back home because I ruined her sale."

He frowned. "What sale?"

"My father died three weeks ago," she said heavily.

She figured he didn't know, because she hadn't seen any signs of life at the house down the road until she'd watched his truck go by just recently. "She had all his things taken to the landfill because I insisted on a real funeral, not a cremation, and now she's trying to sell his stamp collection. It's all I have left of him. I ruined the sale. The man left. She hit me…"

He turned his head. It was the first time he'd noticed the side of her face that looked almost blistered. His eyes narrowed. "Get in the truck."

She stared at him. "I'm all dusty."

"It's a dusty truck. It won't matter."

She got to her feet. "Are you abducting me?"

"Yes."

She sighed. "Okay." She glanced at him ruefully. "If you don't mind, I'd really like to go to Mars. Since I'm being abducted, I mean."

He managed a rough laugh.

She went around to the passenger side. He opened the door for her.

"You're Mr. Brandon," she said when he climbed into the driver's seat and slammed the door.

"Yes."

She drew in a breath. "I'm Michelle."

"Michelle." He chuckled. "There was a song with that name. My father loved it. One of the lines was 'Michelle, *ma belle*.'" He glanced at her. "Do you speak French?"

"A little," she said. "I have it second period. It means something like 'my beauty.'" She laughed. "And that has nothing to do with me, I'm afraid. I'm just plain."

He glanced at her with raised eyebrows. Was she serious? She was gorgeous. Young, and untried, but her creamy complexion was without a blemish. She was nicely shaped and her hair was a pale blond. Those soft gray eyes reminded him of a fog in August…

He directed his eyes to the road. She was just a child, what was he thinking? "Beauty, as they say, is in the eye of the beholder."

"Do you speak French?" she asked, curious.

He nodded. "French, Spanish, Portuguese, Afrikaans, Norwegian, Russian, German and a handful of Middle Eastern dialects."

"Really?" She was fascinated. "Did you work as a translator or something?"

He pursed his lips. "From time to time," he said, and then laughed to himself.

"Cool."

He started the truck and drove down the road to the house he owned. It wasn't far, just about a half mile. It was a ranch house, set back off the road. There were oceans of flowers blooming around it in the summer, planted by the previous owner, Mrs. Eller, who had died. Of course, it was still just February, and very cold. There were no flowers here now.

"Mrs. Eller loved flowers."

"Excuse me?"

"She lived here all her life," she told him, smiling as they drove up to the front porch. "Her husband worked as a deputy sheriff. They had a son in the military, but he was killed overseas. Her husband died soon afterward. She planted so many flowers that you could never even see the house. I used to come over and visit her when I was little, with my grandfather."

"Your people are from here?"

"Oh, yes. For three generations. Daddy went to medical school in Georgia and then he set up a practice in cardiology in San Antonio. We lived there. But I spent every summer here with my grandparents while they were alive. Daddy kept the place up, after, and it was like a vacation home while Mama was alive." She swallowed. That loss had been harsh. "We still had everything, even the furniture, when Daddy decided to move us down here and take early retirement. She hated it from the first time she saw it." Her face hardened. "She's selling it. My stepmother, I mean. She's already talked about it."

He drew in a breath. He knew he was going to regret this. He got out, opened the passenger door and waited for her to get out. He led the way into the house, seated her in the kitchen and pulled out a pitcher of iced tea. When he had it in glasses, he sat down at the table with her.

"Go ahead," he invited. "Get it off your chest."

"It's not your problem…"

"You involved me in an attempted suicide," he said with a droll look. "That makes it my problem."

She grimaced. "I'm really sorry, Mr. Brandon…"

"Gabriel."

She hesitated.

He raised an eyebrow. "I'm not that old," he pointed out.

She managed a shy smile. "Okay."

He cocked his head. "Say it," he said, and his liquid black eyes stared unblinking into hers.

She felt her heart drop into her shoes. She swallowed down a hot wave of delight and hoped it didn't show. "Ga… Gabriel," she obliged.

His face seemed to soften. Just a little. He smiled, showing beautiful white teeth. "That's better."

She flushed. "I'm not…comfortable with men," she blurted out.

His eyes narrowed on her face, her averted eyes. "Does your stepmother have a boyfriend?"

She swallowed, hard. The glass in her hand trembled.

He took the glass from her and put it on the table. "Tell me."

It all poured out. Finding Roberta in Bert's arms just after the funeral, finding them on the couch together that day, the way Bert looked and her and tried to touch her, the visit from her minister…

"And I thought my life was complicated," he said heavily. He shook his head. "I'd forgotten what it was like to be young and at the mercy of older people."

She studied him quietly. The expression on his face was…odd.

"You know," she said softly. "You understand."

"I had a stepfather," he said through his teeth. "He was always after my sister. She was very pretty, almost fourteen. I was a few years older, and I was bigger than he was. Our mother loved him, God knew why. We'd moved back to Texas because the international company he worked for promoted him and he had to go to Dallas for the job. One day I heard my sister scream. I went into her room, and there he was. He'd tried to…" He stopped. His face was like stone. "My mother had to get a neighbor to pull me off him. After that, after she knew what had been going on, she still defended him. I was arrested, but the public defender got an earful. He spoke to my sister. My stepfather was arrested, charged, tried. My mother stood by him, the whole time. My sister was victimized by the defense attorney, after what she'd already suffered at our stepfather's hands. She was so traumatized by the experience that she doesn't even date."

She winced. One small hand went shyly to cover his clenched fist on the table. "I'm so sorry."

He seemed to mentally shake himself, as if he'd been locked into the past. He met her soft, concerned gaze. His big hand turned, curled around hers. "I've never spoken of it, until now."

"Maybe sometimes it's good to share problems. Dark memories aren't so bad when you force them into the light."

"Seventeen going on thirty?" he mused, smiling at her. It didn't occur to her to wonder how he knew her age.

She smiled. "There are always people who are in worse shape than you are. My friend Billy has an alcoholic father who beats him and his mother. The police are over there all the time, but his mother will never press charges. Sheriff Carson says the next time, he's going to jail, even if he has to press charges himself."

"Good for the sheriff."

"What happened, after the trial?" she prodded gently.

He curled his fingers around Michelle's, as if he enjoyed their soft comfort. She might have been fascinated to know that he'd never shared these memories with any other woman, and that, as a rule, he hated having people touch him.

"He went to jail for child abuse," he said. "My mother was there every visiting day."

"No, what happened to you and your sister?"

"My mother refused to have us in the house with her. We were going to be placed in foster homes. The public defender had a maiden aunt, childless, who was suicidal. Her problems weren't so terrible, but she tended to depression and she let them take her almost over the edge. So he thought we might be able to help each other. We went to live with Aunt Maude." He chuckled. "She was not what you think of as anybody's maiden aunt. She drove a Jaguar, smoked like a furnace, could drink any grown man under the table, loved bingo parties and cooked like a gourmet. Oh, and she spoke about twenty languages. In her youth, she was in the army and mustered out as a sergeant."

"Wow," she exclaimed. "She must have been fascinating to live with."

"She was. And she was rich. She spoiled us rotten. She got my sister into therapy, for a while at least, and me into the army right after I graduated." He smiled. "She was nuts about Christmas. We had trees that bent at the ceiling, and the limbs groaned under all the decorations. She'd go out and invite every street person she could find over to eat with us." His face sobered. "She said she'd seen foreign countries where the poor were treated better than they were here. Ironically, it was one of the same people she invited to Christmas dinner who stabbed her to death."

She winced. "I'm so sorry!"

"Me, too. By that time, though, Sara and I were grown. I was in the…military," he said, hoping she didn't notice the involuntary pause, "and Sara had her own apartment. Maude left everything she had to the two of us and her nephew. We tried to give our share back to him, as her only blood heir, but he just laughed and said he got to keep his aunt for years longer because of us. He went into private practice and made a fortune defending drug lords, so he didn't really need it, he told us."

"Defending drug lords." She shook her head.

"We all do what we do," he pointed out. "Besides, I've known at least one so-called drug lord who was better than some upright people."

She just laughed.

He studied her small hand. "If things get too rough for you over there, let me know. I'll manage something."

"It's only until graduation this spring," she pointed out.

"In some situations, a few months can be a lifetime," he said quietly.

She nodded.

"Friends help each other."

She studied his face. "Are we? Friends, I mean?"

"We must be. I haven't told anyone else about my stepfather."

"You didn't tell me the rest of it."

His eyes went back to her hand resting in his. "He got out on good behavior six months after his conviction and decided to make my sister pay for testifying against him. She called 911. The police shot him."

"Oh, my gosh."

"My mother blamed both of us for it. She moved back to Canada, to Alberta, where we grew up."

"Are you Canadian?" she asked curiously.

He smiled. "I'm actually Texas born. We moved to Canada to stay with my mother's people when my father was in the military and stationed overseas. Sara was born in Calgary. We lived there until just after my mother married my stepfather."

"Did you see your mother again, after that?" she asked gently.

He shook his head. "Our mother never spoke to us again. She died a few years back. Her attorney tracked me down and said she left her estate, what there was of it, to the cousins in Alberta."

"I'm so sorry."

"Life is what it is. I had hoped she might one day realize what she'd done to my sister. She never did."

"We can't help who we love, or what it does to mess us up."

He frowned. "You really are seventeen going on thirty."

She laughed softly. "Maybe I'm an old soul."

"Ah. Been reading philosophy, have we?"

"Yes." She paused. "You haven't mentioned your father."

He smiled sadly. "He was in a paramilitary group overseas. He stepped on an antipersonnel mine."

She didn't know what a paramilitary group was, so she just nodded.

"He was from Dallas," he continued. "He had a small ranch in Texas that he inherited from his grandfather. He and my mother met at the Calgary Stampede. He trained horses and he'd sold several to be used at the stampede. She had an uncle who owned a ranch in Alberta and also supplied livestock to the stampede." He stared at her small hand in his. "Her people were French-Canadian. One of my grandmothers was a member of the Blackfoot Nation."

"Wow!"

He smiled.

"Then, you're an American citizen," she said.

"Our parents did the whole citizenship process. In

short, I now have both Canadian and American citizenship."

"My dad loved this Canadian television show, *Due South*. He had the whole DVD collection. I liked the Mountie's dog. He was a wolf."

He laughed. "I've got the DVDs, too. I loved the show. It was hilarious."

She glanced at the clock on the wall. "I have to go. If you aren't going to run over me, I'll have to fix supper in case she comes home to eat. It's going to be gruesome. She'll still be furious about the stamp collection." Her face grew hard. "She won't find it. I've got a hiding place she doesn't know about."

He smiled. "Devious."

"Not normally. But she's not selling Daddy's stamps."

He let go of her hand and got up from his chair. "If she hits you again, call 911."

"She'd kill me for that."

"Not likely."

She sighed. "I guess I could, if I had to."

"You mentioned your minister. Who is he?"

"Jake Blair. Why?"

His expression was deliberately blank.

"Do you know him? He's a wonderful minister. Odd thing, my stepmother was intimidated by him."

He hesitated, and seemed to be trying not to laugh. "Yes. I've heard of him."

"He told her that his daughter was going to pick me up and bring me home from church every week. His daughter works for the Jacobsville police chief."

"Cash Grier."

She nodded. "He's very nice."

"Cash Grier?" he exclaimed. "Nice?"

"Oh, I know people talk about him, but he came to speak to my civics class once. He's intelligent."

"Very."

He helped her back into the truck and drove her to her front door.

She hesitated before she got out, turning to him. "Thank you. I don't think I've ever been so depressed. I've never actually tried to kill myself before."

His liquid black eyes searched hers. "We all have days when we're ridden by the 'black dog.'"

She blinked. "Excuse me?"

He chuckled. "Winston Churchill had periods of severe depression. He called it that."

She frowned. "Winston Churchill…"

"There was this really big world war," he said facetiously, with over-the-top enthusiasm, "and this country called England, and it had a leader during—"

"Oh, give me a break!" She burst out laughing.

He grinned at her. "Just checking."

She shook her head. "I know who he was. I just had to put it into context is all. Thanks again."

"Anytime."

She got out and closed the door, noting with relief that Roberta hadn't come home yet. She smiled and waved. He waved back. When he drove off, she noticed that he didn't look back. Not at all.

SHE HAD SUPPER ready when Roberta walked in the door. Her stepmother was still fuming.

"I'm not eating beef," she said haughtily. "You know I hate it. And are those mashed potatoes? I'll bet you crammed them with butter!"

"Yes, I did," Michelle replied quietly, "because you always said you liked them that way."

Roberta's cheeks flushed. She shifted, as if the words, in that quiet voice, made her feel guilty.

In fact, they did. She was remembering her behavior with something close to shame. Her husband had only been dead three weeks. She'd tossed his belongings, refused to go to the funeral, made fun of her stepdaughter at every turn, even slapped her for messing up the sale of stamps which Alan had left to Michelle. And after all that, the child made her favorite food. Her behavior should be raising red flags, but her stepdaughter was, thankfully, too naive to notice it. Bert's doing, she thought bitterly. All his fault.

"You don't have to eat it," Michelle said, turning away.

Roberta made a rough sound in her throat. "It's all right," she managed tautly. She sat down at the table. She glanced at Michelle, who was dipping a tea bag in a cup of steaming water. "Aren't you eating?"

"I had soup."

Roberta made inroads into the meat loaf and mashed potatoes. The girl had even made creamed peas, her favorite.

She started to put her fork down and noticed her hand trembling. She jerked it down onto the wood and pulled her hand back.

It was getting worse. She needed more and more. Bert was complaining about the expense. They'd had a fight. She'd gone storming up to his apartment in San Antonio to cry on his shoulder about her idiot stepdaughter and he'd started complaining when she dipped into his stash. But after all, he was the one who'd gotten her hooked in the first place.

It had taken more money than she'd realized to keep up, and Alan had finally figured out what she was doing. They'd argued. He'd asked her for a divorce, but she'd pleaded with him. She had no place to go. She knew Bert wouldn't hear of her moving in with him. Her whole family was dead.

Alan had agreed, but the price of his agreement was that she had to move down to his hometown with him after he sold his very lucrative practice in San Antonio.

She'd thought he meant the move to be a temporary one. He was tired of the rat race. He wanted something quieter. But they'd only been in his old family homestead for a few days when he confessed that he'd been diagnosed with an inoperable cancer. He wanted to spend some time with his daughter before the end. He wanted to run a free clinic, to help people who had no money for doctors. He wanted his life to end on a positive note, in the place where he was born.

So here was Roberta, stuck after his death with a habit she could no longer afford and no way to break it. Stuck with Cinderella here, who knew about as much about life as she knew about men.

She glared at the girl. She'd really needed the money from those stamps. There was nothing left that she could liquidate for cash. She hadn't taken all of Alan's things to the landfill. She'd told Michelle that so she wouldn't look for them. She'd gone to a consignment shop in San Antonio and sold the works, even his watch. It brought in a few hundred dollars. But she was going through money like water.

"What did you do with the stamps?" Roberta asked suddenly.

Michelle schooled her features to give away nothing, and she turned. "I hitched a ride into town and asked Cash Grier to keep them for me."

Roberta sucked in her breath. Fear radiated from her. "Cash Grier?"

Michelle nodded. "I figured it was the safest place. I told him I was worried about someone stealing them while I was at school."

Which meant she hadn't told the man that Roberta had slapped her. Thank God. All she needed now was an assault charge. She had to be more careful. The girl was too stupid to recognize her symptoms. The police chief wouldn't be. She didn't want anyone from law enforcement on the place. But she didn't even have the grace to blush when Michelle made the comment about someone possibly "stealing" her stamp collection.

She got up from the table. She was thirsty, but she knew it would be disastrous to pick up her cup of coffee. Not until she'd taken what she needed to steady her hands.

She paused on her way to the bathroom, with her back to Michelle. "I'm… I shouldn't have slapped you," she bit off.

She didn't wait for a reply. She was furious with herself for that apology. Why should the kid's feelings matter to her, anyway? She pushed away memories of how welcoming Michelle had been when she first started dating Alan. Michelle had wanted to impress her father's new friend.

Well, that was ancient history now. She was broke and Alan had died, leaving her next to nothing. She picked up her purse from the side table and went into the bathroom with it.

Michelle cleaned off the table and put the dishes into the dishwasher. Roberta hadn't come out of the bathroom even after she'd done all that, so she went to her room.

MICHELLE HAD BEEN surprised by the almost-apology. But once she thought about it, she realized that Roberta might think she was going to press charges. She was afraid of her stepmother. She had violent mood swings and she'd threatened to hit Michelle several times.

It was odd, because when she'd first married Dr. Alan Godfrey, Michelle had liked her. She'd been fun to be around. But she had a roving eye. She liked men. If they went to a restaurant, someone always struck up a conversation with Roberta, who was exquisitely groomed and dressed and had excellent manners. Roberta enjoyed masculine attention, without being either coarse or forward.

Then, several months ago, everything had changed. Roberta had started going out at night alone. She told her husband that she'd joined an exercise club at a friend's house, a private one. They did aerobics and Pilates and things like that. Just women.

But soon afterward, Roberta became more careless about her appearance. Her manners slipped, badly. She complained about everything. Alan wasn't giving her enough spending money. The house needed cleaning, why wasn't Michelle doing more when she wasn't in school? She wasn't doing any more cooking, she didn't like it, Michelle would have to take over for her. And on it went. Alan had been devastated by the change.

So had Michelle, who had to bear the brunt of most of Roberta's fury.

"Some women have mood swings as they get older," Alan had confided to his daughter, but there was something odd in his tone of voice. "But you mustn't say anything about it to her. She doesn't like thinking she's getting on in years. All right?"

"All right, Daddy," she'd agreed, with a big smile.

He'd hugged her close. "That's my girl."

ROBERTA HAD GONE away for a few weeks after that. Then, not too long after her return, they'd moved to Comanche Wells, into the house where Michelle had spent so many happy weeks with her grandparents every summer.

The elderly couple had died in a wreck only a few years after Michelle's mother had died of a stroke. It had been a blow. Her father had gone through terrible grief. But then, so had Michelle.

Despite the double tragedy, Comanche Wells and this house seemed far more like home than San Antonio ever had, because it was so small that Michelle knew almost every family who lived in it. She knew people in Jacobsville, too, of course, but it was much larger. Comanche Wells was tiny by comparison.

Michelle loved the farm animals that her grandparents had kept. They always had dogs and cats and chickens for her to play with. But by the time Alan moved his family down here, there was only the small herd of beef cattle. Now the herd had been sold and was going to a local rancher who was going to truck the steers over to his own ranch.

Her door opened suddenly. Roberta looked wild-eyed. "I'm going back up to San Antonio for the night. I have to see Bert."

"All…" She had started to say "all right," but the door slammed. Roberta went straight out to her car, revved it up and scattered gravel on the way to the road.

It was odd behavior, even for her.

Michelle felt a little better than she had. At least she and Roberta might be able to manage each other's company until May, when graduation rolled around.

But Gabriel had helped her cope with what she thought was unbearable. She smiled, remembering his kindness, remembering the strong, warm clasp of his fingers. Her heart sailed at the memory. She'd almost never held hands with a boy. Once, when she was twelve, at a school dance. But the boy had moved away, and she was far too shy and old-fashioned to appeal to most of the boys in her high school classes. There had been another boy, at high school, but that date had ended in near disaster.

Gabriel was no boy. He had to be at least in his midtwenties. He would think of her as a child. She grimaced. Well, she was growing up. One day…who knew what might happen?

She opened her English textbook and got busy with her homework. Then she remembered with a start what she'd told Roberta, that lie about having Cash Grier keep the stamp book. What if Roberta asked him?

Her face flamed. It would be a disaster. She'd lied, and Roberta would know it. She'd tear the house apart looking for that collection…

Then Michelle calmed down. Roberta seemed afraid of Cash Grier. Most people were. She doubted very seriously that her stepmother would approach him. But just to cover her bases, she was going to stop by his office after school. She could do it by pretending to ask Carlie what time she would pick her up for church services. Then maybe she could work up the nerve to tell him what she'd done. She would go without lunch. That would give her just enough money to pay for a cab home from Jacobsville, which was only a few miles away. Good thing she already had her lunch money for the week, because Roberta had told her there wouldn't be any more. She was going to have to do without lunch from now on, apparently. Or get a job. And good luck to that, without a car or a driver's license.

She sighed. Her life was more complicated than it had ever been. But things might get better. Someday.

CHAPTER THREE

MICHELLE GOT OFF the school bus in downtown Jacobsville on Friday afternoon. She had to stop by the newspaper office to ask Minette Carson if she'd give her a reference for the scholarship she was applying for. The office was very close to police chief Grier's office, whom she also needed to see. And she had just enough money to get the local cab company to take her home.

Minette was sitting out front at her desk when Michelle walked in. She grinned and got up to greet her.

"How's school?" she asked.

"Going very well," Michelle said. "I wanted to ask if I could put you down as a reference. I'm applying for that journalism scholarship we spoke about last month, at Marist College in San Antonio."

"Of course you can."

"Thanks. I'm hoping I can keep my grades up so I'll have a shot at it."

"You'll do fine, Michelle. You have a way with words." She held up a hand when Michelle looked as if she might protest. "I never lie about writing. I'm brutally honest. If I thought you didn't have the skill, I'd keep my mouth shut."

Michelle laughed. "Okay. Thanks, then."

Minette perched on the edge of her desk. "I was

wondering if you might like to work part-time for me. After school and Saturday morning."

Michelle's jaw dropped. "You mean, work here?" she exclaimed. "Oh, my gosh, I'd love to!" Then the joy drained out of her face. "I can't," she groaned. "I don't drive, and I don't have cab fare home. I mean, I do today, but I went without lunch…" Her face flamed.

"Carlie lives just past you," she said gently. "She works until five. So do we. I know she'd let you ride with her. She works Saturday mornings, too."

The joy came back into her features. "I'll ask her!"

Minette chuckled. "Do that. And let me know."

"I will, I promise."

"You can start Monday, if you like. Do you have a cell phone?" Minette asked.

Michelle hesitated and shook her head with lowered eyes.

"Don't worry about it. We'll get you one."

"Oh, but…"

"I'll have you phoning around town for news. Junior reporter stuff," she added with a grin. "A cell's an absolute necessity."

"In that case, okay, but I'll pay you back."

"That's a deal."

"I'll go over and talk to Carlie."

"Stop back by and let me know, okay?"

"Okay!"

She didn't normally rush, but she was so excited that her feet carried her across the street like wings.

She walked into the police station. Cash Grier was perched on Carlie's desk, dictating from a paper he held in his hand. He stopped when he saw Michelle.

"Sorry," Michelle said, coloring. She clutched her

textbooks to her chest almost as a shield. "I just needed to ask Carlie something. I can come back later…"

"Nonsense," Cash said, and grinned.

She managed a shy smile. "Thanks." She hesitated. "I told a lie to my stepmother," she blurted out. "I think you should know, because it involved you."

His dark eyebrows arched. "Really? Did you volunteer me for the lead in a motion picture or something? Because I have to tell you, my asking price is extremely high…"

She laughed with pure delight. "No. I told her I gave you my father's stamp collection for safekeeping." She flushed again. "She was going to sell it. She'd already thrown away all his stuff. He and I worked on the stamp collection together as long as I can remember. It's all I have left of him." She swallowed. Hard.

Cash got up. He towered over her. He wasn't laughing. "You bring it in here and I'll put it in the safe," he said gently. "Nobody will touch it."

"Thanks." She was trying not to cry. "That's so kind…"

"Now, don't cry or you'll have me in tears. What would people think? I mean, I'm a big, tough cop. I can't be seen standing around sobbing all over the place. Crime would flourish!"

That amused her. She stopped biting her lip and actually grinned.

"That's better." His black eyes narrowed quizzically. "Your stepmother seems to have some issues. I got an earful from your minister this morning."

She nodded sadly. "She was so different when we lived in San Antonio. I mean, we went shopping together, we took turns cooking. Then we moved down here and she got mixed up with that Bert person." She shivered. "He gives me cold chills, but she's crazy about him."

"Bert Sims?" Cash asked in a deceptively soft tone.

"That's him."

Cash didn't say anything else. "If things get rough over there, call me, will you? I know you're outside the city limits, but I can get to Hayes Carson pretty quick if I have to, and he has jurisdiction."

"Oh, it's nothing like that..."

"Isn't it?" Cash asked.

She felt chilled. It was as if he was able to see Roberta through her eyes, and he saw everything.

"She did apologize. Sort of. For hitting me, I mean."

"Hitting you?" Cash stood straighter. "When?"

"I messed up the sale of Daddy's stamps. She was wild-eyed and screaming. She just slapped me, is all. She's been excitable since before Daddy died, but now she's just...just...nuts. She talks about money all the time, like she's dying to get her hands on some. But she doesn't buy clothes or cosmetics, she doesn't even dress well anymore."

"Do you know why?"

She shook her head. She drew in a breath. "She doesn't drink," she said. "I know that's what you're thinking. She and Daddy used to have drinks every night, and she had a problem for a little while, but she got over it."

Cash just nodded. "You let me know if things get worse. Okay?"

"Okay, Chief. Thanks," she added.

The phone rang. Carlie answered it. "It's your wife," she said with a big grin.

Cash's face lit up. "Really? Wow. A big-time movie

star calling me up on the phone. I'm just awed, I am."
He grinned. Everybody knew his wife, Tippy, had been
known as the Georgia Firefly when she'd been a super-
model and, later, an actress. "I'll take it in my office.
With the door closed." He made a mock scowl. "And
no eavesdropping."

Carlie put her hand over her heart. "I swear."

"Not in my office, you don't," he informed her.
"Swearing is a misdemeanor."

She stuck out her tongue at his departing back.

"I saw that," he said without looking behind him.
He went into his office and closed the door on two gig-
gling women.

"He's a trip to work for," Carlie enthused, her green
eyes sparkling in a face framed by short, dark, wavy
hair. "I was scared to death of him when I interviewed
for the job. At least, until he accused me of hiding his
bullets and telling his men that he read fashion magazines in the bathroom."

Michelle laughed.

"He's really funny. He says he keeps files on aliens
in the filing cabinet and locks it so I won't peek." The
smile moderated. "But if there's an emergency, he's the
toughest guy I've ever known. I would never cross him,
if I was a criminal."

"They say he chased a speeder all the way to San
Antonio once."

She laughed. "That wasn't the chief. That was Kilraven, who worked here undercover." She leaned forward. "He really belongs to a federal agency. We're not
supposed to mention it."

"I won't tell," Michelle promised.

"However, the chief—" she nodded toward his closed

door "—got on a plane to an unnamed foreign country, tossed a runaway criminal into a bag and boated him to Miami. The criminal was part of a drug cartel. He killed a small-town deputy because he thought the man was a spy. He wasn't, but he was just as dead. Then the feds got involved and the little weasel escaped into a country that didn't have an extradition treaty with us. However, once he was on American soil, he was immediately arrested by Dade County deputies." She grinned. "The chief denied ever having seen the man, and nobody could prove that it was him on the beach. And," she added darkly, "you never heard that from me. Right?"

"Right!"

Carlie laughed. "So what can I do for you?"

"I need a ride home from work."

"I've got another hour to go, but…"

"Not today," Michelle said. "Starting Monday. Minette Carson just offered me a part-time job, but I don't have a way to get home. And she said I could work part-time Saturday, but I can't drive and I don't have a car."

"You can ride with me, and I'd welcome the company," Carlie said easily.

"I'll chip in for the gas."

"That would really help! Have you seen what I drive?" She groaned. "My dad has this thing about cars. He thinks you need an old truck to keep you from speeding, so he bought me a twelve-year-old tank. At least, it looks like a tank." She frowned. "Maybe it was a tank and he had it remodeled. Anyway, it barely gets twelve miles to a gallon and it won't go over fifty." She shook her head. "He drives a vintage Ford Cobra," she added with a scowl. "One of the neatest rides on the planet and I'm not allowed to touch it, can you believe that?"

Michelle just grinned. She didn't know anything about cars. She did recall the way the minister had peeled out of the driveway, scattering gravel. That car he drove had one big engine.

"Your dad scared my stepmother." Michelle laughed. "She wasn't letting me go to church. Your dad said I could ride with you." She stopped and flushed. "I really feel like I'm imposing. I wish I could drive. I wish I had a car…"

"It's really not imposing," Carlie said softly, smiling. "As I said, I'd like the company. I go down lots of back roads getting here from Comanche Wells. I'm not spooky or anything, but this guy did try to kill my Dad with a knife." She lowered her eyes. "I got in the way."

Michelle felt guilty that she hadn't remembered. "I'll learn karate," she promised. "We can go to a class together or something, and if anybody attacks us we can fight back!"

"Bad idea," Cash said, rejoining them. "A few weeks of martial arts won't make you an expert. Even an expert," he added solemnly, "knows better than to fight if he can get away from an armed man."

"That isn't what the ads say," Carlie mused, grinning.

"Yes, I know," Cash replied. "Take it from me, disarming someone with a gun is difficult even for a black belt." He leaned forward. "Which I am."

Carlie stood up, bowed deeply from the waist, and said, "Sensei!" Cash lost it. He roared with laughter.

"You could teach us," Michelle suggested. "Couldn't you?"

Cash just smiled. "I suppose it wouldn't hurt. Just a

few basics for an emergency. But if you have an armed opponent, you run," he said firmly. "Or if you're cornered, scream, make a fuss. Never," he emphasized, "get into a car with anyone who threatens to kill you if you don't. Once he's got you in a car, away from help, you're dead, anyway."

Michelle felt chills run down her spine. "Okay."

Carlie looked uncomfortable. She knew firsthand about an armed attacker. Unconsciously, she rubbed the shoulder where the knife had gone in. She'd tried to protect her father. Her assailant had been arrested, but had died soon afterward. She never knew why her father had been the target of an attack by a madman.

"Deep thoughts?" Michelle asked her.

She snapped back. "Sorry. I was remembering the guy who attacked my father." She frowned. "What sort of person attacks a minister, for goodness' sake!"

"Come on down to federal lockup with me, and I'll show you a baker's dozen who have," Cash told her. "Religious arguments quite often lead to murder, even in families. That's why," he added, "we don't discuss politics or religion in the office." He frowned. "Well, if someone died in here, we'd probably say a prayer. And if the president came to see me, and why wouldn't he, we'd probably discuss his foreign policy."

"Why would the president come to see you?" Michelle asked innocently.

Cash pursed his lips. "For advice, of course. I have some great ideas about foreign policy."

"For instance?" Carlie mused.

"I think we should declare war on Tahiti."

They both stared at him.

"Well, if we do, we can send troops, right?" he continued. "And what soldier in his right mind wouldn't want to go and fight in Tahiti? Lush tropical flowers, fire-dancing, beautiful women, the ocean..."

"Tahiti doesn't have a standing army, I don't think," Michelle ventured.

"All the better. We can just occupy it for like three weeks, let them surrender, and then give them foreign aid." He glowered. "Now you've done it. You'll repeat that everywhere and the president will hear about it and he'll never have to come and hear me explain it. You've blown my chances for an invitation to the White House," he groaned. "And I did so want to spend a night in the Lincoln bedroom!"

"Listen, break out those files on aliens that you keep in your filing cabinet and tell the president you've got them!" Carlie suggested, while Michelle giggled. "He'll come right down here to have a look at them!"

"They won't let him," Cash sighed. "His security clearance isn't high enough."

"What?" Carlie exclaimed.

"Well, he's only in the office for four years, eight tops. So the guys in charge of the letter agencies—the really secretive ones—allegedly keep some secrets to themselves. Particularly those dealing with aliens." He chuckled.

The girls, who didn't know whether to believe him or not, just laughed along with him.

MICHELLE STOPPED BACK by Minette's office to tell her the good news, and to thank her again for the job.

"You know," she said, "Chief Grier is really nice."

"Nice when he likes you," Minette said drily. "There

are a few criminals in maximum-security prisons who might disagree."

"No doubt there."

"So, will Monday suit you, to start to work?" Minette asked.

"I'd really love to start yesterday." Michelle laughed. "I'm so excited!"

Minette grinned. "Monday will come soon enough. We'll see you then."

"Can you write me a note? Just in case I need one?" She was thinking of how to break it to Roberta. That was going to be tricky.

"No problem." Minette went to her desk, typed out an explanation of Michelle's new position, and signed it. She handed it to the younger woman. "There you go."

"Dress code?" Michelle asked, glancing around the big open room where several people were sitting at desks, to a glass-walled room beyond in which big sheets of paper rested on a long section like a chalkboard.

"Just be neat," Minette said easily. "I mostly kick around in jeans and T-shirts, although I dress up when I go to political meetings or to interviews with state or federal politicians. You'll need to learn how to use a camera, as well. We have digital ones. They're very user-friendly."

"This is very exciting," Michelle said, her gray eyes glimmering with delight.

Minette laughed. "It is to me, too, and I've done this since I was younger than you are. I grew up running around this office." She looked around with pure love in her eyes. "It's home."

"I'm really looking forward to it. Will I just be reporting news?"

"No. Well, not immediately, at least. You'll learn every aspect of the business, from selling ads to typing copy to composition. Even subscriptions." She leaned forward. "You'll learn that some subscribers probably used to be doctors, because the handwriting looks more like Sanskrit than English."

Michelle chuckled. "I'll cope. My dad had the worst handwriting in the world."

"And he was a doctor," Minette agreed, smiling.

The smile faded. "He was a very good doctor," she said, trying not to choke up. "Sorry," she said, wiping away a tear. "It's still hard."

"It takes time," Minette said with genuine sympathy. "I lost my mother, my stepfather, my stepmother—I loved them all. You'll adjust, but you have to get through the grief process first. Tears are healing."

"Thanks."

"If you need to talk, I'm here. Anytime. Night or day."

Michelle wiped away more tears. "That's really nice of you."

"I know how it feels."

The phone rang and one of the employees called out. "For you, boss. The mayor returning your call."

Minette grimaced. "I have to take it. I'm working on a story about the new water system. It's going to be super."

"I'll see you after school Monday, then. And thanks again."

"My pleasure."

MICHELLE WENT HOME with dreams of journalism dancing in her head. She'd never been so happy. Things were really looking up.

She noted that Roberta's car was in the driveway and she mentally braced herself for a fight. It was suppertime and she hadn't been there to cook. She was going to be in big trouble.

Sure enough, the minute she walked in the door, Roberta threw her hands up and glared at her. "I'm not cooking," she said furiously. "That's your job. Where the hell have you been?"

Michelle swallowed. "I was in…in town."

"Doing what?" came the tart query.

She shifted. "Getting a job."

"A job?" She frowned, and her eyes didn't seem to quite focus. "Well, I'm not driving you to work, even if somebody was crazy enough to hire you!"

"I have a ride," she replied.

"A job," she scoffed. "As if you're ever around to do chores as it is. You're going to get a job? Who's going to do the laundry and the housecleaning and the cooking?"

Michelle bit her tongue, trying not to say what she was thinking. "I have to have money for lunch," she said, thinking fast.

Roberta blinked, then she remembered that she'd said Michelle wasn't getting any more lunch money. She averted her eyes.

"Besides, I have to save for college. I'll start in the fall semester."

"Jobs. College." Roberta looked absolutely furious. "And you think I'm going to stay down here in this hick town while you sashay off to college in some big city, do you?"

"I graduate in just over three months…"

"I'm putting the house on the market," Roberta shot back. She held up a hand. "Don't even bother arguing.

I'm listing the house with a San Antonio broker, not one from here." She gave Michelle a dirty look. "They're all on your side, trying to keep the property off the market. It won't work. I need money!"

For just one instant, Michelle thought about letting her have the stamps. Then she decided it was useless to do that. Roberta would spend the money and still try to sell the house. She comforted herself with what the local Realtor had told her—that it would take time for the will to get through probate. If there was a guardian angel, perhaps hers would drag out the time required for all that. And even then, there was a chance the house wouldn't sell.

"I don't imagine a lot of people want to move to a town this small," Michelle said out loud.

"Somebody local might buy it. One of those ranchers." She made it sound like a dirty word.

That made Michelle feel better. If someone from here bought the house, they might consider renting it to her. Since she had a job, thanks to Minette, she could probably afford reasonable rent.

Roberta wiped her face. She was sweating.

Michelle frowned. "Are you all right?"

"Of course I'm all right, I'm just hungry!"

"I'll make supper." She went to her room to put her books away and stopped short. The place was in shambles. Drawers had been emptied, the clothes from the shelves in the closet were tossed haphazardly all over the floor. Michelle's heart jumped, but she noticed without looking too hard that the baseboards in the closet were still where they should be. She looked around but not too closely. After all, she'd told Roberta that Chief Grier had her father's stamp collection. It hadn't stopped

Roberta from searching the room. But it was obvious that she hadn't found anything.

She went back out into the hall, where her stepmother was standing with folded arms, a disappointed look on her face. She'd expected that the girl would go immediately to where she'd hidden the stamps. The fact that she didn't even search meant they weren't here. Damn the luck, she really had taken them to the police chief. And even Roberta wasn't brash enough to walk up to Cash Grier and demand the stamp collection back, although she was probably within her legal rights to do so.

"Don't tell me," Michelle said, staring at her. "Squirrels?"

Roberta was disconcerted. Without meaning to, she burst out laughing at the girl's audacity. She turned away, shaking her head. "All right, I just wanted to make sure the stamp collection wasn't still here. I guess you were telling the truth all along."

"Roberta, if you need money so much, why don't you get a job?"

"I had a job, if you recall," she replied. "I worked in retail."

That was true. Roberta had worked at the cosmetics counter in one of San Antonio's most prestigious department stores.

"But I'm not going back to that," Roberta scoffed. "Once I sell this dump of a house, I'll be able to go to New York or Los Angeles and find a man who really is rich, instead of one who's just pretending to be," she added sarcastically.

"Gosh. Poor Bert," Michelle said. "Does he know?"

Roberta's eyes flashed angrily. "If you say a word to him…!"

Michelle held up both hands. "Not my business."

"Exactly!" Roberta snapped. "Now, how about fixing supper?"

"Sure," Michelle agreed. "As soon as I clean up my room," she added in a bland tone.

Her stepmother actually flushed. She took a quick breath. She was shivering. "I need…more…" she mumbled to herself. She went back into her own room and slammed the door.

THEY ATE TOGETHER, but Michelle didn't taste much of her supper. Roberta read a fashion magazine while she spooned food into her mouth.

"Where are you getting a job? Who's going to even hire a kid like you?" she asked suddenly.

"Minette Carson."

The magazine stilled in her hands. "You're going to work for a newspaper?"

"Of course. I want to study journalism in college."

Roberta looked threatened. "Well, I don't want you working for newspapers. Find something else."

"I won't," Michelle said firmly. "This is what I want to do for a living. I have to start somewhere. And I have to save for college. Unless you'd like to volunteer to pay my tuition…"

"Ha! Fat chance!" Roberta scoffed.

"That's what I thought. I'm going to a public college, but I still have to pay for books and tuition."

"Newspapers. Filthy rags." Her voice sounded slurred. She was picking at her food. Her fork was moving in slow motion. And she was still sweating.

"They do a great deal of good," Michelle argued. "They're the eyes and ears of the public."

"Nosy people sticking their heads into things that don't concern them!"

Michelle looked down at her plate. She didn't mention that people without things to hide shouldn't have a problem with that.

Roberta took her paper towel and mopped her sweaty face. She seemed disoriented and she was flushed, as well.

"You should see a doctor," Michelle said quietly. "There's that flu still going around."

"I'm not sick," the older woman said sharply. "And my health is none of your business!"

Michelle grimaced. She sipped milk instead of answering.

"It's too hot in here. You don't have to keep the thermostat so high!"

"It's seventy degrees," Michelle said, surprised. "I can't keep it higher or we couldn't afford the gas bill." She paid the bills with money that was grudgingly supplied by Roberta from the joint bank account she'd had with Michelle's father. Roberta hadn't lifted a finger to pay a bill since Alan had died.

"Well, it's still hot!" came the agitated reply. She got up from the table. "I'm going outside. I can't breathe in here."

Michelle watched her go with open curiosity. Odd. Roberta seemed out of breath and flushed more and more lately. She had episodes of shaking that seemed very unusual. She acted drunk sometimes, but Michelle knew she wasn't drinking. There was no liquor in the house. It probably was the flu. She couldn't understand why a person who was obviously sick wouldn't just go to the doctor in the first—

There was a loud thud from the general direction of the front porch.

CHAPTER FOUR

MICHELLE GOT UP from her chair and went out onto the porch. It sounded as if Roberta had flung a chair against the wall, maybe in another outburst of temper.

She opened the door and stopped. Roberta was lying there, on her back on the porch, gasping for breath, her eyes wide, her face horrified.

"It's all right, I'll call 911!" She ran for the phone and took it outside with her while she pushed in the emergency services number.

Roberta was grimacing. "The pain!" she groaned. "Hurts…so…bad! Michelle…!"

Roberta held out her hand. Michelle took it, held it, squeezed it comfortingly.

"Jacobs County 911 Center," came a gentle voice on the line. "Is this an emergency?"

"Yes. This is Michelle Godfrey. My stepmother is complaining of chest pain. She's short of breath and barely conscious."

"We'll get someone right out there. Stay on the line."

"Yes, of course."

"Help me," Roberta sobbed.

Michelle's hand closed tighter around her stepmother's. "The EMTs are on the way," she said gently. "It will be all right."

"Bert," Roberta choked. "Damn Bert! It's…his…fault!"

"Please don't try to get up," Michelle said, holding the older woman down. "Lie still."

"I'll…kill him," Roberta choked. "I'll kill him…!"

"Roberta, lie still," Michelle said firmly.

"Oh, God, it hurts!" Roberta sobbed. "My chest…my chest…!"

Sirens were becoming noticeable in the distance.

"They're almost there, dear," the operator said gently. "Just a few more minutes."

"Yes, I hear them," Michelle said. "She says her chest hurts."

There was muffled conversation in the background, on the phone.

Around the curve, the ambulance shot toward her leaving a wash of dust behind it. Roberta's grip on Michelle's hand was painful.

The older woman was white as a sheet. The hand Michelle was holding was cold and clammy. "I'm…sorry," Roberta bit off. Tears welled in her eyes. "He said it wasn't…pure! He swore…! It was too…much…" She gasped for breath. "Don't let Bert…get away…with it…" Her eyes closed. She shivered. The hand holding Michelle's went slack.

The ambulance was in the driveway now, and a man and a woman jumped out of it and ran toward the porch.

"She said her chest hurt." Michelle faltered as she got out of the way. "And she couldn't breathe." Tears were salty in her eyes.

Roberta had never been really kind to her, except at the beginning of her relationship with Michelle's father.

But the woman was in such pain. It hurt her to see anyone like that, even a mean person.

"Is she going to be all right?" Michelle asked.

They ignored her. They were doing CPR. She recognized it, because one of the Red Cross people had come to her school and demonstrated it. In between compressions one EMT ran to the truck and came back with paddles. They set the machine up and tried to restart Roberta's heart. Once. Twice. Three times. In between there were compressions of the chest and hurried communications between the EMTs and a doctor at the hospital.

After a few minutes, one EMT looked at the other and shook his head. They stood up. The man turned to Michelle. "I'm very sorry."

"Sorry. Sorry?" She looked down at the pale, motionless woman on the dusty front porch with a blank expression. "You mean, she's…?"

They nodded. "We'll call the coroner and have him come out, and we'll notify the sheriff's department, since you're outside the city limits. We can't move her until he's finished. Do you want to call the funeral home and make arrangements?"

"Yes, uh, yes." She pushed her hair back. She couldn't believe this. Roberta was dead? How could she be dead? She just stood there, numb, while the EMTs loaded up their equipment and went back out to the truck.

"Is there someone who can stay with you until the coroner gets here?" the female EMT asked softly, staring worriedly at Michelle.

She stared back at the woman, devoid of thought. Roberta was dead. She'd watched her die. She was in shock.

Just as the reality of the situation really started to hit

her, a pickup truck pulled up into the driveway, past the EMT vehicle, and stopped. A tall, good-looking man got out of it, paused to speak to the male EMT and then came right up to the porch.

Without a word, he pulled Michelle into his arms and held her, rocked her. She burst into tears.

"I'll take care of her," he told the female EMT with a smile.

"Thanks," she said. "She'll need to make arrangements…"

"I'll handle it."

"We've notified the authorities," the EMT added. "The sheriff's department and the coroner should arrive shortly." The EMTs left, the ambulance silent and grim now, instead of alive with light and sound, as when it had arrived.

Michelle drank in the scent that clung to Gabriel, the smells of soap and spicy cologne, the leather smell of his jacket. Beneath that, the masculine odor of his skin. She pressed close into his arms and let the tears fall.

ZACK TALLMAN ARRIVED just behind the coroner. Michelle noted the activity on the front porch, but she didn't want to see Roberta's body again. She didn't go outside.

She heard Gabriel and the lawman and the coroner discussing things, and there was the whirring sound a camera made. She imagined that they were photographing Roberta. She shivered. It was so sudden. They'd just had supper and Roberta went outside because she was hot. And then Roberta was dead. It didn't seem real, somehow.

A few minutes later, she heard the coroner's van

drive away. Gabriel and Zack Tallman came in together. Zack was handsome, tall, lean and good-looking. His eyes were almost as dark as Gabriel's, but he looked older than Gabriel did.

"The coroner thinks it was a heart attack," Zack was saying. "They'll have to do an autopsy, however. It's required in cases of sudden death."

"HAYES TOLD ME that Yancy Dean went back to Florida," Gabriel said. "He was the only investigator you had, wasn't he?"

"He was," Zack said, "so when he resigned, I begged Hayes on my knees for the investigator's position. It's a peach of a job."

"Pays about the same as a senior deputy," Gabriel mused, tongue in cheek.

"Yes, but I get to go to seminars and talk to forensic anthropologists and entomologists and do hard-core investigative work," he added. He chuckled. "I've been after Yancy's job forever. Not that he was bad at it—he was great. But his parents needed him in Florida and he was offered his old job back with Dade County SO," he added, referring to the sheriff's office.

"Well, it worked out for both of you, then," Gabriel said.

"Yes." He sobered as Michelle came into the living room from the kitchen. "Michelle, I'm sorry about your stepmother. I know it must be hard, coming so close on the heels of your father passing."

"Thanks, Mr. Tallman," she replied gently. "Yes, it is." She shook her head. "I still have to talk to the funeral director."

"I'll take care of that for you," Gabriel told her.

"Thanks," she added.

"Michelle, can you tell me how it happened?" Zack asked her.

"Of course." She went through the afternoon, ending with Roberta feeling too hot and going out on the porch to cool off.

He stopped her when she mentioned what Roberta had said about Bert and had her repeat Roberta's last words. He frowned. "I'd like to see her room."

Michelle led the way. The room was a mess. Roberta never picked anything up, and Michelle hadn't had time to do any cleaning. She was embarrassed at the way it looked. But Zack wasn't interested in the clutter. He started going through drawers until he opened the one in the bedside table.

He pulled out his digital camera and shot several photos of the drawer and its contents before he put on a pair of gloves, reached into it and pulled out an oblong case. He dusted the case for fingerprints before he opened it on the table and photographed that, too, along with a small vial of white powder. He turned to Gabriel who exchanged a long look with him.

"That explains a lot," Zack said. "I'll take this up to the crime lab in San Antonio and have them run it for us, but I'm pretty sure what it is and where she got it."

"What is it?" Michelle asked, curious.

"Something evil," Zack said.

Michelle wasn't dense. "Drugs," she said icily. "It's drugs, isn't it?"

"Hard narcotics," Zack agreed.

"That's why she was so crazy all the time," Michelle said heavily. "She drank to excess when we lived in San Antonio. Dad got her into treatment and made her quit. I was sure she was okay, because we didn't have any liquor here. But she had these awful mood swings, and sometimes she hit me. " She bit her lip.

"Well, people under the influence aren't easy to live with," Zack replied heavily. "Not at all."

ZACK SAT DOWN with Michelle and Gabriel at the kitchen table and questioned Michelle further about Roberta's recent routine, including trips to see Bert Sims in San Antonio. Roberta's last words were telling. He wrote it all down and gave Michelle a form to fill out with all the pertinent information about the past few hours. When she finished, he took it with him.

There was no real crime scene, since Roberta died of what was basically a heart attack brought on by a drug overdose. The coroner's assistant took photos on the front porch, adding to Zack's, so there was a record of where Roberta died. But the house wasn't searched, beyond Zack's thorough documentation of Roberta's room.

"Bert Sims may try to come around to see if Roberta had anything left, to remove evidence," Zack said solemnly to Michelle. "It isn't safe for you to be here alone."

"I've got that covered," Gabriel said with a smile. "Nobody's going to touch her."

Zack smiled. "I already had that figured out," he mused, and Gabriel cleared his throat.

"I have a chaperone in mind," Gabriel replied. "Just so you know."

Zack patted him on the back. "I figured that out already, too." He nodded toward Michelle. "Sorry again."

"Me, too," Michelle said sadly.

MICHELLE MADE COFFEE while Gabriel spoke to his sister, Sara, on the phone. She couldn't understand what he

was saying. He was speaking French. She recognized
it, but it was a lot more complicated than, "My brother
has a brown suit," which was about her level of skill
in the language.

His voice was low, and urgent. He spoke again, listened, and then spoke once more. *"C'est bien,"* he concluded, and hung up.

"That was French," Michelle said.

"Yes." He sat down at the table and toyed with the
thick white mug she'd put in front of him. There was
good china, too—Roberta had insisted on it when she
and Alan first married. But the mug seemed much more
Gabriel's style than fancy china. She'd put a mug at her
place, as well. She had to have coffee in the morning or
she couldn't even get to school.

"This morning everything seemed much less complicated," she said after she'd poured coffee. He refused
cream and sugar, and she smiled. She didn't take them,
either.

"You think you're going in a straight line, and life
puts a curve in the way," he agreed with a faint smile.
"I know you didn't get along with her. But she was part
of your family. It must sting a bit."

"It does," she agreed, surprised at his perception.
"She was nice to me when she and Daddy were dating,"
she added. "Taught me how to cook new things, went
shopping with me, taught me about makeup and stuff."
She grimaced. "Not that I ever wear it. I hate the way
powder feels on my face, and I don't like gunking up
my eyes and mouth with pasty cosmetics." She looked
at him and saw an odd expression on his face. "That
must sound strange…"

He laughed and sipped coffee before he spoke. "Actually, I was thinking how sane it sounded." He quietly studied her for a couple of moments. "You don't need makeup. You're quite pretty enough without it."

She gaped at him.

"Michelle, *ma belle,*" he said in an odd, soft, deep tone, and he smiled.

She went scarlet. She knew her heart was shaking her to death, that he could see it, and she didn't care. He was simply the most gorgeous man she'd ever seen, and he thought she was pretty. A stupid smile turned her lips up, elongating the perfect bow shape they made.

"Sorry," he said gently. "I was thinking out loud, not hitting on you. This is hardly the time."

"Would you like to schedule a time?" she asked with wide, curious eyes. "Because my education in that department is really sad. This one boy tried to kiss me and missed and almost broke my nose. After that, I didn't get another date until the junior prom." She leaned forward. "He was gay and so sweet and shy about it…well, he asked me and told me the reason very honestly. And I said I'd go with him to the prom because of the way my other date had ended. I mean, he wasn't likely to try to kiss me and break my nose and all… Why are you laughing?"

"Marshmallow," he accused, and his smile was full of affectionate amusement.

"Well, yes, I guess I am. But he's such a nice boy. Several of us know about him, but there are these two guys on the football squad that he's afraid of. They're always making nasty remarks to him. He thought if he went with a girl to a dance, they might back off."

"Did they?" he asked, curious.

"Yes, but not because he went with me," she said. She

glowered at the memory. "One of them made a nasty remark to him when we were dancing, next to the refreshment table, and I filled a big glass with punch and threw it in his face." She grinned. "I got in big trouble until the gym coach was told why I did it. His brother's gay." The grin got bigger. "He said next time I should use the whole pitcher."

He burst out laughing. "Well, your attitude toward modern issues is…unique. This is a very small town," he explained when her eyebrows went up.

"Oh, I see. You think we treat anybody different like a fungus." She nodded.

"Not exactly. But we hear things about small towns," he began.

"No bigots here. Well, except for Chief Grier."

He blinked. "Your police chief is a bigot?"

She nodded. "He is severely prejudiced against people from other planets. You should just hear him talk about how aliens are going to invade us one day to get their hands on our cows. He thinks they have a milk addiction, and that's why you hear about cattle mutilations… You're laughing again."

He wiped his eyes. She couldn't know that he rarely laughed. His life had been a series of tragedies. Humor had never been part of it. She made him feel light inside, almost happy.

"I can see the chief's point," he managed.

"Cow bigot," she accused, and he almost fell on the floor.

She wrapped her cold hands around her mug. "I guess I shouldn't be cracking jokes, with Roberta dead…" Her eyes burned with tears. "I still can't believe it. Roberta's gone. She's gone." She drew in a breath and sipped coffee. "We've done nothing but argue since Daddy died. But she wanted me to hold her hand and she was scared. She said she was sorry." She looked at him. "She said it was Bert's fault. Do you think she was delirious?"

"Not really," he replied quietly.

"Why?"

"That can wait a bit." He grew somber. "You don't have any other family?"

She shook her head. She looked around. "But surely I can stay here by myself? I mean, I'm eighteen now..."

He frowned. "I thought you were seventeen."

She hesitated. Her eyes went to the calendar and she grimaced. "I just turned eighteen. Today is my birthday," she said. She hadn't even realized it, she'd been so busy. Tears ran down her cheeks. "What an awful one this is."

He caught her hand in his and held it tight. "No cousins?"

She shook her head. "I have nobody."

"Not quite true. You have me," he said firmly. "And Sara's on her way down here."

"Sara. Your sister?"

He nodded.

"She'll stay with me?" she asked.

He smiled. "Not exactly. You'll stay with us, in my house. I won't risk your reputation by having you move in with just me."

"But...we're strangers," she pointed out.

"No, we're not," he said, and he smiled. "I told you about my stepfather. That's a memory I've never shared with anyone. And you won't mention it to Sara, right?"

"Of course not." She searched his black eyes. "Why would you do this for me?"

"Who else is there?" he asked.

She searched her mind for a logical answer and couldn't find one. She had nobody. Her best friend, Amy, had moved to New York City with her parents during the summer. They corresponded, and they were still friends, but Michelle didn't want to live in New York, even if Amy's parents, with their five children, were to offer her a home.

"If you're thinking of the local orphanage," he said, tongue in cheek, "they draw the line at cow partisans."

She managed a laugh. "Oh. Okay."

"You can stay with us until you graduate and start college."

"I can't get in until fall semester, even if they accept me," she began.

"Where do you want to go?"

"Marist College in San Antonio. There's an excellent journalism program."

He pulled out his cell phone, punched a few buttons and made a phone call. Michelle listened with stark shock. He was nodding, laughing, talking. Then he thanked the man and hung up.

"You called the governor," she said, dumbfounded.

"Yes. We were in the same fraternity in college. He's on the board of trustees at Marist. You're officially accepted. They'll send a letter soon."

"But they don't have my grades…!"

"They will have, by the time you go. What's on the agenda for summer?" he continued.

"I… Well, I have a job. Minette Carson hired me for the rest of the school year, after school and on Saturdays. And I'm sure she'll let me work this summer, so I can save for college."

"You won't need to do that."

"What?"

He shrugged. "I drive a truck here because it helps me fit in. But I have an apartment in San Antonio with a garage. In the garage, there's a brand-new Jaguar XKE." He raised an eyebrow. "Does that give you a hint about my finances?"

She had no idea what an XKE was, but she knew what a Jaguar was. She'd priced them once, just for fun. If it was new…gosh, people could buy houses around here for less, she thought, but she didn't say it.

"But, I'm a stranger," she persisted.

"Not for long. I'm going to petition the court to become your temporary legal guardian. Sara will go with us to court. You can wear a dress and look helpless and tragic and in desperate need of assistance." He pursed his lips. "I know, it will be a stretch, but you can manage it."

She laughed helplessly.

"Then we'll get you through school."

"I'll find a way to pay you back," she promised.

He smiled. "No need for that. Just don't ever write about me," he added. It sounded facetious, but he didn't smile when he said it.

"I'd have to make up something in order to do that." She laughed.

She didn't know, and he didn't tell her, that there was more to his life than she'd seen, or would ever see. Sara knew, but he kept his private life exactly that—private.

Just for an instant, he worried about putting her in the line of fire. He had enemies. Dangerous enemies, who wouldn't hesitate to threaten anyone close to him. Of course, there was Sara, but she'd lived in Wyoming for the past few years, away from him, on a ranch they co-owned. Now he was putting her in jeopardy along with Michelle.

But what could he do? The child had nobody. Now that her idiot stepmother was dead, she was truly on her own. It was dangerous for a young woman to live alone, even in a small community. And there was Roberta's boyfriend, Bert.

Gabriel knew things about the man that he wasn't eager to share with Michelle. The man was part of a criminal organization, and he knew Michelle's habits. He also had a yen for her, if what Michelle had blurted out to him once was true—and he had no indication that she would lie about it. He might decide to come and try his luck with her now that her stepmother was out of the picture. That couldn't be allowed.

He was surprised by his own affection for Michelle. It wasn't paternal. She was, of course, far too young for anything heavy, being eighteen to his twenty-four. She was a beauty, kind and generous and sweet. She was the sort of woman he usually ran from. No, strike that, she was no woman. She was still unfledged, a dove without flight feathers. He had to keep his interest hidden. At least, until she was grown up enough that it wouldn't hurt his conscience to pursue her. Afterward…well, who knew the future?

At the moment, however, his primary concern was to make sure she had whatever she needed to get through high school and, then, through college. Whatever it took.

SARA CALLED HIM BACK. She wouldn't be able to get a flight to Texas for two days, which meant that Michelle would be on her own at night. Gabriel wasn't about to leave her, not with Bert Sims still out there. But he couldn't risk her reputation by having her stay alone with him.

"You don't want to be alone with me," Michelle guessed when he mentioned Sara's dilemma and frowned.

"It wouldn't look right," he said. "You have a spotless reputation here. I'm not going to be the first to put a blemish on it."

She smiled gently. "You're a very nice man."

He shrugged. "Character is important, regardless of the mess some people make of theirs in public and brag about it."

"My dad used to say that civilization rested on the bedrock of morality, and that when morality went, destruction followed," she recalled.

"A student of history," he said approvingly.

"Yes. He told me that first go the arts, then goes religion, then goes morality. After that, you count down the days until the society fails. Ancient Egypt. Rome. A hundred other governments, some more recently than others," she said.

"Who's right? I don't know. I like the middle of the road, myself. We should live the way that suits us and leave others to do the same."

She grinned. "I knew I liked you."

He chuckled. He finished his coffee. "We should stop discussing history and decide what to do with you tonight."

She stared at her own cooling coffee in the thick mug. "I could stay here by myself."

"Never," he said shortly. "Bert Sims might show up, looking for Roberta's leftovers, like Zack said."

She managed a smile. "Thanks. You could sleep in Roberta's room," she offered.

"Only if there's someone else in the house, too." He pursed his lips. "I have an idea." He pulled out his cell phone.

CARLIE BLAIR WALKED in the door with her overnight bag and hugged Michelle close. "I'm so sorry," she said. "I know you and your stepmother didn't get along, but it's got to be a shock, to have it happen like that."

"It was." Michelle dashed away tears. "She apologized when she was dying. She said one other thing," she added, frowning, as she turned to Gabriel. "She said don't let Bert get away with it. You never told me what you thought that meant."

Gabriel's liquid black eyes narrowed. "Did she say anything else?"

She nodded slowly, recalling the odd statement. "She said he told her it wasn't pure and he lied. What in the world did that mean?"

Gabriel was solemn. "That white powder in the vial was cocaine," he explained. "Dealers usually cut it with something else, dilute it. But if it's pure and a user doesn't know, it can be lethal if they don't adjust the dose." He searched Michelle's eyes. "I'm betting that Bert gave her pure cocaine and she didn't know."

Carlie was surprised. "Your stepmother was using drugs?" she asked her friend.

"That's what they think," Michelle replied. She turned back to Gabriel. "Did he know it was pure? Was he trying to kill her?"

"That's something Zack will have to find out."

"I thought he cared about her. In his way," she faltered.

"He might have, even if it was only because she was a customer."

Michelle bit her lower lip. "That would explain why she was so desperate for money. I did wonder, you know, because she didn't buy new clothes or expensive cosmetics or things like she used to when Daddy was alive." She frowned. "She never bought anything, but she never had any money and she was always desperate for more. Like when she tried to sell my father's stamp collection."

"It's a very expensive habit," Gabriel said quietly.

"But… Bert might have meant to kill her…?"

"It's possible. Maybe she made threats, maybe she tried to quit or argued over the price. But, whether he meant to kill her or not, he's going to find himself in a lot of hot water pretty soon."

"Why?" Michelle asked curiously.

He grimaced. "I'm sorry. That's all I can say. This is more complicated than it seems."

She sighed. "Okay. I won't pry. Keep your secrets." She managed a smile. "But don't you forget that I'm a reporter in training," she added. "One day, I'll have learned how to find out anything I want to know." She grinned.

"Now you're scaring me," he teased.

"Good."

He just shook his head. "I have to go back to my place and get a razor. I'll be right back. Lock the door," he told Michelle, "and don't open it for anybody. If Bert Sims shows up, you call me at once. Got that?"

"Got it," she said.

"Okay."

He left. Carlie got up from the sofa, where she'd been perched on the arm, and hugged Michelle. "I know this is hard for you. I'm so sorry."

"Me, too." Michelle gave way to tears. "Thanks for coming over. I hope I'm not putting you in any danger."

"Not me," Carlie said. "And neither of us is going to be in danger with that tall, dark, handsome man around. He is so good-looking, isn't he?" she added with a theatrical sigh.

Michelle dried her tears. "He really is. My guardian angel."

"Some angel."

She tried to think of something that might restore a little normalcy into her routine. Roberta was lying heavily on her mind. "I have to do dishes. Want to dry?"

"You bet!"

CHAPTER FIVE

CARLIE AND MICHELLE shared the double bed in Michelle's room, while Gabriel slept in Roberta's room. Michelle had insisted on changing the bed linen first. She put Roberta's clothes in the washing machine, the ones that had been scattered all over the room. When she'd washed them, she planned to donate them to charity. Michelle couldn't have worn them even if she'd liked Roberta's flamboyant style, which she didn't.

The next morning, Gabriel went to the local funeral home and made the arrangements for Roberta. She had an older sister in Virginia. The funeral home contacted her, but the woman wanted nothing to do with any arrangements. She and Roberta had never gotten along, and she couldn't care less, she said, whether they cremated her or buried her or what. Gabriel arranged for her to be cremated, and Reverend Blair offered a plot in the cemetery of his church for her to be interred. There would be no funeral service, just a graveside one. Michelle thought they owed her that much, at least.

Reverend Blair had invited Michelle to come and stay at his house with Carlie, but Michelle wanted familiar things around her. She also wanted Gabriel, on whom she had come to rely heavily. But she couldn't stay with Gabriel alone. It would not look right in the tiny community of Comanche Wells, where time hadn't moved into the twenty-first century yet.

"Sara will be here tomorrow," Gabriel told the girls as they sat down to supper, which Michelle and Carlie had prepared together. He smiled as he savored hash browns with onions, perfectly cooked, alongside a tender cut of beef and a salad. "You two can cook," he said with admiration. "Hash browns are hard to cook properly. These are wonderful."

"Thanks," they said in unison, and laughed.

"She did the hash browns," Carlie remarked, grinning at Michelle. "I never could get the hang of them. Mine just fall apart and get soggy."

"My mother used to make them," Michelle said with a sad smile. "She was a wonderful cook. I do my best, but I'm not in her league."

"Where do your parents live, Gabriel?" Carlie asked innocently.

Gabriel's expression went hard.

"I made a cherry pie for dessert," Michelle said, quickly and neatly deflecting Carlie's question. "And we have vanilla ice cream to go on it."

Carlie flushed, realizing belatedly that she'd made a slight faux pas with her query. "Michelle makes the best cherry pie around," she said with enthusiasm.

Gabriel took a breath. "Don't look so guilty," he told Carlie, and smiled at her. "I'm touchy about my past, that's all. It was a perfectly normal question."

"I'm sorry, just the same," Carlie told him. "I get nervous around people and I babble." She flushed again. "I don't…mix well."

Gabriel laughed softly. "Neither do I," he confessed.

Michelle raised her hand. "That makes three of us," she remarked.

"I feel better," Carlie said. "Thanks," she added, intent on her food. "I have a knack for putting my foot into my mouth."

"Who doesn't?" Gabriel mused.

"I myself never put my foot into my mouth," Michelle said, affecting a haughty air. "I have never made a single statement that offended, irritated, shocked or bothered a single person."

The other two occupants of the table looked at her with pursed lips.

"Being perfect," she added with a twinkle in her eyes, "I am unable to understand how anyone could make such a mistake."

Carlie picked up her glass of milk. "One more word…" she threatened.

Michelle grinned at her. "Okay. Just so you remember that I don't make mistakes."

Carlie rolled her eyes.

IT WAS CHILLY OUTSIDE. Michelle sat on the porch steps, looking up at the stars. They were so bright, so perfectly clear in cold weather. She knew it had something to do with the atmosphere, but it was rather magical. There was a dim comet barely visible in the sky. Michelle had looked at it through a pair of binoculars her father had given her. It had been winter, and most hadn't been visible to the naked eye.

The door opened and closed behind her. "School is going to be difficult on Monday," she said. "I dread it. Everyone will know…you sure you don't mind giving me rides home after work?" she added.

"That depends on where you want to go," came a deep, amused masculine voice from behind her.

She turned quickly, shocked. "Sorry," she stammered. "I thought you were Carlie."

"She found a game show she can't live without. She's sorry." He chuckled.

"Do you like game shows?" she wondered.

He shrugged. He came and sat down beside her on the step. He was wearing a thick black leather jacket with exquisite beadwork. She'd been fascinated with it when he retrieved it from his truck earlier.

"That's so beautiful," she remarked, lightly touching the colorful trim above the long fringes with her fingertips. "I've never seen anything like it."

"Souvenir from Canada," he said. "I've had it for a long time."

"The beadwork is gorgeous."

"A Blackfoot woman made it for me," he said.

"Oh." She didn't want to pursue that. The woman he mentioned might have been a lover. She didn't want to think of Gabriel with a woman. It was intensely disturbing.

"My cousin," he said, without looking down at her. "She's sixty."

"Oh." She sounded embarrassed now.

He glanced at her with hidden amusement. She was so young. He could almost see the thoughts in her mind. "You need somebody young to cut your teeth on, kid. They'd break on my thick hide."

She flushed and started to jump up, but he caught her hand in his big, warm one, and pulled her gently back down.

"Don't run," he said softly. "No problem was ever

solved by retreat. I'm just telling you how it is. I'm not involved with anyone. I haven't been for years. You're a bud, just opening on a rosebush, testing the air and the sunlight. I like my roses in full bloom."

"Oh."

He sighed. His fingers locked into hers. "These one syllable answers are disturbing," he mused.

She swallowed. The touch of his big, warm hand was causing some odd sensations in her young body. "I see."

"Two syllables. Better." He drew in a long breath. "Until you graduate, we're going to be living in close proximity, even with Sara in the house. I'll be away some of the time. My job takes me all over the world. But there are going to have to be some strict ground rules when I'm home."

"Okay," she faltered. "What?"

"No pajamas or nightgowns when you walk around the house. You put them on when you go to bed, in your room. No staying up late alone. Stuff like that."

She blinked. "I feel like Mata Hari."

"You feel like a spy? An old one, at that." He chuckled.

"A femme fatale, then," she amended. "Gosh, I don't even own pajamas or a gown..."

"You don't wear clothes in bed?" He sounded shocked.

"Oh, get real," she muttered, glad he couldn't see her face. "I wear sweats."

"To bed?" he exclaimed.

"They're comfortable," she said. "Nobody who wanted a good night's sleep ever wore a long gown, they just twist you up and constrict you. And pajamas usually have lace or thick embroidery. It's irritating to my skin."

"Sweats." Of all the things he'd pictured his young companion in at night, that was the last thing.

She looked down at his big hand in the light from the living room. It burned out onto the porch like yellow sun in the darkness, making shadows of the chairs behind them on the dusty boards of the porch. He had good hands, big and strong-looking, with square nails that were immaculate. "I guess the women you know like frilly stuff."

They did, but he wasn't walking into that land mine. He turned her hand in his. "Do you date?"

Her heart jumped. "Not since the almost-broken-nose thing."

He laughed softly. "Sorry. I forgot about that."

"There aren't a lot of eligible boys in my school who live in the dark ages like I do," she explained. "At least two of the ones who go to my church are wild as bucks and go to strip parties with drugs." She grimaced. "I don't fit in. Anywhere. My parents raised me with certain expectations of what life was all about." She turned to look at him. "Is it wrong, to have a belief system? Is it wrong to think morality is worth something?"

"Those are questions you should be asking Carlie's dad," he pointed out.

"Do you believe in…in a higher power?"

His fingers contracted around hers. "I used to."

"But not anymore?"

His drawn breath was audible. "I don't know what I believe anymore, *ma belle,*" he said softly. "I live in a world you wouldn't understand, I go to places where you couldn't survive."

"What kind of work do you do?" she asked.

He laughed without humor. "That's a discussion we may have in a few years."

"Oh, I see." She nodded. "You're a cannibal."

He stilled. "I'm…a what?"

"Your work embarrasses you," she continued, unabashed, "which means you don't work in a bank or drive trucks. If I had a job that embarrassed me, it would be involved with cannibalism."

He burst out laughing. "Pest," he muttered.

She grinned.

His big thumb rubbed her soft fingers. "I haven't laughed so much in years, as I do with you."

She chuckled. "I might go on the stage. If I can make a hardcase like you laugh, I should be able to do it for a living."

"And here I thought you wanted to be a reporter."

"I do," she said. She smiled. "More than anything. I can't believe I'm actually going to work for a newspaper starting Monday," she said. "Minette is getting me my own cell phone and she's going to teach me to use a camera…it's like a dream come true. I only asked her for a reference for college. And she offered me a job." She shook her head. "It's like a dream."

"I gather you'll be riding with Carlie."

"Yes. I'm going to help with gas."

He was silent for a minute. "You keep your eyes open on the road, when you're coming home from work."

"I always do. But why?"

"I don't trust Roberta's boyfriend. He's dangerous. Even Carlie is in jeopardy because of what happened to her father, so you both have to be careful."

"I don't understand why someone would want to harm a minister," she said, shaking her head. "It makes no sense."

He turned his head toward her. "Michelle, most ministers started out as something else."

"Something else?"

"Yes. In other words, Reverend Blair wasn't always a reverend."

She hesitated, listening to make sure Carlie wasn't at the door. "What did he do before?" she asked.

"Sorry. That's a confidence. I never share them."

She curled her hand around his. "That's reassuring. If I ever tell you something dreadful in secret, you won't go blabbing it to everyone you know."

He laughed. "That's a given." His hand contracted. "The reverse is also applicable," he added quietly. "If you overhear anything while you're under my roof, it's privileged information. Not that you'll hear much that you can understand."

"You mean, like when you were talking to Sara in French," she began.

"Something like that." His eyes narrowed. "Did you understand what I said?"

"I can say, where's the library and my brother has a brown suit," she mused. "Actually, I don't have a brother, but that was in the first-year French book. And it's about the scope of my understanding. I love languages, but I have to study very hard to learn anything."

He relaxed a little. He'd said some things about Michelle's recent problems to Sara that he didn't want her to know. Not yet, anyway. It would sound as if he were gossiping about her to his sister.

"The graveside service is tomorrow," she said. "Will Sara be here in time, do you think?"

"She might. I'm having a car pick her up at the airport and drive her down here."

"A car?"

"A limo."

Her lips parted. "A limousine? Like those long, black cars you see politicians riding around in on television? I've only seen one maybe once or twice, on the highway when I was on the bus!"

He laughed softly at her excitement. "They also have sedans that you can hire to transport people," he told her. "I use them a lot when I travel."

He was talking about another world. In Michelle's world, most cars were old and had plenty of mechanical problems. She'd never even looked inside a limousine. She'd seen them on the highway in San Antonio. Her father told her that important businessmen and politicians and rich people and movie stars rode around in them. Not ordinary people. Of course, Gabriel wasn't ordinary. He'd said he owned a new Jaguar. Certainly he could afford to ride in a limousine.

"Do you think they'd let me look inside, when it brings her here?" she asked.

Gabriel was amused at her innocence. She knew nothing of the world at large. He couldn't remember being that young, or that naive about life. He hoped she wouldn't grow up too quickly. She made him feel more masculine, more capable, more intriguing than he really was. He liked her influence. She made him laugh. She made him want to be all the things she thought he was.

"Yes," he said after a minute. "Certainly you can look inside."

"Something to put in my diary," she mused.

"You keep a diary?" he asked, with some amusement.

"Oh, yes," she said. "I note all the cows I've seen abducted, and the strange little men who come out of the pasture at night…"

"Oh, cool it." He chuckled.

"Actually, it's things like how I did on tests, and memories I have of my father and mother," she confessed. "And how I feel about things. There's a lot about Roberta and Bert in there, and how disgusting I thought they were," she added.

"Well, Roberta's where she can't hurt you. And Bert is probably trying to find a way out of the country, if he's smart."

"What do you mean?" she asked.

He stood up and pulled her up beside him. "That's a conversation for another time. Let's go see if Carlie's game show is off."

"Don't you like game shows?" she wondered aloud.

"I like the History Channel, the Nature Channel, the Military Channel, and the Science Channel."

"No TV shows?"

"They're not TV shows. They're experiments in how to create attention deficit disorders in the entire population with endless commercials and ads that pop up right in the middle of programs. I only watch motion pictures or DVDs, unless I find something interesting enough to suffer through. I like programs on World War II history and science."

She pondered that. "I guess there's five minutes of program to fifteen minutes of commercials," she agreed.

"As long as people put up with it, that will continue, too." He chuckled. "I refuse to be part of the process."

"I like history, too," she began.

"There was this big war…" he began with an exaggerated expression.

She punched his arm affectionately. "No cherry pie and ice cream for you."

"I take it back."

She grinned up at him. "Okay. You can have pie and ice cream."

He smiled and opened the door for her.

She hesitated in the opening, just staring up at him, drinking in a face that was as handsome as any movie star's, at the physique that could have graced an athlete.

"Stop ogling me, if you please," he said with exaggerated patience. "You have to transfer that interest to someone less broken."

She made a face at him. "You're not broken," she pointed out. "Besides, there's nobody anywhere who could compare with you." She flushed at her own boldness. "Anyway, you're safe to cut my teeth on, and you know it." She grinned. "I'm off-limits, I am."

He laughed. "Off-limits, indeed, and don't you forget it."

"Spoilsport."

She went inside ahead of him. He felt as if he could fly. Dangerous, that. More dangerous, his reaction to her. She was years too young for anything more than banter. But, he reminded himself, the years would pass. If he lived long enough, after she graduated from college, who knew what might happen?

THERE WAS A grim memorial service at the Comanche Wells Cemetery. It was part of the land owned by the Methodist church where Reverend Blair was the minister. He stood over the small open grave, with an open Bible in his hands, reading the service for the dead. The urn containing Roberta's ashes was in the open grave, waiting for the funeral home's maintenance man, standing nearby, to close after the ceremony.

Gabriel stood beside Michelle, close, but not touching. He was wearing a suit, some expensive thing that fit him with delicious perfection. The navy darkness of the suit against the spotless white shirt and blue patterned tie only emphasized his good looks. His wavy black hair was unruly in the stiff breeze. Michelle's own hair was tormented into a bun because of the wind. But it blew tendrils down into her eyes and mouth while she tried to listen to the service, while she tried even harder to feel something for the late Roberta.

It was sad that the woman's own sister didn't care enough to even send a flower. Total strangers from Jacobs County had sent sprays and wreathes and potted plants to the funeral home that had arranged for the cremation. The flowers were spread all around the grave. Some of them would go to the local hospital and nursing home in Jacobsville, others for the evening church service here. A few of the potted plants would go home with Michelle.

She remembered her father, and how much he'd been in love with Roberta at first. She remembered Roberta in the days before Bert. More recently, she remembered horrible arguments and being slapped and having Roberta try to sell the very house under her feet. There had been more bad times than good.

But now that part of her life was over. She had a future that contained Gabriel, and the beginning of a career as a journalist. It was something to look forward to, something to balance her life against the recent death of her father and Roberta's unexpected passing.

Sara's plane had been held up due to an electrical fault. She'd phoned Gabriel just before he and Michelle went to the funeral with Carlie, to apologize and give an updated arrival time. Michelle looked forward to meeting her. From what Gabriel had said about his sister, she sounded like a very sweet and comfortable person.

Reverend Blair read the final verses, closed the Bible, bowed his head for prayer. A few minutes later, he paused to speak to Michelle, where she stood with Gabriel and Carlie, thanking the few local citizens who'd taken time to attend. There hadn't been time for the newspaper to print the obituary, so services had been announced on the local radio station. Everybody listened to it, for the obituaries and the country-western music. They also listened for the school closings when snow came. That didn't happen often, but Michelle loved the rare times when it did.

"I'm sorry for your loss," Reverend Blair said, holding Michelle's hand and smiling gently. "No matter how contrary some people are, we get used to having them in our lives."

"That's true," Michelle said gently. "And my father loved her," she added. "For a time, she made him happy." She grimaced. "I just don't understand how she changed so much, so quickly. Even when she drank too much—" she hesitated, looking around to make sure she wasn't overheard before she continued "—she was never really mean."

Gabriel and the minister exchanged enigmatic glances.

Michelle didn't notice. Her eyes were on the grave. "And she said not to let Bert get away with it," she added slowly.

"There are some things going on that you're better off not knowing about," Reverend Blair said softly. "You can safely assume that Bert will pay a price for what he did. If not in this life, then in the next."

"But what did he do?" Michelle persisted.

"Bad things." Reverend Blair smiled.

"My sister will be here in an hour," Gabriel said, reading the screen of his cell phone, with some difficulty because of the sun's glare. He grinned at the reverend. "You can have your daughter back tonight."

Reverend Blair grinned. "I must say, I miss the little touches. Like clean dishes and laundry getting done." He made a face. "She's made me lazy." He smiled with pure affection at his daughter, who grinned.

"I'll make you fresh rolls for supper," Carlie promised him.

"Oh, my, and I didn't get you anything," he quipped.

She hugged him. "You're just the best dad in the whole world."

"Pumpkin, I'm glad you think so." He let her go. "If you need anything, you let us know, all right?" he asked Michelle. "But you're in good hands." He smiled at Gabriel.

"She'll be safe, at least." Gabriel gave Reverend Blair a complicated look. "Make sure about those new locks, will you? I've gotten used to having you around."

The other man made a face. "Locks and bolts won't keep out the determined," he reminded him. "I put my trust in a higher power."

"So do I," Gabriel replied. "But I keep a Glock by the bed."

"Trust in Allah, but tie up your camel."

Everybody looked at Michelle, who blushed.

"Sorry," she said. "I was remembering something I read in a nonfiction book about the Middle East. It was written by a former member of the French Foreign Legion."

Now the stares were more complicated, from the two males at least.

"Well, they fascinate me," she confessed, flushing a little. "I read true crime books and biographies of military men and anything I can find about the Special Air Services of Great Britain and the French Foreign Legion."

"My, my," Gabriel said. He chuckled with pure glee, a reaction that was lost on Michelle.

"I lead a sheltered life." Michelle glanced at the grave. The maintenance man, a little impatient, had started to fill the grave. "We should go."

"Yes, we should." Reverend Blair smiled. "Take care."

"Thanks. The service was very nice," Michelle said.

"I'm glad you thought so."

Gabriel took her arm and led her back to the car. He drove her home first, so that she could change back into more casual clothes and get her overnight bag. Then he drove her to his own house, where Sara was due to arrive any minute.

Michelle had this picture of Sara. That she'd be dark-haired and dark-eyed, with a big smile and a very tender nature. Remembering what Gabriel had told her in confidence, about the perils Sara had survived when they were in school, she imagined the other woman would be a little shy and withdrawn.

So it came as something of a shock when a tall, beautiful woman with long black hair and flashing black eyes stepped out of the back of the limousine and told the driver where he could go and how fast.

CHAPTER SIX

"I AM VERY SORRY, LADY," the driver, a tall lanky man, apologized. "I truly didn't see the truck coming…"

"You didn't look!" she flashed at him in a terse but sultry tone. "How dare you text on your cell phone while driving a customer!"

He was very flushed by now. "I won't do it again, I swear."

"You won't do it with me in the car, and I am reporting you to the company you work for," she concluded.

Gabriel stepped forward as the driver opened the trunk. He picked up the single suitcase that Sara had brought with her. Something in the way Gabriel looked at the man had him backing away.

"Very sorry, again," he said, flustered. "If you'd just sign the ticket, ma'am…"

He fetched a clipboard and handed it to her, eyeing Gabriel as if he expected him to leap on him any second. Sara signed it. The man obviously knew better than to look for a tip. He nodded, turned, jumped into the car and left a trail of dust as he sped away.

"That could have gone better," Sara said with a grim smile. She hugged Gabriel. "So good to see you again."

"You, too," he replied. His face changed as he looked at the younger woman. He touched her hair. "You only grow more beautiful with age."

"You only think so because you're my brother." She laughed musically. She looked past him at Michelle, who stood silent and wary.

"And you must be Michelle." Sara went to her, smiled and hugged her warmly. "I have a nasty temper. The silly man almost killed us both, texting some woman."

"I'm so glad he didn't," Michelle said, hugging her back. "It's very kind of both of you to do this for me," she added. "I…really don't have anyplace to go. I mean, the Reverend Blair said I could stay with him and Carlie, but…"

"You certainly do have someplace to go," Gabriel said with a grin. "Sara needed the change of scenery. She was vegetating up in Wyoming."

Sara sighed. "In a sense, I suppose so, although I like it better there than in British Columbia. I left our foreman in charge at the ranch in Catelow. That's in Wyoming," Sara told Michelle with a smile. "Anything that needs doing for the sale, I can do online." Her black eyes, so like Gabriel's, had a sad cast. "The change of scenery will do me good. I love to ride. Do you?" she asked the younger woman.

"I haven't been on a horse in years," Michelle confessed. "Mostly, horses try to scrape me off or dislodge me. I'm sort of afraid of them."

"My horses are very tame," Gabriel told her. "They'll love you."

"I hope you have coffee made," Sara sighed as they made their way into the sprawling house. "I'm so tired! Flying is not my favorite mode of travel."

"I've never even been on a plane," Michelle confessed.

Sara stopped and stared at her. "Never?"

"Never."

"She wanted to look inside the limo." Gabriel chuckled. "She's never seen one of those, either."

"I'm so sorry!" Sara exclaimed. "I made a fuss…"

"You should have made a fuss," Michelle replied. "There will be other times."

"I'll make sure of that." Sara smiled, and it was like the sun coming out.

SCHOOL HAD BEEN rough in the days after Roberta's death. People were kind, but there were so many questions about how she died. Gossip ran rampant. One of the girls she sat near in history class told her that Roberta's boyfriend was a notorious drug dealer. At least two boys in their school got their fixes from him.

Now the things Roberta had said started to make sense. And Michelle was learning even more about the networks and how they operated from Minette since she'd started working for the Jacobsville newspaper.

"It's a vile thing, drug dealing," Minette said harshly. "Kids overdose and die. The men supplying the drugs don't even care. They only care about the profit." She hesitated. "Well, maybe some of them have good intentions…"

"A drug dealer with good intentions?" Michelle laughed. "You have got to be kidding."

"Actually, I'm not. You've heard of the man they call El Jefe?"

"Who hasn't?" Michelle replied. "We heard that he helped save you and Sheriff Carson," she added.

"He's my father."

Michelle gaped at her. "He's…?"

"My father," Minette repeated. "I didn't know who my real father was until very recently. My life was in danger, even more than Hayes's was when he was shot, because my father was in a turf war with a rival who was the most evil man I ever knew."

"Your life is like a soap opera," Michelle ventured.

Minette laughed. "Well, yes, it is."

"I wish mine was more exciting. In a good way," she clarified. She drew in a long breath. "Okay, what about this camera?" she asked. It had more dials and settings than a spaceship.

"I know, it's a little intimidating. Let me show you how it works."

She did. It took a little time, and when they finished, a phone call was waiting for Minette. She motioned to Michelle. "I have a new reporter. I'm going to let her take this down, if you don't mind. Her name is Michelle... That's right. It's a deal. Thanks!" She put her hand over the receiver so that the caller wouldn't hear. "This is Ben Simpson. He's our Jacobs County representative in District 3 for the Texas Soil and Water Conservation Board. He wants us to do a story on a local rancher who won Rancher of the Year for the Jacobs County Soil and Water Conservation District for his implementation of natural grasses and ponds. The award was made just before Christmas, but the rancher has been out of the country until now. I'm going to let you take down the details, and then I'll send you out to his ranch to take a photo of him with the natural grasses in the background. Are you up to it?" she teased.

Michelle was almost shaking, but she bit her lip and nodded. "Yes, ma'am," she said.

Minette grinned. "Go for it!"

MICHELLE WAS USED to taking copious notes in school. She did well in her schoolwork because she was thorough. She took down the story, pausing to clarify the spelling of names, and when she was through she had two sheets of notes and she'd arranged a day and time to go out to photograph the rancher.

She hung up. Minette was still in the doorway. "Did I do that okay?" she asked worriedly.

"You did fine. I was listening on the other phone. I took notes, too, just in case. You write the story and we'll compare your notes to mine."

"Thanks!" Michelle said fervently. "I was nervous."

"No need to be. You'll do fine." She indicated the computer at the desk. "Get busy." She smiled. "I like the way you are with people, even on the phone. You have an engaging voice. It will serve you well in this business."

"That's nice of you to say," Michelle said.

"Write the story. Remember, short, concise sentences, nothing flowery or overblown. I'll be out front if you need me."

She started to thank Minette again, but it was going to get tedious if she kept it up, so she just nodded and smiled.

WHEN SHE TURNED in the story, she stood gritting her teeth while Minette read it and compared it with her own notes.

"You really are a natural," she told the younger woman. "I couldn't have done better myself. Nice work."

"Thank you!"

"Now go home," she said. "It's five, and Carlie will be peeling rubber any minute to get home."

Michelle laughed. "I think she may. I'll see you tomorrow, then. Do I go out to photograph the man tomorrow, too?"

"Yes."

Michelle bit her lip. "But I don't have a license or own a car...there's only Roberta's and she didn't leave it to me. I don't think she even had a will...and I can't ask Carlie to take off from work..." The protests came in small bursts.

"I'll drive you out there," Minette said softly. "We might drop by some of the state and federal offices and I'll introduce you to my sources."

"That sounds very exciting! Thanks!" She sounded relieved, and she was.

"One more thing," Minette said.

"Yes?"

"I'm printing the conservation story under your own byline."

Michelle caught her breath. "My first one. That's so kind of you."

"You'll have others. This is just the first." She grinned. "Have a good night."

"I will. Sara's making homemade lasagna. It's my favorite."

"Sara?"

"Gabriel's sister. She's so beautiful." Michelle shook her head. "The two of them have been lifesavers for me. I didn't want to have to pick up and move somewhere else. I couldn't have stayed here to finish school without them."

"Not quite true," Minette replied. "You could have come to us. Even Cash Grier mentioned that they could make room for you, if you needed a place to stay."

"So many," Michelle said, shaking her head. "They hardly know me."

"They know you better than you think," was the

reply. "In small communities like ours, there are no se-crcts. Your good deeds are noted by many."

"I guess I lived in the city for too long. Daddy had patients but no real friends, especially after Roberta came into our lives. It was just the three of us." She smiled. "I love living here."

"So do I, and I've been here all my life." She cocked her head. "Gabriel seems an odd choice to be your guardian. He isn't what you think of as a family man."

"He's not what he seems," Michelle replied. "He was kind to me when I needed it most." She made a face. "I was sitting in the middle of the road hoping to get hit by a car. It was the worst day of my life. He took me home with him and talked to me. He made everything better. When Roberta…died…he was there to comfort me. I owe him a lot. He even got Sara down here to live with him so that he could be my legal guardian with no raised eyebrows around us."

Minette simply said, "I see." What she did see, she wasn't going to share. Apparently Gabriel had a little more than normal interest in this young woman, but he wasn't going to risk her reputation. It was going to be all by the book. Minette wondered what he had in mind for Michelle when she was a few years older. And she also wondered if Michelle had any idea who Gabriel really was, and how he earned his living. That was a secret she wasn't going to share, either. Not now.

"Well, I'll see you tomorrow, then," Michelle added.

"Tomorrow."

CARLIE WAS WAITING for her at the front door the next morning, which was Friday. She looked out of breath.

"Is something wrong?" Michelle asked.

"No. Of course not. Let's go."

Carlie checked all around the truck and even looked under it before she got behind the wheel and started it.

"Okay, now, what's going on?" Michelle asked.

"Daddy got a phone call earlier," Carlie said, looking both ways before she pulled carefully out of the driveway.

"What sort of call?"

"From some man who said Daddy might think he was out of the woods, but somebody else was coming to pay him a visit, and he'll never see it coming." She swallowed. "Daddy told me to check my truck out before I drove it. I forgot, so I looked underneath just in case." She shook her head. "It's like a nightmare," she groaned. "I have no idea in this world why anyone would want to harm a minister."

"It's like our police chief said," Michelle replied quietly. "There are madmen in the world. I guess you can't ever understand what motivates them to do the things they do."

"I wish things were normal again," Carlie said in a sad tone. "I hate having to look over my shoulder when I drive and look for bombs under my car." She glanced at Michelle. "I swear, I feel like I'm living in a combat zone."

"I know the feeling, although I've never been in any real danger. Not like you." She smiled. "Don't you worry. I'll help you keep a lookout."

"Thanks." She smiled. "It's nice, having someone to ride with me. These back roads get very lonely."

"They do, indeed." Michelle sighed as she looked out over the barren flat landscape toward the horizon as the car sped along. "I just wrote my first story for the newspaper," she said with a smile. "And Minette is taking me out to introduce me to people who work for the state and federal government. It's the most exciting thing that's ever happened to me," she added, her eyes starry with pleasure. "I get my own byline." She shook her head. "It really is true…"

"What's true?" Carlie asked.

"My dad said that after every bad experience, something wonderful happens to you. It's like you pay a price for great happiness."

"I see what you mean." She paused. "I really do."

MINETTE DROVE MICHELLE out to the Patterson ranch, to take photographs for her story and to see the rancher's award for conservation management. She also wanted a look at his prize Santa Gertrudis bull. The bull had been featured in a cattle magazine because he was considered one of the finest of his breed, a stud bull whose origins, like all Santa Gertrudis, was the famous King Ranch in Texas. It was a breed native to Texas that had resulted from breeding Shorthorn and Hereford cattle with Brahman cattle. The resulting breed was named for the Spanish land grant where Richard King founded the cattle empire in the nineteenth century: Santa Gertrudis.

Wofford Patterson was tall, intimidating. He had jet-black hair, thick and straight, and an olive complexion. His eyes, surprisingly, were such a pale blue that they seemed to glitter like Arctic ice. He had big hands and big feet and his face looked as if it had been carved from solid stone. It was angular. Handsome, in its way, but not conventionally handsome.

There were scars on his hands. Michelle stared at

them as she shook his hand, and flushed when she saw his keen, intelligent eyes noting the scrutiny.

"Sorry," she said, although she hadn't voiced her curiosity.

"I did a stint with the FBI's Hostage Rescue Team," he explained, showing her the palms of both big hands. "Souvenirs from many rappels down a long rope from a hovering chopper," he added with a faint smile. "Even gloves don't always work."

Her lips fell open. This was not what she'd expected when Minette said they'd take pictures of a rancher. This man wasn't what he appeared to be.

"No need to look threatened," he told her, and his pale eyes twinkled as he shoved his hands into the pockets of his jeans. "I don't have arrest powers anymore." He scowled. "Have you done something illegal? Is that why you look intimidated?"

"Oh, no, sir," she said quickly. "It's just that I was listening for the sound of helicopters." She smiled vacantly.

He burst out laughing. He glanced at Minette. "I believe you said she was a junior reporter? You didn't mention that she was nuts, did you?"

"I am not nuts, I have read of people who witnessed actual alien abductions of innocent cows," she told him solemnly. But her eyes were twinkling, like his.

"I haven't witnessed any," he replied, "but if I ever do, I'll phone you to come out and take pictures."

"Would you? How kind!" She glanced at Minette, who was grinning from ear to ear. "Now about that conservation award, Mr. Patterson…"

"Mr. Patterson was my father," he corrected. "And he was Mister Patterson, with a capital letter. He's gone now, God rest his soul. He was the only person alive I was really afraid of." He chuckled. "You can call me Wolf."

"Wolf?"

"Wofford… Wolf," he said. "They hung that nickname on me while I worked for the Bureau. I have something of a reputation for tracking."

"And a bit more," Minette interrupted, tongue in cheek.

"Yes, well, but we mustn't put her off, right?" he asked in return, and he grinned.

"Right."

"Come on and I'll show you Patterson's Lone Pine Red Diamond. He won a 'bull of the year' award for conformation, and I'm rolling in the green from stud fees. He has nicely marbled fat and large—" he cleared his throat "—assets."

Minette glanced at Michelle and shook her head when Wolf wasn't looking. Michelle interpreted that as an "I'll tell you later" look.

The bull had his own stall in the nicest barn Michelle had ever seen. "Wow," she commented as they walked down the bricked walkway between the neat wooden stalls. There was plenty of ventilation, but it was comfortably warm in here. A tack room in back provided any equipment or medicines that might be needed by the visiting veterinarian for the livestock in the barn.

There were two cows, hugely pregnant, in two of the stalls and a big rottweiler, black as coal, lying just in front of the tack room door. The animal raised his head at their approach.

"Down, Hellscream," he instructed. The dog lay back down, wagging its tail.

"Hellscream?" Michelle asked.

He grinned. "I don't have a social life. Too busy with the bloodstock here. So in my spare time, I play World of Warcraft. The leader of the Horde—the faction that fights the Alliance—is Garrosh Hellscream. I really don't like him much, so my character joined the rebellion to throw him out. Nevertheless, he is a fierce fighter. So is my girl, there," he indicated the rottweiler. "Hence, the name."

"Winnie Kilraven's husband is a gaming fanatic," Minette mused.

"Kilraven plays Alliance," Wolf said in a contemptuous tone. "A Paladin, no less." He pursed his lips. "I killed him in a battleground, doing player versus player. It was very satisfying." He grinned.

"I'd love to play, but my husband is addicted to the Western Channel on TV when he's not in his office being the sheriff," Minette sighed. "He and the kids watch cartoon movies together, too. I don't really mind. But gaming sounds like a lot of fun."

"Trust me, it is." Wolf stopped in front of a huge, sleek red-coated bull. "Isn't he a beaut?" he asked the women, and actually sighed. "I'd let him live in the house, but I fear the carpets would never recover."

The women looked at each other. Then he laughed at their expressions, and they relaxed.

"I read about a woman who kept a chicken inside once," Michelle said with a bland expression. "I think they had to replace all the carpets, even though she had a chicken diaper."

"I'd like to see a cow diaper that worked." Wolf chuckled.

"That's a product nobody is likely to make," Michelle said.

"Can we photograph you with the bull?" Michelle asked.

"Why not?"

He went into the stall with the bull and laid his long arm around his neck. "Smile, Red, you're going to be even more famous," he told the big animal, and smoothed his fur.

He and the bull turned toward the camera. Michelle took several shots, showing them to Minette as they went along.

"Nice," Minette said. She took the digital camera, pulled up the shots, and showed them to Wolf.

"They'll do fine," Wolf replied. "You might want to mention that the barn is as secure as the White House, and anyone who comes here with evil intent will end up in the backseat of a patrol car, handcuffed." He pursed his lips. "I still have my handcuffs, just in case."

"We'll mention that security is tight." Minette laughed.

"He really is a neat bull," Michelle added. "Thanks for letting us come out and letting us take pictures."

He shrugged broad shoulders. "No problem. I'm pretty much available until next week."

"What happens next week?" Michelle asked.

"A World Event on World of Warcraft," he mused. "The 'Love Is in the Air' celebration. It's a hoot."

"A world event?" Michelle asked, curious.

"We have them for every holiday. It's a chance for people to observe them in-game. This is the equivalent of Valentine's Day." He laughed. "There's this other player I pal around with. I'm pretty sure she's a girl.

We do battlegrounds together. She gets hung on trees, gets lost, gets killed a lot. I enjoy playing with her."

"Why did you say that you think she's a girl?" Michelle asked.

"People aren't what they seem in video games," he replied. "A lot of the women are actually men. They think of it as playing with a doll, dressing her up and stuff."

"What about women, do they play men?" she persisted.

He laughed. "Probably. I've come across a few whose manners were a dead giveaway. Women are mostly nicer than some of the guys."

"What class is your Horde character?" Minette broke in.

"Oh, you know about classes, huh?"

"Just what I overheard when Kilraven was raving about them to my husband," she replied, chuckling.

"I play a Blood Elf death knight," he said. "Two-handed sword, bad attitude, practically invincible."

"What does the woman play?" Michelle asked, curious.

"A Blood Elf warlock. Warlocks cast spells. Deadliest class there is, besides mages," he replied. "She's really good. I've often wondered where she lives. Somewhere in Europe, I think, because she's on late at night, when most people in the States are asleep."

"Why are you on so late yourself?" Michelle asked.

He shrugged. "I have sleep issues." And for an instant, something in his expression made her think of wounded things looking for shelter. He searched her eyes. "You're staying with the Brandons, aren't you?"

"Well, yes," she said hesitantly.

He nodded. "Gabriel's a good fellow." His face tautened. "His sister, however, could drop houses on people."

She stared at him. "Excuse me?"

"I was backing out of a parking space at the county courthouse and she came flying around the corner and hit the back end of my truck." He was almost snarling. "Then she gets out, cussing a blue streak, and says it's my fault! She was the one speeding!"

Michelle almost bit her tongue off trying not to say what she was thinking.

"So your husband—" he nodded to Minette "—comes down the courthouse steps and she's just charming to him, almost in tears over her poor car, that I hit!" He made a face. "I get hit with a citation for some goldarned thing, and my insurance company has to fix her car and my rates go up."

"Was that before or after you called her a broom-riding witch and indicated that she didn't come from Wyoming at all, but by way of Kansas…?"

"Sure, her and the flying monkeys," he muttered.

Michelle couldn't keep from laughing. "I'm sorry," she defended herself. "It was the flying monkey bit…" She burst out laughing again.

"Anyway, I politely asked her which way she was going and if she was coming back to town, so I could park my truck somewhere while she was on the road. Set her off again. Then she started cussing me in French. I guess she thought some dumb country hick like me wouldn't understand her."

"What did you do?" Michelle asked.

He shrugged. "Gave it back to her in fluent and formal French. That made her madder, so she switched to

Farsi." He grinned. "I'm also fluent in that, and I know the slang. She called on the sheriff to arrest me for obscenity, but he said he didn't speak whatever language we were using so he couldn't arrest me." He smiled blithely. "I like your husband," he told Minette. "He was nice about it, but he sent her on her way. Her parting shot, also in Farsi, was that no woman in North America would be stupid enough to marry a man like me. She said she'd rather remain single forever than to even consider dating someone like me."

"What did you say to her then?" Michelle wanted to know.

"Oh, I thanked her."

"What?" Minette burst out.

He shrugged. "I said that burly masculine women didn't appeal to me whatsoever, and that I'd like a nice wife who could cook and have babies."

"And?" Minette persisted.

"And she said I wanted a malleable female I could chain to the bed." He shook his head.

"What did you say about that?"

"I said it would be too much trouble to get the stove in there."

Michelle almost doubled up laughing. She could picture Sara trying to tie this man up in knots and failing miserably. She wondered if she dared repeat the conversation when she got home.

Wolf anticipated her. He shook his finger at her. "No carrying tales, either," he instructed. "You don't arm the enemy."

"But she's nice," she protested.

"Nice. Sure she is. Does she keep her pointed hat

in the closet or does she wear it around the house?" he asked pleasantly.

"She doesn't own a single one, honest."

"Make her mad," he invited. "Then stand back and watch the broom and the pointy hat suddenly appear."

"You'd like her if you got to know her," Michelle replied.

"No, thank you. No room in my life for a woman who shares her barn with flying monkeys."

MICHELLE AND MINETTE laughed all the way back to the office.

"Oh, what Sara's missing," Minette said, wiping tears of mirth from her eyes. "He's one of a kind."

"He really is."

"I wish I could tell her what he said. I wouldn't dare. She's already scored a limousine driver. I expect she could strip the skin off Wofford Patterson at ten paces."

"A limousine?"

Michelle nodded. "The driver was texting someone at the wheel and almost wrecked the car. She reported him to the agency that sent him."

"Good for her," Minette said grimly. "There was a wreck a few months ago. A girl was texting a girlfriend and lost control of the car she was driving. She killed a ten-year-old boy and his grandmother who were walking on the side of the road."

"I remember that," Michelle said. "It was so tragic."

"It's still tragic. The girl is in jail, pending trial. It's going to be very hard on her parents, as well as those of the little boy."

"You have sympathy for the girl's parents?" Michelle ventured.

"When you work in this business for a while, you'll learn that there really are two sides to every story. Normal people can do something impulsive and wrong and end up serving a life term. Many people in jail are just like you and me," she continued. "Except they have less control of themselves. One story I covered, a young man had an argument with his friend while he was skinning a deer they'd just killed in the woods. Impulsively, he stabbed his friend with the knife. He cried at his trial. He didn't mean to do it. He had one second of insanity and it destroyed his life. But he was a good boy. Never hurt an animal, never skipped school, never did anything bad in his life. Then he killed his best friend on an impulse that he regretted immediately."

"I never thought of it like that," Michelle said, dazed.

"Convicted felons have families," she pointed out. "Most of them are as normal as people can be. They go to church, give to charity, help their neighbors, raise good children. They have a child do something stupid and land in jail. They're not monsters. Although I must confess I've seen a few parents who should be sitting in jail." She shook her head. "People are fascinating to me, after all these years." She smiled. "You'll find that's true for you, as well."

Michelle leaned back. "Well, I've learned something. I've always been afraid of people in jail, especially when they work on the roadways picking up trash."

"They're just scared kids, mostly," Minette replied. "There are some bad ones. But you won't see them out on the highways. Only the trusted ones get to do that sort of work."

"The world is a strange place."

"It's stranger than you know." Minette chuckled. She

pulled up in front of the newspaper office. "Now, let's get those photos uploaded and cropped and into the galleys."

"You bet, boss," Michelle said with a grin. "Thanks for the ride, too."

"You need to learn to drive," Minette said.

"For that, you need a car."

"Roberta had one. I'll talk to Blake Kemp. He's our district attorney, but he's also a practicing attorney. We'll get him going on probate for you."

"Thanks."

"Meanwhile, ask Gabriel about teaching you. He's very experienced with cars."

"Okay," she replied. "I'll ask him." It didn't occur to her to wonder how Minette knew he was experienced with cars.

CHAPTER SEVEN

"NO, NO, NO!" Gabriel said through gritted teeth. "Michelle, if you want to look at the landscape, for God's sake, stop and get out of the car first!"

She bit her lower lip. "Sorry. I wasn't paying attention."

The truck, his truck, was an inch away from going into a deep ditch.

"Put it in Reverse, and back up slowly," he instructed, forcing his voice to seem calm.

"Okay." She did as instructed, then put it in gear, and went forward very slowly. "How's this?"

"Better," he said. He drew in a breath. "I don't understand why your father never taught you."

Mention of her father made her sad. "He was too busy at first and then too sick," she said, her voice strained. "I wanted to learn, but I didn't pester him."

"I'm sorry," he said deeply. "I brought back sad memories for you."

She managed a faint smile. "It's still not that long since he, well, since he was gone," she replied. She couldn't bring herself to say "died." It was too harsh a word. She concentrated on the road. "This is a lot harder than it looks," she said. She glanced up in the rearview mirror. "Oh, darn."

He glanced behind them. A car was speeding toward

them, coming up fast. The road was straight and clear, however. "Just drive," he told her. "He's got plenty of room to pass if he wants to."

"Okay."

The driver slowed down suddenly, pulled around them and gave her a sign that made her flush.

"And that was damned well uncalled for," Gabriel said shortly. He pulled out his cell phone, called the state highway police, gave them the license plate number and offered to press charges if they caught the man. "She's barely eighteen and trying to learn to drive," he told the officer he was speaking to. "The road was clear, he had room to pass. He was just being a jerk because she was female."

He listened, then chuckled. "I totally agree. Thanks."

He closed the cell phone. "They're going to look for him."

"I hope they explain manners to him. So many people seem to grow up without any these days," she sighed. She glanced at her companion. It had made him really angry, that other man's rudeness.

He caught her staring. "Watch the road."

"Sorry."

"What's wrong?"

"Nothing. I was just…well, it was nice of you, to care that someone insulted me."

"Nobody's picking on you while I'm around," he said with feeling.

She barely turned her head and met his searching black eyes. Her heart went wild. Her hands felt like ice on the wheel. She could barely get her breath.

"Stop that," he muttered, turning his head away. "You'll kill us both."

She cleared her throat. "Okay."

He drew in a breath. "You may be the death of me, anyway," he mused, giving her a covert glance. She was very pretty, with her blond hair long, around her shoulders, with that creamy complexion and those soft gray eyes. He didn't dare pay too much attention. But when she was fully grown, she was going to break hearts. His jaw tautened. He didn't like to think about that, for some reason.

"Now make a left turn onto the next road. Give the signal," he directed. "That's right. Look both ways. Good. Very good."

She grinned. "This is fun."

"No, fun is when you streak down the interstate at a hundred and twenty and nobody sees you. That's fun."

"You didn't!" she gasped.

He shrugged. "Jags like to run. They purr when you pile on the gas."

"They do not."

"You'll see." He smiled to himself. He already had plans for her graduation day. He and Sara had planned it very well. It was only a couple of months away. He glanced at his companion. She was going to be absolutely stunned when she knew what they had in mind.

THE PIECE ON Wofford Patterson ran with Michelle's byline, along with photos of his native grasses, his water conservation project and his huge bull. People she didn't even know at school stopped her in the hall to talk to her. And not only other students. Teachers paid her more attention, as well. She felt like a minor celebrity.

"I actually had someone to sit with at lunch," she told Sara, all enthusiasm, when she got home from school that day. "Mostly I'm always by myself. But one little article in the paper with my name and just look!"

Sara managed a smile. "It was well written. You did a good job. Considering the material you had to work with," she added with smoldering black eyes.

Then Michelle remembered. Wofford Patterson. Mortal enemy. Sara's nemesis.

"Sorry," she said, flushing.

"The man is a total lunatic," Sara muttered, slamming pans around as she looked for something to boil pasta in. Her beautiful complexion was flushed. "He backed into me and tried to blame me for it! Then he said I rode a broom and kept flying monkeys in the barn!"

Michelle almost bit through her lower lip. She couldn't laugh. She couldn't laugh…

Sara glanced at her, rolled her eyes, and dragged out a big pot. "You like him, I gather?"

"Well, he didn't accuse me of keeping flying monkeys," Michelle said reasonably. "He's very handsome, in a rough-cut sort of way, and he loves animals."

"Probably because he is one," Sara said under her breath.

"He has this huge rottweiler. You wouldn't believe what he calls her!"

"Have you seen my hammer?" Gabriel interrupted suddenly.

Both women turned.

"Don't you keep it in the toolbox?" Michelle asked.

"Yes. Where's my toolbox?" he amended.

The two women looked at each other blankly. Then Sara flushed.

"I, uh, had to find a pair of pliers to turn the water

spigot on outside. Not my fault," she added. "You have big hands and when you turn the water off, I can't turn it back on. I took the whole toolbox with me so I'd have access to whatever I needed."

"No problem. But where is it?" Gabriel added.

"Um," Sara frowned. "I think I remember…just a sec." She headed out the back door.

"Don't, for God's sake, tell her the name of Patterson's dog!" Gabriel said in a rough whisper.

She stared at him. "Why?"

He gave her a speaking look. "Who do you think Patterson's unknown buddy in World of Warcraft is?" he asked patiently.

Her eyes widened with glee. "You mean, they're buddies online and they don't know it?"

"In a nutshell." He grinned. "Two lonely people who can't stand each other in person, and they're soul mates online. Let them keep their illusions, for the time being."

"Of course." She shook her head. "She'd like him if she got to know him."

"I know. But first impressions die hard."

Sara was back, carrying a beat-up brown toolbox. "Here." She set it down on the table. "Sorry," she added sheepishly.

"I don't mind if you borrow stuff. Just put it back, please." He chuckled.

She shrugged. "Sometimes I do. I'm just scatterbrained."

"Listen," he said, kissing the top of her head, "nobody who speaks six languages fluently could even remotely be called scatterbrained. You just have a lot on your mind all the time."

"What a nice way to put it. No wonder you're my favorite brother!"

He gave Michelle a droll look.

"Well, if I had other brothers, you'd still be my favorite," Sara amended.

"Are we going to drive some more today?" Michelle asked him hopefully.

"Maybe tomorrow," he said after a minute. He forced a smile. He left, quickly.

Michelle sighed. "I can't follow orders," she explained while Sara put water on to boil and got out spaghetti.

"He's just impatient," Sara replied. "He always was, even when we were kids." She shook her head. "Some habits you never grow out of."

Michelle knew a lot about Sara, and her childhood. But she was too kindhearted to mention any of what Gabriel had told her. She just smiled and asked what she could do to help.

GRADUATION WAS ONLY days away. So much had happened to Michelle that she could hardly believe how quickly the time had gone by. Marist College had accepted her, just as Gabriel had told her. She was scheduled for orientation in August, and she'd already had a conversation online with her faculty advisor.

"I'm so excited," she told Gabriel. They were sitting on the front porch, watching a meteor shower. There were a couple of fireballs, colorful and rare. "I'll be in college. I can't believe it."

He smiled. "You'll grow. College changes people. You see the world in a different way when you've studied courses like Western Civilization and math."

"I'm not looking forward to the math," she sighed. "People say college trig is a nightmare."

"Only if you don't have a tutor."

"But I don't…"

He glanced down at her. "I made straight A's."

"Oh." She grinned. "Okay. Thanks in advance."

He stretched. "No problem. Maybe you'll do better at math than you do at driving."

She thumped his arm. "Stop that. I can drive."

"Sort of."

"It takes practice," she reminded him. "How can I practice if you're always too busy to ride in the truck with me?"

"You could ask Sara," he pointed out.

She glowered at him. "I did."

"And?"

"She's always got something ready to cook." She pursed her lips. "In fact, she has pots and pans lined up, ready, in case I look like I'm even planning to ask her to ride with me." Her eyes narrowed suspiciously. "I have reason to believe you've been filling her head with irrelevant facts about how many times I've run into ditches."

"Lies."

"It was only one ditch," she pointed out.

"That reminds me." He pulled out his cell phone and checked a text message. He nodded. "I have a professional driving instructor coming out to work with you, starting Saturday afternoon."

"Coward," she accused.

He grinned. "I don't teach."

"I thought you were doing very well, except for the nonstop cursing."

"I thought you were doing well, except for the non-stop near accidents."

She threw up her hands and sighed. "Okay. Just push me off onto some total stranger who'll have a heart attack if I miss a turn. His family will sue us and we'll end up walking everywhere…"

He held up a hand. "I won't change my mind. I can't teach you how to drive with any efficiency. These people have been doing it for a long time."

She gave in. "Okay. I'll give it a shot." She looked up at him. "You and Sara are coming to graduation, aren't you?"

He smiled down at her. "I wouldn't miss it for the whole world, *ma belle*."

Her heart jumped up into her throat. She could walk on air, because Gabriel teased her in that deep, soft tone that he used only with her.

He touched her long hair gently. "You're almost grown. Just a few more years."

"I'm eighteen."

He let go of her hair. "I know." He turned away. She was eighteen years old. Years too young for what he was thinking of. He had to let her go, let her grow, let her mature. He couldn't hold her back out of selfishness. In a few years, when she was through college, when she had a good job, when she could stand alone—then, yes, perhaps. Perhaps.

"You're very introspective tonight," she remarked.

"Am I?" He chuckled. "I was thinking about cows."

"Cows?"

"It's a clear night. If a UFO were to abduct a cow, we would probably see it."

"How exciting! Let's go looking for them. I'll drive!"

"Not on your life, and don't you have homework? Finals are coming up, I believe?"

She made a face. "Yes, they are, and I can't afford to make a bad grade." She glanced at him. "Spoilsport."

He shrugged. "I want you to graduate."

She folded her hands on her jeans-clad thighs. "I've never told you how much I appreciate all you and Sara have done for me," she said quietly. "I owe you so much…"

"Stop that. We were happy to help."

It had just occurred to her that she was going away, very soon, to college. She was going to live in the dormitory there. She wouldn't live with Sara and Gabriel again. Her holidays would be spent with fellow students, if anyone even stayed on campus—didn't the campus close for holidays?

"I can see the wheels turning," he mused, glancing down at her. "You'll come to us for holidays and vacations," he said. "Sara and I will be here. At least until you're through college. Okay?"

"But Sara has a place in Wyoming—" she began.

"We have a place in Wyoming, and we have a competent manager in charge of it," he interrupted. "Besides, she likes it here in Texas."

"I did notice she was up very late last night on the computer," she said under her breath.

"New expansion on her game," he whispered. "She and her unknown pal are running battlegrounds together. She's very excited."

Michelle laughed softly. "We should probably tell her."

"No way. It's the first time I've seen her happy, really happy, in many years," he said wistfully. "Dreams are precious. Let her keep them."

"I suppose it won't hurt," she replied. "But she's not getting a lot of sleep."

"She hasn't slept well in a long time, despite therapy and prescriptions. This gaming might actually solve a few problems for her."

"You think?"

"We can wait and see, at least." He glanced at his watch, the numbers glowing in the darkness. "I have some paperwork to get through. You coming in?"

"In just a minute. I do love meteor showers."

"So do I. If you like astronomy, we'll have to buy a telescope."

"Could we?" she asked enthusiastically.

"Of course. I'll see about it."

"I would love to look at Mars!"

"So would I."

"I would love to go there," she ventured.

He shrugged. "Not going to happen."

"It was worth a try."

He chuckled, ruffled her hair and went back inside.

GRADUATION DAY WAS going to be long and exciting. Michelle had gone to the rehearsal, which had to be held inside because it was pouring rain that day. She had hoped it wouldn't rain on graduation day.

Her gown and cap fit perfectly. She wasn't going to graduate with honors, but she was at least in the top 10 percent of her class. Her grades had earned her a small scholarship, which would pay for textbooks. She didn't want Gabriel and Sara to be out of pocket on her account, regardless of their financial worth.

Her gown was white. It made her look almost angelic, with her long blond hair down to her waist, her peaches-and-cream complexion delicately colored, her gray eyes glittering with excitement.

She didn't see Gabriel and Sara in the audience, but that wasn't surprising. There was a huge crowd. They were able to graduate outside because the skies cleared up. They held the graduation ceremonies on the football field, with faculty and students and families gathered for the occasion.

Michelle accepted her diploma from the principal, grinned at some of her fellow students and walked off the platform. On the way down, she remembered what a terrifying future she was stepping into. For twelve years, she'd gone to school every day—well, thirteen years if you counted kindergarten. Now, she was free. But with freedom came responsibility. She had to support herself. She had to manage an apartment. She had to pay bills...

Maybe not the bills part, totally. She would have to force Gabriel and Sara to let her pay rent. That would help her pride. She'd go off to college, to strangers, to a dormitory that might actually be unisex. That was a scary thought.

She ran to Gabriel and Sara, to be hugged and congratulated.

"You are now a free woman." Sara chuckled. "Well, mostly. Except for your job, and college upcoming."

"If it's going to be a unisex dorm," Michelle began worriedly.

"It's not," Gabriel assured her. "Didn't you notice? It's a Protestant college. They even have a chaplain."

"Oh. Oh!" She burst out laughing, and flushed. "No,

I didn't really notice, until I thought about having to share my floor with men who are total strangers."

"No way would that happen," Gabriel said solemnly, and his dark eyes flashed. "I'd have you driven back and forth first."

"So would I," Sara agreed. "Or I'd move up to San Antonio, get an apartment and you could room with me."

Tears stung Michelle's cheeks. She was remembering how proud her father had been of her grades and her ambitions, how he'd looked forward to seeing her graduate. He should have been here.

"Now, now," Gabriel said gently, as if he could see the thoughts in her mind. He brushed the tears away and kissed her eyelids closed. "It's a happy occasion," he whispered.

She was tingling all over from the unexpectedly intimate contact. Her heart went wild. When he drew back, everything she felt and thought was right there, in her eyes. His own narrowed, and his tall, muscular body tensed.

Sara coughed. She coughed again, to make sure they heard her.

"Lunch," Gabriel said at once, snapping out of it. "We have reservations."

"At one of the finest restaurants in the country, and we still have to get to the airport."

"Restaurant? Airport?" Michelle was all at sea.

Gabriel grinned. "It's a surprise. Someone's motioning to you." He indicated a female student who was waving like crazy.

"It's Yvonne," Michelle told them. "I promised to

have my picture taken with her and Gerrie. They were in my geography class. Be right back!"

They watched her go, her face alive with pleasure.

"Close call, masked man," Sara said under her breath.

He stuffed his hands into his slacks and his expression hardened.

"You have to be patient," Sara added gently, and touched his chest with a small hand. "Just for a little while."

"Just for years," he said curtly. "While she meets men and falls in love…"

"Fat chance."

He turned and looked down at her, his face guarded but full of hope.

"You know how she feels," Sara said softly. "That isn't going to change. But she has to have time to grow up, to see something of the world. The time will pass."

He grimaced and then drew in a breath. "Yes. I suppose so." He laughed hollowly. "Maybe in the meantime, I can work up to how I'm going to explain my line of work to her. Another hurdle."

"By that time, she'll be more likely to understand."

He nodded. "Yes."

She hugged him impulsively. "You're a great guy. She already knows it."

He hugged her back. "I'll be her best friend."

"You already are." She drew back, smiling. The smile faded and her eyes sparked with temper as she looked past him.

"My, my, did you lose your broom?" came a deep, drawling voice from behind Gabriel.

"The flying monkeys are using it right now," Sara snarled at the tall man. "Are you just graduating from high school, too?" she added. "And I didn't get you a present."

He shrugged. "My foreman's daughter graduated. I'm her godfather."

"So many responses come to mind. But choosing just one." She pondered for a minute. She pursed her full lips. "Do you employ a full-time hit man, or do you have to manage with pickups?"

He raised his thick eyebrows. "Oh, full-time, definitely," he said easily, hands deep in his jean pockets. He cocked his head. "But he doesn't do women. Pity."

Sara was searching for a comeback when Michelle came running back.

"Oh, hi, Mr. Patterson!" she said with a grin. "How's that bull doing?"

"Eating all he can get and looking better by the day, Miss Godfrey," he replied, smiling. "That was a good piece you wrote on the ranch."

"Thanks. I had good material to work with."

Sara made a sound deep in her throat.

"What was that? Calling the flying monkeys in some strange guttural language?" Wolf asked Sara with wide, innocent eyes.

She burst out in Farsi, things that would have made Michelle blush if she understood them.

"Oh, my, what a thing to say to someone!" Wolf said with mock surprise. He looked around. "Where's a police officer when you need one?"

"By all means, find one who speaks Farsi," Sara said with a sarcastic smile.

"Farsi?" Jacobsville police chief Cash Grier strolled up with his wife, Tippy. "I speak Farsi."

"Great. Arrest her," Wolf said, pointing at Sara. "She

just said terrible things about my mother. Not to mention several of my ancestors."

Cash glanced at Sara, who was glowering at Wolf, and totally unrepentant.

"He started it," Sara said angrily. "I do not ride a broom, and I have never seen a flying monkey!"

"I did, once," Cash said, nodding. "Of course, a man threw it at me…"

"Are you going to arrest her?" Wolf interrupted.

"You'd have to prove that she said it," Cash began.

"Gabriel heard her say it," Wolf persisted.

Cash looked at Gabriel. So did Sara and Michelle and Tippy.

"I'll burn the pasta for a week," Sara said under her breath.

Gabriel cleared his throat. "Gosh, I'm sorry," he said. "I wasn't paying attention. Would you like to say it again, and this time I'll listen?" he asked his sister.

"Collusion," Wolf muttered. He glowered at Sara. "I still have my handcuffs from my FBI days…"

"How very kinky," Sara said haughtily.

Cash turned away quickly. His shoulders were shaking.

Tippy hit him.

He composed himself and turned back. "I'm sorry, but I really can't be of any assistance in this particular matter. Congratulations, Michelle," he added.

"Thanks, Chief Grier," she replied.

"Why are you here?" Wolf asked the chief.

"One of my young brother-in-law's older gaming friends is graduating," he replied with a smile. "We came to watch him graduate." He shook his head. "He's awesome at the Halo series on Xbox 360."

"So am I," Wolf said with a grin. He glanced at Gabriel. "Do you play?"

Gabriel shook his head. "I don't really have time."

"It's fun. I like console games. But I also like…" Wolf began.

"The reservations!" Gabriel interrupted, checking his watch. "Sorry, but we've got a flight to catch. Graduation present," he added with a grin and a glance at Michelle. "See you all later."

"Sure," Wolf replied. He glanced at Sara and his eyes twinkled. "An airplane, huh? Having mechanical problems with the broom…?"

"We have to go, right now," Gabriel said, catching Sara before she could move toward Wolf.

He half dragged her away, to the amusement of the others.

"YOU SHOULD HAVE let me hit him," Sara fumed as they sat comfortably in the business-class section of an aircraft bound for New Orleans. "Just one little slap…"

"In front of the police chief, who would have been obliged to arrest you," Gabriel pointed out. "Not a good thing on Michelle's graduation day."

"No." She smiled at Michelle, who looked as amused as Gabriel did. "Sorry. That man just rubs me the wrong way."

"It's okay," Michelle said. "I can't believe we're flying to New Orleans for lunch." She laughed, shaking her head. "I've never been on a plane before in my life. The takeoff was so cool!" she recalled, remembering the burst of speed, the clouds coming closer, the land falling away under the plane as she looked out the window. They'd given her the window seat, so that she had a better view.

"It was fun, seeing it through your eyes," Sara replied, smiling. "I tend to take it for granted. So does he." She indicated Gabriel, who laughed.

"I spend most of my life on airplanes, of one type or another," Gabriel confessed. "I must admit, my flights aren't usually this relaxed."

"You never did tell me what you do," Michelle said.

"I'm sort of a government contractor," he said easily. "An advisor. I go lots of places in that capacity. I deal with foreign governments." He made it sound conventional. It really wasn't.

"Oh. Like businessmen do."

"Something like that," he lied. He smiled. "You have your first driving lesson tomorrow," he reminded her.

"Sure you wouldn't like to do it instead?" she asked. "I could try really hard to avoid ditches."

He shook his head. "You need somebody better qualified than I am."

"I hope he's got a good heart."

"I'm sure he'll be personable…"

"I hope he's in very good health," she amended.

Gabriel just chuckled.

THEY ATE AT a five-star restaurant downtown. The food was the most exquisite Michelle had ever tasted, with a Cajun spiced fare that teased the tongue, and desserts that almost made her cry they were so delicious.

"This is one of the best restaurants I've ever frequented," Gabriel said as they finished second cups of coffee. "I always stop by when I'm in the area." He looked around at the elegant decor. "They had some problems during Hurricane Katrina, but they've remodeled and regrouped. It's better than ever."

"It was delicious," Michelle said, smiling. "You guys are spoiling me rotten."

"We're enjoying it," Sara replied. "And there's an even bigger surprise waiting when we get home," she added.

"Another one? But this was the best present I've ever had! You didn't need to…"

"Oh, but we did," Gabriel replied. He leaned back in his chair, elegant in a navy blue jacket with a black turtleneck and dark slacks. Sara was wearing a simple black dress with pearls that made her look both expensive and beautiful. Michelle, in contrast, was wearing the only good dress she had, a simple sheath of off-white, with her mother's pearls. She felt dowdy compared to her companions, but they didn't even seem to notice that the dress was old. They made her feel beautiful.

"What is it?" Michelle asked suddenly.

She was met with bland smiles.

"Wait and see," Gabriel said with twinkling black eyes.

CHAPTER EIGHT

IT WAS VERY late when they got back to the ranch. There, sitting in the driveway, was a beautiful little white car with a big red ribbon tied around it.

Michelle gaped at it. Her companions urged her closer.

She touched the trunk, where a sleek silver Jaguar emblem sat above the keyhole.

"It's a Jag," she stammered.

"It's not the most expensive one," Sara said quickly when Michelle gave them accusing glances. "In fact, it's a midrange automobile. But it's one of the safest cars on the road. Which is why we got it for you. Happy Graduation!"

She hugged Michelle.

"It's too much," Michelle stammered, touching the body with awe. She fought tears. "I never dreamed… Oh, it's so…beautiful!" She turned and threw herself into Sara's arms, hugging her close. "I'll take such good care of it! I'll polish it by the inch, with my own hands…!"

"Don't I get a hug, too? It was my idea," Gabriel said.

She laughed, turned and hugged him close. "Of course you do. Thank you! Gosh, I never dreamed you'd get me a car as a present!"

"You needed one," Gabriel said at the top of her head.

"You have to be able to drive to work for Minette in the summer. And you'll need one to commute from college to home on weekends. If you want to come home that often," he added.

"Why would I want to stay in the city when I can come down here and ride horses?" she asked, smiling up at him. He was such a dish, she thought dreamily.

Gabriel looked back at her with dark, intent eyes. She was beautiful. Men would want her. Other men.

"Well, try it out," Sara said, interrupting tactfully. "I'll help you untie the ribbon."

"I'm never throwing the ribbon away!" Michelle laughed. "Oh. Wait!" She pulled out her cell phone and took a picture of the car in its bow.

"Stand beside it. We'll get one of you, too," Gabriel said, pulling out his own cell phone. He took several shots, smiling all the time. "Okay. Now get inside and try it out."

"Who's riding shotgun?" Michelle asked.

They looked worriedly at each other.

"It's too late to take it out of the driveway," Gabriel said finally. "Just start it up."

Michelle stood at the door. It wouldn't open.

"The key," Sara prompted Gabriel.

"The key. Duh." He chuckled. He dug it out of his pants pocket and handed it to Michelle. It was still warm from his body.

She looked at the fob in the light from the porch. "There's no key."

"You don't need one."

She unlocked the car and got inside. "There's no gearshift!"

"See the start button?" Gabriel prompted. "Press it."

She did. Nothing happened.

"Hold down the brake with your foot and then press it," he added.

She did. The car roared to life. She caught her breath as the vents opened and the gearshift rose up out of the console. "Oh!" she exclaimed. She looked at the controls, at the instrument panel, at the leather seats. "Oh!" she said again.

Gabriel squatted by the door, on the driveway. "Its creator said something like, 'We will never come closer to building something that is alive.' Each Jaguar is unique. Each has its own little idiosyncrasies. I've been driving them for years, and I still learn new things about them. They purr when they're happy, they growl when they want the open road." He laughed self-consciously. "Well, you'll see."

She leaned over and brushed her soft mouth against his cheek, very shyly. "Thanks."

He chuckled and got to his feet. "You're welcome."

"Thanks, Sara," she called to the other woman.

"It was truly our pleasure." Sara yawned. "And now we really should get to bed, don't you think? Michelle has an early morning, and I'm quite tired." She hesitated. "Perhaps we should check to make sure the flying monkeys are locked up securely…?"

They both laughed.

THE DRIVING INSTRUCTOR'S name was Mr. Moore. He had a small white round patch of hair at the base of his skull. Michelle wondered if his hair loss was from close calls by students.

He was very patient. She had a couple of near-misses, but was able to correct in time and avoid an accident.

He told her that it was something that much practice would fix. She only needed to drive, and remember her lessons.

So she drove. But it was Sara, not Gabriel, who rode with her that summer. Gabriel had packed a bag, told the women goodbye, and rushed out without another word.

"Where is he going?" Michelle had asked Sara.

The other woman smiled gently. "We're not allowed to know. Some of what he does is classified. And you must never mention it to anyone. Okay?"

"Of course not," Michelle replied. She bit her lip. "What he does—it's just office stuff, right? I mean he advises. That's talking to people, instructing, right?"

Sara hesitated only a beat before she replied, "Of course."

MICHELLE PUT IT out of her mind. Gabriel didn't phone home. He'd been gone several weeks. During that time, Michelle began to perfect her driving skills, with Sara's help. She got her driver's license, passing the test easily, and now she drove alternately to work with Carlie.

"This is just so great," Carlie enthused on the way to work. "They bought you a Jaguar! I can't believe it!" She sighed, smoothing her hand over the soft leather seat. "I wish somebody would buy me a Jaguar."

Michelle chuckled. "It was a shock to me, too, let me tell you. I tried to give it back, but they wouldn't hear of it. They said I needed something safe. Like a big Ford truck wouldn't be safe?" she mused.

"I'd love a big brand-new Ford truck," Carlie sighed. "One of those F-Series ones. Or a Dodge Ram. Or a Chevy Silverado. I've never met a truck I didn't love."

"I like cars better," Michelle said. "Just a personal

preference." She glanced at her friend. "I'm going to miss riding with you when I go to college."

"I'll miss you, too." Carlie glanced out the window. "Just having company keeps me from brooding."

"Carson is still giving you fits, I gather?" Michelle asked gently.

Carlie looked down at her hands. "I don't understand why he hates me so much," she said. "I haven't done anything to him. Well, except make a few sarcastic comments, but he starts it," she added with a scowl.

"Maybe he likes you," Michelle ventured. "And he doesn't want to."

"Oh, sure, that's the reason." She shook her head. "No. That isn't it. He'd throw me to the wolves without a second thought."

"He spends a lot of time in Cash Grier's office."

"They're working on something. I'm not allowed to know what, and the chief makes sure I can't overhear him when he talks on the phone." She frowned. "My father's in there a lot, too. I can't imagine why. Carson isn't the praying sort," she added coldly, alluding to her father's profession. He was, after all, a minister.

"I wouldn't think the chief is the praying sort, either," Michelle replied. "Maybe it's something to do about that man who attacked your father."

"I've wondered about that," her companion replied. "Dad won't tell me anything. He just clams up if I mention it."

"You could ask the chief."

Carlie burst out laughing. "You try it," she replied with a grin. "He changes the subject, picks up the phone, drags someone passing by into the office to chat—he's a master at evasion."

"You might try asking Carson," she added.

The smile faded. "Carson would walk all over me."

"You never know."

"I know, all right." Carlie flushed a little, and stared out the window again.

"Sorry," Michelle said gently. "You don't want to talk about him. I understand."

"It's okay." She turned her head. "Is Gabriel coming back soon?"

"We don't know. We don't even know where he is," Michelle said sadly. "Some foreign country, I gather, but he didn't say." She shook her head. "He's so mysterious."

"Most men are." Carlie laughed.

"At least what he does is just business stuff," came the reply. "So we don't have to worry about him so much."

"A blessing," Carlie agreed.

MICHELLE DID A story about the local fire department and its new fire engine. She learned a lot from the fire chief about how fires were started and how they were fought. She put it all into a nice article, with photos of the firemen. Minette ran it on the front page.

"Favoritism," Cash Grier muttered when she stopped by to get Carlie for the drive home that Friday afternoon.

"Excuse me?" Michelle asked him.

"A story about the fire department, on the front page," he muttered. He glared at her. "You haven't even done one about us, and we just solved a major crime!"

"A major crime." Michelle hadn't heard of it.

"Yes. Someone captured old man Jones's chicken,

put it in a doll dress, and tied it to his front porch." He grinned. "We captured the perp."

"And?" Michelle prompted. Carlie was listening, too.

"It was Ben Harris's granddaughter." He chuckled. "Her grandmother punished her for overfilling the bathtub by taking away her favorite dolly. So there was this nice red hen right next door. She took the chicken inside, dressed it up, and had fun playing with it while her grandparents were at the store. Then she realized how much more trouble she was going to be in when they noticed what the chicken did, since it wasn't wearing a diaper."

Both women were laughing.

"So she took the chicken back to Jones's house, but she was afraid it might run off, so she tied it to the porch rail." He shook his head. "The doll's clothes were a dead giveaway. She's just not cut out for a life of crime."

"What did Mr. Jones do?" Michelle asked.

"Oh, he took pictures," he replied. "Want one? They're pretty cool. I'm thinking of having one blown up for my office. To put on my solved-crime wall." He grinned.

They were laughing so hard, tears were rolling down their cheeks.

"And the little girl?" Michelle persisted.

"She's assigned to menial chores for the next few days. At least, until all the chicken poop has been cleaned off the floors and furniture. They did give her back the doll, however," he added, tongue in cheek. "To prevent any future lapses. Sad thing, though."

"What is?"

"The doll is naked. If she brings it out of the house,

as much as I hate it, I'll have to cite it for indecent exposure…"

The laughter could be heard outside the door now. The tall man with jet-black hair hanging down to his waist wasn't laughing.

He stopped, staring at the chief and his audience.

"Something?" Cash asked, suddenly all business.

"Something." Carson's black eyes slid to Carlie's face and narrowed coldly. "If you can spare the time."

"Sure. Come on in."

"If you don't need me, I'll go home," Carlie said at once, flushed, as she avoided Carson's gaze.

"I don't need you." Carson said it with pure venom.

She lifted her chin pugnaciously. "Thank God," she said through her teeth.

He opened his mouth, but Cash intervened. "Go on home, Carlie," he said, as he grabbed Carson by the arm and steered him into the office.

"SO THAT'S CARSON," Michelle said as she drove toward Carlie's house.

"That's Carson."

Michelle drew in a breath. "A thoroughly unpleasant person."

"You don't know the half of it."

"He really has it in for you."

Carlie nodded. "Told you so."

There really didn't seem to be anything else to say. Michelle gave her a sympathetic smile and kept her silence until they pulled up in front of the Victorian house she shared with her father.

"Thanks for the ride," Carlie said. "My turn to drive tomorrow."

"And my turn to buy gas." She chuckled.

"You don't hear me arguing, do you?" Carlie sighed, smiling. "Gas is outrageously high."

"So is most everything else. Have a good night. I'll see you tomorrow."

"Sure. Thanks again."

MICHELLE PARKED HER car in front of the house, noted that she really needed to take it through the car wash, and started toward the front door. Sara's car was missing. She hadn't mentioned being away. Not a problem, however, since Michelle had a key.

She started to put it into the lock, just as it opened on its own. And there was Gabriel, tanned and handsome and smiling.

"Gabriel!" She threw herself into his arms, to be lifted, and hugged, and swung around once, twice, three times, in an embrace so hungry that she never wanted to be free again.

"When did you get home?" she asked at his ear.

"About ten minutes ago," he murmured into her neck. "You smell of roses."

"New perfume. Sara bought it for me." She drew back just enough to see his face, her arms still around his neck, his arms still holding her close. She searched his eyes at point-blank range and felt her heart go into overdrive. She could barely breathe. He felt like heaven in her arms. She looked at his mouth, chiseled, perfect, and wondered, wondered so hard, how it would feel if she moved just a little, if she touched her lips to it…

His hand caught in her long hair and pulled. "No," he said through his teeth.

She met his eyes. She saw there, or thought she saw,

the same burning hunger that was beginning to tauten her young body, to kindle needs she'd never known she had.

Her lips parted on a shaky breath. She stared at him. He stared back. There seemed to be no sound in the world, nothing except the soft rasp of her breathing and the increasing heaviness of his own. Against her flattened breasts, she could feel the warm hardness of his chest, the thunder of his heartbeat.

One of his hands slid up and down her spine. His black eyes dropped to her mouth and lingered there until she almost felt the imprint of them, like a hard, rough kiss. Her nails bit into him where her hands clung.

She wanted him. He could feel it. She wanted his mouth, his hands, his body. Her breath was coming in tiny gasps. He could feel her heartbeat behind the soft, warm little breasts pressed so hard to his chest. Her mouth was parted, moist, inviting. He could grind his own down into it and make her moan, make her want him, make her open her arms to him on the long, soft sofa that was only a few steps away...

She was eighteen. She'd never lived. There hadn't been a serious romance in her young life. He could rob her of her innocence, make her a toy, leave her broken and hurting and old.

"No," he whispered. He forced himself to put her down. He held her arms, tightly, until he could force himself to let go and step back.

She was shaky. She felt his hunger. He wasn't impervious to her. But he was cautious. He didn't want to start anything. He was thinking about her age. She knew it.

"I won't...always be eighteen," she managed.

He nodded, very slowly. "One day," he promised. "Perhaps."

She brightened. It was like the sun coming out. "I'll read lots of books."

His eyebrows arched.

"You know. On how to do…stuff. And I'll buy a hope chest and fill it up with frothy little black things."

The eyebrows arched even more.

"Well, it's a hope chest. As in, I hope I'll need it one day when you think I'm old enough." She pursed her lips and her gray eyes twinkled. "I could fake my ID…"

"Give it up." He chuckled.

She shrugged. "I'll grow up as fast as I can," she promised. She glowered at him. "I won't like it if I hear about you having orgies with strange women."

"Most women are strange," he pointed out.

She hit his chest. "Not nice."

"How's the driving?" he asked, changing the subject.

"I haven't hit a tree, run off the road or approached a ditch since you left," she said smugly. "I haven't even dinged the paint."

"Good girl," he said, chuckling. "I'm proud of you. How's the job coming along?"

"It's great! I'm working on this huge story! It may have international implications!"

Odd, how worried he looked for a few seconds. "What story?"

"It involves a kidnapping," she continued.

He frowned.

"A chicken was involved," she added, and watched his face clear and become amused. "A little girl whose doll was taken away for punishment stole a chicken and dressed it in doll's clothes. I understand she'll be cleaning the house for days to come."

He laughed heartily. "The joys of small-town reporting," he mused.

"They never end. How was your trip?"

"Long," he said. "And I'm starving."

"Sara made a lovely casserole. I'll heat you up some."

He sat down at the kitchen table and watched her work. She made coffee and put a mug of it, black, at his place while she dealt with reheating the chicken casserole.

She warmed up a piece of French bread with butter to go with it. Then she sat down and watched him eat while she sipped her own coffee.

"It sure beats fried snake," he murmured.

She blinked. "What?"

"Well, we eat what we can find. Usually, it's a snake. Sometimes, if we're lucky, a big bird or some fish."

"In an office building?" she exclaimed.

He glanced at her with amusement. "It's not always in an office building. Sometimes we have to go out and look at…projects, wherever they might be. This time, it was in a jungle."

"Wow." She was worried now. "Poisonous snakes?"

"Mostly. It doesn't really affect the taste," he added.

"You could get bitten," she persisted.

"I've been bitten, half a dozen times," he replied easily. "We always carry antivenin with us."

"I thought you were someplace safe."

He studied her worried face and felt a twinge of guilt. "It was just this once," he lied, and he smiled. "What I do is rarely dangerous." Another lie. A bigger one. "Nothing to concern you. Honest."

She propped her face in her hands, her elbows on the table, and watched him finish his meal and his coffee.

"Stop that," he teased. "I can take care of myself. I've been doing it for twenty-odd years."

She grimaced. "Okay. Just checking."

"I promise not to get killed."

"If you do, I'm coming after you. Boy, will you be sorry, too."

He laughed. "I hear you."

"Want dessert? We have a cherry pie."

He shook his head. "Maybe later. Where's Sara?"

"I have no idea. She didn't even leave a note."

He pulled out his cell phone and pressed the speed dial. He got up and poured more coffee into his cup while he waited.

"Where are you?" he asked after a minute.

There was a reply. He glanced at Michelle, his lips pursed, his eyes twinkling. "Yes, she's right here."

Another silence. He sat back down. He was nodding.

"No, I think it's a very good idea. But you might have asked for my input first... No, I agree, you have exquisite taste... Yes, that's true, returns are possible. I won't tell her. How long?... Okay. See you then." He smiled. "Me, too. Thanks."

He hung up.

"Where is she?" she asked.

"On her way home. With a little surprise."

"Something for me?" she asked, and her face brightened.

"I'd say so."

"But you guys have already given me so much," she began, protesting.

"You can take that up with my sister," he pointed out. "Not that it will do you much good. She's very stubborn."

She laughed. "I noticed." She paused. "What is it?"

"You'll have to wait and see."

SARA PULLED UP into the driveway and got out of her car. She popped the truck and dragged out several big shopping bags. She handed some to Gabriel and one to Michelle. She was grinning from ear to ear.

"What in the world…?" Michelle exclaimed.

"Just a few little odds and ends that you're going to need to start college. Come on inside and I'll show you. Gabriel, get your nose out of that bag, it's private!"

He laughed and led the way into the house.

MICHELLE WAS SPEECHLESS. Sara had exquisite taste in clothing, and it showed in the items she'd purchased for their houseguest. There was everything from jeans and sweats to dresses and handbags and underwear, gossamer gowns and an evening gown that brought tears to Michelle's eyes because it was the loveliest thing she'd ever seen.

"You like them?" Sara asked, a little worried.

"I've never had things like this," she stammered. "Daddy was so sick that he never thought of shopping with me. And when Roberta took me, it was just for bras and panties, never for nice clothes." She hugged Sara impulsively. "Thank you. Thank you so much!"

"You might try on that gown. I wasn't sure about the size, but we can exchange it if it doesn't fit. I'll go have coffee with Gabriel while you check the fit." She smiled, and left Michelle with the bags.

THEY WERE SIPPING coffee in the kitchen when Michelle came nervously to the doorway. She'd fixed her hair, put on shoes and she was wearing the long, creamy evening gown with its tight fit and cap sleeves, revealing soft cleavage. There was faint embroidery on the bodice and around the hem. The off-white brought out the highlights in Michelle's long, pale blond hair, and accentuated her peaches-and-cream complexion. In her softly powdered face, her gray eyes were exquisite.

Gabriel turned his head when he caught movement in his peripheral vision. He sat like a stone statue, just staring. Sara followed his gaze, and her face brightened.

"It's perfect!" she exclaimed, rising. "Michelle, it's absolutely perfect! Now you have something to wear to a really formal occasion."

"Thanks," she replied. "It's the most beautiful thing I've ever owned." She glanced at Gabriel, who hadn't spoken. His coffee cup was suspended in his hand in midair, as if he'd forgotten it. "Does it…look okay?" she asked him, wanting reassurance.

He forced his eyes away. "It looks fine." He put the mug down and got to his feet. "I need to check the livestock." He went out the back door without a glance behind him.

Michelle felt wobbly. She bit her lower lip. "He didn't like it," she said miserably.

Sara touched her cheek gently. "Men are strange. They react in odd ways. I'm sure he liked it, but he's not demonstrative." She smiled. "Okay?"

Michelle relaxed. "Okay."

OUT IN THE BARN, Gabriel was struggling to regain his composure. He'd never seen anything in his life more beautiful than Michelle in that dress. He'd had to force himself out the door before he reacted in a totally inappropriate way. He wanted to sweep her up in his arms and kiss her until her mouth went numb. Not a great idea.

He stood beside one of his horses, stroking its muzzle gently, while he came to grips with his hunger. It was years too soon. He would have to manage the long wait. Meanwhile, he worried about the other men, young men, who would see Michelle in that gown and want her, as he wanted her. But they would be her age, young and untried, without his jaded past. They would be like her, full of passion for life.

It wasn't fair of him to try to keep her. He must distance himself from her, give her the chance to grow away from him, to find someone more suitable. It was going to be hard, but he must manage it. She deserved the chance.

THE NEXT MORNING, he was gone when Michelle went into the kitchen to help Sara fix breakfast.

"His truck's gone," Michelle said, her spirits dropping hard.

"Yes. I spoke to him late last night," Sara replied, not looking at her. "He has a new job. He said he might be away for a few weeks." She glanced at the younger woman and managed a smile. "Don't worry about him. He can take care of himself."

"I'm sure he can. It's just…" She rested her hand on the counter. "I miss him, when he's away."

"I'm sure you do." She hesitated. "Michelle, you haven't started to live yet. There's a whole world out there that you haven't even seen."

Michelle turned, her eyes old and wise. "And you think I'll find some young man who'll sweep me off my feet and carry me off to a castle." She smiled. "There's only one man I'll ever want to do that, you know."

Sara grimaced. "There are so many things you don't know."

"They won't matter," Michelle replied very quietly. She searched Sara's eyes. "None of it will matter."

Sara couldn't think of the right words. So she just hugged Michelle instead.

CHAPTER NINE

MICHELLE WAS VERY NERVOUS. It was the first day of the semester on campus, and even with a map, it was hard to find all her classes. Orientation had given the freshmen an overview of where everything was off the quad, but it was so confusing.

"Is Western Civilization in Sims Hall or Waverly Hall?" she muttered to herself, peering at the map.

"Waverly," came a pleasant male voice from just behind her. "Come on, I'll walk you over. I'm Randy. Randy Miles."

"Michelle Godfrey," she said, shaking his hand and smiling. "Thanks. Are you in my class?"

He shook his head. "I'm a junior."

"Should you be talking to me?" she teased. "After all, I'm pond scum."

He stopped and smiled. He had dark hair and pale eyes. He was a little pudgy, but nice. "No. You're not pond scum. Trust me."

"Thanks."

"My pleasure. Are you from San Antonio?"

"My family is from Jacobsville, but I lived here with my parents while they were alive."

"Sorry."

"They were wonderful people. The memories get

easier with time." She glanced around. "This is a huge campus."

"They keep adding to it," he said. "Sims Hall is brand-new. Waverly is old. My father had history with old Professor Barlane."

"Really?"

He nodded. "Just a word of warning, never be late for his class. You don't want to know why."

She grinned. "I'll remember."

On the way to Waverly Hall, Randy introduced Michelle to two of his friends, Alan Drew and Marjory Wills. Alan was distantly pleasant. Marjory was much more interested in talking to Randy than being introduced to this new student.

"You're going to be late for class, aren't you?" Alan asked Michelle, checking his watch. "I'll walk you the rest of the way."

"Nice to have met you," Randy said pleasantly. Marjory just nodded.

Michelle smiled and followed Alan to the towering building where her class was located.

"Thanks," she said.

He shrugged and smiled. "Those two." He rolled his eyes. "They're crazy about each other, but neither one will admit it. Don't let them intimidate you, especially Marjory. She has…issues."

"No problem. I guess I'll see you around."

"You will." He leaned forward, grinning. "I'm in the class you're going to right now. And we'd better hurry!"

THEY BARELY MADE it before the bell. The professor, Dr. Barlane, was old and cranky. He gave the class a dismissive look and began to lecture. Michelle was grateful that she'd learned how to take notes, because she had a feeling that this class was going to be one of the more demanding ones.

Beside her, Alan was scribbling on scraps of paper instead of a notebook, like Michelle. He wasn't bad-looking. He had dark hair and eyes and a nice smile, but in her heart, there was only Gabriel. She might like other men as friends, but there was never going to be one to compare with Gabriel.

After class, Alan left her with a smile and whistled as he continued on to his next class. Michelle looked at her schedule, puzzled out the direction to go and went along the walkway to the next building.

"WELL, HOW WAS IT?" Sara asked that night on the phone.

"Very nice," she replied. "I made a couple of friends."

"Male ones?" Sara teased.

"What was that?" Gabriel spoke up in the background.

"She made friends," Sara called to him. "Don't have a cow."

He made a sarcastic sound and was quiet.

"How do you like your roommate?" Sara continued.

Michelle glanced into the next room, where Darla was searching frantically for a blouse she'd unpacked and couldn't find, muttering and ruffling her red hair.

"She's just like me. Disorganized and flighty," Michelle said, a little loudly.

"I heard that!" Darla said over her shoulder.

"I know!" Michelle laughed. Darla shook her head, laughing, too.

"We're going to get along just fine," Michelle told Sara. "Neither of us has half a mind, and we're so disorganized that we're likely to be thrown out for creating a public eyesore."

"Not likely," Sara replied. "Well, I'm glad things are going well. If you need us, you know where we are, sweetie."

"I do. Thanks. Thanks for everything."

"Keep in touch. Good night."

"Good night."

"Your family?" Darla asked, poking her head into the room.

Michelle hesitated, but only for a second. She smiled. "Yes. My family."

MICHELLE ADJUSTED TO college quite easily. She made some friends, mostly distant ones, and one good one—her roommate, Darla. She and Darla were both religious, so they didn't go to boozy parties or date promiscuous boys. That meant they spent a lot of time watching rented movies and eating popcorn in their own dorm room.

One thing Sara had said was absolutely true; college changed her. She learned things that questioned her own view of the world and things about other cultures. She saw the rise and fall of civilizations, the difference in religions, the rise of science, the fascination of history. She continued her study of French—mainly because she wanted to know what Sara and Gabriel spoke about that they didn't want her to hear—and she sweated first-year biology. But by and large, she did well in her classes.

ALL TOO SOON, final exams arrived. She sat in the library with other students, she and Darla trying to absorb what they needed to know to pass their courses.

She'd already lived in the biology lab for several days after school with a study group, going over material that was certainly going to come up when they were tested.

"I'm going to fail," she moaned softly to Darla. "I'll go home in disgrace. I'll have to hide my head in a paper sack…"

"Shut up," Darla muttered. "You're going to pass! So am I. Be quiet and study, girl!"

Michelle sighed. "Thanks. I needed that."

"I'm going to fail," one of the boys nearby moaned to Darla. "I'll go home in disgrace…"

She punched him.

"Thanks." He chuckled, and went back to his books.

MICHELLE DID PASS, with flying colors, but she didn't know it when she went back to Comanche Wells for the holidays.

"I'll have to sweat it out until my grades come through," she said to Sara, hugging her warmly. "But I think I did okay." She looked past Sara and then at her, curious.

"He's out of the country," Sara said gently. "He was really sorry, he wanted to be home for the holidays. But it wasn't possible. This was a rush thing."

Michelle's heart fell. "I guess he has to work."

"Yes, he does. But he got your presents, and mine, and wrapped them before he left." Her dark eyes twinkled. "He promised that we'd love the gifts."

"I'd love a rock, if he picked it out for me," Michelle sighed. "Can we go shopping? Minette said I could work for her over the holidays while I'm home, so I'll have a little money of my own."

"Whenever you like, dear," Sara promised.

"Thanks!"

"Now come and have hot chocolate. I want to hear all about college!"

MINETTE HAD SOME interesting assignments for Michelle. One was to interview one of Jacobsville's senior citizens about Christmas celebrations in the mid-twentieth century, before the internet or space travel. It had sounded rather boring, honestly. But when she spoke to Adelaide Duncan, the old woman made the past come alive in her soft, mellow tones.

"We didn't have fancy decorations for the Christmas tree," Mrs. Duncan recalled, her pale blue eyes dancing with delightful memories. "We made them from construction paper. We made garlands of cranberries. We used candles set on the branches to light the tree, and we used soap powder mixed with a little water for snow. Presents were practical things, mostly fruit or nuts or handcrafted garments. One year I got oranges and a knit cap. Another, I got a dress my mother had made me in a beautiful lemon color. My husband kissed me under the mistletoe when we were still in school together, long before we married." Her face was wistful. "He was seventeen and I was fifteen. We danced to music that our parents and relatives made with fiddles and guitars. I wore the lemon-yellow dress, ruffled and laced, and I felt like I had possession of the whole world's treasures." She sighed. "We were married for fifty-five years," she added wistfully. "And one day, not too long away now, I'll see him again. And we'll dance together…"

Michelle had to fight tears. "Fifty-five years," she repeated, and couldn't imagine two people staying together for so long.

"Oh, yes. In my day, people got married and then had children." She shook her head. "The world has changed, my dear. Marriage doesn't seem to mean the same as it used to. History tends to repeat itself, and I fear when the stability of a civilization is lost, society crumbles. You'll study the results in your history classes in college," she added, nodding. "Do you have Dr. Barlane for history by any chance?"

"Yes," Michelle said, stunned.

The old woman laughed. "He and I graduated together from Marist College, both with degrees in history. But he went on to higher education and I got married and had a family. By and large, I think my life was happier than his. He never married."

"Do your children live here?" she asked.

"Oh, no, they're scattered around the world." She laughed. "I visit with them on Skype and we text back and forth every day, though. Modern technology." She shook her head. "It really is a blessing, in this day and time."

Michelle was surprised. "You text?" she asked.

"My dear," the old lady mused, laughing, "I not only text, I tweet and surf, and I am hell on wheels with a two-handed sword in World of Warcraft. I own a guild."

The younger woman's idea of elderly people had gone up in a blaze of disbelief. "You…play video games?"

"I eat them up." She shrugged. "I can't run and jump and play in real life, but I can do it online." She grinned from ear to ear. "Don't you dare tell Wofford Patterson, but I creamed one of his Horde toons last night on a battleground."

Michelle almost fell over laughing.

"And you thought you were going to interview some

dried up old hulk who sat in a rocking chair and knitted, I bet," the woman mused with twinkling eyes.

"Yes, I did," Michelle confessed, "and I am most heartily sorry!"

"That's all right, dear," Mrs. Duncan said, patting her hand. "We all have misconceptions about each other."

"Mine were totally wrong."

"How nice of you to say so!"

Michelle changed gears and went back to the interview. But what she learned about elderly people that day colored her view of them forever.

"She plays video games," Michelle enthused to Minette, back at the office. She'd written her story and turned it in, along with her photos, while Minette was out of the office. Now she was elaborating on the story, fascinated with what she'd learned.

"Yes, there have been a lot of changes in the way we perceive the elderly," Minette agreed. "I live with my great-aunt. She doesn't play video games, but I did catch her doing Tai Chi along with an instructor on public television. And she can text, too."

"My grandparents sat and rocked on the porch after supper," Michelle recalled. "He smoked a pipe and she sewed quilt tops and they talked." She shook her head. "It's a different world."

"It is." She hesitated. "Has Gabriel come home?"

Michelle shook her head. "It's almost Christmas, too. We don't know where he is, or what he's doing."

Minette, who did, carefully concealed her knowledge. "Well, he might surprise you and show up on Christmas day. Who knows?"

Michelle forced a smile. "Yes."

SHE AND SARA decorated the tree. Two of the men who worked for Gabriel part-time, taking care of the horses and the ranch, had come in earlier with a big bucket, holding a tree with the root ball still attached.

"I can't bear to kill a tree," Sara confided as the men struggled to put it in place in the living room. "Sorry, guys," she added.

"Oh, Miss Sara, it's no trouble at all," the taller of the two cowboys said at once, holding his hat to his heart. He grinned. "It was our pleasure."

"Absolutely," the shorter one agreed.

They stood smiling at Sara until one thumped the other and reminded him that they had chores to do. They excused themselves, still smiling.

"You just tie them up in knots." Michelle laughed, when they were out of the room. "You're so pretty."

Sara made a face. "Nonsense."

"Hide your head in the sand, then. What are we going to decorate it with?" she added.

"Come with me."

Sara pulled down the ladder and the two women climbed carefully up into the attic.

Michelle caught her breath when she saw the heart of pine rafters. "My goodness, it's almost a religious experience to just look at them!" she exclaimed. "Those rafters must be a hundred years old!"

Sara glanced at her with amusement. "I believe they are. Imagine you, enthralled by rafters!"

"Heart of pine rafters," she replied. "My grandfather built houses when he was younger. He took me with him a time or two when he had to patch a roof or fix a leak. He was passionate about rafters." She laughed. "And especially those made of heart of pine. They're rare, these days, when people mostly build with green lumber that hasn't been properly seasoned."

"This house has a history," Sara said. "You probably already know it, since your people came from Jacobs County."

Michelle nodded, watching Sara pick up two boxes of ornaments and stack them together. "It belonged to a Texas Ranger."

"Yes. He was killed in a shoot-out in San Antonio. He left behind two sons, a daughter and a wife. There's a plaque in city hall in Jacobsville that tells all about him."

"I'll have to go look," Michelle said. "I haven't done any stories that took me there, yet."

"I'm sure you will. Minette says you're turning into a very good reporter."

"She does?" Michelle was all eyes. "Really?"

Sara looked at her and smiled. "You must have more confidence in yourself," she said gently. "You must believe in your own abilities."

"That's hard."

"It comes with age. You'll get the hang of it." She handed Michelle a box of ornaments. "Be careful going down the steps."

"Okay."

THEY SPENT THE afternoon decorating the tree. When they finally plugged in the beautiful, colored fairy lights, Michelle caught her breath.

"It's the most breathtaking tree I've ever seen," she enthused.

"It is lovely, isn't it?" Sara asked. She fingered a branch. "We must keep it watered, so that it doesn't die.

When Christmas is over, I'll have the men plant it near the front steps. I do so love white pines!"

"Do you ever miss Wyoming?" Michelle asked, a little worried because she knew Sara was only here so that Michelle could come home, so that she wouldn't be alone with Gabriel.

Sara turned to her. "A little. I lived there because Gabriel bought the ranch and one of us needed to run it. But I had no real friends. I'm happier here." Her dark eyes were soft. She smoothed over an ornament. "This belonged to my grandmother," she said softly. It was a little house, made of logs, hanging from a red silk ribbon. "My grandfather whittled it for her, when they were dating." She laughed. "Wherever I am, it always makes me feel at home when the holidays come."

"Your mother's parents?"

Sara's face went hard. "No. My father's."

"I'm sorry."

Sara turned back to her. In her lovely face, her dark eyes were sad. "I don't speak of my mother, or her people. I'm sorry. It's a sore spot with me."

"I'll remember," Michelle said quietly. "It's like my stepmother."

"Exactly."

Michelle didn't betray her secret knowledge of Sara's early life, of the tragedy she and Gabriel had lived through because of their mother's passion for their stepfather. She changed the subject and asked about the other ornaments that Sara had placed on the tree.

But Sara wasn't fooled. She was very quiet. Later, when they were sipping hot chocolate in the kitchen, her dark eyes pinned Michelle.

"How much did he tell you?" she asked suddenly.

In her hands, the mug jumped, almost enough to spill the hot liquid on her fingers.

"Careful, it's hot," Sara said. "Come on, Michelle. How much did Gabriel tell you?"

Michelle grimaced.

Sara took in a long breath. "I see." She sipped the liquid gingerly. "He never speaks of it at all. Yet he told you." Her soft eyes lifted to Michelle's worried gray ones. "I'm not angry. I'm surprised."

"That he told me?"

"Yes." She smiled sadly. "He doesn't warm to people. In fact, he's cold and withdrawn with almost everyone. You can't imagine how shocked I was when he phoned me and asked me to come down here because of a young girl he was going to get custody of." She laughed, shaking her head. "I thought he was joking."

"But he's not. Cold and withdrawn, I mean." Michelle faltered.

"Not with you." She stared into Michelle's eyes earnestly. "I haven't heard Gabriel laugh in years," she added softly. "But he does it all the time with you. I don't understand it. But you give him peace, Michelle."

"That would be nice, if it were true. I don't know if it is," Michelle replied.

"It's fairly obvious what you feel for him."

She flushed. She couldn't lift her eyes.

"He won't take advantage of it, don't worry," Sara added gently. "That's why I'm here." She laughed. "He's taking no chances."

"He doesn't want to get involved with a child," Michelle said heavily.

"You won't be a child for much longer," the other woman pointed out.

"I'm sure he meets beautiful women all the time," Michelle said.

"I'm sure it doesn't matter what they look like," Sara replied. She smiled. "You'll see."

Michelle didn't reply to that. She just sipped her hot chocolate and felt warm inside.

IT WAS THE week before Christmas, a Friday about lunchtime, when the women heard a truck pull up in the driveway.

Michelle, who was petting one of the horses in the corral, saw the truck and gasped and ran as fast as she could to the man getting out of it.

"Gabriel!" she cried.

He turned. His face lit up like floodlights. He held out his arms and waited until she ran into them to pick her up and whirl her around, holding her so close that she felt they were going to be joined together forever.

"Oh, I've missed you," she choked.

"I've missed you." His voice was deep at her ear. He lifted his head and set her on her feet. His black eyes were narrow, intent on her face. He touched her mouth with just the tip of his forefinger, teasing it apart. His eyes fell to it and lingered there while her heart threatened to jump right out of her throat.

"Ma belle," he whispered roughly.

He framed her oval face in his big hands and searched her eyes. *"Ma belle,"* he repeated. His eyes fell to her mouth. "It's like falling into fire…"

As he spoke, his head started to bend. Michelle's heart ran away. She could hear her own breathing, feel his breath going into her mouth, taste the coffee and the faint odor of tobacco that came from him, mingled with some masculine cologne that teased her senses.

"Gabriel," she whispered, hanging at his mouth, aching to feel it come crashing down on her lips, crushing them, devouring him, easing the ache, the hunger that pulsed through her young, untried body...

"Gabriel!"

Sara's joyful cry broke them apart just in the nick of time. Gabriel cleared his throat, turned to his sister and hugged her.

"It's good to have you home," Sara said against his chest.

"It's good to be home." He was struggling to sound normal. His mind was still on Michelle's soft mouth and his hunger to break it open under his lips, back her into a wall and devour her.

"Have you eaten? I just made soup," Sara added.

"No. I'm starved." He made an attempt not to look at Michelle when he said that. He even smiled.

"I could eat, too," Michelle said, trying to break the tension.

"Let's go in." Sara took his arm. "Where did you come from?"

"Dallas, this time," he said. "I've been in the States for a couple of days, but I had business there before I could get home." He hesitated. "I got tickets to the ballet in San Antonio when I came through there this morning." He glanced at Michelle. "Want to go see *The Nutcracker* with me?" he added with a grin.

"Oh, I'd love to," she said fervently. "What do we wear?"

"A very dressy evening outfit," Sara said. "I bought you one once, and you never even wore it."

Michelle grinned. "Well, I haven't been anywhere I'd need to wear it," she replied, not guessing what it told Gabriel, whose eyes twinkled brightly.

Michelle flushed and then grinned at him. "No, I'm not dating anybody at college," she said. She shrugged. "I'm too busy studying."

"Is that so?" Gabriel laughed, and was relieved.

"When are you leaving?" Sara asked.

"At six, and you'd better start dressing as well, because we're all three going," Gabriel added, and he exchanged a speaking look with Sara.

"All of us? Oh. Oh! That's nice!" Michelle worked at sounding enthusiastic.

Sara just winked at her. "I'd better go through my closet."

Gabriel looked down at Michelle with the Christmas tree bright and beautiful behind her. "I wouldn't dare take you out alone, *ma belle,*" he said under his breath. "You know it. And you know why."

Her eyes searched his hungrily. She knew. She'd felt it, when he held her beside the truck. She knew that he wanted her.

She'd had no idea what wanting really was, until Gabriel had come into her life. Now she was aware of a hunger that came around when he was close, that grew and surged in her when he looked at her, when he spoke to her, when he touched her...

"Yes, you know, don't you?" he breathed, standing a little too close. He rubbed his thumb against her lips, hard enough to make her gasp and shiver with delight. His black eyes narrowed. "It's too soon. You know that, too."

She ground her teeth together as she looked at him. He was the most perfect thing in her life. He was preaching caution when all she wanted to do was push him down on the floor and spread her body over him and...

She didn't know what would come next. She'd read books, but they were horribly lacking in preliminaries.

"What are you thinking about so hard?" he asked.

"About pushing you down on the floor," she blurted out, and flushed. "But I don't know what comes next, exactly…"

He burst out laughing.

"You stop that," she muttered. "I'll bet you weren't born knowing what to do, either."

"I wasn't," he confessed. He touched her nose with the tip of his finger. "It's just as well that you don't know. Yet. And we aren't going to be alone. Yet."

She drew in a long sigh and smiled. "Okay."

He chuckled.

"I've never been to the ballet," she confessed.

"High time you went," he replied, and he laughed. "Go on."

SARA HAD LAID out the most beautiful black velvet dress Michelle had ever seen. It had a discreet rounded neckline and long sleeves, and it fell to the ankles, with only a slight tuck where the waistline was.

"It's gorgeous!" Michelle enthused.

"And you'll look gorgeous in it," Sara replied. She hugged Michelle. "It's yours. I have shoes and a purse to match it."

"But, I have a dress," Michelle began.

"A summer dress," Sara said patiently, and smiled. "This one is more suitable for winter. I have one similar to it that I'm wearing. We'll look like twins." She grinned.

"Okay, then. And thank you!" Michelle said heartily.

"You're very welcome."

CHAPTER TEN

GABRIEL WORE A dress jacket with dark slacks and a black turtleneck sweater. He looked classy and elegant. Sara wore a simple sheath of navy blue velvet with an expensive gold necklace and earrings and looked exquisite, with her silky black hair loose almost to her waist and her big, dark eyes soft in her beautiful face.

Michelle in her black velvet dress felt like royalty. The trio drew eyes as they filed into the auditorium where the ballet was being performed.

Up front, in the orchestra pit, the musicians were tuning up their instruments. Gabriel found their seats and let the women go in first before he took his place on the aisle.

"There's quite a crowd," Michelle remarked as more people filed in.

"Oh, dear." Sara's voice was full of consternation.

Before Michelle could ask what was wrong, she saw it for herself. Wofford Patterson, in a dinner jacket with a white tie and black slacks was escorting a beautiful blonde, in an elegant green velvet gown, down the aisle—directly to the seats beside Sara.

"Mr. Brandon," Wolf said, nodding. "This is Elise Jorgansen. Elise, Gabriel Brandon. That's his sister, Sara. And that's his ward, Michelle."

"Nice to meet you," Elise said, and smiled at them all with genuine warmth.

"I believe our seats are right there," Wolf told the pretty woman. He escorted her past Gabriel and the women with apologies, because it was a tight squeeze. He sat next to Sara, with Elise on his other side.

Sara tensed and glared straight ahead. Wolf grinned.

"I didn't know that you liked the ballet, Miss Brandon," Wolf said politely.

"I like this one. It's *The Nutcracker,*" she added with a venomous look at the man beside her.

He pursed his lips. "Left the flying monkeys at home, did we?"

"I'd love to drop a house on you, dear man," she said under her breath.

"Now, now, it's the ballet," he pointed out. "We must behave like civilized people."

"You'd need so much instruction for that, Mr. Patterson," Sara said, her voice dripping honey.

"Isn't the music lovely?" Michelle broke in.

The music was the instruments being tuned, but it shattered the tension and everyone laughed.

"Behave," Gabriel whispered to his sister.

She gave him an irritated look, but she kept her hands in her lap and sat quietly as the ballerinas came onstage one by one and the performance began, to Michelle's utter fascination and delight. She'd never seen a live performance of the ballet, which was her favorite.

At intermission, Sara excused herself and left the row.

"I'm not getting up," Wolf said. "I'd never get back in here."

"Neither am I," Gabriel mused. "It's quite a crowd."

"You seem to be enjoying the music, Miss Godfrey," Wolf said politely.

"I've never been to a ballet before," she replied, laughing. "It's so beautiful!"

"You should see it in New York City, at the American Ballet Company," Gabriel said gently.

"They do an excellent performance," Wolf agreed. "Have you seen it at the Bolshoi?" he added.

"Yes," Gabriel agreed. "Theirs is unbelievably beautiful."

"That's in Russia, isn't it?" Michelle asked, wide-eyed.

"Yes," Gabriel said. He smiled down at her. "One day, Sara and I will have to take you traveling."

"You should see the world," Elise agreed, from beside Wolf. "Or at least, some of it. Travel broadens your world."

"I can't think of anything I'd love more," Michelle replied, smiling back at the woman.

"Elise studied ballet when she was still in school," Wolf said. "She was in line to be a prima ballerina with the company she played with in New York."

"Don't," Elise said gently.

"Sorry," Wolf said, patting her hand. "Bad memories. I won't mention it again."

"That life is long over," she replied. "But I still love going to see the ballet and the theater and opera. We have such a rich cultural heritage here in San Antonio."

"We do, indeed," Gabriel agreed.

The musicians began tuning their instruments again, just as Sara came back down the aisle, so graceful and poised that she drew male eyes all the way.

"Your sister has an elegance of carriage that is quite rare," Elise said to Gabriel as she approached.

"She also studied ballet," Gabriel replied quietly. "But the stress of dancing and trying to get through college became too much. She gave up ballet and got her degree in languages." He laughed. "She still dances, though," he added. "She just doesn't put on a tutu first."

"It wouldn't go with the broom," Sara said to Wolf, and smiled coldly as she sat down.

"Broom?" Elise asked, curious.

"Never mind. I'll explain it to you later," Wolf replied.

Sara gave him a look that might have curdled milk and turned her attention to the stage as the curtain began to rise.

"WELL, IT WAS a wonderful evening," Michelle said dreamily as she followed them out to the car. "Thank you so much for taking us," she added to Gabriel.

He studied her in the lovely dress, smiling. "It was my pleasure. We'll have to do this more often."

"Expose you to culture, he means," Sara said in a stage whisper. "It's good for you."

"I really had a good time."

"I would have, except for the company," Sara muttered. She flushed. "Not you two," she said hastily when they gaped at her. "That…man! And his date."

"I thought Elise was very nice," Michelle ventured.

Sara clammed up.

Gabriel just chuckled.

CHRISTMAS EVE WAS MAGICAL. They sat around the Christmas tree, watching a program of Christmas music on television, sipping hot chocolate and making s'mores in the fireplace, where a sleepy fire flamed every now and then.

In all her life, Michelle couldn't remember being so happy. Her eyes kept darting to Gabriel, when she thought he wasn't looking. Even in jeans and a flannel shirt, he was the stuff of dreams. It was so hard not to appear starstruck.

They opened presents that night instead of the next morning, because Sara announced that she wasn't getting up at dawn to see what Santa had left.

She gave Michelle a beautiful scarf of many colors, a designer one. Michelle draped it around her neck and raved over it. Then she opened Gabriel's gift. It was pearls, a soft off-white set in a red leather box. They were Japanese. He'd brought them home from his last trip and hidden them to give at Christmas. The necklace was accompanied by matching drop earrings.

"I was right," he mused as Michelle tried them on enthusiastically. "They're just the right shade."

"They are, indeed. And thank you for mine, also, my sweet." Sara kissed his tan cheek, holding a strand of white ones in her hand. They suited her delicate coloring just as the off-white ones suited Michelle's.

"I like mine, too." He held up a collection of DVDs of shows he particularly liked from Michelle and a black designer turtleneck from Sara.

Sara loved her handmade scarf from Michelle. It was crocheted and had taken an age to finish. It was the softest white knit, with tassels. "I'll wear it all winter," she promised Michelle, and kissed her, too.

Michelle had hung mistletoe in strategic places, but she hadn't counted on Gabriel's determined reticence.

He kissed her on the cheek, smiled and wished her the happiest of Christmases and New Years. She pretended that it didn't matter that he didn't drag her into an empty room and kiss her half to death. He was determined not to treat her as an adult. It was painful. But in some sense, she did understand.

So THREE YEARS went by, more quickly than Michelle had dreamed they would. She got a job part-time with a daily newspaper in San Antonio and did political pieces for it while she got through her core courses and into serious journalism in college.

She went to class during summer to speed up her degree program, although she came home for the holidays. Gabriel was almost always away now. Sara was there, although she spent most of her time in Wyoming at the ranch she and Gabriel owned. Michelle had gone up there with her one summer for a couple of weeks during her vacation. It was a beautiful place. Sara was different somehow. Something had happened between her and Wofford Patterson. She wouldn't talk about it, but she knew that it had changed Sara. Gabriel had mentioned something about Sara going back into therapy and there had been an argument in French that Michelle couldn't follow.

Wofford Patterson had also moved up to Catelow, Wyoming. He bought a huge ranch there near Sara's. He kept his place in Comanche Wells, but he put in a foreman to manage it for him. He had business interests in Wyoming that took up much of his time, he said, and it was hard to commute. Sara didn't admit that she was glad to have him as a neighbor. But Michelle suspected that she did.

Sara was still playing her online game with her friend, and they fought battles together late into the night. She still didn't know who he really was, either. Gabriel had made sure of it.

"He's such a gentleman," Sara mused over coffee one morning, her face bright with pleasure. "He wants to meet me in person." She hesitated. "I'm not sure about that."

"Why not, if you like him?" Michelle asked innocently, although she didn't dare let on that she knew exactly who Sara's friend was, and she knew that Sara would have a stroke if she saw him in person. It would be the end of a lovely online relationship.

"People aren't what they seem," Sara replied, and pain was in her eyes. "If it seems too good to be true, it usually is."

"He might be a knight in shining armor," Michelle teased. "You should find out."

"He might be an ogre who lives in a cave with bats, too." Sara chuckled. "No. I like things the way they are. I really don't want to try to have a relationship with a man in real life." Her face tensed. "I never wanted to."

Michelle grimaced. "Sara, you're so beautiful…"

"Beautiful!" She laughed coldly. "I wish I'd been born ugly. It would have made my life so much easier. You don't know…" She drew in a harsh breath. "Well, actually, you do know." She managed a soft smile. "We're all prisoners of our childhoods, Michelle. Mine was particularly horrible. It warped me."

"You should have been in therapy," Michelle said gently.

"I tried therapy. It only made things worse. I can't talk to total strangers."

"Maybe you just talked to the wrong person."

Sara's eyes were suddenly soft and dreamy and she flushed. "I think I did. So much has changed," she added softly.

Michelle, who had a good idea what was going on up in Wyoming, just grinned.

Sara's eyes took on an odd, shimmering softness. "Life is so much sweeter than I dreamed it could be." She smiled to herself and looked at her watch. "I have some phone calls to make. I love having you around." She added, "Thanks."

"For what?"

"For caring," Sara said simply.

MICHELLE WAS LOOKING forward to her last Christmas in college. She got talked into a blind date with Darla's boyfriend's friend. He turned out to be a slightly haughty man who worked as a stockbroker and never stopped talking on his cell phone for five seconds. He was at it all through dinner. Bob, Darla's boyfriend, looked very uncomfortable and apologetic.

"Bob feels awful," Darla whispered to Michelle in the restroom after they'd finished eating. "Larry seemed to be a normal guy."

"He just lives and breathes his job. Besides," she added, "you know there's only one man who interests me at all. And it's never going to be someone like Larry."

"Having seen your Mr. Brandon, I totally understand." Darla giggled. She shook her head. "He is a dreamboat."

"I think so."

"Well, we'll stop by the bar for a nightcap and go

home. Maybe we can pry Larry away from his phone long enough to say good-night."

"I wish I was riding with you and Bob," Michelle sighed. "At least he stops talking while he's driving."

"Curious, that he didn't want to ride with Bob," Darla said. "Well, that's just men, I guess."

But Larry had an agenda that the girls weren't aware of. He knew that Bob and Darla were going dancing and wouldn't be home soon. So when he walked Michelle to the door of the apartment she and Darla shared, he pushed his way in and took off his jacket.

"Finally, alone together," he enthused, and reached for her. "Now, sweetie, let's have a little payback for the meal and the drinks…"

"Are you out of your mind?" she gasped, avoiding his grasping arms.

"I paid for the food," he said, almost snarling. "You owe me!"

"I owe you? Like hell I owe you!" She got to the door and opened it. "I'll send you a check for my part of the meal! Get out!"

"I'm not leaving. You just want to play hard to get." He started to push the door closed. And connected with a steely big hand that caught him by the arm, turned him around and booted him out into the night.

"Gabriel!" Michelle gasped.

"You can't do that to me…!" Larry said angrily, getting to his feet.

Gabriel fell into a fighting stance. "Come on," he said softly. "I could use the exercise."

Larry came to his senses. He glanced at Michelle. She went back inside, got his jacket, and threw it at him.

"Dinner doesn't come with bed," she told him icily.

Larry started to make a reply, but Gabriel's expression was a little too unsettling. He muttered something under his breath, turned, slammed into his car and roared away.

Gabriel went inside with Michelle, who was tearing up now that the drama had played itself out.

"Ah, no, *ma belle,*" he whispered. "There's no need for tears." He pulled her into his arms, bent his head, and kissed her so hungrily that she forgot to breathe.

He lifted his head. His black eyes were smoldering, so full of desire that they mesmerized Michelle. She tasted him on her mouth, felt the heavy throb of his heart under her hands.

"Finally," he breathed, pulling her close. He brushed his lips over her soft mouth. "Finally!"

She opened her mouth to ask what he meant, and the kiss knocked her so off balance that she couldn't manage a single word in reply. She held on with all her might, clung to him, pushed her body into his so that she could feel every movement of his powerful body against her. He was aroused, very quickly, and even that didn't intimidate her. She moaned. Which only made matters worse.

He picked her up, still kissing her, and laid her out on the couch, easing his body down over hers in a silence that throbbed with frustrated desire.

"Soft," he whispered. "Soft and sweet. All mine."

She would have said something, but he was kissing her again, and she couldn't think at all. She felt his big, rough hands go under her dress, up and up, touching and exploring, testing softness, finding her breasts under the lacy little bra.

"You feel like silk all over," he murmured. He found the zipper and eased her out of the dress and the half slip under it, then out of the bra, so that all she had left on were her briefs. He kissed his way down her body, lingering on her pert breasts with their tight little crowns, savoring her soft, helpless cries of pleasure.

It excited him to know that she'd never done this. He ate her up like candy, tasting her hungrily. He nuzzled her breasts, kissing their soft contours with a practiced touch that made her rise up in an aching arch to his lips.

Somehow, his jacket and shirt ended up on the floor. She felt the rough, curling hair on his chest against her bare breasts as his body covered hers. His powerful legs eased between her own, so that she could feel with him an intimacy she'd never shared with anyone.

She cried out as he moved against her. Sensations were piling on each other, dragging her under, drowning her in pleasure. She clung to him, pleading for more, not even knowing exactly what she wanted, but so drawn with tension that she was dying for it to ease.

She felt hot tears run down her cheeks as his mouth moved back onto hers. He touched her as he never had before. She shivered. The touch came again. She sobbed, and opened her mouth under his. She felt his tongue go into her mouth, as his hands moved on her more intimately.

Suddenly, like a fall of fire, a flash of agonized pleasure convulsed the soft body under his. He groaned and had to fight the instinctive urge to finish what he started, to go right into her, push inside her, take what was his, what had always been his.

But she was a virgin. His exploration had already told him that. He'd known already, by her reactions.

She was very much a virgin. He didn't want to do this. Not yet. She was his. It must be done properly, in order, in a way that wouldn't shame her to remember somewhere down the line.

So he forced his shivering body to bear the pain. He held her very close while she recovered from her first ecstasy. He wrapped her up tight, and held her while he endured what he must to spare her innocence.

She wept. He kissed away the tears, so tenderly that they fell even harder, hot and wet on her flushed cheeks.

She was embarrassed and trying not to let him see.

He knew. He smiled and kissed her eyes shut. "It had to be with me," he whispered. "Only with me. I would rather die than know you had such an experience with any other man."

She opened her eyes and looked up into his. "Really?"

"Really." He looked down at her nudity, his eyes hungry again at the sight of her pink-and-peach skin, silky and soft and fragrant. He touched her breasts tenderly. "You are the most beautiful woman I will ever see."

Her lips parted on a shaky breath.

He bent and kissed her breasts. "And now we have to get up."

She stared at him.

"Or not get up," he murmured with a laugh. "Because I can't continue this much longer."

"It would be…all right," she whispered. "If you wanted to," she added.

"I want to," he said huskily. "But you won't be happy afterward. And you know it. Not like this, *ma belle*. Not our first time together. It has to be done properly."

"Properly?"

"You graduate from college, get a job, go to work.

I come to see you bringing flowers and chocolates," he mused, tracing her mouth. "And then, eventually, a ring."

"A ring."

He nodded.

"An…engagement…ring?"

He smiled.

"People do it all the time, even before they get engaged," she said.

He got to his feet. "They do. But we won't."

"Oh."

He dressed her, enjoying the act of putting back onto her lovely body the things he'd taken off it. He laughed at her rapt expression. "You have a belief system that isn't going to allow a more modern approach to sex," he said blandly. "So we do it your way."

"I could adjust," she began, still hungry.

"Your happiness means a lot to me," he said simply. "I'm not going to spoil something beautiful with a tarnished memory. Not after I've waited so long."

She stared up into his black eyes. "I've waited for you, too," she whispered.

"I know." He smoothed back her hair just as they heard a car door slam and footsteps approaching.

Michelle looked horrified, thinking what could have happened, what condition they could have been in as Darla put her key into the lock.

Gabriel burst out laughing at her expression. "Now was I right?" he asked.

The door opened. Darla stopped with Bob in tow and just stared at Gabriel. Then she grinned. "Wow," she said. "Look what Larry changed into!"

And they all burst out laughing.

Michelle graduated with honors. Gabriel and Sara were both there for the ceremony, applauding when she walked down the aisle to accept her diploma. They went out to eat afterward, but once they were home, Gabriel couldn't stay. He was preoccupied, and very worried, from the look of things.

"Can you tell me what's wrong?" Michelle asked.

He shook his head. He bent to kiss her, very gently. "I'm going to have to be out of the country for two or three months."

"No!" she exclaimed.

"Only that. Then I have a job waiting, one that won't require so much travel," he promised. "Bear with me. I'm sorry. I have to do this."

She drew in a long breath. "Okay. If you have to go."

"You've got a job waiting in San Antonio, anyway," he reminded her with a smile. "On a daily newspaper. It has a solid reputation for reporting excellence. Make a name for yourself. But don't get too comfortable there," he added enigmatically. "Because when I get back, we need to talk."

"Talk." She smiled.

"And other things."

"Oh, yes, especially, other things," she whispered, dragging his mouth down to hers. She kissed him hungrily. He returned the kiss, but drew back discreetly when Sara came into the room. He hugged her, too.

He paused in the doorway and looked back at them, smiling. "Take care of each other." He grinned at his sister. "Happy?" he asked, referring to the changes in her life.

Sara laughed, tossing her long hair. "I could die of it," she sighed.

"I'll be back before you miss me," he told Michelle, who was looking sad. He wanted to kiss her, right there in front of the world. But it wasn't the time. And he wasn't sure he could stop.

"Impossible," Michelle said softly. "I miss you already."

He winked and closed the door.

MICHELLE LIKED THE JOB. She had a desk and three years of solid education behind her to handle the assignments she was given.

A big story broke the second month she'd been with the newspaper. There was a massacre of women and children in a small Middle Eastern nation, perpetrated, it was said, by a group of mercenaries led by a Canadian national named Angel Le Veut. He had ties to an anti-terrorism school run by a man named Eb Scott in, of all places, Jacobsville, Texas.

Michelle went on the offensive at once, digging up everything she could find about the men in the group who had killed the women and children in the small Muslim community that was at odds with a multinational occupation force.

The name of the man accused of leading the assault was ironic. One of the languages she'd studied was French. And if loosely translated, the man's name came out as "Angel wants it." It was an odd play on words that was used most notably in the sixteenth century by authorities when certain cases were tried and a guilty verdict was desired. The phrase *"Le Roi le Veut"* meant that the king wanted the accused found guilty—whether or not he really was, apparently. The mysterious Angel was obviously an educated man with a knowledge of

European history. Michelle was puzzled over why such a man would choose a lifestyle that involved violence.

HER FIRST STOP was Jacobsville, Texas, where she arranged an interview with Eb Scott, the counterterrorism expert, whose men had been involved in the massacre. Michelle knew him, from a distance.

Her father had gone to school with him and they were acquaintances. Her father had said there wasn't a finer man anywhere, that Eb was notorious for backing lost causes and fighting for the underdog. That didn't sound like a man who would order the murder of helpless women and children.

Eb shook her hand and invited her into his house. His wife and children were gone for the day, shopping in San Antonio for summer clothing. It was late spring already.

"Thank you for seeing me," Michelle said when they were seated. "Especially under the circumstances."

"Hiding from the press is never a good idea, but at times, in matters like this, it's necessary, until the truth can be ferreted out," Eb said solemnly. His green eyes searched hers. "You're Alan Godfrey's daughter."

"Yes," she said, smiling.

"You used to spend summers in Comanche Wells with your grandparents." He smiled back. "Minette Carson speaks well of you. She did an interview with me yesterday. Hopefully, some of the truth will trickle down to the mass news media before they crucify my squad leader."

"Yes. This man, Angel," she began, looking over her notes while Eb Scott grimaced and tried not to reveal what he really knew about the man, "his name is quite odd."

"Le Veut?" He smiled again. "He gets his way. He's something of an authority on sixteenth-century European history. He and Kilraven, one of the feds who's married to a local girl, go toe-to-toe over whether or not Mary Queen of Scots really helped Lord Bothwell murder her husband."

"Has this man worked for you, with you, for a long time?" she asked.

He nodded. "Many years. He's risked his life time and time again to save innocents. I can promise you that when the truth comes out, and it will, he'll be exonerated."

She was typing on her small notebook computer as he spoke. "He's a Canadian national?"

"He has dual citizenship, here and in Canada," he corrected. "But he's lived in the States most of his life."

"Does he live in Jacobsville?"

Eb hesitated.

She lifted her hands from the keyboard. "You wouldn't want to say, would you?" she asked perceptibly. "If he has family, it could hurt them, as well. There wouldn't be a place they could go where the media wouldn't find them."

"The media can be like a dog after a juicy bone," Eb said with some irritation. "They'll get fed one way or the other, with truth or, if time doesn't permit, with lies. I've seen lives ruined by eager reporters out to make a name for themselves." He paused. "Present company excepted," he added gently. "I know all about you from Minette."

She smiled gently. "Thanks. I always try to be fair

and present both sides of the story without editorializing. I don't like a lot of what I see on television, presented as fair coverage. Most of the commentators seem quite biased to me. They convict people and act as judge, jury and executioner." She shook her head. "I like the paper I work for. Our editor, even our publisher, are fanatics for accurate and fair coverage. They fired a reporter last month whose story implicated an innocent man. He swore he had eyewitnesses to back up the facts, and that he could prove them. Later, when the editor sent other reporters out to recheck—after the innocent man's attorneys filed a lawsuit—they found that the reporter had ignored people who could verify the man's whereabouts at the time of the crime. The reporter didn't even question them."

Eb sighed, leaning back in his recliner. "That happens all too often. Even on major newspapers," he added, alluding to a reporter for one of the very large East Coast dailies who'd recently been let go for fabricating stories.

"We try," Michelle said quietly. "We really try. Most reporters only want to help people, to point out problems, to help better the world around us."

"I know that. It's the one bad apple in the barrel that pollutes the others," he said.

"This man, Angel, is there any way I could interview him?"

He almost bit through his lip. He couldn't tell her that. "No," he said finally. "We've hidden him in a luxury hotel in a foreign country. The news media will have a hell of a time trying to ferret him out. We have armed guards in native dress everywhere. Meanwhile, I've hired an investigative firm out of Houston—Dane

Lassiter's—to dig out the truth. Believe me, there's no one in the world better at it. He's a former Houston policeman."

"I know of him," she replied. "His son was involved in a turf war between drug lords in the area, wasn't he?"

"Yes, he was. That was a while back."

"Well, tell me what you can," she said. "I'll do my best not to convict the man in print. The mercenaries who were with Angel," she added, "are they back in the States?"

"That's another thing I can't tell you right now," he replied. "I'm not trying to be evasive. I'm protecting my men from trial by media. We have attorneys for all of them, and our investigator hopes to have something concrete for us, and the press, very soon."

"That's fair enough."

"Here's what we know right now," Eb said. "My squad leader was given an assignment by a State Department official to interview a local tribesman in a village in Anasrah. The man had information about a group of terrorists who were hiding in the village—protected by a high-ranking government official, we were told. My squad leader, in disguise, took a small team in to interview him, but when he and his men arrived, the tribesman and his entire family were dead. One of the terrorists pointed the finger at Angel and accused his team of the atrocity. I'm certain the terrorist was paid handsomely to do it."

Michelle frowned. "You believe that?"

Eb stared her down with glittering green eyes. "Miss Godfrey, if you knew Angel, you wouldn't have to ask me that question."

"Sorry," she said. "It's my job, Mr. Scott."

He let out a breath. "You can't imagine how painful this is for me," he said. "Men I trained, men I've worked with, accused of something so inhuman." His face hardened. "Follow the money. It's all about the money, I assure you," he added curtly. "Someone stands to lose a lot of it if the truth comes out."

"I can only imagine how bad it must be," she said, and not without sympathy.

She asked questions, he answered them. She was impressed by him. He wasn't at all the sort of person that she'd pictured when she heard people speak of mercenaries. Even the word meant a soldier for hire, a man who sold his talents to the highest bidder. But Eb Scott's organization trained men in counterterrorism. He had an enormous operation in Jacobsville, and men and women came from around the world to learn from his experts. There were rumors that a few government agents had also availed themselves of his expertise.

The camp was state-of-the-art, with every electronic gadget known to modern science—and a few things that were largely experimental. They taught everything from evasive driving techniques to disarming bombs, improvised weapons, stealth, martial arts, the works. Michelle was allowed to photograph only a small section of the entire operation, and she wasn't allowed to photograph any of his instructors or the students. But even with the reservations on what she was shown, what she learned fascinated her.

"Well, I'll never think of mercenaries the same way again, Mr. Scott," she said when she was ready to leave. "This operation is very impressive."

"I'm glad you think so."

She paused at the door and turned. "You know, the

electronic media have resources that those of us in print journalism don't. I mean, we have a digital version of our paper online, like most everyone does. But the big networks employ dozens of experts who can find out anything. If they want to find your man, they will. And his family."

"Miss Godfrey, for the sake of a lot of innocent people, I hope you're wrong."

The way he said it stayed on her mind for hours after she left.

CHAPTER ELEVEN

MICHELLE WROTE THE STORY, and she did try to be fair. But when she saw the photographs of the massacre, the bodies of small children with women and men weeping over them, her heart hardened. If the man was guilty, he should be hanged for this.

She didn't slant the story. She presented the facts from multiple points of view. She interviewed a man in Saudi Arabia who had a friend in Anasrah with whom he'd recently spoken. She interviewed a representative of the State Department, who said that one of their staff had been led into the village by a minor government official just after the attack and was adamant that the mercenaries had been responsible for the slaughter. She also interviewed an elder in the village, through an interpreter, who said that an American had led the attack.

There was another man, also local, who denied that a foreigner was responsible. He was shouted down by the others, but Michelle managed to get their representative in Saudi Arabia to go to Anasrah, a neighboring country, and interview the man in the village. His story contradicted the others. He said that it was a man well-known in terrorist circles who had come into the village and accused the tribesmen of betraying their own people by working with the government and foreigners. He said that if it continued, an example, a horrible example, would be made, he would see to it personally.

The local man said that he could prove that the terrorists themselves had perpetrated the attack, if he had time.

Michelle made the first big mistake of her career in journalism by discounting the still, small voice in the wilderness. The man's story didn't ring true. She took notes, and filed them on her computer. But when she wrote the story, she left out what sounded like a made-up tale.

THE STORY BROKE with the force of bombs. All of a sudden, it was all anyone heard on the media. The massacre in Anasrah, the children murdered by foreigners, the mercenaries who had cut them down with automatic weapons while their parents pleaded for mercy. On television, the weeping relatives were interviewed. Their stories brought even hardened commentators to tears on-screen.

Michelle's story, with its unique point of view and Eb Scott's interview—which none of the national media had been able to get, because he refused to talk to them—put her in the limelight for the first time. Her story was reprinted partially in many national papers, and she was interviewed by the major news networks, as well. She respected Eb Scott, she added, and she thought he was sincere, but she wept for the dead children and she thought the mercenary responsible should be tried in the world court and imprisoned for the rest of his life.

Her impulsive comment was broadcast over and over. And just after that came the news that the mercenary had a sister, living in Wyoming. They had her name, as well. Sara.

IT COULD HAVE been a coincidence. Except that suddenly she remembered that the man, Angel, had both American and Canadian citizenship. Now she learned that he had a sister named Sara. Gabriel was gone for long periods of time overseas on jobs. Michelle still tried to persuade herself that it wasn't, couldn't, be Gabriel.

Until Sara called her on the phone.

"I couldn't believe it when they said you broke the story," she said in a cold tone. "How could you do this to us?"

"Sara, it wasn't about anyone you know," she said quickly. "It was about a mercenary who gunned down little children in a Middle Eastern village…!"

"He did nothing of the sort," Sara said, her voice dripping ice. "It was the tribesman's brother-in-law, one of the terrorists, who killed the man and his family and then blamed it on Angel and his men."

"Do you know this man Angel?" Michelle asked, a sick feeling in her stomach because Sara sounded so harsh.

"Know him." Her laugh was as cold as death. "We both know him, Michelle. He uses Angel as an alias when he goes on missions for Eb Scott's clients. But his name is Gabriel."

Michelle felt her blood run cold. Images flashed through her mind. Dead children. The one dissenting voice, insisting that it was the terrorists not the Americans who perpetrated the horror. Her refusal to listen, to print the other side of the story. Gabriel's side. She'd convinced herself that it couldn't be Gabriel. Now she had to face facts.

"I didn't know," she said, her voice breaking. "Sara, believe me, I didn't know!"

"Eb told you it wasn't him," Sara said furiously. "But you wouldn't listen. I had a contact in the State Department send a man to tell your newspaper's agent about the dead man's brother-in-law. And you decided not to print it. Didn't you? God forbid you should run against the voice of the world press and risk your own glowing reputation as a crusader for justice by dissenting!"

"I didn't know," Michelle repeated through tears.

"You didn't know! If Gabriel ends up headfirst in a ditch somewhere, it will be all right, because you didn't know! Would you like to see the road in front of our ranch here in Wyoming, Michelle?" she added. "It looks like a tent city, surrounded by satellite trucks. They're certain they'll wear me down and I'll come out and accuse my brother for them!"

"I'm so sorry." Michelle didn't have to be told that Gabriel was innocent. She knew he was. But she'd helped convict him.

"You're sorry. I'll be certain to tell him when, and if, I see him again." There was a harshly indrawn breath. "He phoned me two days ago," she said in a haunted voice. "They're hunting him like an animal, thanks to you. When I told him who sold him out, he wouldn't believe me. It wasn't until I sent him a link to your story that he saw for himself."

Michelle felt every drop of blood draining out of her face. "What…did he say?"

"He said," Sara replied, enunciating every word, "that he'd never been so wrong about anyone in his life. He thought that you, of all people, would defend him even against the whole world. He said," she added coldly, "that he never wanted to see you or hear from you again as long as he lived."

The words were like bullets. She could actually feel their impact.

"I loved you like my own sister," Sara said, her voice breaking. "And I will never, never forgive you!" She slammed down the phone.

Michelle realized after a minute that she hadn't broken the connection. She hung up her own telephone. She sat down heavily and heard the recriminations break over her head again and again.

She remembered Eb Scott's certainty that his man would never do such a thing. Sara's fierce anger. It had been easy to discount them while Angel was a shadowy figure without substance. But Michelle knew Gabriel. And she was certain, absolutely certain, that the man who'd saved her from suicide would never put another human being in harm's way.

IT TOOK TWO days for the effects of Sara's phone call to wear off enough that she could stop crying and blaming herself. The news media was having a field day with the story, running updates about it all day, every day, either in newscasts or in banners under the anchor people. Michelle finally had to turn off the television to escape it, so that she could get herself back together.

She wanted, so desperately, to make up for what she'd done. But she didn't even know where to start. The story was everywhere. People were condemning the American mercenaries on every news program in the world.

But Gabriel was innocent. Michelle had helped convict him in the press, without knowing who she was writing about. Now it was her turn to do her job properly, and give both sides of the story, however unpopular. She had to save him, if she could, even if he hated her forever for what she'd done.

So she went back to work. Her first act was to contact the newspaper's man in Saudi Arabia and ask him to repeat the story his informant in Anasrah had told him. Then she contacted Eb Scott and gave him the information, so that he could pass it on to his private investigator. Before she did that, she asked him to call her back on a secure line, because she knew how some of the tabloid news bureaus sometimes had less scrupulous agents digging out information.

"You're learning, Miss Godfrey," Eb said solemnly.

"Not soon enough. I know who Angel is now," she added heavily. "His sister hates me. He told her that he never wanted to see or speak to me again, either. And I deserve that. I wasn't objective, and people are paying for my error. But I have to do what I can to undo the mess I helped make. I'm sorry I didn't listen."

"Too little, and almost too late," he said brutally. "Learn from it. Sometimes the single dissenting voice is the right one."

"I won't forget," she said.

He hung up.

She tried to phone Sara back and apologize once again, to tell her she was trying to repair the damage. But Sara wouldn't accept the first phone call and after that, her number was blocked. She was heartsick. The Brandons had been so good to her. They'd made sacrifices to get her through school, through college, always been there when she needed help. And she'd repaid them like this. It wounded her as few things in life ever had.

When she tried to speak to her editor in confidence, to backtrack on the story she'd written, he laughed it off. The man was obviously guilty, he said, why make waves now? She'd made a name for herself in investigative reporting, it was all good.

She told him that Angel wasn't the sort of person to ever harm a child. Then he wanted to know how she knew that. She wouldn't reveal her source, she said, falling back on a tried and true response. But the man was innocent.

Her editor had just laughed. So she thought the guy was innocent, what did it matter? The news was the thing that mattered, scooping all the other media and being first and best at delivering the story. She'd given the facts of the matter, that was the end of it. She should just enjoy her celebrity status while it lasted.

Michelle went back to her apartment that night saddened and weary, with a new sense of disillusionment about life and people.

THE NEXT MORNING, she phoned Minette Carson and asked if she had an opening for a reporter who was certain she wasn't cut out for the big dailies.

Minette was hesitant.

"Look, never mind," Michelle said gently. "I know I've made a lot of enemies in Jacobsville with the way I covered the story. It's okay. I can always teach journalism. I'll be a natural at showing students what not to do."

"We all have to start somewhere when we learn how to do a job," Minette replied. "Usually, it's a painful process. Eb Scott called and asked me, before you did the interview, if you knew who Gabriel really was. I told him no. I knew you'd have said something long before this. I should have told you."

"I should have suspected something," came the sad reply. "He was away from home for long stretches, he spoke a dozen impossible languages, he was secretive about what sort of work he did—I just wasn't paying attention."

"It amused everyone when he took you in as his ward," Minette said. "He was one of the coldest men Eb Scott ever hired—well, after Carson, who works for Cy Parks, that is." She chuckled. "But once you came along, all of a sudden Gabriel was smiling."

"He won't be anymore," Michelle said, feeling the pain to the soles of her feet.

"Give it time," was the older woman's advice. "First, you have some work to do."

"I know. I'm going to do everything in my power to prove him innocent. Whatever it takes," Michelle added firmly.

"That's more like it. And about the job," she replied. "Once you've proven that you aren't running away from an uncomfortable assignment, we'll have a place for you here. That's a promise."

"Thanks."

"You're welcome."

MICHELLE CONVINCED EB SCOTT to let her talk to his detective. It worked out well, because Dane Lassiter was actually in San Antonio for a seminar that week and he agreed to meet with her in a local restaurant.

He wasn't exactly what she'd expected. He was tall, dark-haired and dark-eyed, with an easygoing manner and a wife who was thirtysomething and very attractive. She, like Michelle, was blonde.

"We always go together when he has to give seminars." Tess laughed. "At least once I've had to chase a pursuing woman out of his room." She shook her head, sighing as she met her husband's amused gaze. "Well, after all, I know he's a dish. Why shouldn't other women notice?"

Michelle laughed with them, but her heart wasn't in it. There had been a snippet of news on television the night before, showing a camp of journalists on the road that led to the Brandons' Wyoming property. They were still trying to get Sara to talk to them. But this time they were met with a steely-eyed man Michelle recognized as Wofford Patterson, who was advising them to decamp before some of Sara's friends loosed a few bears on the property in a conservation project. Patterson had become Sara's personal protector and much more, after many years of antagonism.

"I've been watching the press reports on Brandon," Dane said, having guessed the train of her thoughts. "You watch six different reports and get six different stories."

"Yes," Michelle said sadly. "Not everyone tries for accuracy. And I can include myself in that company, because I should have gone the extra mile and presented the one dissenting opinion. It was easy to capitulate, because I didn't think I had any interest in the outcome," she added miserably.

Tess's pale eyes narrowed. "Mr. Brandon was your guardian."

She nodded. He was more, but she wasn't sharing that news with a virtual stranger. "I sold him out. I didn't mean to. I had no idea Angel was Gabriel. It was hard, going against a majority opinion. Everyone said he was guilty as sin. I saw the photographs of the women and children." Her face hardened. "It was easy to believe it, after that."

"I've seen similar things," Dane said, sipping black coffee. "But I can tell you that things are rarely what they seem."

She told him about her contacts, and he took notes, getting names and telephone numbers and putting together a list of people to interview.

He put up his pen and notebook. "This is going to be a lot of help to the men who were blamed for the tragedy," he said finally. "There's a violent element in the country in question, dedicated to rooting out any hint of foreign influence, however beneficial. But at the same time, in their ranks are a few who see a way to quick profit, a way to fund their terrorism and inflict even more horror on our overseas personnel. This group that put your friend in the middle of the controversy is made up of a few money-hungry profiteers. Our State Department has worked very hard to try to stifle them. We have several oil corporations with offices there, and a good bit of our foreign oil is shipped from that country. We depend on the goodwill of the locals to keep the oil companies' officials and workers safe. The terrorists know that, and they see a way to make a quick profit through kidnappings and other attacks. Except that instead of holding people for ransom, they threaten violence if their demands aren't met. It's almost like a protection racket…"

"That's what he meant," Michelle said suddenly.

"Excuse me?"

"Eb Scott said, 'follow the money,'" she recalled.

"Eb's sharp. Yes, that's apparently what's behind all this. The terrorist leader wanted millions in bribes to protect oil company executives in his country. The brother-in-law of the leader was selling him out to our State Department. A lot of local men work for the oil companies and don't want any part of the terrorists' plans. It's a poor country, and the oil companies provide a secure living for the village. But nobody makes waves and gets away with it. The terrorist leader retaliated, in the worst possible way, and blamed it on Angel and his men—a way of protecting his own men, whom he ordered to kill his brother-in-law to keep him from talking. It was also a way of notifying foreigners that this is how any future attempts to bypass his authority would be handled."

"I'm not telling you anything you didn't already know," she said suddenly.

"I knew it. I couldn't prove it," he added. "But you've given me contacts who can back up the protester's story. I'll have my investigators check them out and our attorneys will take depositions that will hold up in court. It will give the State Department's representatives the leverage they need to deal with the terrorists. And it will provide our news media with a week of guaranteed stories," he added coldly.

She sighed. "I think I'm in the wrong business."

"Good reporters can do a lot of good in the world," Tess interrupted. "It's just that there's more profit in digging up dirt on people."

"Amen," Dane said.

"Well, if I can help dig Gabriel out of the hole I put

him into, I'll be happy," Michelle told him. "It's little enough in the way of apology."

"If you hear anything else, through your sources, you can call me anytime," he told her.

"I'll remember."

DANE WENT TO pay the check, against Michelle's protests.

Tess smiled at her. "You really care about the mercenary, don't you?" she asked.

"More than you know," Michelle replied. "He and his sister sacrificed a lot for me. I'll never be able to pay them back. And now, this has happened…"

"At least you're trying to make up for it," she replied. "That's worth something."

"I hope it's worth enough. I'm grateful to you and your husband for meeting with me."

"It was a nice interlude between the rehashing of horrible cases." Tess laughed. "I work as a skip tracer, something Dane would never let me do before. My father planned to marry his mother, but they were killed in a wreck, so Dane became sort of responsible for me," she added surprisingly. "He wasn't very happy about it. We had a rocky road to the altar." She smiled. "But a son and a daughter later, we're very content."

"You don't look old enough to have two children." Michelle laughed. "Either of you."

"Thanks. But believe me, we are."

Dane was back, putting away his wallet. He handed Michelle a business card. "My cell's on there, as well as the office number."

"I'll cross my fingers, that our contacts can help you get Gabriel and his men off the hook," Michelle said.

His eyes narrowed. "I'm surprised that the national

news media hasn't been camped on your doorstep," he remarked.

"Gabriel didn't advertise his involvement with me," she replied. "And nobody in Jacobsville, Texas, will tell them a thing, believe me."

He smiled. "I noticed the way the locals shut them out when they waltzed into town with their satellite trucks. Amazing, that the restaurants all ran out of food and the motels were all full and nobody had a single room to rent out at any price."

She smiled angelically. "I'm sure that was mostly true."

"They did try Comanche Wells, I hear," Dane added.

"Well, see, Comanche Wells doesn't have a restaurant or a motel at all."

"That explains it."

SHE WENT BACK to work, only to find her desk piled high with notes.

"Hey, Godfrey, can't you get your answering machine to work?" Murphy, one of the older reporters whose desk was beside hers, asked. "My old hands are too gnarled to take notes from all your darned callers."

"Sorry, Murph," she said. She was frowning when she noticed who the notes were from. "They want to send a limo for me and have me stay at the Plaza?" she exclaimed.

"What it is to be a celebrity." Murph shook his head. "Hey, there was this cool video that Brad Paisley did, about being a celebrity…!"

"I saw it. Thanks," she said, waving the notes at him. She picked up her purse and left the building, just avoiding her editor on the way out the door.

Apparently the news media had found somebody in Jacobsville who was willing to talk to them. She wondered with droll cynicism what the informant had been paid.

SHE DISCOVERED THAT if she agreed to do an exclusive interview with just one station, the others would have to leave her alone. Before she signed any papers, she spoke with an attorney and had him check out the agreement.

"It says that I agree to tell them my story," she said.

"Exactly," he replied.

She pursed her lips. "It doesn't specify which story."

"I think they'll assume it means the story they want to hear," he replied. "Although that's implied rather than stated."

"Ah."

"And I would advise caution when they ask you to name the person overseas whom your newspaper provided as a reference regarding the informer," he added. "That may be a protected source."

"I was hoping you'd notice that. It is a protected source."

He only smiled.

SHE SAT DOWN in front of the television cameras with a well-known, folksy interviewer who was calm, gentle and very intelligent. He didn't press her for details she couldn't give, and he understood that some sources of information that she had access to were protected.

"I understand from what you told our correspondent that you don't believe the men in question actually perpetrated the attack, which resulted in the deaths of several women and small children," he began.

"That's correct."

"Would you tell me why?"

"When I first broke the story, I went on the assumption that because the majority of the interviewees placed the blame on the American mercenaries, they must be guilty. There was, however, one conflicting opinion. A villager, whom I cannot name, said that extortion was involved and that money was demanded for the protection of foreign workers. When a relative of the extortionist threatened to go to the authorities and reveal the financial aspect, he and his family were brutally murdered as a warning. These murders were blamed on the Americans who had, in fact, been working for the government trying to uncover a nest of terrorists threatening American oil company employees there."

The interviewer was frowning. "Then the massacre was, in fact, retaliation for the villager's threat to expose the extortionist."

"That is my information, yes."

He studied a sheet of paper. "I see here that the newspaper which employs you used its own foreign sources to do interviews about this story."

"Those sources are also protected," Michelle replied. "I can't name them."

He pursed his lips and, behind his lenses, his blue eyes twinkled. "I understand. But I believe the same sources have been named, in the press, by attorneys for the men allegedly implicated by the international press for the atrocities."

She smiled. "I believe so."

"In which case," he added, "we have elicited permission to quote one of the sources. He has signed an affidavit, which is in the hands of our State Department. Please welcome Mr. David Arbuckle, who is liaison for the U.S. Department of State in Anasrah, which is at the center of this matter. Mr. Arbuckle, welcome."

"Thank you, Mr. Price," a pleasant-looking, middle-aged man replied. He was in a studio in Washington, D.C., his image provided via satellite.

"Now, from what Ms. Godfrey has told us—and we have validated her story—a terrorist cell had infiltrated the village in question and made threats against foreign nationals including ours. Is this true?"

"It is," Mr. Arbuckle said solemnly. "We're very grateful to Ms. Godfrey for bringing this matter to our attention. We were told that a group of mercenaries muscled their way into the village, demanding tribute and killed people when their demands were not met. This is a very different story than we were able to verify by speaking, under offer of protection, to other men in the same village."

He coughed, then continued, "We were able to ascertain that a terrorist cell with links to another notorious international organization was going to fund itself by extorting money from oil corporations doing business near the village. They were using the village itself for cover, posing as innocent tribesmen."

"Abominable," the host replied.

"Yes, killing innocents to prove a point is a particularly bloodthirsty manner in which to operate. The local people were terrified to say anything, after the massacre, although they felt very sad that innocent men were blamed for it. In fact, the so-called mercenaries had provided medical supplies and treatment for many children and elderly people and even helped buy food for them."

"A laudable outreach effort."

"Indeed," Mr. Arbuckle replied grimly. "Suffice it to say that we have used our influence to make sure that the terrorists no longer have a foothold in the village, and the international community has moved people in to assure the safety of the tribesmen who provided us with this information."

"Then the American mercenaries are being cleared of any involvement with the massacre?"

"I can assure you that they have been," Mr. Arbuckle replied. "We were provided with affidavits and other documents concerning the massacre by an American private detective working in concert with the mercenaries' attorneys. They were allowed to leave the country last night and are en route to a secure location while we deal with the terrorists in question. The terrorists responsible for the massacre will be brought to trial for the murders and held accountable. And the mercenaries will return to testify against them."

"I'm sure our viewers will be happy to hear that."

"We protect our people overseas," Mr. Arbuckle replied. "All of them. And in fact, the mercenaries in question were private contractors working for the United States government, not the sort of soldiers for hire that often involve themselves in foreign conflicts."

"Another surprise," Mr. Price said with a smile.

"In this day and time, we all have to be alert about our surroundings abroad," Mr. Arbuckle said. "We take care of our own," he added with a smile.

"Thank you for your time, Mr. Arbuckle."

"Thank you for yours, Mr. Price."

Mr. Price turned back to Michelle. "It was a very brave thing you did, Ms. Godfrey, going up against the weight of the international press to defend these men. I understand that you know some of them."

"I know Eb Scott, who runs an international school of counterterrorism," Michelle corrected, unwilling to say more. "He has great integrity. I can't imagine that any agents he trained would ever go against basic humanitarianism."

"He has a good advocate here." He chuckled.

"I learned a lesson from this, as well," she replied quietly. "That you don't discount the single small voice in the wilderness when you write a story that can cost lives and reputations. It is one I hope I never have to repeat." She paused. "I'd like to thank my editor for standing by me," she added, lying because he hadn't, "and for teaching me the worth of integrity in reporting."

Mr. Price named the newspaper in San Antonio and thanked her for appearing on his program.

BACK IN THE OFFICE, her editor, Len Worthington, was ecstatic. "That was the nicest plug we ever got from anybody! Thanks, kid!" he told her, shaking her hand.

"You're welcome. Thanks for not firing me for messing up so badly."

"Hey, what are friends for?"

He'd never know, she thought, but she only smiled. She'd seen a side of journalism that left her feeling sick. It wasn't pretty.

SHE DIDN'T TRY to call Sara again. The poor woman probably hadn't seen the program Michelle was on. It was likely that she was avoiding any sort of press coverage of what had happened. That wasn't hard anymore, because there was a new scandal topping the news now, and all the satellite trucks had gone in search of other prey. Michelle's phone had stopped ringing. There were no more notes on her desk, no more offers of limos and five-star hotels. She didn't mind at all.

She only hoped that one day Sara and Gabriel would forgive her. She went back to work on other stories, mostly political ones, and hoped that she'd never be in a position again where she'd have to sell out her nearest and dearest for a job. Not that she ever would. Nor would she have done it, if she'd had any idea who Gabriel really was.

MICHELLE HAD THOUGHT about asking Minette for a job again. She wasn't really happy living in the city and she cringed every time someone mentioned her name in connection with the past big news story.

She still hadn't heard from Gabriel or Sara. She didn't expect to. She'd hoped that they might contact her. But that was wishful thinking.

She now owned the home where her father and, before him, her grandparents had lived in Comanche Wells. She couldn't bear to drive the Jaguar that Gabriel and Sara had given her...driving it made her too sad. So she parked it at Gabriel's house and put the key in the mail slot. One day, she assumed, he'd return and see it. She bought a cute little VW bug, with which she could commute from Jacobsville to work in San Antonio. She moved back home.

At first, people were understandably a little stand-offish. She was an outsider, even though she was born in Jacobs County. Perhaps they thought she was going to go all big-city on them and start poking her nose into local politics.

When she didn't do that, the tension began to ease a little. When she went into Barbara's Café to have lunch on Saturdays, people began to nod and smile at her. When she went grocery shopping in the local supermarket, the cashier actually talked to her. When she got gas at the local station, the attendant finally stopped asking for identification when she presented her credit card. Little by little, she was becoming part of Jacobs County again.

CARLIE CAME TO visit occasionally. She was happily married, and expecting her first child. They weren't as close as they had been, but it made Michelle feel good to know that her friend was settled and secure.

She only wished that she could be, settled and secure. But as months went by with no word of or from the Brandons, she gave up all hope that she might one day be forgiven for the things she'd written.

She knew that Sara had a whole new life in Wyoming from the cashier at the grocery store who had known her. Michelle didn't blame her for not wanting to come back to Texas. After all, she'd only lived in Comanche Wells as a favor to Gabriel, so that he could be Michelle's guardian.

Guardian no more, obviously. He'd given up that before, of course, when she turned twenty-one. But sometimes Michelle wished that she still had at least a relationship with him. She mourned what could have been, before she lost her way. Gabriel had assured her that they had a future. But that was before.

She was hanging out sheets in the yard, fighting the fierce autumn breeze to keep them from blowing away, when she heard a vehicle coming down the long road. It was odd, because nobody lived out this way except Michelle. It was Saturday. The next morning, she'd planned to go to church. She'd missed it for a couple of Sundays while she worked on a hot political story.

These days, not even the Reverend Blair came visiting much. She didn't visit other people, either. Her job occupied much of her time, because a reporter was always on call. But Michelle still attended services most Sundays.

So she stared at the truck as it went past the house. Its windows were tinted, and rolled up. It was a new truck, a very fancy one. Perhaps someone had bought the old Brandon place, she concluded, and went back to hanging up clothes. It made her sad to think that Gabriel would sell the ranch. But, after all, what would he need it for? He only had a manager there to care for it, so it wasn't as if he needed to keep it. He had other things to do.

She'd heard from Minette that Gabriel was part of an international police force now, one that Eb Scott had contracted with to provide security for those Middle Eastern oilmen who had played such a part in Gabriel's close call.

She wondered if he would ever come back to Comanche Wells. But she was fairly certain he wouldn't. Too many bad memories.

CHAPTER TWELVE

MICHELLE FINISHED HANGING up her sheets in the cool breeze and went back into the house to fix herself a sandwich.

There were rumors at work that a big story was about to break involving an oil corporation and a terrorist group in the Middle East, one that might have local ties. Michelle, now her editor's favorite reporter for having mentioned him on TV, was given the assignment. It might, he hinted, involve some overseas travel. Not to worry, the paper would gladly pay her expenses.

She wondered what sort of mess she might get herself into this time, poking her nose into things she didn't understand. Well, it was a job, and she was lucky to even have one in this horrible economy.

She finished her sandwich and drank a cup of black coffee. For some reason she thought of Gabriel, and how much he'd enjoyed her coffee. She had to stop thinking about him. She'd almost cost him his life. She'd destroyed his peace of mind and Sara's, subjected them both to cameras and reporters and harassment. It was not really a surprise that they weren't speaking to her anymore. Even if she'd gone the last mile defending them, trying to make up for her lack of foresight, it didn't erase the damage she'd already done.

She was bored to death. The house was pretty. She'd

made improvements—she'd redecorated Roberta's old room and had the whole place repainted. She'd put up new curtains and bought new furniture. But the house was cold and empty.

Back when her father was alive, it still held echoes of his parents, of him. Now, it was a reminder of old tragedies, most especially her father's death and Roberta's.

She carried her coffee into the living room and looked around her. She ought to sell it and move into an apartment in San Antonio. She didn't have a pet, not even a dog or cat, and the livestock her father had owned were long gone. She had nothing to hold her here except a sad attachment to the past, to dead people.

But there was something that kept her from letting go. She knew what it was, although she didn't want to remember. It was Gabriel. He'd eaten here, slept here, comforted her here. It was warm with memories that no other dwelling place would ever hold.

She wondered if she couldn't just photograph the rooms and blow up the photos, make posters of them, and sacrifice the house.

Sure, she thought hollowly. Of course she could.

She finished her coffee and turned on the television. Same old stories. Same programs with five minutes of commercials for every one minute of programming. She switched it off. These days she only watched DVDs or streamed movies from internet websites. She was too antsy to sit through a hundred commercials every half hour.

She wondered why people put up with it. If everyone stopped watching television, wouldn't the advertisers be forced to come up with alternatives that compromised a bit more? Sure. And cows would start flying any day.

That reminded her of the standing joke she'd had with Grier and Gabriel about cows being abducted by aliens, and it made her sad.

Outside, she heard the truck go flying past her house. It didn't even slow down. Must be somebody looking at Gabriel's house. She wondered if he'd put it on the market without bothering to put a for-sale sign out front. Why not? He had no real ties here. He'd probably moved up to Wyoming to live near Sara.

She went into the kitchen, put her coffee cup in the sink, and went back to her washing.

SHE WORE A simple beige skirt and a short-sleeved beige sweater to church with pretty high heels and a purse to match. She left her hair long, down her back, and used only a trace of makeup on her face.

She'd had ample opportunities for romance, but all those years she'd waited for Gabriel, certain that he was going to love her one day, that she had a future with him. Now that future was gone. She knew that one day, she'd have to decide if she really wanted to be nothing more than a career woman with notoriety and money taking the place of a husband and children and a settled life.

There was nothing wrong with ambition. But the few career women she'd known seemed empty somehow, as if they presented a happy face to the world but that it was like a mask, hiding the insecurities and loneliness that accompanied a demanding lifestyle. What would it be like to grow old, with no family around you, with only friends and acquaintances and business associates to mark the holidays? Would it make up for the continuity of the next generation and the generation after that, of seeing your features reproduced down through your children and grandchildren and great-grandchildren? Would it make up for laughing little voices and busy little hands, and soft kisses on your cheek at bedtime?

That thought made her want to cry. She'd never thought too much about kids during her school days, but when Gabriel had kissed her and talked about a future, she'd dreamed of having his children. It had been a hunger unlike anything she'd ever known.

She had to stop tormenting herself. She had to come to grips with the world the way it was, not the way she wanted it to be. She was a grown woman with a promising career. She had to look ahead, not behind her.

SHE SLID INTO her usual pew, listened to Reverend Blair's sermon and sang along with the choir as they repeated the chorus of a well-loved old hymn. Sometime during the offering, she was aware of a tingling sensation, as if someone were watching her. She laughed silently. Now she was getting paranoid.

As the service ended, and they finished singing the final hymn, as the benediction sounded in Reverend Blair's clear, deep voice, she continued to have the sensation that someone was watching her.

Slowly, as her pew filed out into the aisle, she glanced toward the back of the church. But there was no one there, no one looking at her. What a strange sensation.

REVEREND BLAIR SHOOK her hand and smiled at her. "It's nice to have you back, Miss Godfrey," he teased.

She smiled back. "Rub it in. I had a nightmare of a political story to follow. I spent so much time on it that I'm thinking I may run for public office myself. By now, I know exactly what not to do to get elected," she confided with a chuckle.

"I know what you mean. It was a good story."

"Thanks."

"See you next week."

"I hope." She crossed her fingers. He just smiled.

SHE WALKED TO her car and clicked the smart key to unlock it when she felt, rather than saw, someone behind her.

She turned and her heart stopped in her chest. She looked up into liquid black eyes in a tanned, hard face that looked as if it had never known a smile.

She swallowed. She wanted to say so many things. She wanted to apologize. She wanted to cry. She wanted to throw herself into his arms and beg him to hold her, comfort her, forgive her. But she did none of those things. She just looked up at him hopelessly, with dead eyes that looked as if they had never held joy.

His square chin lifted. His eyes narrowed on her face. "You've lost weight."

She shrugged. "One of the better consequences of my profession," she said quietly. "How are you, Gabriel?"

"I've been better."

She searched his eyes. "How's Sara?"

"Getting back to normal."

She nodded. She swallowed again and dropped her eyes to his chest. It was hard to find something to say that didn't involve apologies or explanations or pleas for forgiveness.

The silence went on for so long that she could hear pieces of conversation from other churchgoers. She could hear the traffic on the highway, the sound of children playing in some yard nearby. She could hear the sound of her own heartbeat.

This was destroying her. She clicked the key fob again deliberately. "I have to go," she said softly.

"Sure."

He moved back so that she could open the door and get inside. She glanced at him with sorrow in her face, but she averted her eyes so that it didn't embarrass him. She didn't want him to feel guilty. She was the one who should feel that emotion. In the end she couldn't meet his eyes or even wave. She just started the car and drove away.

WELL, AT LEAST the first meeting was over with, she told herself later. It hadn't been quite as bad as she'd expected. But it had been rough. She felt like crying, but her eyes were dry. Some pain was too deep to be eased by tears, she thought sadly.

She changed into jeans and a red T-shirt and went out on the front porch to water her flowers while a TV dinner microwaved itself to perfection in the kitchen.

Her flowers were going to be beautiful when they bloomed, she decided, smiling as they poked their little heads up through the dirt in an assortment of ceramic pots all over the wooden floor.

She had three pots of chrysanthemums and one little bonsai tree named Fred. Gabriel had given it to her when she first moved in with them, a sort of welcome present. It was a tiny fir tree with a beautiful curving trunk and feathery limbs. She babied it, bought it expensive fertilizer, read books on how to keep it healthy and worried herself to death that it might accidentally die if she forgot to water it. That hadn't happened, of course, but she loved it dearly. Of all the things Gabriel had given her, and there had been a lot, this was her favorite. She left it outside until the weather grew too cold, then she carried it inside protectively.

The Jaguar had been wonderful. But she'd still been driving it when she did the story that almost destroyed Gabriel's life and after that, she could no longer bear to sit in it. The memories had been killing her.

She missed the Jag. She missed Gabriel more. She wondered why he'd come back. Probably to sell the house, she decided, to cut his last tie with Comanche Wells. If he was working for an international concern, it wasn't likely that he'd plan to come back here. He'd see the Jag in the driveway, she thought, and understand why she'd given it back. At least, she hoped he would.

That thought, that he might leave Comanche Wells forever, was really depressing. She watered Fred, put down the can, and went back into the house. It didn't occur to her to wonder what he'd been doing at her church.

WHEN SHE WENT into the kitchen to take her dinner out of the microwave, a dark-haired man was sitting at the table sipping coffee. There were two cups, one for him and one for her. The dinner was sitting on a plate with a napkin and silverware beside it.

He glanced up as she came into the room. "It's getting cold," he said simply.

She stood behind her chair, just staring at him, frowning.

He raised an eyebrow as he studied her shirt. "You know, most people who wore red shirts on the original *Star Trek* ended up dead."

She cocked her head. "And you came all this way to give me fashion advice?"

He managed a faint smile. "Not really." He sipped coffee. He let out a long breath. "It's been a long time, Michelle."

She nodded. Slowly, she pulled out the chair and sat down. The TV dinner had the appeal of mothballs. She pushed it aside and sipped the black coffee he'd put at her place. He still remembered how she took it, after all this time.

She ran her finger around the rim. "I learned a hard lesson," she said after a minute. "Reporting isn't just about presenting the majority point of view."

He lifted his eyes to hers. "Life teaches very hard lessons."

"Yes, it does." She drew in a breath. "I guess you're selling the house."

His eyebrows lifted. "Excuse me?"

"I saw a truck go out there yesterday. And I read that you're working with some international police force now. So since Sara's living in Wyoming, I assumed you'd probably be moving up there near her. For when you're home in the States, I mean."

"I'd considered it," he said after a minute. He sipped more coffee.

She wondered if her heart could fall any deeper into her chest. She wondered how in the world he'd gotten into the house so silently. She wondered why he was there in the first place. Was he saying goodbye?

"Did you find the keys to the Jag?" she asked.

"Yes. You didn't want to keep it?"

She swallowed hard. "Too many bad memories, of what I did to you and Sara," she confessed heavily.

He shook his head. After a minute, he stared at her bent head. "I don't think you've really looked at me once," he said finally.

She managed a tight smile. "It's very hard to do that, after all the trouble I caused you," she said. "I rehearsed it, you know. Saying I was sorry. Working up all sorts of ways to apologize. But there really isn't a good way to say it."

"People make mistakes."

"The kind I made could have buried you." She said it tautly, fighting tears. It was harder than she'd imagined. She forced down the rest of the coffee. "Look, I've got things to do," she began, standing, averting her face so he couldn't see her eyes.

"Ma belle," he whispered, in a voice so tender that her control broke the instant she heard it. She burst into tears.

He scooped her up in his arms and kissed her so hungrily that she just went limp, arching up to him, so completely his that she wouldn't have protested anything he wanted to do to her.

"So it's like that, is it?" he whispered against her soft, trembling mouth. "Anything I want? Anything at all?"

"Anything," she wept.

"Out of guilt?" he asked, and there was an edge to his tone now.

She opened her wet eyes and looked into his. "Out of...love," she choked.

"Love."

"Go ahead. Laugh..."

He buried his face in her throat. "I thought I'd lost you for good," he breathed huskily. "Standing there at your car, looking so defeated, so depressed that you couldn't even meet my eyes. I thought, I'll have to leave, there's nothing left, nothing there except guilt and sorrow. And then I decided to have one last try, to come here and talk to you. You walked into the room and every single thing you felt was there, right there, in your eyes when you looked at me. And I knew, then, that it wasn't over at all. It was only beginning."

Her arms tightened around his neck. Her eyes were pouring with hot tears. "I loved you...so much," she choked. "Sara said you never wanted to see me again. She hated me. I knew you must hate me, too...!"

He kissed the tears away. He sat down on the sofa with Michelle in his lap and curled her into his chest. "Sara has a quick, hot temper. She loses it, and it's over. She's sorry that she was so brutal with you. She was frightened and upset and the media was hunting her. She's had other problems as well, that you don't know about. But she's ashamed that she took it all out on you, blamed you for something you didn't even do deliberately." He lifted his head and smoothed the long, damp hair away from her cheek. "She wanted to apologize, but she's too ashamed to call you."

"That's why?" she whispered. "I thought I would never see her again. Or you."

"That would never happen," he said gently. "You're part of us."

She bit her lower lip. "I sold you out...!"

"You did not. You sold out a mercenary named Angel, someone you didn't know, someone you thought had perpetrated a terrible crime against innocent women and children," he said simply. He brushed his mouth over her wet eyes. "You would never have sold me out in a million years, even if you had thought I was guilty as sin." He lifted his head and looked into her eyes. "Because you love me. You love me enough to forgive anything, even murder."

The tears poured out even hotter. She couldn't stop crying.

He wrapped her up close, turned her under him on the sofa, slid between her long legs and began to kiss her with anguished hunger. The kisses grew so long and so hard and so hot that she trembled and curled her legs around the back of his, urging him into greater intimacy, pleading with him to ease the tension that was putting her young body on the rack.

"If you don't stop crying," he threatened huskily, "this is going to end badly."

"No, it isn't. You want to," she whispered, kissing his throat.

"Yes, I do," he replied deeply. "But you're going to need a lot of time that I can't give you when I'm out of control," he murmured darkly. "You won't enjoy it."

"Are you sure?" she whispered.

He lifted his head. His eyes were hot and hungry on her body. His hands had pushed up the red shirt and the bra, and he was staring at her pert, pretty breasts with aching need. "I am absolutely sure," he managed.

"Oh."

The single word and the wide-eyed, hopeless look in her eyes broke the tension and he started laughing. "That's it? 'Oh'?"

She laughed, too. "Well, I read a lot and I watch movies, but it's not quite the same thing…"

"Exactly."

He forced himself to roll off her. "If you don't mind, could you pull all this back down?" he asked, indicating her breasts. He averted his eyes. "And I'll try deep breaths and mental imagery of snow covered hills."

"Does it work?"

"Not really."

She pulled down her shirt and glanced at him with new knowledge of him and herself, and smiled.

"That's a smug little look," he accused.

"I like knowing I can throw you off balance," she said with a wicked grin.

"I'll enjoy letting you do it, but not until we're used to each other," he replied. He pulled her close. "The first time has to be slow and easy," he whispered, brushing his mouth over hers. "So that it doesn't hurt so much."

"If you can knock me off balance, I won't care if it hurts," she pointed out.

His black eyes twinkled. "I'll remember that."

She lay back on the sofa and looked up at him with wide, wondering eyes. "I thought it was all over," she whispered. "That I had nothing left, nothing to live for..."

"I felt the same way," he returned, solemn and quiet. "Thank God I decided to make one more attempt to get through to you."

She smiled gently. "Fate."

He smiled back. "Yes. Fate."

"Where are you going? Come back here." She pulled him back down.

He pursed his lips. "We need to discuss things vertically, not horizontally."

"I'm not going to seduce you, honest. I have something very serious I need to talk to you about."

"Okay. What?"

She pursed her own lips and her eyes twinkled. "Cow abductions."

He burst out laughing.

THEY WERE MARRIED in the Methodist church two weeks later by Reverend Blair. Michelle wore a conventional white gown with lace inserts and a fingertip veil, which Gabriel lifted to kiss her for the first time as his wife. In the audience were more mercenaries and ex-military and feds than anyone locally had seen in many a year.

Eb Scott and his wife, along with Dr. Micah Steele and Callie, and Cy Parks and Lisa, were all in the front row with Minette Carson and her husband Hayes. Carlie and her husband were there, too.

There was a reception in the fellowship hall and Jacobsville police chief Cash Grier kept looking around restlessly.

"Is something going on that we should know about?" Gabriel asked with a grin.

"Just waiting for the riot to break out."

"What riot?" Michelle asked curiously.

"You know, somebody says something, somebody else has too much to drink and takes offense, blows are exchanged, police are called in to break up the altercation…"

"Chief Grier, just how many riots at weddings have you seen?" she wanted to know.

"About half a dozen," he said.

"Well, I can assure you, there won't be any here," Michelle said. "Because there's no booze!"

Cash gaped at her. "No booze?"

"No."

"Well, damn," he said, glowering at her.

"Why do you say that?" she asked.

"How can you have altercations without booze?" He threw up his hands. "And I had so looked forward to a little excitement around here!"

"I could throw a punch at Hayes," Gabriel offered, grinning at the sheriff. "But then he'd have to arrest me, and Michelle would spend our honeymoon looking for bail bondsmen..."

Cash chuckled. "Just kidding. I like the occasional quiet wedding." He leaned forward. "When you're not busy, you might want to ask Blake Kemp about *his* wedding reception, though," he added gleefully. "Jacobsville will never forget that one, I swear!"

MICHELLE LAY TREMBLING in Gabriel's arms, hot and damp in the aftermath of something so turbulent and thrilling that she knew she could live on the memory of it for the rest of her life.

"I believe the chief wanted a little excitement?" She laughed hoarsely. "I don't think anyone could top this. Ever."

He trailed his fingers up her body, lingering tenderly on a distended nipple. He stroked it until she arched and gasped. "I don't think so, either." He bent his head and slipped his lips over the dusky peak, teasing it until it grew even harder and she shivered. He suckled it, delighting in the sounds that came out of her throat.

"You like that, do you?" he whispered. He moved over her. "How about this?"

"Oh...yes," she choked. "Yes!"

He slid a hand under her hips and lifted her into the slow penetration of his body, moving restlessly as she accepted him, arched to greet him, shivered again as she felt the slow, hungry depth of his envelopment.

"It's easier now," he whispered. "Does it hurt?"

"I haven't…noticed yet," she managed, shuddering as he moved on her.

He chuckled.

"I was afraid," she confessed in a rush of breath.

"I know."

She clung to him as the rhythm lifted her, teased her body into contortions of pure, exquisite pleasure. "I can't believe… I was afraid!"

His hips moved from side to side and she made a harsh, odd little cry that was echoed in the convulsion of her hips.

"Yes," he purred. "I can make you so hungry that you'll do anything to get me closer, can't I, *ma belle?*"

"Any…thing," she agreed.

He ground his teeth together. "It works…both ways… too," he bit off. He groaned harshly as the pleasure bit into him, arched him down into her as the rhythm grew hard and hot and deep. He felt his heartbeat in his head, slamming like a hammer as he drove into her welcoming body, faster and harder and closer until suddenly, like a storm breaking, a silver shaft of pleasure went through him like a spear, lifting him above her in an arch so brittle that he thought he might shatter into a thousand pieces.

"Like…dying," he managed as the pleasure took him.

She clung to him, too involved to even manage a reply, lifting and pleading, digging her nails into his hard back as she welcomed the hard, heavy push of his body, welcomed the deep, aching tension that grew and swelled and finally burst like rockets going off inside her.

She cried out helplessly, sobbing, as the ecstasy washed over her like the purest form of pleasure imaginable and then, just as quickly, was gone. Gone. Gone!

They clung together, damp with sweat, sliding against each other in the aftermath, holding on to the echoes of the exquisite satisfaction that they'd shared.

"Remind me to tell you one day how rare it is for two people to find completion at the same time," he whispered, sliding his mouth over her soft, yielding body. "Usually, the woman takes a long time, and the man only finds his satisfaction when hers is over."

She lifted an eyebrow. "And you would know this, how?" she began.

He lifted his head and looked into her eyes with a rakish grin. "Oh, from the videos I watched and the books I read and the other guys I listened to..."

"Is that so?" she mused, with a suspicious look.

He kissed her accusing eyes shut. "It was long before I knew you," he whispered. "And after the first day I saw you, sitting in the road waiting for me to run over you, there was no one. Ever."

Her eyes flew open. "Wh-what?"

He brushed the hair from her cheeks. "I knew then that I would love you one day, forever," he said quietly. "So there were no other women."

Her face flushed. "Gabriel," she whispered, overcome.

He kissed her tenderly. "The waiting was terrible," he groaned. "I thought I might die of it, waiting until you grew up, until you knew something of the world and men so that I didn't rob you of that experience." He lifted his head. "Always, I worried that you might find a younger man and fall in love…"

She put her fingers over his chiseled mouth. "I loved you from the day I met you," she whispered. "When I stared at you, that day in town with my grandfather, before I was even sixteen." She touched his cheek with her fingertips. "I knew, too, that there could never be anyone else."

He nibbled her fingers. "So sweet, the encounter after all the waiting," he whispered.

"Sweeter than honey," she agreed, her eyes warm and soft on his face.

"There's just one thing," he murmured.

She raised her eyebrows.

He opened a drawer and pulled out an item that he'd placed there earlier. An item that they'd forgotten to use.

She just smiled.

After a minute, he smiled back and dropped the item right back into the drawer.

SARA WAS OVERJOYED. "I can't wait to come down there and see you both," she exclaimed. "But you've only been married six weeks," she added.

Gabriel was facing the computer with Michelle at his side, holding her around the waist, his big hands resting protectively over her slightly swollen belly as they talked on Skype with Sara in Wyoming. "We were both very sure that it was what we wanted," he said simply.

"Well, I'm delighted," Sara said. She smiled. "The only way I could be more delighted is if it was me who was pregnant. But, that will come with time," she said complacently, and smiled. "I'm only sorry I couldn't be at the wedding," she added quietly. "I was very mean to you, Michelle. I couldn't face you, afterward."

"I understood," Michelle said gently. "You're my sister. Really my sister now," she added with a delighted laugh. "We're going to get a place near yours in Wyoming so that we can be nearby when the baby comes."

"I can't wait!"

"Neither can I," Michelle said. "We'll talk to you soon."

"Very soon." Sara smiled and cut the connection.

"Have you ever told her?" Michelle asked after a minute, curling up in Gabriel's lap.

He kissed her. "We did just tell her, my love…"

"Not about the baby," she protested. "About Wolf. About who he really is."

"You mean, her gaming partner for the past few years?" He grinned. "That's a story for another day."

"If you say so."

He kissed her. "I do say so. And now, how about a nice pickle and some vanilla ice cream?"

Her eyebrows lifted. "You know, that sounds delicious!"

He bent his head and kissed the little bump below her waist. "He's going to be extraordinary," he whispered.

"Yes. Like his dad," she replied with her heart in her eyes.

And they both grinned.

* * * * *

COLTRAIN

To Darlene, Cindy and Melissa

CHAPTER ONE

THE LITTLE BOY's leg was bleeding profusely. Dr. Louise Blakely knew exactly what to do, but it was difficult to get the right pressure on the cut so that the nicked artery would stop emptying onto the brown, dead December grass.

"It hurts!" the little boy, Matt, cried. "Ow!"

"We have to stop the bleeding," she said reasonably. She smiled at him, her dark eyes twinkling in a face framed by thick, medium blond hair. "Maybe your mom could get you an ice cream after we've patched you up." She glanced at the white-faced lady beside them, who nodded enthusiastically. "Okay?"

"Well…" He grimaced, holding his leg above where Lou was putting pressure to bear.

"Only a minute more," she promised, looking around for the ambulance she'd asked a bystander to call. It was on the way. She could hear the siren. Even in a small town like Jacobsville, there was an efficient ambulance service. "You're going to get to ride in a real ambulance," she told the child. "You can tell your friends all about it on Monday at school!"

"Will I have to go back?" he asked, enthusiastic now. "Maybe I could stay in the hospital for a whole week?"

"I really think the emergency room is as far as you're going to get this time." Lou chuckled. "Now pay atten-

tion while they're loading you up, so that you can remember everything!"

"I sure will!" he said.

She stood up as the ambulance pulled alongside the
police car and two attendants jumped out. They started
loading the boy onto a stretcher. Lou had a brief word
with the female EMT and described the boy's injuries
and gave instructions. She was on staff at the local hospital where he would be taken, and she planned to follow the ambulance in her own car.

The police officer who'd been citing the reckless
driver for hitting the small boy on the bicycle came
over to talk to Lou. "Good thing you were having lunch
in the café," he remarked with a grin. "That was a bad
cut."

"He'll be okay," Lou said as she closed her medical
bag. She always had it in the car when she left the office, and this time it had paid off.

"You're Dr. Coltrain's partner, aren't you?" he asked
suddenly.

"Yes." She didn't add anything to that. The expression on the officer's face said enough. Most people
around Jacobsville knew that Dr. Coltrain had as little
use for his partner as he had for alcohol. He'd made it
all too evident in the months she'd been sharing his
practice.

"He's a good man," the officer added. "Saved my
wife when her lung collapsed." He smiled at the memory. "Nothing shakes him up. Nor you, either, judging
by what I just saw. You're a good hand in an emergency."

"Thanks." She gave him a brief smile and went to her
small gray Ford to follow the ambulance to the hospital.

THE EMERGENCY ROOM was full, as usual. It was Saturday and accidents always doubled on weekends. She nodded to a couple of her patients that she recognized, and she kept walking, right behind the trolley that was taking young Matt to a treatment room.

Dr. Coltrain was on his way back from surgery. They met in the hall. The green surgical uniform looked sloppy on some of the surgeons, but not on Coltrain. Despite the cap that hid most of his thick red hair, he looked elegant and formidable.

"Why are you here on Saturday? I'm supposed to be doing rounds today for both of us," he asked sharply.

Here he goes again, practicing Coltrain's First Law...jump to conclusions, she thought. She didn't grin, but she felt like it.

"I wound up at a car accident scene," she began.

"The hospital pays EMTs to work wrecks," he continued, glaring at her while hospital personnel came and went around them.

"I did not go out to—" she began hotly.

"Don't let this happen again, or I'll have a word with Wright, and you'll be taken off staff here. Is that clear?" he added coldly. Wright was the hospital administrator and Coltrain was medical chief of staff. He had the authority to carry out the threat.

"Will you listen?" she asked irritably. "I didn't go out with the ambulance...!"

"Doctor, are you coming?" one of the EMTs called to her.

Coltrain glanced toward the EMT and then back at Louise, irritably jerking off his cap and mask. His pale blue eyes were as intimidating as his stance. "If your

social life is this stale, Doctor, perhaps you need to consider a move," he added with biting sarcasm.

She opened her mouth to reply, but he was already
walking away. She threw up her hands furiously. She
couldn't ever get a word in, because he kept talking,
or interrupted her, and then stormed off without giving her a chance to reply. It was useless to argue with
him, anyway. No matter what she said or did, she was
always in the wrong.

"One day you'll break something," she told his re-
treating back. "And I'll put you in a body cast, so help
me God!"

A passing nurse patted her on the shoulder. "There,
there, Doctor, you're doing it again."

She ground her teeth together. It was a standing joke
in the hospital staff that Louise Blakely ended up talking to herself every time she argued with Dr. Coltrain.
That meant that she talked to herself almost constantly.
Presumably he heard her from time to time, but he never
gave a single indication that he had.

With a furious groan deep in her throat, she turned
down the hall to join the EMT.

IT TOOK AN hour to see to the boy, who had more than
one cut that needed stitches. His mother was going to
have to buy him a lot of ice cream to make up for the
pain, Lou thought, and she'd been wrong about another
thing, too—he did have to stay overnight in the hospital. But that would only give him status among his
peers, she thought, and left him smiling with a caution-
ary word about the proper way to ride a bicycle in town.

"No need to worry about that," his mother said

firmly. "He won't be riding his bike across city streets anymore!"

She nodded and left the emergency room, her bag in hand. She looked more like a teenager on holiday than a doctor, she mused, in her blue jeans and T-shirt and sneakers. She'd pulled her long blond hair up into its habitual bun and she wore no makeup to enhance her full mouth or her deep brown eyes. She had no man to impress, except the one she loved, and he wouldn't notice if she wore tar and feathers to the office they shared. "Copper" Coltrain had no interest in Lou Blakely, except as an efficient co-worker. Not that he ever acknowledged her efficiency; instead he found fault with her constantly. She wondered often why he ever agreed to work with her in the first place, when he couldn't seem to stand the sight of her. She wondered, too, why she kept hanging on where she wasn't wanted. The hunger her poor heart felt for him was her only excuse. And one day, even that wouldn't be enough.

Dr. Drew Morris, the only friend she had on staff, came down the hall toward her. Like Coltrain, he'd been operating, because he was wearing the same familiar green surgical clothing. But where Coltrain did chest surgery, Drew's talents were limited to tonsils, adenoids, appendices and other minor surgeries. His speciality was pediatrics. Coltrain's was chest and lungs, and many of his patients were elderly.

"What are you doing here? It's too early or too late for rounds, depending on your schedule," he added with a grin. "Besides, I thought Copper was doing them today."

Copper, indeed. Only a handful of people were privileged to call Dr. Coltrain by that nickname, and she wasn't numbered among them.

She grimaced at him. He was about her height, although she was tall, and he had dark hair and eyes and was a little overweight. He was the one who'd phoned her at the Austin hospital where she was working just after her parents' deaths, and he'd told her about the interviews Coltrain was holding for a partner. She'd jumped at the chance for a new start, in the hometown where her mother and father had both been born. And amazingly, in light of his ongoing animosity toward her, Coltrain had asked her to join him after a ten-minute interview.

"There was an accident in front of the café," she said. "I was having lunch there. I haven't been to the grocery store yet," she added with a grimace. "I hate shopping."

"Who doesn't?" He smiled. "Doing okay?"

She shrugged. "As usual."

He stuck his hands on his hips and shook his head. "It's my fault. I thought it would get better, but it hasn't, has it? It's been almost a year, and he still suffers you."

She winced. She didn't quite avert her face fast enough to hide it.

"You poor kid," he said gently. "I'm sorry. I suppose I was too enthusiastic about getting you here. I thought you needed a change, after...well, after your parents' deaths. This looked like a good opportunity. Copper's one of the best surgeons I've ever known, and you're a skilled family practitioner. It seemed a good match of talent, and you've taken a load off him in his regular practice so that he could specialize in the surgery he's so skilled at." He sighed. "How wrong can a man be?"

"I signed a contract for one year," she reminded him. "It's almost up."

"Then what?"

"Then I'll go back to Austin."

"You could work the E.R.," he teased. It was a standing joke between them. The hospital had to contract out the emergency room staff, because none of the local doctors wanted to do it. The job was so demanding that one young resident had walked out in the middle of the unnecessary examination of a known hypochondriac at two in the morning and never came back.

Lou smiled, remembering that. "No, thanks. I like private practice, but I can't afford to set up and equip an office of my own just yet. I'll go back to the drawing board. There's bound to be a practice somewhere in Texas."

"You're fit for this one," he said shortly.

"Not to hear my partner tell it," she said curtly. "I'm never right, didn't you know?" She let out a long breath. "Anyway, I'm in a rut, Drew. I need a change."

"Maybe you do, at that." He pursed his lips and smiled. "What you really need is a good social life. I'll be in touch."

She watched him walk away with grave misgivings. She hoped that he didn't mean what it sounded like he meant. She wanted nothing to do with Drew in a romantic way, although she did like him. He was a kind man, a widower who'd been in love with his wife and was still, after five years, getting over her. Drew was a native of Jacobsville, and knew Lou's parents. He'd been very fond of her late mother. He'd met up with them again in Austin—that's where Lou had met him.

Lou decided not to take Drew's teasing seriously because she knew about his devotion to his wife's memory. But he'd looked very solemn when he'd remarked that her social life needed uplifting.

She was probably imagining things, she told herself. She started out to the parking lot and met Dr. Coltrain, dressed in an expensive gray vested suit, bent on the same destination. She ground her teeth together and slowed her pace, but she still reached the doors at the same time he did.

He spared her a cold glance. "You look unprofessional," he said curtly. "At least have the grace to dress decently if you're going to cruise around with the ambulance service."

She stopped and looked up at him without expression. "I wasn't cruising anywhere. I don't have a boat, so how could I cruise?"

He just looked at her. "They don't need any new EMTs…"

"You shut up!" she snapped, surprising him speechless. "Now you listen to me for a change, and don't interrupt!" she added, holding up her hand when his thin lips parted. "There was an accident in town. I was in the café, so I gave assistance. I don't need to hang out with the ambulance crew for kicks, Doctor! And how I dress on my days off is none of your—" she almost turned blue biting back the curse "—*business, Doctor!*"

He was over his shock. His hand shot out and caught the wrist of her free hand, the one that wasn't holding her black medical bag, and jerked. She caught her breath at the shock of his touch and squirmed, wrestling out of his grip. The muted violence of it brought back protective instincts that she'd almost forgotten. She stood very still, holding her breath, her eyes the size of saucers as she looked at him and waited for that hand to tighten and twist...

But it didn't. He, unlike her late father, never seemed to lose control. He released her abruptly. His blue eyes narrowed. "Cold as ice, aren't you?" he drawled mockingly. "You'd freeze any normal man to death. Is that why you never married, Doctor?"

It was the most personal thing he'd ever said to her, and one of the most insulting.

"You just think what you like," she said.

"You might be surprised at what I think," he replied.

Her own eyebrows lifted. "Really?" She laughed and walked off to her car, happy to have seen him stiffen. She walked past his Mercedes without even a glance. Take that, she thought furiously. She didn't care what he thought about her, she told herself. She spent most of her free time telling herself that. But she did care about him, far too much. That was the whole problem.

He thought she was cold, but she wasn't. It was quite the reverse where he was concerned. She always jerked away when he came too close, when he touched her infrequently. It wasn't because she found him repulsive but because his touch excited her so much. She trembled when he was too close, her breathing changed. She couldn't control her shaky legs or her shaky voice. The only solution had been to distance herself physically from him, and that was what she'd done.

There were other reasons, too, why she avoided physical involvement. They were none of his business, or anyone else's. She did her job and avoided trouble as much as possible. But just lately, her job was becoming an ordeal.

She drove home to the small dilapidated white house

on the outskirts of town. It was in a quiet neighborhood that was just beginning to go downhill. The rent was cheap. She'd spent weekends painting the walls and adding bits and pieces to the house's drab interior. She had it all but furnished now, and it reflected her own quiet personality. But there were other dimensions to the room, like the crazy cat sculpture on the mantel and the colorful serapes on the chairs, and the Indian pottery and exotic musical instruments on the bookshelf. The paintings were her own, disturbingly violent ones with reds and blacks and whites in dramatic chaos. A visitor would have found the combinations of flowers amid those paintings confusing. But, then, she'd never had a visitor. She kept to herself.

Coltrain did, too, as a rule. He had visitors to his ranch from time to time, but his invitations even when they included the medical staff invariably excluded Louise. The omission had caused gossip, which no one had been brave enough to question to his face. Louise didn't care if he never invited her to his home. After all, she never invited him to hers.

Secretly she suspected that he was grieving for Jane Parker, his old flame who'd just recently married Todd Burke. Jane was blond and blue-eyed and beautiful, a former rodeo star with a warm heart and a gentle personality.

Lou often wondered why he'd ever agreed to work with someone he disliked so much, and on such short acquaintance. He and Dr. Drew Morris were friends, and she'd tried to question Drew about her sudden acceptance, but Drew was a clam. He always changed the subject.

Drew had known her parents in Jacobsville and he

had been a student of her father's at the Austin teaching hospital where he'd interned. He'd become an ally of her mother during some really tough times, but he didn't like Lou's father. He knew too much about his home life, and how Lou and her mother were treated.

There had been one whisper of gossip at the Jacobsville hospital when she'd first gone there on cases. She'd heard one of the senior nurses remark that it must disturb "him" to have Dr. Blakely's daughter practicing at this hospital and thank God she didn't do surgery. Lou had wanted to question the nurse, but she'd made herself scarce after that and eventually had retired.

Louise had never found out who "he" was or what was disturbing about having another Blakely practice at the Jacobsville hospital. But she did begin to realize that her father had a past here.

"What did my father do at this hospital, Drew?" she'd asked him one day suddenly, while they were doing rounds at the hospital.

He'd seemed taken aback. "He was a surgeon on staff, just as I am," he said after a hesitation.

"He left here under a cloud, didn't he?" she persisted.

He shook his head. "There was no scandal, no cloud on his reputation. He was a good surgeon and well respected, right until the end. You know that. Even if he was less than admirable as a husband and father, he was an exceptional surgeon."

"Then why the whispers about him when I first came here?"

"It was nothing to do with his skill as a surgeon," he replied quietly. "It's nothing that really even concerns you, except in a roundabout way."

"But what…?"

They'd been interrupted and he'd looked relieved. She hadn't asked again. But she wondered more and more. Perhaps it had affected Dr. Coltrain in some way and that was why he disliked Lou. But wouldn't he have mentioned it in a whole year?

She didn't ever expect to understand the so-controlled Dr. Coltrain or his venomous attitude toward her. He'd been much more cordial when she first became his partner. But about the time she realized that she was in love with him, he became icy cold and antagonistic. He'd been that way ever since, raising eyebrows everywhere.

The remark he'd made this morning about her coldness was an old one. She'd jerked back from him at a Christmas party, soon after she'd come to work in his office in Jacobsville, to avoid a kiss under the mistletoe. She could hardly have admitted that even then the thought of his hard, thin mouth on hers made her knees threaten to buckle. Her attraction to him had been explosive and immediate, a frightening experience to a woman whose whole life had been wrapped around academic excellence and night upon night of exhaustive studying. She had no social life at all—even in high school. It had been the one thing that kept her father's vicious sarcasm and brutality at bay, as long as she made good grades and stayed on the dean's list.

Outside achievements had been the magic key that kept the balance in her dysfunctional family. She studied and won awards and scholarships and praise, and her father basked in it. She thought that he'd never felt much for her, except pride in her ability to excel. He was a cruel man and grew crueler as his addiction climbed year after year to new heights. Drugs had caused the plane crash. Her mother had died with him. God knew, that was fitting, because she'd loved him to the point of blindness, overlooking his brutality, his addiction, his cruelty in the name of fidelity.

Lou wrapped her arms around herself, feeling the chill of fear. She'd never marry. Any woman could wake up in a relationship that damaging. All she had to do was fall in love, lose control, give in to a man's dominance. Even the best man could become a predator if he sensed vulnerability in a woman. So she would never be vulnerable, she assured herself. She would never be at a man's mercy as her mother had been.

But Copper Coltrain made her vulnerable, and that was why she avoided any physical contact with him. She couldn't give in to the feelings he roused in her, for fear of becoming a victim. Loneliness might be a disease, but it was certainly a more manageable one than love.

The ringing of the telephone caught her attention.

"Dr. Blakely?" Brenda, her office nurse, queried. "Sorry to bother you at home, but Dr. Coltrain said there's been a wreck on the north end of town and they'll be bringing the victims to the emergency room. Since he's on call, you'll have to cover the two-hour Saturday clinic at the office."

"I'll be right over," she promised, wasting no more time in conversation.

THE CLINIC WAS almost deserted. There was a football game at the local high school that night, and it was sunny and unseasonably warm outside for early December. It didn't really surprise Lou that she only needed to see a handful of patients.

"Poor Dr. Coltrain," Brenda said with a sigh as they

finished the last case and closed up the office. "I'll bet he won't be in until midnight."

"It's a good thing he isn't married," Lou remarked. "He'd have no home life at all, as hard as he works."

Brenda glanced at her, but with a kind smile. "That is true. But he should be thinking about it. He's in his thirties now, and time is passing him by." She turned the key in the lock. "Pity about Miss Parker marrying that Burke man, isn't it? Dr. Coltrain was sweet on her for so many years. I always thought—I guess most people here did—that they were made for each other. But she was never more than friendly. If you saw them together, it was obvious that she didn't feel what he did."

In other words, Dr. Coltrain had felt a long and unrequited love for the lovely blond former rodeo cowgirl, Jane Parker. That much, Lou had learned from gossip. It must have hurt him very badly when she married someone else.

"What a pity that we can't love to order," Lou remarked quietly, thinking how much she'd give to be unscarred and find Dr. Coltrain as helplessly drawn to her as she was to him. That was the stuff of fantasy, however.

"Wasn't it surprising about Ted Regan and Coreen Tarleton, though?" Brenda added with a chuckle.

"Indeed it was," Lou agreed, smiling as she remembered having Ted for a patient. "She was shaking all over when she got him to me with that gored arm. He was cool. Nothing shakes Ted. But Coreen was as white as milk."

"I thought they were already married," Brenda groaned. "Well, I was new to the area and I didn't know them. I do now," she added, laughing. "I pass them at least once a week on their way to the obstetrician's office. She's due any day."

"She'll be a good mother, and Ted will certainly be a good father. Their children will have a happy life."

Brenda caught the faint bitterness in the words and glanced at Lou, but the other woman was already calling her goodbyes and walking away.

She went home and spent the rest of the weekend buried in medical journals and the latest research on the new strain of bacteria that had, researchers surmised, mutated from a deadly scarlet fever bacterium that had caused many deaths at the turn of the century.

CHAPTER TWO

MONDAY MORNING BROUGHT a variety of new cases, and Louise found herself stuck with the most routine of them, as usual. She and Coltrain were supposed to be partners, but when he wasn't operating, he got the interesting, challenging illnesses. Louise got fractured ribs and colds.

He'd been stiff with her this morning, probably because he was still fuming over the argument they'd had about his mistaken idea of her weekend activities. Accusing her of lollygagging with the EMTs for excitement; really!

She watched his white-coated back disappear into an examination room down the hall in their small building and sighed half-angrily as she went back to check an X-ray in the files. The very worst thing about unrequited love, she thought miserably, was that it fed on itself. The more her partner in the medical practice ignored and antagonized her, the harder she had to fight her dreams about him. She didn't want to get married; she didn't even want to get involved. But he made her hungry.

He'd spent a lot of time with Jane Parker until she married that Burke man, and Lou had long ago given up hope that he would ever notice her in the same way he always noticed Jane. The two of them had grown up together, though, whereas Lou had only been in partnership with him for a year. She was a native of Austin, not Jacobsville. Small towns were like extended families. Everybody knew each other, and some families had been friends for more than one generation. Lou was a true outsider here, even though she *was* a native Texan. Perhaps that was one of many reasons that Dr. Coltrain found her so forgettable.

She wasn't bad looking. She had long, thick blond hair and big brown eyes and a creamy, blemish-free complexion. She was tall and willowy, but still shorter than her colleague. She lacked his fiery temper and his authoritarian demeanor. He was tall and whipcord lean, with flaming red hair and blue eyes and a dark tan from working on his small ranch when he wasn't treating patients. That tan was odd in a redhead, although he did have a smattering of freckles over his nose and the backs of his big hands. She'd often wondered if the freckles went any farther, but she had yet to see him without his professional white coat over his very formal suit. He wasn't much on casual dressing at work. At home, she was sure that he dressed less formally.

That was something Lou would probably never know. She'd never been invited to his home, despite the fact that most of the medical staff at the local hospital had. Lou was automatically excluded from any social gathering that he coordinated.

Other people had commented on his less than friendly behavior toward her. It puzzled them, and it puzzled her, because she hadn't become his partner in any underhanded way. He had known from the day of her application that she was female, so it couldn't be that. Perhaps, she thought wistfully, he was one of those old-line dominating sort of men who thought women had no place in medicine. But he'd been instrumental in getting women into positions of authority at the hospital, so that theory wasn't applicable, either. The bottom line was that he simply did not like Louise Blakely, medical degree or no medical degree, and she'd never known why.

She really should ask Drew Morris why, she told herself with determination. It had been Drew, a surgeon and friend of her family, who'd sent word about the opening in Coltrain's practice. He'd wanted to help Lou get a job near him, so that he could give her some moral support in the terrible days following the deaths of her parents. She, in turn, had liked the idea of being in practice in a small town, one where she knew at least one doctor on the staff of the hospital. Despite growing up in Austin, it was still a big city and she was lonely. She was twenty-eight, a loner whose whole life had been medicine. She'd made sure that her infrequent dates never touched her heart, and she was innocent in an age when innocence was automatically looked on with disdain or suspicion.

Her nurse stuck her head in the doorway. "There's a call for you. Dr. Morris is on line two."

"Thanks, Brenda."

She picked up the receiver absently, her finger poised over the designated line. But when she pressed it, before she could say a word, the sentence she'd intercepted accidentally blared in her ear in a familiar deep voice.

"...told you I wouldn't have hired her in the first place, if I had known who she was related to. I did you a favor, never realizing she was Blakely's daughter. You can't imagine that I'll ever forgive her father for what he did to the girl I loved, do you? She's been a constant reminder, a constant torment!"

"That's harsh, Copper," Drew began.

"It's how I feel. She's nothing but a burden here. But to answer your question, hell no, you're not stepping on my toes if you ask her out on a date! I find Louise Blakely repulsive and repugnant, and an automaton with no attractions whatsoever. Take her with my blessing. I'd give real money if she'd get out of my practice and out of my life, and the sooner the better!" There was a click and the line, obviously open, was waiting for her.

She clicked the receiver to announce her presence and said, as calmly as she could, "Dr. Lou Blakely."

"Lou! It's Drew Morris," came the reply. "I hope I'm not catching you at a bad moment?"

"No." She cleared her throat and fought to control her scattered emotions. "No, not at all. What can I do for you?"

"There's a dinner at the Rotary Club Thursday. How about going with me?"

She and Drew occasionally went out together, in a friendly but not romantic way. She would have refused, but what Coltrain had said made her mad. "Yes, I would like to, thanks," she said.

Drew laughed softly. "Great! I'll pick you up at six on Thursday, then."

"See you then."

She hung up, checked the X-ray again meticulously, and put it away in its file. Brenda ordinarily pulled the X-rays for her, but it was Monday and, as usual, they were overflowing with patients who'd saved their weekend complaints for office hours.

She went back to her patient, her color a little high, but no disturbance visible in her expression.

She finished her quota of patients and then went into her small office. Mechanically she picked up a sheet of letterhead paper, with Dr. Coltrain's name on one side and hers on the other. Irrelevantly, she thought that the stationery would have to be replaced now.

She typed out a neat resignation letter, put it in an envelope and went to place it on Dr. Coltrain's desk. It was lunchtime and he'd already left the building. He made sure he always did, probably to insure that he didn't risk having Lou invite herself to eat with him.

Brenda scowled as her boss started absently toward the back door. "Shouldn't you take off your coat first?" she asked hesitantly.

Lou did, without a word, replaced it in her office, whipped her leather fanny pack around her waist and left the building.

It would have been nice if she'd had someone to talk to, she thought wistfully, about this latest crisis. She sat alone in the local café, drinking black coffee and picking at a small salad. She didn't mingle well with people. When she wasn't working, she was quiet and shy, and she kept to herself. It was difficult for strangers to approach her, but she didn't realize that. She stared into her coffee and remembered every word Coltrain had said to Drew Morris about her. He hated her. He couldn't possibly have made it clearer. She was repugnant, he'd said.

Well, perhaps she was. Her father had told her so, often enough, when he was alive. He and her mother were from Jacobsville but hadn't lived in the area for years. He had never spoken of his past. Not that he spoke to Lou often, anyway, except to berate her grades and tell her that she'd never measure up.

"Excuse me?"

She looked up. The waitress was staring at her. "Yes?" she asked coolly.

"I don't mean to pry, but are you all right?"

The question surprised Lou, and touched her. She managed a faint smile through her misery. "Yes. It's been a…long morning. I'm not really hungry."

"Okay." The waitress smiled again, reassuringly, and went away.

Just as Lou was finishing her coffee, Coltrain came in the front door. He was wearing the elegant gray suit that looked so good on him, and carrying a silver belly Stetson by the brim. He looked furiously angry as his pale eyes scanned the room and finally spotted Lou, sitting all alone.

He never hesitated, she thought, watching him walk purposefully toward her. There must be an emergency…

He slammed the opened envelope down on the table in front of her. "What the hell do you mean by that?" he demanded in a dangerously quiet tone.

She raised her dark, cold eyes to his. "I'm leaving," she explained and averted her gaze.

"I know that! I want to know why!"

She looked around. The café was almost empty, but the waitress and a local cowboy at the counter were glancing at them curiously.

Her chin came up. "I'd rather not discuss my private business in public, if you don't mind," she said stiffly.

His jaw clenched, and his eyes grew glittery. He stood back to allow her to get up. He waited while she paid for her salad and coffee and then followed her out to where her small gray Ford was parked.

Her heart raced when he caught her by the arm before she could get her key out of her jeans pocket. He jerked her around, not roughly, and walked her over to Jacobsville's small town square, to a secluded bench in a grove of live oak and willow trees. Because it was barely December, there were no leaves on the trees and it was cool, despite her nervous perspiration. She tried to throw off his hand, to no avail.

He only loosened his grip on her when she sat down on a park bench. He remained standing, propping his boot on the bench beside her, leaning one long arm over his knee to study her. "This is private enough," he said shortly. "Why are you leaving?"

"I signed a contract to work with you for one year. It's almost up, anyway," she said icily. "I want out. I want to go home."

"You don't have anyone left in Austin," he said, surprising her.

"I have friends," she began.

"You don't have those, either. You don't have friends at all, unless you count Drew Morris," he said flatly.

Her fingers clenched around her car keys. She looked at them, biting into the flesh even though not a speck of emotion showed on her placid features.

His eyes followed hers to her lap and something moved in his face. There was an expression there that puzzled her. He reached down and opened her rigid hand, frowning when he saw the red marks the keys had made in her palm.

She jerked her fingers away from him.

He seemed disconcerted for a few seconds. He stared

at her without speaking and she felt her heart beating wildly against her ribs. She hated being helpless

He moved back, watching her relax. He took another step and saw her release the breath she'd been holding. Every trace of anger left him.

"It takes time for a partnership to work," he said abruptly. "You've only given this one a year."

"That's right," she said tonelessly. "*I've* given it a year."

The emphasis she placed on the first word caught his attention. His blue eyes narrowed. "You sound as if you don't think I've given it any time at all."

She nodded. Her eyes met his. "You didn't want me in the practice. I suspected it from the beginning, but it wasn't until I heard what you told Drew on the phone this morning that—"

His eyes flashed oddly. "You heard what I said?" he asked huskily. "You heard…all of it!" he exclaimed.

Her lips trembled just faintly. "Yes," she said.

He was remembering what he'd told Drew Morris in a characteristic outburst of bad temper. He often said things in heat that he regretted later, but this he regretted most of all. He'd never credited his cool, unflappable partner with any emotions at all. She'd backed away from him figuratively and physically since the first day she'd worked at the clinic. Her physical withdrawal had maddened him, although he'd always assumed she was frigid.

But in the past five minutes, he'd learned disturbing things about her without a word being spoken. He'd hurt her. He didn't realize she'd cared that much about his opinion. Hell, he'd been furious because he'd just had to diagnose leukemia in a sweet little boy of four. It had hurt him to do that, and he'd lashed out at Morris over Lou in frustration at his own helplessness. But he'd had no idea that she'd overheard his vicious remarks. She was going to leave and it was no less than he deserved. He was genuinely sorry. She wasn't going to believe that, though. He could tell by her mutinous expression, in her clenched hands, in the tight set of her mouth.

"You did Drew a favor and asked me to join you, probably over some other doctor you really wanted," she said with a forced smile. "Well, no harm done. Perhaps you can get him back when I leave."

"Wait a minute," he began shortly.

She held up a hand. "Let's not argue about it," she said, sick at knowing his opinion of her, his real opinion. "I'm tired of fighting you to practice medicine here. I haven't done the first thing right, according to you. I'm a burden. Well, I just want out. I'll go on working until you can replace me." She stood up.

His hand tightened on the brim of his hat. He was losing this battle. He didn't know how to pull his irons out of the fire.

"I had to tell the Dawes that their son has leukemia," he said, hating the need to explain his bad temper. "I say things I don't mean sometimes."

"We both know that you meant what you said about me," she said flatly. Her eyes met his levelly. "You've hated me from almost the first day we worked together. Most of the time, you can't even be bothered to be civil to me. I didn't know that you had a grudge against me from the outset..."

She hadn't thought about that until she said it, but there was a subtle change in his expression, a faint distaste that her mind locked on.

"So you heard that, too." His jaw clenched on words he didn't want to say. But maybe it was as well to say them. He'd lived a lie for the past year.

"Yes." She gripped the wrought-iron frame of the park bench hard. "What happened? Did my father cause someone to die?"

His jaw tautened. He didn't like saying this. "The girl I wanted to marry got pregnant by him. He performed a secret abortion and she was going to marry me anyway." He laughed icily. "A fling, he called it. But the medical authority had other ideas, and they invited him to resign."

Lou's fingers went white on the cold wrought iron. Had her mother known? What had happened to the girl afterward?

"Only a handful of people knew," Coltrain said, as if he'd read her thoughts. "I doubt that your mother did. She seemed very nice—hardly a fit match for a man like that."

"And the girl?" she asked levelly.

"She left town. Eventually she married." He rammed his hands into his pockets and glared at her. "If you want the whole truth, Drew felt sorry for you when your parents died so tragically. He knew I was looking for a partner, and he recommended you so highly that I asked you. I didn't connect the name at first," he added on a mocking note. "Ironic, isn't it, that I'd choose as a partner the daughter of a man I hated until the day he died."

"Why didn't you tell me?" she asked irritably. "I would have resigned!"

"You were in no fit state to be told anything," he replied with reluctant memories of her tragic face when she'd arrived. His hands clenched in his pockets. "Besides, you'd signed a one-year contract. The only way out was if you resigned."

It all made sense immediately. She was too intelligent not to understand why he'd been so antagonistic. "I see," she breathed. "But I didn't resign."

"You were made of stronger stuff than I imagined," he agreed. "You wouldn't back down an inch. No matter how rough it got, you threw my own bad temper back at me." He rubbed his fingers absently over the car keys in his pocket while he studied her. "It's been a long time since anyone around here stood up to me like that," he added reluctantly.

She knew that without being told. He was a holy terror. Even grown men around Jacobsville gave him a wide berth when he lost his legendary temper. But Lou never had. She stood right up to him. She wasn't fiery by nature, but her father had been viciously cruel to her. She'd learned early not to show fear or back down, because it only made him worse. The same rule seemed to apply to Coltrain. A weaker personality wouldn't have lasted in his office one week, much less one year, male or female.

She knew now that Drew Morris had been doing what he thought was a good deed. Perhaps he'd thought it wouldn't matter to Coltrain after such a long time to have a Blakely working for him. But he'd obviously underestimated the man. Lou would have realized at once, on the shortest acquaintance, that Coltrain didn't forgive people.

He stared at her unblinkingly. "A year. A whole year, being reminded every day I took a breath what your father cost me. There were times when I'd have done anything to make you leave. Just the sight of you was painful." He smiled wearily. "I think I hated you, at first."

That was the last straw. She'd loved him, against her will and all her judgment, and he was telling her that all he saw when he looked at her was an ice woman whose father had betrayed him with the woman he loved. He hated her.

It was too much all at once. Lou had always had impeccable control over her emotions. It had been dangerous to let her father know that he was hurting her, because he enjoyed hurting her. And now here was the one man she'd ever loved telling her that he hated her because of her father.

What a surprise it would be for him to learn that her father, at the last, had been little more than a high-class drug addict, stealing narcotics from the hospital where he worked in Austin to support his growing habit. He'd been as high as a kite on narcotics, in fact, when the plane he was piloting went down, killing himself and his wife.

Tears swelled her eyelids. Not a sound passed her lips as they overflowed in two hot streaks down her pale cheeks.

He caught his breath. He'd seen her tired, impassive, worn-out, fighting mad, and even frustrated. But he'd never seen her cry. His lean hand shot out and touched the track of tears down one cheek, as if he had to touch them to make sure they were real.

She jerked back from him, laughing tearfully. "So that was why you were so horrible to me." She choked out the words. "Drew never said a word…no wonder you suffered me! And I was silly enough to dream…!" The laughter was harsher now as she dashed away the tears, staring at him with eyes full of pain and loss. "What a fool I've been," she whispered poignantly. "What a silly fool!"

She turned and walked away from him, gripping the car keys in her hand. The sight of her back was as eloquently telling as the words that haunted him. She'd dreamed...what?

FOR THE NEXT few days, Lou was polite and remote and as courteous as any stranger toward her partner. But something had altered in their relationship. He was aware of a subtle difference in her attitude toward him, in a distancing of herself that was new. Her eyes had always followed him, and he'd been aware of it at some subconscious level. Perhaps he'd been aware of more than covert glances, too. But Lou no longer watched him or went out of her way to seek him out. If she had questions, she wrote them down and left them for him on his desk. If there were messages to be passed on, she left them with Brenda.

The one time she did seek him out was Thursday afternoon as they closed up.

"Have you worked out an advertisement for someone to replace me?" she asked him politely.

He watched her calm dark eyes curiously. "Are you in such a hurry to leave?" he asked.

"Yes," she said bluntly. "I'd like to leave after the Christmas holidays." She turned and would have gone out the door, but his hand caught the sleeve of her white jacket. She slung it off and backed away. "At the first of the year."

He glared at her, hating the instinctive withdrawal

that came whenever he touched her. "You're a good doctor," he said flatly. "You've earned your place here."

High praise for a man with his grudges. She looked over her shoulder at him, her eyes wounded. "But you hate me, don't you? I heard what you said to Drew, that every time you looked at me you remembered what my father had done and hated me all over again."

He let go of her sleeve, frowning. He couldn't find an answer.

"Well, don't sweat it, Doctor," she told him. "I'll be gone in a month and you can find someone you like to work with you."

She laughed curtly and walked out of the office.

SHE DRESSED SEDATELY that evening for the Rotary Club dinner, in a neat off-white suit with a pink blouse. But she left her blond hair long around her shoulders for once, and used a light dusting of makeup. She didn't spend much time looking in the mirror. Her appearance had long ago ceased to matter to her.

Drew was surprised by it, though, and curious. She looked strangely vulnerable. But when he tried to hold her hand, she drew away from him. He'd wanted to ask her for a long time if there were things in her past that she might like to share with someone. But Louise was an unknown quantity, and she could easily shy away. He couldn't risk losing her altogether.

Drew held her arm as they entered the hall, and Lou was disconcerted to find Dr. Coltrain there. He almost never attended social functions unless Jane Parker was in attendance. But a quick glance around the room ascertained that Jane wasn't around. She wondered if the doctor had brought a date. It didn't take long to have that question answered, as a pretty young brunette came up beside him and clung to his arm as if it was the ticket to heaven.

Coltrain wasn't looking at her, though. His pale, narrow eyes had lanced over Lou and he was watching her closely. He hadn't seen her hair down in the year they'd worked together. She seemed more approachable tonight than he'd ever noticed, but she was Drew's date. Probably Drew's woman, too, he thought bitterly, despite her protests and reserve.

But trying to picture Lou in Drew's bed was more difficult than he'd thought. It wasn't at all in character. She was rigid in her views, just as she was in her mode of dress and her hairstyle. Just because she'd loosened that glorious hair tonight didn't mean that she'd suddenly become uninhibited. Nonetheless, the change disturbed him, because it was unexpected.

"Copper's got a new girl, I see," Drew said with a grin. "That's Nickie Bolton," he added. "She works as a nurse's aide at the hospital."

"I didn't recognize her out of uniform," Lou murmured.

"I did," he said. "She's lovely, isn't she?"

She nodded amiably. "Very young, too," she added with an indulgent smile.

He took her hand gently and smiled down at her. "You aren't exactly over the hill yourself," he teased.

She smiled up at him with warm eyes. "You're a nice man, Drew."

Across the room, a redheaded man's grip tightened ominously on a glass of punch. For over a year, Louise had avoided even his lightest touch. A few days ago, she'd thrown off his hand violently. But there she stood not only allowing Drew to hold her hand, but actually smiling at him. She'd never smiled at Coltrain that way; she'd never smiled at him any way at all.

His companion tapped him on the shoulder.

"You're with me, remember?" she asked with a pert smile. "Stop staring daggers at your partner. You're off duty. You don't have to fight all the time, do you?"

He frowned slightly. "What do you mean?"

"Everyone knows you hate her," Nickie said pleasantly. "It's common gossip at the hospital. You rake her over the coals and she walks around the corridors, red in the face and talking to herself. Well, most of the time, anyway. Once, Dr. Simpson found her crying in the nursery. But she doesn't usually cry, no matter how bad she hurts. She's pretty tough, in her way. I guess she's had to be, huh? Even if there are more women in medical school these days, you don't see that many women doctors yet. I'll bet she had to fight a lot of prejudice when she was in medical school."

That came as a shock. He'd never seen Lou cry until today, and he couldn't imagine her being upset at any temperamental display of his. Or was it, he pondered uneasily, just that she'd learned how not to show her wounds to him?

CHAPTER THREE

AT DINNER, Lou sat with Drew, as far away from Coltrain and his date as she could get. She listened attentively to the speakers and whispered to Drew in the spaces between speakers. But it was torture to watch Nickie's small hand smooth over Coltrain's, to see her flirt with him. Lou didn't know how to flirt. There were a lot of things she didn't know. But she'd learned to keep a poker face, and she did it very well this evening. The one time Coltrain glanced down the table toward her, he saw nothing on her face or in her eyes that could tell him anything. She was unreadable.

After the meeting, she let Drew hold her hand as they walked out of the restaurant. Behind them, Coltrain was glaring at her with subdued fury.

When they made it to the parking lot, she found that the other couple had caught up with them.

"Nice bit of surgery this morning, Copper," Drew remarked. "You do memorable stitches. I doubt if Mrs. Blake will even have a scar to show around."

He managed a smile and held Nickie's hand all the tighter. "She was adamant about that," he remarked. "It seems that her husband likes perfection."

"He'll have a good time searching for it in this imperfect world," Drew replied. "I'll see you in the morning. And I'd like your opinion on my little strep-throat patient. His mother wants the whole works taken out, tonsils and adenoids, but he doesn't have strep often and I don't like unnecessary surgery. Perhaps she'd listen to you."

"Don't count on it," Copper said dryly. "I'll have a look if you like, though."

"Thanks."

"My pleasure." He glanced toward Lou, who hadn't said a word. "You were ten minutes late this morning," he added coldly.

"Oh, I overslept," she replied pleasantly. "It wears me out to follow the EMTs around looking for work."

She gave him a cool smile and got into the car before he realized that she'd made a joke, and at his expense.

"Be on time in the morning," he admonished before he walked away with Nickie on his arm.

"On time," Lou muttered beside Drew in the comfortable Ford he drove. Her hands crushed her purse. "I'll give him on time! I'll be sitting in *his* parking spot at eight-thirty on the dot!"

"He does it on purpose," he told her as he started the car. "I think he likes to make you spark at him."

"He's overjoyed that I'm leaving," she muttered. "And so am I!"

He gave her a quick glance and hid his smile. "If you say so."

She twisted her small purse in her lap, fuming, all the way back to her small house.

"I haven't been good company, Drew," she said as he walked her to the door. "I'm sorry."

He patted her shoulder absently. "Nothing wrong with the company," he said, correcting her. He smiled down at her. "But you really do rub Copper the wrong way, don't you?" he added thoughtfully. "I've noticed that antagonism from a distance, but tonight is the first time I've seen it at close range. Is he always like that?"

She nodded. "Always, from the beginning. Well, not quite," she confessed, remembering. "From last Christmas."

"What happened last Christmas?"

She studied him warily.

"I won't tell him," he promised. "What happened?"

"He tried to kiss me under the mistletoe and I, well, I sort of ducked and pulled away." She flushed. "He rattled me. He does, mostly. I get shaky when he comes too close. He's so forceful, and so physical. Even when he wants to talk to me, he's forever trying to grab me by the wrist or a sleeve. It's as if he knows how much it disturbs me, so he does it on purpose, just to make me uncomfortable."

He reached down and caught her wrist very gently, watching her face distort and feeling the instinctive, helpless jerk of her hand.

He let go at once. "Tell me about it, Lou."

With a wan smile, she rubbed her wrist. "No. It's history."

"It isn't, you know. Not if it makes you shaky to have people touch you…"

"Not everyone, just him," she muttered absently.

His eyebrows lifted, but she didn't seem to be aware of what she'd just confessed.

She sighed heavily. "I'm so tired," she said, rubbing the back of her neck. "I don't usually get so tired from even the longest days."

He touched her forehead professionally and frowned. "You're a bit warm. How do you feel?"

"Achy. Listless." She grimaced. "It's probably that virus that's going around. I usually get at least one every winter."

"Go to bed and if you aren't better tomorrow, don't go in," he advised. "Want me to prescribe something?"

She shook her head. "I'll be okay. Nothing does any good for a virus, you know that."

He chuckled. "Not even a sugarcoated pill?"

"I can do without a placebo. I'll get some rest. Thanks for tonight. I enjoyed it."

"So did I. I haven't done much socializing since Eve died. It's been five long years and I still miss her. I don't think I'll ever get over her enough to start a new relationship with anyone. I only wish we'd had a child. It might have made it easier."

She was studying him, puzzled. "It's said that many people marry within months of losing a mate," she began.

"I don't fit that pattern," he said quietly. "I only loved once. I'd rather have my memories of those twelve years with Eve than a hundred years with someone else. I suppose that sounds old-fashioned."

She shook her head. "It sounds beautiful," she said softly. "Lucky Eve, to have been loved so much."

He actually flushed. "It was mutual."

"I'm sure it was, Drew. I'm glad to have a friend like you."

"That works both ways." He smiled ruefully. "I'd like to take you out occasionally, so that people will stop thinking of me as a mental case. The gossip is beginning to get bad."

"I'd love to go out with you," she replied. She smiled. "I'm not very worldly, you know. It was books and exams and medicine for eight long years, and then internship. I was an honor student. I never had much time for men." Her eyes darkened. "I never wanted to have much time for them. My parents' marriage soured me. I never knew it could be happy or that people could love each other enough to be faithful—" She stopped, embarrassed.

"I knew about your father," he said. "Most of the hospital staff did. He liked young girls."

"Dr. Coltrain told me," she said miserably.

"He what?"

She drew in a long breath. "I overheard what he said to you on the telephone the other day. I'm leaving. My year is up after New Year's, anyway," she reminded him. "He told me what my father had done. No wonder he didn't want me here. You shouldn't have done it, Drew. You shouldn't have forced him to take me on."

"I know. But it's too late, isn't it? I thought I was helping, if that's any excuse." He searched her face. "Maybe I hoped it would help Copper, too. He was infatuated with Jane Parker. She's a lovely, sweet woman, and she has a temper, but she was never a match for Copper. He's the sort who'd cow a woman who couldn't stand up to him."

"Just like my father," she said shortly.

"I've never mentioned it, but one of your wrists looks as if it's suffered a break."

She flushed scarlet and drew back. "I have to go in now. Thanks again, Drew."

"If you can't talk to me, you need to talk to someone," he said. "Did you really think you could go through life without having the past affect the future?"

She smiled sweetly. "Drive carefully going home."

He shrugged. "Okay. I'll drop it."

"Good night."

"Good night."

She watched him drive away, absently rubbing the wrist he'd mentioned. She wouldn't think about it, she told herself. She'd go to bed and put it out of her mind.

Only it didn't work that way. She woke up in the middle of the night in tears, frightened until she remembered where she was. She was safe. It was over. But she felt sick and her throat was dry. She got up and found a pitcher, filling it with ice and water. She took a glass along with her and went back to bed. Except for frequent trips to the bathroom, she finally slept soundly.

THERE WAS A LOUD, furious knock at the front door. It kept on and on, followed by an equally loud voice. What a blessing that she didn't have close neighbors, she thought drowsily, or the police would be screaming up the driveway.

She tried to get up, but surprisingly, her feet wouldn't support her. She was dizzy and weak and sick at her stomach. Her head throbbed. She lay back down with a soft groan.

A minute later, the front door opened and a furious redheaded man in a lab coat came in the bedroom door.

"So this is where you are," he muttered, taking in her condition with a glance. "You couldn't have called?"

She barely focused on him. "I was up most of the night..."

"With Drew?"

She couldn't even manage a glare. "Being sick," she corrected. "Have you got anything on you to calm my stomach? I can't keep down anything to stop the nausea."

"I'll get something."

He went back out, grateful that she kept a key under the welcome mat. He didn't relish having to break down doors, although he had in the past to get to a patient.

He got his medical bag and went back into the bedroom. She was pale and she had a fever. He turned off the electronic thermometer and checked her lungs. Clear, thank God.

Her pulse was a little fast, but she seemed healthy enough. "A virus," he pronounced.

"No!" she exclaimed with weak sarcasm.

"You'll live."

"Give me the medicine, please," she asked, holding out a hand.

"Can you manage?"

"If you'll get me to the bathroom, sure."

He helped her up, noticing the frailty of her body. She didn't seem that thin in her clothing, but she was wearing silky pajamas that didn't conceal the slender lines of her body. He supported her to the door, and watched the door close behind her.

Minutes later, she opened the door again and let him help her back into bed.

He watched her for a minute and then, with resolution, he picked up the telephone. He punched in a number. "This is Dr. Coltrain. Send an ambulance out to Dr. Blakely's home, 23 Brazos Lane. That's right. Yes. Thank you."

She glared at him. "I will not…!"

"Hell, yes, you will," he said shortly. "I'm not leaving you out here alone to dehydrate. At the rate you're losing fluids, you'll die in three days."

"What do you care if I die?" she asked furiously.

He reached down to take her pulse again. This time, he caught the left wrist firmly, but she jerked it back. His blue eyes narrowed as he watched her color. Drew had been holding her right hand. At the table, it was her right hand he'd touched. But most of the time, Copper automatically reached for the left one…

He glanced down to where it lay on the coverlet and he noticed what Drew had; there was a definite break there, one which had been set but was visible.

She clenched her fist. "I don't want to go to the hospital."

"But you'll go, if I have to carry you."

She glared at him. It did no good at all. He went into the kitchen to turn off all the appliances except the refrigerator. On his way back, he paused to look around the living room. There were some very disturbing paintings on her walls, side by side with beautiful pastel drawings of flowers. He wondered who'd done them.

The ambulance arrived shortly. He watched the paramedics load her up and he laid the small bag she'd asked him to pack on the foot of the gurney.

"Thank you so much," she said with her last lucid breath. The medicine was beginning to take effect, and it had a narcotic in it to make her sleep.

"My pleasure, Dr. Blakely," he said. He smiled, but it didn't reach his eyes. They were watchful and thoughtful. "Do you paint?" he asked suddenly.

Her dark eyes blinked. "How did you know?" she murmured as she drifted off.

SHE AWOKE HOURS later in a private room, with a nurse checking her vital signs. "You're awake!" the nurse said with a smile. "Feeling any better?"

"A little." She touched her stomach. "I think I've lost weight."

"No wonder, with so much nausea. You'll be all right now. We'll take very good care of you. How about some soup and Jell-O and tea?"

"Coffee?" she asked hopefully.

The nurse chuckled. "Weak coffee, perhaps. We'll see." She charted her observations and went to see about supper.

It was modest fare, but delicious to a stomach that had hardly been able to hold anything. Imagine being sent to the hospital with a twenty-four-hour virus, Lou thought irritably, and wanted to find Dr. Coltrain and hit him.

Drew poked his head in the door while he was doing rounds. "I told you you felt feverish, didn't I?" he teased, smiling. "Better?"

She nodded. "But I would have been just fine at home."

"Not to hear your partner tell it. I expected to find your ribs sticking through your skin," he told her, chuckling. "I'll check on you later. Stay put."

She groaned and lay back. Patients were stacking up and she knew that Brenda had probably had to deal with angry ones all day, since Dr. Coltrain would have been operating in the morning. Everyone would be sitting in the waiting room until long after dark, muttering angrily.

It was after nine before he made rounds. He looked worn, and she felt guilty even if it couldn't be helped.

"I'm sorry," she said irritably when he came to the bedside.

He cocked an eyebrow. "For what?" He reached

down and took her wrist—the right one—noticing that she didn't react while he felt her pulse.

"Leaving you to cope with my patients as well as your own," she said. The feel of his long fingers was disturbing. She began to fidget.

He leaned closer, to look into her eyes, and his hand remained curled around her wrist. He felt her pulse jump as his face neared hers and suddenly a new thought leaped into his shocked mind and refused to be banished.

She averted her gaze. "I'm all right," she said. She sounded breathless. Her pulse had gone wild under his searching fingers.

He stood up, letting go of her wrist. But he noticed the quick rise and fall of her chest with new interest. What an odd reaction for a woman who felt such antagonism toward him.

He picked up her chart, still frowning, and read what was written there. "You've improved. If you're doing this well in the morning, you can go home. Not to work," he added firmly. "Drew's going to come in and help me deal with the backlog in the morning while he has some free time."

"That's very kind of him."

"He's a kind man."

"Yes. *He* is."

He chuckled softly. "You don't like me, do you?" he asked through pursed lips. "I've never given you any reason to. I've been alternately hostile and sarcastic since the day you came here."

"Your normal self, Doctor," she replied.

His lips tugged up. "Not really. You don't know me."

"Lucky me."

His blue eyes narrowed thoughtfully. She'd reacted to him from the first as if he'd been contagious. Every approach he'd made had been met with instant withdrawal. He wondered why he'd never questioned her reactions. It wasn't revulsion. Oh, no. It was something much more disturbing on her part. She was vulnerable, and he'd only just realized it, when it was too late. She would leave before he had the opportunity to explore his own feelings.

He stuck his hands into his pockets and his eyes searched her pale, worn face. She wasn't wearing a trace of makeup. Her eyes held lingering traces of fever and her hair was dull, lackluster, disheveled by sleep. But even in that condition, she had a strange beauty.

"I know how I look, thanks," she muttered as she saw how he was looking at her. "You don't need to rub it in."

"Was I?" He studied her hostile eyes.

She dropped her gaze to her slender hands on the sheets. "You always do." Her eyes closed. "I don't need you to point out my lack of good looks, Doctor. My father never missed an opportunity to tell me what I was missing."

Her father. His expression hardened as the memories poured out. But even as they nagged at his mind, he began to remember bits and pieces of gossip he'd heard about the way Dr. Fielding Blakely treated his poor wife. He'd dismissed it at the time, but now he realized that Mrs. Blakely had to be aware of her husband's affairs. Had she not minded? Or was she afraid to mind...

He had more questions about Lou's family life than he had answers, and he was curious. Her reticence with him, her broken wrist, her lack of self-esteem—they began to add up.

His eyes narrowed. "Did your mother know that your father was unfaithful to her?" he asked.

She stared at him as if she didn't believe what she'd heard. "What?"

"You heard me. Did she know?"

She drew the sheet closer to her collarbone. "Yes." She bit off the word.

"Why didn't she leave him?"

She laughed bitterly. "You can't imagine."

"Maybe I can." He moved closer to the bed. "Maybe I can imagine a lot of things that never occurred to me before. I've looked at you for almost a year and I've never seen you until now."

She fidgeted under the cover. "Don't strain your imagination, Doctor," she said icily. "I haven't asked for your attention. I don't want it."

"Mine, or any other man's, right?" he asked gently.

She felt like an insect on a pin. "Will you stop?" she groaned. "I'm sick. I don't want to be interrogated."

"Is that what I'm doing? I thought I was showing a belated interest in my partner," he said lazily.

"I won't be your partner after Christmas."

"Why?"

"I've resigned. Have you forgotten? I even wrote it down and gave it to you."

"Oh. That. I tore it up."

Her eyes popped. "You what?"

"Tore it up," he said with a shrug. "I can't do without you. You have too many patients who won't come back if they have to see me."

"You had a fine practice…"

"Too fine. I never slept or took vacations. You've

eased the load. You've made yourself indispensable. You have to stay."

"I do not." She shot her reply back instantly. "I hate you!"

He studied her, nodding slowly. "That's healthy. Much healthier than withdrawing like a frightened clam into a shell every time I come too close."

She all but gasped at such a blunt statement. "I do not...!"

"You do." He looked pointedly at her left wrist. "You've kept secrets. I'm going to worry you to death until you tell me every last one of them, beginning with why you can't bear to have anyone hold you by the wrist."

She couldn't get her breath. She felt her cheeks becoming hot as he stared down at her intently. "I'm not telling you any secrets," she assured him.

"Why not?" he replied. "I don't ever tell what I know."

She knew that. If a patient told him anything in confidence, he wouldn't share it.

She rubbed the wrist absently, wincing as she remembered how it had felt when it was broken, and how.

Coltrain, watching her, wondered how he could ever have thought her cold. She had a temper that was easily the equal of his own, and she never backed away from a fight. She'd avoided his touch, but he realized now that it was the past that made her afraid, not the present.

"You're mysterious, Lou," he said quietly. "You hold things in, keep things back. I've worked with you for a year, but I know nothing about you."

"That was your choice," she reminded him coolly. "You've treated me like a leper in your life."

He started to speak, took a breath and finally, nodded. "Yes. Through no fault of your own, I might add. I've held grudges."

She glanced at his hard, lean face. "You were entitled," she admitted. "I didn't know about my father's past. I probably should have realized there was a reason he never went back to Jacobsville, even to visit, while his brother was still alive here. Afterward, there wasn't even a cousin to write to. We all lost touch. My mother never seemed to mind that we didn't come back." She looked up at him. "She probably knew..." She flushed and dropped her eyes.

"But she stayed with him," he began.

"She had to!" The words burst out. "If she'd tried to leave, he'd have..." She swallowed and made a futile gesture with her hand.

"He'd have what? Killed her?"

She wouldn't look at him. She couldn't. The memories came flooding back, of his violence when he used narcotics, of the threats, her mother's fear, her own. The weeping, the cries of pain...

She sucked in a quick breath, and all the suffering was in the eyes she lifted to his when he took her hand.

His fingers curled hard around hers and held them, as if he could see the memories and was offering comfort.

"You'll tell me, one day," he said abruptly, his eyes steady on her own. "You'll tell me every bit of it."

She couldn't understand his interest. She searched his eyes curiously and suddenly felt a wave of feeling encompass her like a killing tide, knocking her breathless. Heat surged through her slender body, impaling her, and in his hard face she saw everything she knew of love, would ever know of it.

But he didn't want her that way. He never would. She was useful to the practice, but on a personal level, he was still clutching hard at the past; at the girl her father had taken from him, at Jane Parker. He was sorry for her, as he would be for anyone in pain, but it wasn't a personal concern.

She drew her hand away from his slowly and with a faint smile. "Thanks," she said huskily. "I... I think too hard sometimes. The past is long dead."

"I used to think so," he said, watching her. "Now, I'm not so sure."

She didn't understand what he was saying. It was just as well. The nurse came in to do her round and any personal conversation was banished at once.

CHAPTER FOUR

THE NEXT DAY, Lou was allowed to go home. Drew had eaten breakfast with her and made sure that she was well enough to leave before he agreed with Copper that she was fit. But when he offered to drive her home, Coltrain intervened. His partner, he said, was his responsibility. Drew didn't argue. In fact, when they weren't looking, he grinned.

Copper carried her bag into the house and helped her get settled on the couch. It was lunchtime and he hesitated, as if he felt guilty about not offering to take her out for a meal.

"I'm going to have some soup later," she murmured without looking at him. "I'm not hungry just yet. I expect you are."

"I could eat." He hesitated again, watching her with vague irritation. "Will you be all right?"

"It was only a virus," she said, making light of it. "I'm fine. Thank you for your concern."

"You might as well enjoy it, for novelty value if nothing else," he said without smiling. "It's been a long time since I've given a damn about a woman's comfort."

"I'm just a colleague," she replied, determined to show him that she realized there was nothing personal in their relationship. "It isn't the same thing."

"No, it isn't," he agreed. "I've been very careful to

keep our association professional. I've never even asked you to my home, have I?"

He was making her uneasy with that unblinking stare. "So what? I've never asked you to mine," she replied. "I wouldn't presume to put you in such an embarrassing situation."

"Embarrassing? Why?"

"Well, because you'd have to find some logical excuse to refuse," she said.

He searched her quiet face and his eyes narrowed thoughtfully. "I don't know that I'd refuse. If you asked me."

Her heart leaped and she quickly averted her eyes. She wanted him to go, now, before she gave herself away. "Forgive me, but I'm very tired," she said.

She'd fended him off nicely, without giving offense. He wondered how many times over the years she'd done exactly that to other men.

He moved closer to her, noticing the way she tensed, the telltale quickening of her breath, the parting of her soft lips. She was affected by his nearness and trying valiantly to hide it. It touched him deeply that she was so vulnerable to him. He could have cursed himself for the way he'd treated her, for the antagonism that made her wary of any approach now.

He stopped when there was barely a foot of space between them, with his hands in his pockets so that he wouldn't make her any more nervous.

He looked down at her flushed oval face with curious pleasure. "Don't try to come in tomorrow if you don't feel like it. I'll cope."

"All right," she said in a hushed tone.

"Lou."

He hadn't called her by her first name before. It surprised her into lifting her eyes to his face.

"You aren't responsible for anything your father did," he said. "I'm sorry that I've made things hard for you. I hope you'll reconsider leaving."

She shifted uncomfortably. "Thank you. But I think I'd better go," she said softly. "You'll be happier with someone else."

"Do you think so? I don't agree." His hand lowered slowly to her face, touching her soft cheek, tracing it down to the corner of her mouth. It was the first intimate contact she'd ever had with him, and she actually trembled.

Her reaction had an explosive echo in his own body. His breath jerked into his throat and his teeth clenched as he looked at her mouth and thought he might die if he couldn't have it. But it was too soon. He couldn't…!

He drew back his hand as if she'd burned it. "I have to go," he said tersely, turning on his heel. Her headlong response had prompted a reaction in him that he could barely contain at all. He had to distance himself before he reached for her and ruined everything.

Lou didn't realize why he was in such a hurry to leave. She assumed that he immediately regretted that unexpected caress and wanted to make sure that she didn't read anything into it.

"Thank you for bringing me home," she said formally.

He paused at the door and looked back at her, his eyes fiercely intent on her slender body in jeans and sweatshirt, on her loosened blond hair and exquisite complexion and dark eyes. "Thank your lucky stars that I'm leaving in time." He bit off the words.

He closed the door on her puzzled expression. He was acting very much out of character lately. She didn't know why, unless he was sorry he'd tried to talk her out of leaving the practice. Oh, well, she told herself, it was no longer her concern. She had to get used to the idea of being out of his life. He had nothing to offer her, and he had good reason to hate her, considering the part her father had played in his unhappy past.

She went into the kitchen and opened a can of to-mato soup. She'd need to replenish her body before she could get back to work.

The can slipped in her left hand and she grimaced. Her dreams of becoming a surgeon had been lost overnight in one tragic act. A pity, her instructor had said, because she had a touch that few surgeons ever achieved, almost an instinctive knowledge of the best and most efficient way to sever tissue with minimum loss of blood. She would have been famous. But alas, the tendon had been severed with the compound fracture. And the best efforts of the best orthopedic surgeon hadn't been able to repair the damage. Her father hadn't even been sorry....

She shook her head to clear away the memories and went back to her soup. Some things were better forgotten.

SHE WAS BACK at work the day after her return home, a bit shaky, but game. She went through her patients efficiently, smiling at the grievance of one small boy whose stitches she'd just removed.

"Dr. Coltrain doesn't like little kids, does he?" he muttered. "I showed him my bad place and he said he'd seen worse!"

"He has," she told the small boy. She smiled at him. "But you've been very brave, Patrick my boy, and I'm giving you the award of honor." She handed him a stick of sugarless chewing gum and watched him grin. "Off with you, now, and mind you don't fall down banks into any more creeks!"

"Yes, ma'am!"

She handed his mother the charge sheet and was showing them out the door of the treatment cubicle just as Coltrain started to come into it. The boy glowered at him, smiled at Lou and went back to his waiting mother.

"Cheeky brat," he murmured, watching him turn the corner.

"He doesn't like you," she told him smugly. "You didn't sympathize with his bad place."

"Bad place." He harrumphed. "Two stitches. My God, what a fuss he made."

"It hurt," she informed him.

"He wouldn't let me take the damn stitches out, either. He said that I didn't know how to do it, but you did."

She grinned to herself at that retort while she dealt with the mess she'd made while working with Patrick.

"You don't like children, do you?" she asked.

He shrugged. "I don't know much about them, except what I see in the practice," he replied. "I deal mostly with adults since you came."

He leaned against the doorjamb and studied her with his hands in the pockets of his lab coat, a stethoscope draped around his neck. His eyes narrowed as he watched her work.

She became aware of the scrutiny and turned, her eyes meeting his and being captured there. She felt her heart race at the way he looked at her. Her hands stilled on her preparations for the next patient as she stood helplessly in thrall.

His lips compressed. He looked at her mouth and traced the full lower lip, the soft bow of the upper, with her teeth just visible where her lips parted. The look was intimate. He was wondering how it would feel to kiss her, and she knew it.

Muffled footsteps caught them unawares, and Brenda jerked open the sliding door of the cubicle. "Lou, I've got the wrong... Oh!" She bumped into Coltrain, whom she hadn't seen standing there.

"Sorry," he muttered. "I wanted to ask Lou if she'd seen the file on Henry Brady. It isn't where I left it."

Brenda grimaced as she handed it to him. "I picked it up mistakenly. I'm sorry."

"No harm done." He glanced back at Lou and went out without another word.

"Not another argument," Brenda groaned. "Honestly, partners should get along better than this."

Lou didn't bother to correct that assumption. It was much less embarrassing than what had really happened. Coltrain had never looked at her in that particular way before. She was glad that she'd resigned; she wasn't sure that she could survive any physical teasing from him. If he started making passes, she'd be a lot safer in Austin than she would be here.

After all he was a confirmed bachelor and there was no shortage of women on his arm at parties. Nickie was the latest in a string of them. And according to rumor, before Nickie, apparently he'd been infatuated with Jane Parker. He might be nursing a broken heart as well, since Jane's marriage.

Lou didn't want to be anybody's second-best girl. Besides, she never wanted to marry. It had been better when Coltrain treated her like the enemy. She wished he'd go back to his former behavior and stop looking at her mouth that way. She still tingled remembering the heat in his blue eyes. A man like that would be just plain hell to be loved by. He would be addictive. She had no taste for addictions and she knew already that Coltrain would break her heart if she let him. No, it was better that she leave. Then she wouldn't have the anguish of a hopeless relationship.

THE ANNUAL HOSPITAL Christmas party was scheduled for Friday night, two weeks before Christmas so that the staff wouldn't be too involved with family celebrations to attend.

Lou hadn't planned to go, but Coltrain cornered her in his office as they prepared to leave that afternoon for the weekend.

"The Christmas party is tonight," he reminded her.

"I know. I'm not going."

"I'll pick you up in an hour," he said, refusing to listen when she tried to protest. "I know you still tire easily after the virus. We won't stay long."

"What about Nickie?" she asked irritably. "Won't she mind if you take your partner to a social event?"

Her antagonism surprised him. He lifted an indignant eyebrow. "Why should she?" he asked stiffly.

"You've been dating her."

"I escorted her to the Rotary Club meeting. I haven't proposed to her. And whatever you've heard to the contrary, she and I are not an item."

"You needn't bite my head off!" She shot the words at him.

His eyes dropped to her mouth and lingered there. "I know something I'd like to bite," he said deep in his throat.

She actually gasped, so stunned by the remark that she couldn't even think of a reply.

His eyes flashed back up to catch hers. He was a bulldozer, she thought, and if she didn't stand up to him, he'd run right over her.

She stiffened her back. "I'm not going to any hospital dance with you," she said shortly. "You've given me hell for the past year. Do you think you can just walk in here and wipe all that out with an invitation? Not even an invitation, at that—a command!"

"Yes, I do," he returned curtly. "We both belong to the hospital staff, and nothing will start gossip quicker than having one of us stay away from an annual event. I do not plan to have any gossip going around here at my expense. I had enough of that in the past, thanks to your philandering father!"

She gripped her coat, furious at him. "You just got through saying that you didn't blame me for what he did."

"And I don't!" he said angrily. "But you're being blind and stupid."

"Thank you. Coming from you, those are compliments!"

He was all but vibrating with anger. He stared at her, glared at her, until her unsteady movement made him realize that she'd been ill.

He became less rigid. "Ben Maddox is going to be there tonight. He's a former colleague of ours from Canada. He's just installed a massive computer system with linkups to medical networks around the world. I think it's too expensive for our purposes, but I agreed to hear him out about it. You're the high-tech expert," he added with faint sarcasm. "I'd like your opinion."

"My opinion? I'm honored. You've never asked for it before."

"I've never given a damn about it before," he retorted evenly. "But maybe there's something to this electronic revolution in medicine." He lifted his chin in a challenge. "Or so you keep telling me. Put your money where your mouth is, Doctor. Convince me."

She glared at him. "I'll drive my own car and see you there."

It was a concession, of sorts. He frowned slightly. "Why don't you want to ride with me? What are you afraid of?" he taunted softly.

She couldn't admit what frightened her. "It wouldn't look good to have us arrive together," she said. "It would give people something to talk about."

He was oddly disappointed, although he didn't quite know why. "All right, then."

She nodded, feeling that she'd won something. He nodded, too, and quietly left her. It felt like a sort of truce. God knew, they could use one.

BEN MADDOX WAS TALL, blond and drop-dead gorgeous. He was also married and the father of three. He had photographs, which he enjoyed showing to any of his old colleagues who were willing to look at them. But in addition to those photographs, he had information on a networking computer system that he used extensively in his own practice. It was an expensive piece of equipment, but it permitted the user instant access to medical experts in every field. As a diagnostic tool and a means of getting second opinions from recognized authorities, it was breathtaking. But so was the price.

Lou had worn a black silk dress with a lace overlay, a demure rounded neckline and see-through sleeves. Her hairstyle, a topknot with little tendrils of blond hair slipping down to her shoulders, looked sexy. So did her long, elegant legs in high heels, under the midknee fitted skirt. She wore no jewelry at all, except for a strand of pearls with matching earrings.

Watching her move, Coltrain was aware of old, unwanted sensations. At the party a year ago, she'd worn something a little more revealing, and he'd deliberately maneuvered her under the mistletoe out of mingled curiosity and desire. But she'd evaded him as if he had the plague, then and since. His ego had suffered a sharp blow. He hadn't felt confident enough to try again, so antagonism and anger had kept her at bay. Not that his memories of her father's betrayal hadn't added to his enmity.

She was animated tonight, talking to Ben about the computer setup as if she knew everything there was to know about the machines.

"Copper, you've got a savvy partner here," Ben remarked when he joined them. "She's computer literate!"

"She's the resident high-tech expert," Copper replied. "I like old-fashioned, hands-on medicine. She'd rather reach for a machine to make diagnoses."

"High tech is the way of the future," Ben said coaxingly.

"It's also the reason medical costs have gone through the roof," came the predictable reply. "The money we spend on these outrageously expensive machines has to be passed on to the patients. That raises our fees, the hospital's fees, the insurance companies' fees…"

"Pessimist!" Ben accused.

"I'm being realistic," Copper told him, lifting his highball glass in a mock toast. He drained it, feeling the liquor.

Ben frowned as his old colleague made his way past the dancers back to the buffet table. "That's odd," he remarked. "I don't remember ever seeing Copper take more than one drink."

Neither did Lou. She watched her colleague pour himself another drink and she frowned.

Ben produced a card from the computer company for her, and while he was explaining the setup procedure, she noticed Nickie going up to Coltrain. She was wearing an electric blue dress that could have started a riot. The woman was pretty anyway, but that dress certainly revealed most of her charms.

Nickie laughed and dragged Coltrain under the mistletoe, looking up to indicate it there, to the amusement of the others standing by. Coltrain laughed softly, whipped a lean arm around Nickie's trim waist and pulled her against his tall body. He bent his head, and the way he kissed her made Lou go hot all over. She'd never been in his arms, but she'd dreamed about it. The fever in that thin mouth, the way he twisted Nickie even closer, made her breath catch. She averted her eyes and flushed at the train of her own thoughts.

"Leave it to Coltrain to draw the prettiest girls." Ben chuckled. "The gossip mill will grind on that kiss for a month. He's not usually so uninhibited. He must be over his limit!"

She could have agreed. Her hand clenched around the piña colada she was nursing. "This computer system, is it reliable?" she asked through tight lips, forcing a smile.

"Yes, except in thunderstorms. Always unplug it, regardless of what they tell you about protective spikes. One good hit, and you could be down for days."

"I'll remember, if we get it."

"The system I have is expensive," Ben agreed, "but there are others available that would be just right for a small practice like yours and Copper's. In fact…"

His voice droned on and Lou tried valiantly to pay attention. She was aware at some level that Coltrain and Nickie were dancing and making the rounds of guests together. It was much later, and well into her second piña colada, when the lavish mistletoe began to get serious workouts.

Lou wasn't in the mood to dance. She refused Ben's offer, and several others. A couple of hours had passed and it felt safe to leave now, before her spirit was totally crushed by being consistently ignored by Coltrain. She put down her half-full glass. "I really do have to go," she told Ben. "I've been ill and I'm not quite back up to par yet." She shook his hand. "It was very nice to have met you."

"Same here. I wonder why Drew Morris didn't show up? I had hoped to see him again while I was here."

"I don't know," she said, realizing that she hadn't heard from Drew since she was released from the hospital. She had no idea where he was, and she hadn't asked.

"I'll check with Copper. He's certainly been elusive this evening. Not that I can blame him, considering his pretty companion over there." He raised his hand to catch the other man's eyes, to Lou's dismay.

Coltrain joined them with Nickie hanging on his arm. "Still here?" he asked Lou with a mocking smile. "I thought you'd be out the door and gone by now."

"I'm just about to leave. Do you know where Drew is?"

"He's in Florida at that pediatric seminar. Didn't Brenda tell you?"

"She was so busy she probably forgot," she said.

"So that's where the old devil has gone," Ben said ruefully. "I'm sorry I missed him."

"I'm sure he will be, too," Lou said. The sight of Nickie and Coltrain together was hurting her. "I'd better be off—"

"Oh, not yet," Copper said with glittery blue eyes. "Not before you've been kissed under the mistletoe, Doctor."

She flushed and laughed nervously. "I'll forgo that little ritual, I think."

"No, you won't." He sounded pleasant enough, but the expression on his face was dangerous. He moved away from Nickie and his lean arm shot around Lou's waist, maneuvering her under a low-hanging sprig of mistletoe tied with a red velvet bow. "You're not getting away this time," he said huskily.

Before she could think, react, protest, his head bent and his thin, cruel mouth fastened on hers with fierce intent. He didn't close his eyes when he kissed, she thought a bit wildly, he watched her all through it. His arm pressed her closer to the length of his muscular body, and his free hand came up so that his thumb could rub sensuously over her mouth while he kissed it, parting her lips, playing havoc with her nerves.

She gasped at the rough pleasure, and inadvertently

gave him exactly what he wanted. His open mouth ground into hers, pressing her lips apart. She tasted him in an intimacy that she'd never shared with a man, in front of the amused hospital staff, while his cold eyes stared straight into hers.

She made a faint sound and he lifted his head, looking down at her swollen lips. His thumb traced over them with much greater tenderness than his mouth had given her, and he held her shocked eyes for a long moment before he reluctantly let her go.

"Merry Christmas, Dr. Blakely," he said in a mocking tone, although his voice was husky.

"And you, Dr. Coltrain," she said shakily, not quite meeting his eyes. "Good night, Ben... Nickie."

She slid away from them toward the door, on shaky legs, with a mouth that burned from his cold, fierce kiss. She barely remembered getting her coat and saying goodbye to the people she recognized on her way to the car park.

Coltrain watched her go with feelings he'd never encountered in his life. He was burning up with desire, and he'd had enough whiskey to threaten his control.

Nickie tugged on his sleeve. "You didn't kiss me like that," she protested, pouting prettily. "Why don't you take me home and we can..."

"I'll be back in a minute," he said, shaking her off.

She glared at him, coloring with embarrassment when she realized that two of the staff had overheard her. Rejection in private was one thing, but it hurt to have him make it so public. He hadn't called her since the night of the Rotary Club meeting. He'd just kissed her very nicely, but it looked different when he'd done it with his partner. She frowned. Something was going on. She followed at a distance. She was going to find out what.

Coltrain, unaware of her pursuit, headed after Lou with no real understanding of his own actions. He couldn't get the taste of her out of his head. He was pretty sure that she felt the same way. He couldn't let her leave until he knew...

Lou kept walking, but she heard footsteps behind her as she neared her car. She knew them, because she heard them every day on the slick tile of the office floor. She walked faster, but it did no good. Coltrain reached her car at the same time she reached it.

His hand came around her, grasping her car key and her fingers, pulling, turning her. She was pressed completely against the car by the warm weight of his body, and she looked up into a set, shadowy face while his mouth hovered just above her own in the starlit darkness.

"It wasn't enough," he said roughly. "Not nearly enough."

He bent and his mouth found hers expertly. His hands smoothed into hers and linked with her fingers. His hips slid sensuously over hers, seductive, refusing to entertain barriers or limits. His mouth began to open, brushing in soft strokes over her lips until they began to part, but she stiffened.

"Don't you know how to kiss?" he whispered, surprised. "Open your mouth, little one. Open it and fit it to mine... Yes, that's it."

She felt his tongue dance at the opening he'd made, felt it slowly ease into her mouth and penetrate, teasing, probing, tasting. Her fingers clutched helplessly at his and she shivered. It was so intimate, so...familiar! She moaned sharply as his hips began to caress hers. She felt him become aroused and her whole body vibrated.

His mouth grew more insistent then. He released one of her hands and his fingers played with her mouth, as they had inside, but now there was the heat and the magic they were generating, and it was no cold, clinical experiment. He groaned against her mouth and she felt his body go rigid all at once.

He bit her lower lip, hard, when her teeth clenched at the soft probing of his tongue. Suddenly she came to her senses and realized what was happening. He tasted blatantly of whiskey. He'd had too much to drink and he'd forgotten which woman he was with. Did he think she was Nickie? she wondered dizzily. Was that why he was making love to her? And that was what it was, she realized with a shock. Only a lover would take such intimacy for granted, be so blind to surroundings and restraint.

CHAPTER FIVE

DESPITE THE PLEASURE she felt, the whiskey on his breath brought back unbearable memories of another man who drank; memories not of kisses, but of pain and fear. Her hands pressed against his warm shirtfront under the open dinner jacket and she pushed, only vaguely aware of thick hair under the silkiness of the fabric.

"No," she whispered into his insistent mouth.

He didn't seem to hear her. His mouth hardened and a sound rumbled out of the back of his throat. "For God's sake, stop fighting me," he whispered fiercely.

The fear in her voice got through the intoxication. His mouth stilled against her cheek, but his body didn't withdraw. She could feel it against every inch of her like a warm, steely brand. His breathing wasn't steady, and over her breasts, his heart was beating like a frenzied bass drum.

It suddenly dawned on him what he was doing, and with whom.

"My God!" he whispered fiercely. His hands tightened for an instant before they fell away from her. A faint shudder went through his powerful body as he slowly, so slowly, pushed himself away from her, balancing his weight on his hands against the car doorframe.

She felt his breath on her swollen mouth as he fought for control. He was still too close.

"You haven't used my given name before," he said as he levered farther away from her. "I didn't know you knew it."

"It's…on our contract," she said jerkily.

He removed his hands from the car and stood upright, dragging in air. "I've had two highballs," he said on an apologetic laugh. "I don't drink. It hit me harder than I realized."

He was apologizing, she thought dazedly. That was unexpected. He wasn't that kind of man. Or was he? She hadn't thought he was the type to get drunk and kiss women in that intimate, fierce way, either. Especially her.

She tried to catch her own breath. Her mouth hurt from the muted violence of his kisses and her legs felt weak. She leaned back against the car, only now noticing its coldness. She hadn't felt it while he was kissing her. She touched her tongue to her lips and she tasted him on them.

She eased away from the car a little, shy now that he was standing back from her.

She was so shaky that she wondered how she was going to drive home. Then she wondered, with even more concern, how *he* was going to drive home.

"You shouldn't drive," she began hesitantly.

In the faint light from the hospital, she saw him smile sardonically. "Worried about me?" he chided.

She shouldn't have slipped like that. "I'd worry about anyone who'd had too much to drink," she began.

"All right, I won't embarrass you. Nickie can drive. She doesn't drink at all."

Nickie. Nickie would take him home and she'd probably stay to nurse him, too, in his condition. God only knew what might happen, but she couldn't afford to interfere. He'd had too much to drink and he'd kissed her, and she'd let him. Now she was ashamed and embarrassed.

"I have to go," she said stiffly.

"Drive carefully," he replied.

"Sure."

She found her keys where they'd fallen to the ground when he kissed her and unlocked the car door. She closed it once she was inside and started it after a bad fumble. He stood back from it, his hands in his pockets, looking dazed and not quite sober.

She hesitated, but Nickie came out the door, calling him. When he turned and raised a hand in Nickie's direction and answered her, laughing, Lou came to her senses. She lifted a hand toward both of them and drove away as quickly as she could. When she glanced back in the rearview mirror, it was to see Nickie holding Coltrain's hand as they went toward the building again.

So much for the interlude, she thought miserably. He'd probably only just realized who he'd kissed and was in shock.

THAT WAS CLOSE to the truth. Coltrain's head was spinning. He'd never dreamed that a kiss could be so explosive or addictive. There was something about Lou Blakely that made his knees buckle. He had no idea why he'd reacted so violently to her that he couldn't even let her leave. God knew what would have happened if she hadn't pushed him away when she did.

Nickie held on to him as they went back inside. "You've got her lipstick all over you," she accused.

He paused, shaken out of his brooding. Nickie was

pretty, he thought, and uncomplicated. She already knew that he wasn't going to get serious however long they dated, because he'd told her so. It made him relax. He smiled down at her. "Wipe it off."

She pulled his handkerchief out of his pocket and did as he asked, smiling pertly. "Want to sample mine again?"

He tapped her on the nose. "Not tonight," he said. "We'd better leave. It's getting late."

"I'm driving," she told him.

"Yes, you are," he agreed.

She felt better. At least she was the one going home with him, not Lou. She wasn't going to give him up without a struggle, not when he was the best thing that had ever happened to her. Wealthy bachelor surgeons didn't come along every day of the week.

LOU DROVE HOME in a similar daze, overcome by the fervor of Coltrain's hard kisses. She couldn't understand why a man who'd always seemed to hate her had suddenly become addicted to her mouth; so addicted, in fact, that he'd followed her to her car. It had been the sweetest night of her life, but she had to keep her head and realize that it was an isolated incident. If Coltrain hadn't been drinking, it would never have happened. Maybe by Monday, she thought, he'd have convinced himself that it hadn't. She wished she could. She was more in love with him than ever, and he was as far out of her reach as he had ever been. Except that now he'd probably go even farther out of reach, because he'd lost his head and he wouldn't like remembering it.

She did her usual housework and answered emergency calls. She got more than her share because Dr.

Coltrain had left word with their answering service that he was going to be out of town until Monday and Dr. Blakely would be covering for him.

Nice of him to ask her first, she thought bitterly, and tell her that he was going to be out of town. But perhaps he'd been reluctant to talk to her after what had happened. If the truth were known, he was more than likely as embarrassed as she was and just wanted to forget the whole thing.

She did his rounds and hers at the hospital, noticing absently that she was getting more attention than usual. Probably, she reasoned, because people were remembering the way Coltrain had kissed her. Maybe they thought something was going on between them.

"How's it going?" Drew asked on Sunday afternoon, grinning at her. "I hear I missed a humdinger of a kiss at the Christmas party," he added wickedly.

She blushed to her hairline. "Lots of people got kissed."

"Not like you did. Not so that he followed you out to the parking lot and damn near made love to you on the hood of your car." He chuckled.

"Who...?"

"Nickie," he said, confirming her worst nightmare. "She was watching, apparently, and she's sweet on Copper. I guess she thought it might turn him off you if there was a lot of gossip about what happened. Rumors fly, especially when they're about two doctors who seem to hate each other."

"He'll walk right into it when he comes back," she said uneasily. "What can I do?"

"Nothing, I'm afraid."

Her eyes narrowed. "That's what you think."

She turned on her heel and went in search of Nickie. She found her in a patient's room and waited calmly while the girl, nervous and very insecure once she saw Lou waiting for her, finished the chore she was performing.

She went out into the hall with Lou, and she looked apprehensive.

Lou clutched a clipboard to her lab jacket. She didn't smile. "I understand you've been feeding the rumor mill. I'll give you some good advice. Stop it while you can."

By now, Nickie's face had gone puce. "I never meant... I was kidding!" she burst out. "That's all, just kidding!"

Lou studied her without emotion. "I'm not laughing. Dr. Coltrain won't be laughing, either, when he hears about it. And I'll make sure he knows where it came from."

"That's spiteful!" Nickie cried. "I'm crazy about him!"

"No, you aren't," Lou said shortly. "You'd never subject him to the embarrassment you have with all this gossip if you really cared."

Nickie's hands locked together. "I'm sorry," she said on a long sigh. "I really am. I was just jealous," she confessed, avoiding Lou's eyes. "He wouldn't even kiss me good-night, but he'd kiss you that way, and he hates you."

"Try to remember that he'd had too much to drink," Lou said quietly. "Only a fool would read anything into a kiss under the mistletoe."

"I guess so," Nickie said, but she wasn't really convinced. "I'm sorry. You won't tell him it was me, will you?" she added worriedly. "He'll hate me. I care so much, Dr. Blakely!"

"I won't tell him," Lou said. "But no more gossip!"

"Yes, ma'am!" Nickie brightened, grinned and went off down the hall, irrepressibly young and optimistic. Watching her, Lou felt ancient.

THE NEXT MORNING was Monday, and Lou went into the office to come face-to-face with a furious partner, who blocked her doorway and glared at her with blue eyes like arctic ice.

"Now what have I done?" she asked before he could speak, and slammed her bag down on her desk, ready to do battle.

"You don't know?" he taunted.

She folded her arms over her breasts and leaned back against the edge of the desk. "There's a terrible rumor going around the hospital," she guessed.

His eyebrow jerked, but the ice didn't leave his eyes. "Did you start it?"

"Of course," she agreed furiously. "I couldn't wait to tell everybody on staff that you bent me back over the hood of my car and ravished me in the parking lot!"

Brenda, who'd started in the door, stood there with her mouth open, intercepted a furious glare from two pairs of eyes, turned on her heel and got out.

"Could you keep your voice down?" Coltrain snapped.

"Gladly, when you stop making stupid accusations!"

He glared at her and she glared back.

"I was drinking!"

"That's it, announce it to everyone in the waiting

room, why don't you, and see how many patients run for their cars!" she raged.

He closed her office door, hard, and leaned back against it. "Who started the rumor?" he asked.

"That's more like it," she replied. "Don't accuse until you ask. I didn't start it. I have no wish to become the subject of gossip."

"Not even to force me to do something about the rumors?" he asked. "Such as announce our engagement?"

Her eyes went saucer-wide. "Please! I've just eaten!"

His jaw went taut. "I beg your pardon?"

"And so you should!" she said enthusiastically. "Marry you? I'd rather chain myself to a tree in an alligator swamp!"

He didn't answer immediately. He stared at her instead while all sorts of impractical ideas sifted through his mind.

A buzzer sounded on her desk. She reached over and pressed a button. "Yes?"

"What about the patients?" Brenda prompted.

"He doesn't *have* any patience," Lou said without thinking.

"Excuse me?" Brenda stammered.

"Oh. That sort of patients. Send my first one in, will you, Brenda? Dr. Coltrain was just leaving."

"No, he wasn't," he returned when her finger left the intercom button. "We'll finish this discussion after office hours."

"After office hours?" she asked blankly.

"Yes. But, don't get your hopes up about a repeat of Friday evening," he said with a mocking smile. "After all, I'm not drunk today."

Her eyes flashed murderously and her lips compressed. But he was already out the door.

LOU WAS NEVER sure afterward how she'd managed to get through her patients without revealing her state of mind. She was furiously angry at Coltrain for his accusations and equally upset with Brenda for hearing what she'd said in retaliation. Now it would be all over the office as well as all over the hospital that she and Coltrain had something going. And they didn't! Despite Lou's helpless attraction to him, it didn't take much imagination to see that Coltrain didn't feel the same. Well, maybe physically he felt something for her, but emotionally he still hated her. A few kisses wouldn't change that!

She checked Mr. Bailey's firm, steady heartbeat, listened to his lungs and pronounced him over the pneumonia she'd been treating him for.

As she started to go, leaving Brenda to help him with his shirt, he called to her.

"What's this I hear about you and Doc Coltrain?" he teased. "Been kissing up a storm at the hospital Christmas party, they say. Any chance we'll be hearing wedding bells?"

He didn't understand, he told Brenda on his way out, why Dr. Blakely had suddenly screamed like that. Maybe she'd seen a mouse, Brenda replied helpfully.

When the office staff went home, Coltrain was waiting at the front entrance for Lou. He'd stationed himself there after checking with the hospital about a patient, and he hadn't moved, in case Lou decided to try to sneak out.

He was wearing the navy blue suit that looked so good on him, lounging against the front door with elegant carelessness, when she went out of her office. His red hair caught the reflection of the overhead light and seemed to burn like flames over his blue, blue eyes. They swept down over her neat gray pantsuit to her long legs encased in slacks with low-heeled shoes.

"That color looks good on you," he remarked.

"You don't need to flatter me. Just say what's on your mind, please, and let me go home."

"All right." His eyes fell to her soft mouth and lingered there. "Who started the rumors about us?"

She traced a pattern on her fanny pack. "I promised I wouldn't tell."

"Nickie," he guessed, nodding at her shocked expression.

"She's young and infatuated," she began.

"Not that young," he said with quiet insinuation.

Her eyes flashed before she could avert them. Her hand dug into the fanny pack for her car keys. "It's a nine-days wonder," she continued. "People will find something else to talk about."

"Nothing quite this spicy has happened since Ted Regan went chasing off to Victoria after Coreen Tarleton and she came home wearing his engagement ring."

"There's hardly any comparison," she said, "considering that everyone knows how we feel about each other!"

"How *do* we feel about each other, Lou?" he replied quietly, and watched her expression change.

"We're enemies," she returned instantly.

"Are we?" He searched her eyes in a silence that grew oppressive. His arms fell to his sides. "Come here, Lou."

She felt her breathing go wild. That could have been

an invitation to bypass him and leave the building. But the look in his eyes told her it wasn't. Those eyes blazed like flames in his lean, tanned face, beckoning, promising pleasures beyond imagination.

He lifted a hand. "Come on, coward," he chided softly, and his lips curled at the edges. "I won't hurt you."

"You're sober," she reminded him.

"Cold sober," he agreed. "Let's see how it feels when I know what I'm doing."

Her heart stopped, started, raced. She hesitated, and he laughed softly and started toward her, with that slow, deliberate walk that spoke volumes about his intent.

"You mustn't," she spoke quickly, holding up a hand.

He caught the hand and jerked her against him, imprisoning her there with a steely arm. "I must." He corrected her, letting his eyes fall to her mouth. "I *have* to know." He bit off the words against her lips.

She never found out what he had to know, because the instant she felt his lips probing her mouth, she went under in a blaze of desire unlike anything she'd felt before. She gasped, opened her lips, yielded to his enveloping arms without a single protest. If anything, she pushed closer into his arms, against that steely body that was instantly aroused by the feel of her.

She tried to speak, to protest, but he pushed his tongue into her mouth with a harsh groan, and his arms lifted her so that she fit perfectly against him from breast to thigh. She fought, frightened by the intimacy and the sensations kindled in her untried body.

Her frantic protest registered at once. He remembered she'd had the same reaction the night of the

Christmas party. His mouth lifted, and his searching eyes met hers.

"You couldn't be a virgin," he said, making it sound more like an accusation than a statement of fact.

She bit her lip and dropped her eyes, shamed and embarrassed. "Rub it in," she growled.

"My God." He eased her back onto her feet and held her by the upper arms so that she wouldn't fall. "My God! How old are you, thirty?"

"Twenty-eight," she said unsteadily, gasping for breath. Her whole body felt swollen. Her dark eyes glowered up at him as she pushed back her disheveled hair. "And you needn't look so shocked, you of all people should know that some people still have a few principles! You're a doctor, after all!"

"I thought virgins were a fairy tale," he said flatly. "Damn it!"

Her chin lifted. "What's wrong, Doctor, did you see me as a pleasant interlude between patients?"

His lips compressed. He rammed his hands into his trouser pockets, all too aware of a throbbing arousal that wouldn't go away. He turned to the door and jerked it open. All weekend he'd dreamed of taking Louise Blakely home with him after work and seducing her in his big king-size bed. She was leaving anyway, and the hunger he felt for her was one he had to satisfy or go mad. It had seemed so simple. She wanted him; he knew she did. People were already talking about them, so what would a little more gossip matter? She'd be gone at the first of the year, anyway.

But now he had a new complication, one he'd never dreamed of having. She was no young girl, but it didn't take an expert to know why she backed away from intimacy like a repressed adolescent. He'd been baiting her with that accusation of virginity, but she hadn't realized it. She'd taken it at face value and she'd given him a truth he didn't even want. She was innocent. How could he seduce her now? On the other hand, how was he going to get rid of this very inconvenient and noticeable desire for her?

Watching him, Lou was cursing her own headlong response. She hated having him know how much she wanted him.

"Any man could have made me react that way!" she flared defensively, red-faced. "Any experienced man!"

His head turned and he stared at her, seeing through the flustering words to the embarrassment.

"It's all right," he said gently. "We're both human. Don't beat your conscience to death over a kiss, Lou."

She went even redder and her hands clenched at her sides. "I'm still leaving!"

"I know."

"And I won't let you seduce me!"

He turned. "I won't try," he said solemnly. "I don't seduce virgins."

She bit her lip and tasted him on it. She winced.

"Why?" he asked quietly.

She glared at him.

"Why?" he persisted.

Her eyes fell under that piercing blue stare. "Because I don't want to end up like my mother," she said huskily.

Of all the answers he might have expected, that was the last. "Your mother? I don't understand."

She shook her head. "You don't need to. It's personal. You and I are business partners until the end of

the month, and then nothing that happened to me will
be any concern of yours."

He didn't move. She looked vulnerable, hurt. "Counseling might be of some benefit," he said gently.

"I don't need counseling."

"Tell me how your wrist got broken, Lou," he said
matter-of-factly.

She stiffened.

"Oh, a layman wouldn't notice, it's healed nicely.
But surgery is my business. I know a break when I see
one. There are scars, too, despite the neat stitching job.
How did it happen?"

She felt weak. She didn't want to talk to him, of all
people, about her past. It would only reinforce what he
already thought of her father, though God only knew
why she should defend such a man.

She clasped her wrist defensively, as if to hide what
had been done to it. "It's an old injury," she said finally.

"What sort of injury? How did it happen?"

She laughed nervously. "I'm not your patient."

He absently jingled the change in his pocket, watching her. It occurred to him that she was a stranger. Despite their heated arguments over the past year, they'd
never come close to discussing personal matters. Away
from the office, they were barely civil to each other. In
it, they never discussed anything except business. But
he was getting a new picture of her, and not a very reassuring one. This was a woman with a painful past,
so painful that it had locked her up inside an antiseptic
prison. He wondered if she'd ever had the incentive to
fight her way out, or why it should matter to him that
she hadn't.

"Can you talk to Drew about it?" he asked suddenly.

She hesitated and then shook her head. Her fingers tightened around her wrist. "It doesn't matter, I tell you."

His hand came out of his pocket and he caught the damaged wrist very gently in his long fingers, prepared for her instinctive jerk. He moved closer, drawing that hand to his chest. He pressed it gently into the thick fabric of his vest.

"There's nothing you can't tell me," he said solemnly. "I don't carry tales, or gossip. Anything you say to me will remain between the two of us. If you want to talk, ever, I'll listen."

She bit her bottom lip. She'd never been able to tell anyone. Her mother knew, but she defended her husband, trying desperately to pretend that Lou had imagined it, that it had never happened. She excused her husband's affairs, his drinking bouts, his drug addiction, his brutality, his sarcasm…everything, in the name of love, while her marriage disintegrated around her and her daughter turned away from her. Obsessive love, one of her friends had called it—blind, obsessive love that refused to acknowledge the least personality flaw in the loved one.

"My mother was emotionally crippled," she said, thinking aloud. "She was so blindly in love with him that he could do no wrong, no wrong at all…" She remembered where she was and looked up at him with the pain still in her eyes.

"Who broke your wrist, Lou?" he asked gently.

She remembered aloud. "He was drinking and I tried to take the bottle away from him, because he'd hit my mother. He hit my wrist with the bottle, and it broke," she added, wincing at the memory of the pain. "And all the while, when they operated to repair the damage, he kept saying that I'd fallen through a glass door, that I'd tripped. Everyone believed him, even my mother. I told her that he did it, and she said that I was lying."

"He? Who did it, Lou?"

She searched his curious eyes. "Why...my father," she said simply.

CHAPTER SIX

COLTRAIN SEARCHED HER dark eyes, although the confession didn't really surprise him. He knew too much about her father to be surprised.

"So that was why the whiskey on my breath bothered you Friday night," he remarked quietly.

She averted her head and nodded. "He was a drunkard at the last, and a drug addict. He had to stop operating because he almost killed a patient. They let him retire and act in an advisory capacity because he'd been such a good surgeon. He was, you know," she added. "He might have been a terrible father, but he was a wonderful surgeon. I wanted to be a surgeon, to be like him." She shivered. "I was in my first year of medical school when it happened. I lost a semester and afterward, I knew I'd never be able to operate. I decided to become a general practitioner."

"What a pity," he said. He understood the fire for surgical work because he had it. He loved what he did for a living.

She smiled sadly. "I'm still practicing medicine. It isn't so bad. Family practice has its place in the scheme of things, and I've enjoyed the time I've spent in Jacobsville."

"So have I," he admitted reluctantly. He smiled at her expression. "Surprised? You've been here long enough to know how a good many people react to me. I'm the original bad boy of the community. If it hadn't been for the scholarship one of my teachers helped me get, I'd probably be in jail by now. I had a hard childhood and I hated authority in any form. I was in constant trouble with the law."

"You?" she asked, aghast.

He nodded. "People aren't always what they seem, are they?" he continued. "I was a wild boy. But I loved medicine and I had an aptitude for it and there were people who were willing to help me. I'm the first of my family to escape poverty, did you know?"

She shook her head. "I don't know anything about your family," she said. "I wouldn't have presumed to ask anyone something so personal about you."

"I've noticed that," he returned. "You avoid sharing your feelings. You'll fight back, but you don't let people close, do you?"

"When people get too close, they can hurt you," she said.

"A lesson your father taught you, no doubt."

She wrapped her arms around her chest. "I'm cold," she said dully. "I want to go home."

He searched her face. "Come home with me."

She hesitated warily.

He made a face. "Shame on you for what you're thinking. You should know better. You're off the endangered list. I'll make chili and Mexican corn bread and strong coffee and we can watch a Christmas special. Do you like opera?"

Her eyes brightened. "Oh, I love it."

His own eyes brightened. "Pavarotti?"

"And Domingo." She looked worried. "But people will talk…"

"They're already talking. Who cares?" he asked. "We're both single adults. What we do together is nobody's business."

"Yes, well, the general consensus of opinion is that we're public property, or didn't you hear what Mr. Bailey said?"

"I heard you scream," he mused.

She cleared her throat. "Well, it was the last straw."

He caught her hand, the undamaged one, and locked her fingers into his, tugging her out the door.

"Dr. Coltrain," she began.

He locked the office door. "You know my name."

She looked wary. "Yes."

He glanced at her. "My friends call me Copper," he said softly, and smiled.

"We're not friends."

"I think we're going to be, though, a year too late." He tugged her toward his car.

"I can drive mine," she protested.

"Mine's more comfortable. I'll drive you home, and give you a lift to work in the morning. Is it locked?"

"Yes, but…"

"Don't argue, Lou. I'm tired. It's been a long day and we've still got to make rounds at the hospital later."

We. He couldn't know the anguish of hearing him link them together when she had less than two weeks left in Jacobsville. He'd said that he'd torn up her resignation, but she was levelheaded enough to know that she had to go. It would be pure torment to be around him all the time and have him treat her as a friend and nothing more. She couldn't have an affair with him, either, so what was left?

He glanced down at her worried face and his fingers contracted. "Stop brooding. I promised not to seduce you."

"I know that!"

"Unless you want me to," he chided, chuckling at her expression. "I'm a doctor," he added in a conspiratorial whisper. "I know how to protect you from any consequences."

"Damn you!"

She jerked away from him, furiously. He laughed at her fighting stance.

"That was wicked," he acknowledged. "But I do love to watch you lose that hot temper. Are you Irish, by any chance?"

"My grandfather was," she muttered. She dashed a strand of blond hair out of her eyes. "You stop saying things like that to me!"

He unlocked her door, still smiling. "All right. No more jokes."

She slid into the leather seat and inhaled the luxurious scent of the upholstery while he got in beside her and started the car. It was dark. She sat next to him in perfect peace and contentment as they drove out to his ranch, not breaking the silence as they passed by farms and ranches silhouetted against the flat horizon.

"You're very quiet," he remarked when he pulled up in front of the Spanish-style adobe house he called home.

"I'm happy," she said without thinking.

He was quiet, then. He helped her out and they walked a little apart on the flagstone walkway that led to the front porch. It was wide and spacious, with gliders and a porch swing.

"It must be heaven to sit out here in the spring," she remarked absently.

He glanced at her curiously. "I never pictured you as the sort to enjoy a porch swing."

"Or walks in the woods, or horseback riding, or baseball games?" she asked. "Because I like those things, too. Austin does have suburbs, and I had friends who owned ranches. I know how to ride and shoot, too."

He smiled. She'd seemed like such a city girl. He'd made sure that he never looked too closely at her, of course. Like father, like daughter, he'd always thought. But she was nothing like Fielding Blakely. She was unique.

He unlocked the door and opened it. The interior was full of Spanish pieces and dark furniture with creams and beiges and browns softened by off-white curtains. It had the look of professional decorating, which it probably was.

"I grew up sitting on orange crates and eating on cracked plates," he commented as she touched a bronze sculpture of a bronc rider. "This is much better."

She laughed. "I guess so. But orange crates and cracked plates wouldn't be so bad if the company was pleasant. I hate formal dining rooms and extravagant place settings."

Now he was getting suspicious. They really couldn't have that much in common! His eyebrow jerked. "Full of surprises, aren't you? Or did you just take a look at my curriculum vitae and tell me what I wanted to hear?" he added in a crisp, suspicious tone.

Her surprise was genuine, and he recognized it immediately. She searched his face. "This was a mistake," she said flatly. "I think I'd like to go…"

He caught her arm. "Lou, I'm constantly on the defensive with women," he said. "I never know, you see…" He hesitated.

"Yes, I understand," she replied. "You don't have to say it."

"All that, and you read minds, too," he said with cool sarcasm. "Well, well."

She drew away from him. She seemed to read his mind quite well, she thought, because she usually knew what he was going to say.

That occurred to him, too. "It used to make me mad as hell when you handed me files before I asked for them," he told her.

"It wasn't deliberate," she said without thinking.

"I know." His jaw firmed as he looked at her. "We know too much about each other, don't we, Lou? We know things we shouldn't, without ever saying them."

She looked up, feeling the bite of his inspection all the way to her toes. "We can't say them," she replied. "Not ever."

He only nodded. His eyes searched hers intently. "I don't believe in happily ever after," he said. "I did, once, until your father came along and shattered all my illusions. She wouldn't let me touch her, you see. But she slept with him. She got pregnant by him. The hell of it was that she was going to marry me without telling me anything." He sighed. "I lost my faith in women on the spot, and I hated your father enough to beat him to his knees. When you came here, and I found out who you were…" He shook his head. "I almost decked Drew for not telling me."

"I didn't know, either," she said.

"I realize that." He smiled. "You were an asset, after I got over the shock. You never complained about long hours or hard work, no matter how much I put on you. And I put a lot on you, at first. I thought I could make you quit. But the more I demanded, the more you gave. After a while, it occurred to me that I'd made a good bargain. Not that I liked you," he added sardonically.

"You made that perfectly clear."

"You fought back," he said. "Most people don't. They knuckle under and go home and fume about it, and think up things they wish they'd said. You just jump in with both feet and give it all you've got. You're a hell of an adversary, Lou. I couldn't beat you down."

"I always had to fight for things," she recalled. "My father was like you." Her face contorted and she turned away.

"I don't get drunk as a rule, and I've never hurt a woman!" he snapped.

"I didn't mean that," she said quickly. "It's just that you're forceful. You demand, you push. You don't ever give up or give in. Neither did he. If he thought he was right, he'd fight the whole world to prove it. But he fought the same when he was wrong. And in his later years, he drank to excess. He wouldn't admit he had a problem. Neither would my mother. She was his slave," she added bitterly. "Even her daughter was dispensable if the great man said so."

"Didn't she love you?"

"Who knows? She loved him more. Enough to lie for him. Even to die for him. And she did." She turned, her face hard. "She got into a plane with him, knowing that he was in no condition to fly. Maybe she had a premonition that he would go down and she wanted to go with him. I'm almost sure that she still would have gone with him if she'd known he was going to crash the plane. She loved him that much."

"You sound as if you can't imagine being loved that much."

"I can't," she said flatly, lifting her eyes. "I don't want that kind of obsessive love. I don't want to give it or receive it."

"What do you want?" he persisted. "A lifetime of loneliness?"

"That's what you're settling for, isn't it?" she countered.

He shrugged. "Maybe I am," he said after a minute. His blue eyes slid over her face and then averted. "Can you cook?" he asked on the way into the kitchen. Like the rest of the house, it was spacious and contained every modern device known to man.

"Of course," she said.

He glanced at her with a grin. "How well do you do chili?" he persisted.

"Well…"

"I've won contests with mine," he said smugly. He slid out of his jacket and vest and tie, opened the top buttons of his shirt and turned to the stove. "You can make the coffee."

"Trusting soul, aren't you?" she murmured as he acquainted her with the coffeemaker and the location of filters, coffee and measuring spoons.

"I always give a fellow cook the benefit of the doubt once," he replied. "Besides, you drink coffee all the time, just like I do. That means you must know how to make it."

She laughed. "I like mine strong," she warned.

"So do I. Do your worst."

Minutes later, the food was on the small kitchen table, steaming and delicious. Lou couldn't remember when she'd enjoyed a meal more.

"That's good chili," she had to admit.

He grinned. "It's the two-time winner of the Jacobsville Chili Cookoff."

"I'm not surprised. The corn bread was wonderful, too."

"The secret to good corn bread is to cook it in an iron skillet," he confessed. "That's where the crispness comes from."

"I don't own a single piece of iron cookware. I'll have to get a pan."

He leaned back, balancing his coffee mug in one hand as he studied her through narrow eyes. "It hasn't all been on my side," he remarked suddenly.

Her eyes lifted to his. "What hasn't?"

"All that antagonism," he said. "You've been as prickly as I have."

Her slender shoulders rose and fell. "It's instinctive to recoil from people when we know they don't like us. Isn't it?"

"Maybe so." He checked his watch and finished his coffee. "I'll get these things in the dishwasher, then we'd better get over to the hospital and do rounds before the Christmas concert comes on the educational channel."

"I don't have my car," she said worriedly.

"We'll go together."

"Oh, that will certainly keep gossip down," she said on a sigh.

He smiled at her. "Damn gossip."

"Was that an adjective or a verb?"

"A verb. I'll rinse, you stack."

They loaded the dishes and he started the dishwasher. He slid back into his jacket, buttoned his shirt and fixed his tie. "Come on. We'll get the chores out of the way."

THE HOSPITAL WAS CROWDED, and plenty of people noticed that Drs. Coltrain and Blakely came in together to make rounds. Lou tried not to notice as she went from patient to patient, checking charts and making conversation.

But when she finished, Coltrain was nowhere in sight. She glanced out the window into the parking lot. His car was still there in his designated space. She went to the doctors' lounge looking for him, and turned the corner just in time to see him with a devastating blond woman in a dress that Lou would love to have been able to afford.

Coltrain saw Lou and he looked grim. He turned toward her with his hands in his pockets, and Lou noticed that the woman was clutching one of his arms tightly in both hands.

"This is my partner," he said, without giving her name. "Lou, this is Dana Lester, an old…friend."

"His ex-fiancée." The woman corrected him in a sweet tone. "How nice to meet you! I've just accepted an appointment as nursing director here, so we'll be seeing a lot of each other!"

"You're a nurse?" Lou asked politely, while she caved in inside.

"A graduate nurse," she said, nodding. "I've been working in Houston, but this job came open and was advertised in a local paper. I applied for it, and here

I am! How lovely it will be to come home. I was born here, you know."

"Oh, really?" Lou said.

"Darling," she told Copper, "you didn't tell me your partner's name."

"It's Blakely," he said evenly. "Dr. Louise Blakely."

"Blakely?" the woman queried, her blue eyes pensive. "Why does that name sound so familiar...." She suddenly went pale. "No," she said, shaking her head. "No, that would be too coincidental."

"My father," Lou said coolly, "was Dr. Fielding Blakely. I believe you...knew him?" she added pointedly.

Dana's face looked like rice paper. She drew away from Coltrain. "I... I must fly, darling," she said. "Things to do while I get settled! I'll have you over for supper one night soon!"

She didn't speak to Lou again, not that it was expected. Lou watched her go with cold, angry eyes.

"You didn't want to tell her my name," Lou accused softly.

His face gave away nothing. "The past is best left alone."

"Did you know about her job here?"

His jaw clenched. "I knew there was an opening. I didn't know she'd been hired. If Selby Wills hadn't just retired as hospital administrator, she wouldn't have gotten the job."

She probed into the pocket of her lab coat without really seeing it. "She's pretty."

"She's blond, too, isn't that what you're thinking?"

She raised her face. "So," she added, "is Jane Parker."

"Jane Burke, now." He corrected her darkly. "I like blondes."

His tone dared her to make another remark She lifted a shoulder and turned. "Some men do. Just don't expect me to welcome her with open arms. I'm sure that my mother suffered because of her. At least my father was less careless with women in his later years."

"It was over a long time ago," Copper said quietly. "If I can overlook your father, you can overlook her."

"Do you think so?"

"What happened between them was nothing to do with you," he persisted.

"He betrayed my mother with her, and it's nothing to do with me?" she asked softly.

He rammed his hands into his pockets, his face set and cold. "Are you finished here?"

"Oh, yes, I'm finished here," she agreed fervently. "If you'll drop me off at my car, I'd like to go home now. We'll have to save the TV Special for another time."

He hesitated, but only for a minute. Her expression told him everything he needed to know, including the futility of having an argument with her right now.

"All right," he agreed, nodding toward the exit. "Let's go."

He stopped at her car in the office parking lot and let her out.

"Thanks for my supper," she said politely.

"You're welcome."

She closed the door and unlocked her own car. He didn't drive away until she was safely inside and heading out toward home.

DANA LESTER'S ARRIVAL in town was met with another spate of gossip, because there were people in Jacobsville who remembered the scandal very well. Lou tried to pay as little attention to it as possible as she weathered the first few days with the new nursing supervisor avoiding her and Coltrain barely speaking to her.

It was, she told herself, a very good thing that she was leaving after the first of January. The situation was strained and getting worse. She couldn't work out if Dana was afraid of her or jealous of her. Gossip about herself and Coltrain had been lost in the new rumors about his ex-fiancée's return, which did at least spare Lou somewhat. She couldn't help but see that Dana spent a fair amount of time following Coltrain around the hospital, and once or twice she phoned him at the office. Lou pretended not to notice and not to mind, but it was cutting her up inside.

The night she'd had supper with her taciturn partner had been something of a beginning. But Dana's arrival had nipped it all in the bud. He'd turned his back on Lou and now he only spoke to her when it was necessary and about business. If he'd withdrawn, so had she. Poor Brenda and the office receptionist worked in an armed camp, walking around like people on eggshells. Coltrain's temper strained at the bit, and every time he flared up, Lou flared right back.

"We hear that Nickie and Dana almost came to blows the other night about who got to take Dr. Coltrain a file," Brenda remarked a few days later.

"Too bad someone didn't have a hidden camera, isn't it?" Lou remarked. She sipped her coffee.

Brenda frowned. "I thought... Well, it did seem that you and the doctor were getting along better."

"A temporary truce, nothing more," she returned. "I'm still leaving after the first of the year, Brenda.

Nothing's really changed except that Coltrain's old flame has returned."

"She was poison," Brenda said. "I heard all about her from some of the older nurses at the hospital. Did you know that at least two threatened to quit when they knew she was taking over as head nurse at the hospital? One of the nurses she worked with in Houston has family here. They said she was about to be fired when she grabbed this job. Her credentials look impressive, but she's not a good administrator, regardless of her college background, and she plays favorites. They'll learn that here, the hard way."

"It's not my problem."

"Isn't it?" Brenda muttered. "Well, they also say that her real purpose in applying for this job was to see if Copper was willing to take her back and try again. She's looking for a husband and he's number one on her list."

"Lucky him," she said blithely. "She's very pretty."

"She's a blond tarantula," she said hotly. "She'll suck him dry!"

"He's a big boy, Brenda," Lou returned imperturbably. "He can take care of himself."

"No man is immune to a beautiful face and figure and having a woman absolutely worship him. You take my word for it, there's going to be trouble."

"I won't be here to see it," Lou reminded her. And for the first time, she was glad. Nickie and Dana could fight over Coltrain and may the best woman win, she thought miserably. At least she wouldn't have to watch the struggle. She'd always known that Coltrain wasn't for her. She might as well accept defeat with good grace and get out while she could.

She went back to work, all too aware of Coltrain's

deep voice in one of the cubicles she passed. She wondered how her life was going to feel when this was all a bad memory, and she wouldn't hear his voice again.

Drew invited her out to eat and she went, gratefully, glad for the diversion. But the restaurant he chose, Jacobsville's best, had two unwelcome diners: Coltrain and his ex-fiancée.

"I'm sorry," Drew said with a smile and a grimace of apology. "I didn't know they'd be here or I'd have chosen another place to take you for supper."

"Oh, I don't mind," she assured him. "I have to see them at the hospital every day, anyway."

"Yes, *see* them being the key word here," he added knowingly. "I understand that they both avoid you."

"God knows why," she agreed. "She's anywhere I'm not when I need to ask her a question, and he only talks to me about patients. I'm glad I'm leaving, Drew. And with all respect to you, I'm sorry I came."

He smiled ruefully. "I'm sorry I got you into this," he said. "Nothing went as I planned."

"What exactly did you plan?" she asked probingly.

He lifted his water glass and took a sip. "Well, I had hoped that Copper would see something in you that he hadn't found anywhere else. You're unique, Lou. So is he, in some respects. You seemed like a match."

She glared at him. "We're chalk and cheese," she said, ignoring the things she and the redheaded doctor did have in common. "And we can't get along for more than five minutes."

"So I see." He looked around and made a face. "Oh, God, more complications!"

She followed his gaze. A determined Nickie, in a skintight dress cut almost to the navel, was dragging an embarrassed intern to a table right beside Coltrain and Dana's.

"That won't do," she remarked, watching Coltrain's blue eyes start to glitter. "He won't like that. And if she thinks he'll forgo a scene, she's very wrong. Any minute now he's going to get up and walk out."

When he did exactly that, leaving an astonished Dana at one table and a shocked Nickie at the other, Drew whistled through his teeth and gave Lou a pointed stare.

"You know him very well," was all he said, though.

"I know him," Lou said simply. "He says I read his mind. Maybe I do, on some level."

He frowned. "Do you realize how rare a rapport that is?"

She shrugged. "Not really. He seems to read my mind, too. I shouldn't feel sorry for him, but I do. Imagine shuffling two women in one restaurant."

He didn't add that it was really three, and that Copper had been watching Lou surreptitiously ever since she and Drew entered the restaurant. But of the three women, Lou was the only one who wasn't blatantly chasing him.

"He's paying the check," he remarked. "And, yes, there he goes, motioning to Dana. Good thing they'd finished dessert, wasn't it? Poor Nickie. She won't forget this in a while."

"I told her she was pushing too hard," Lou remarked. "Too bad. She's so young. I suppose she hasn't learned that you can chase a man too relentlessly and lose him."

"Some women never chase a man at all," he said.

She looked up and saw the teasing expression on

his face. She laughed. "Drew, you are a dear," she said genuinely.

He chuckled. "My wife always said that I was," he agreed. "What are you going to do?"

"Me? What do you mean? What am I going to do about what?"

"About Copper."

"Nothing," she replied. "Right after the holidays, I leave for Austin."

He pursed his lips as he lifted his coffee cup. "You know," he said, "I have a feeling you'll never get out of town."

CHAPTER SEVEN

SATURDAY MORNING, Lou woke to the sound of someone hammering on her front door. Half-asleep, with a pale pink satin robe whipped around her slender body and her hair disheveled, she made her way to open it.

The sight that met her eyes was shocking. Coltrain was standing there, dressed in jeans and boots and a faded cotton shirt under a fleece-lined jacket, with a weather-beaten gray Stetson in one lean hand.

She blinked. "Are we filming a new series called 'Cowboy Doctor'?"

"Cute," he remarked, but he wasn't smiling. "I have to talk to you."

She opened the door, still drowsy. "Come on in. I'll make coffee," she said, stifling a yawn as she shuffled toward the kitchen. She could have gone immediately to change, but she was more than adequately covered and he was a doctor. Besides, she reminded herself, he had two women chasing him relentlessly anyway.

"I'll make the coffee. How about some toast to go with it?"

"Plain or cinnamon?"

"Suit yourself."

She got out butter and cinnamon and, just as the coffee finished brewing, she had the toast ready—piping hot from the oven.

He watched her moving about the kitchen. He was sitting leaning back in one of her kitchen chairs with one booted foot on the floor and the chair propped against the wall. He looked out of humor and wickedly handsome all at the same time.

In the position he was occupying, his jeans clung closely to every powerful line of his long legs. He was muscular without being exaggerated, and with his faded shirt unbuttoned at the throat and his red hair disheveled from the hat, he looked more relaxed than she'd ever seen him.

It occurred to her that this was the way he usually was, except when he was working. It was like a private look into his secret life, and she was unexpectedly pleased to have been given it before she left town for good.

"Here." She put the toast on the table, handed him a plate, put condiments on the spotless white tablecloth and then poured coffee into two cups.

"The Christmas concert was nice," he remarked.

"Was it?" she replied. "I went to bed."

"I had nothing to do with getting Dana down here," he said flatly. "In case you wondered."

"It's none of my business."

"Yes, I know," he said heavily. He sipped coffee and munched toast, but he was preoccupied. "Nickie and Dana are becoming an embarrassment."

"Leave it to you to be irritated when two lovely women compete for your attention," she remarked dryly.

His eyes narrowed on her face. "Irritation doesn't quite cover it. I feel like the stud of the month," he said disgustedly.

She burst out laughing. "Oh, I'm sorry!" she said when he glared at her. "It was the way you said it."

He was ruffled, and looked it. He sipped more coffee. "I wasn't trying to make a joke."

"I know. It must be difficult, especially when you have to make rounds at the hospital, with both of them working there."

"I understand you're having some problems of your own in that regard."

"You might say that," she agreed. "I can't find Dana or Nickie when I need them. I seem to have the plague."

"You know that it can't continue?"

"Of course I do," she assured him. "And when I leave, things will settle down, I'm sure."

He scowled. "What do you mean, when you leave? How will that help? Anyway, we'd already agreed that you were staying."

"We agreed on nothing," she returned. "I gave you my resignation. If you tore it up, that's your problem. I consider it binding."

He stared down into his coffee cup, deep in thought. "I had no idea that you meant it."

"Amazing," she mused, watching him. "You have such a convenient memory, Dr. Coltrain. I can't forget a single word you said to Drew about me, and you can't remember?"

His face hardened. "I didn't know you were listening."

"That makes everything all right?" she asked with mock solemnity.

He ran a hand through his already disheveled hair. "Things came to a head," he replied. "I'd just had to diagnose leukemia in a child who should have had years of happiness to look forward to. I'd had a letter from my father asking for money…"

She shifted against the table. "I didn't know that your parents were still alive."

"My mother died ten years ago," he replied. "My father lives in Tucson. He wrangles horses, but he likes to gamble. When he gets in too deep, he always comes to me for a grubstake." He said it with utter contempt.

"Is that all you mean to him? Money?" she asked gently.

"It was all I ever meant to him." He lifted cold blue eyes to hers. He smiled unpleasantly. "Who do you think put me up to breaking and entering when I was a teenager? I was a juvenile, you know. Juveniles don't go to jail. Oh, we didn't do it here," he added. "Not where he lived. We always went to Houston. He cased the houses and sent me in to do the actual work."

Her gasp was audible. "He should have been arrested!"

"He was," he replied. "He served a year and got probation. We haven't spent any time together since I was placed with a foster family when I was thirteen, long before I started medical school. I put all that behind me. Apparently so did he. But now that I'm making a comfortable living, he doesn't really see any good reason not to ask me for help when he needs it."

What sort of family life had *he* grown up in? she wondered. It was, in some ways, like her own upbringing. "What a pity that we can't choose our parents," she remarked.

"Amen." His broad shoulders shifted against the wall. "I was in a temper already, and Drew's phone call was the last straw. It irritated the hell out of me that you liked him, but you jerked away from my slightest touch as if I might contaminate you."

She hadn't thought he'd noticed. He took her reaction as a sign of her distaste for him, when it was a fierce, painful attraction. It was ironic.

She lowered her eyes. "You said when I first came to work with you that we would have a business relationship."

"So I did. But that didn't mean you should treat me like a leper," he remarked. Oddly, he didn't seem to be concerned about it anymore. He smiled, in fact, his blue eyes sparkling. "But I wouldn't have had you overhear what I told Drew for all the world, Lou. It shamed me when you asked to end our partnership."

She toyed with a fingernail. "I thought it would make you happy."

Her choice of words delighted him. He knew exactly what she felt for him. He'd had suspicions for a while now, but he hadn't been certain until he kissed her. He couldn't let her leave until he was sure about what he felt for her. But how was he going to stop her? His blue eyes ran searchingly over her face and a crazy idea popped into his mind. "If you and I were engaged," he mused aloud, "Dana and Nickie would give up."

The words rambled around in her mind like marbles as she stared at him. The sun was out. It was a nice December day. Her Christmas decorations lined the windows and the tinsel on the Christmas tree in the living room caught the sun through the curtains and glittered.

"Did you hear me?" he asked when she didn't react.

Her cheeks burned. "I don't think that's very funny," she remarked, turning away.

He got to his feet with an audible thud and before

she could move three feet, he had her by the waist from behind. Steely hands pulled her back against him and when she caught them, she felt their warm strength under her cool fingers. She felt his breath against her hair, felt it as his chest moved at her back.

"Shall we stop dancing around it?" he asked roughly. "You're in love with me. I've pretended not to see it, but we both know it's why you're leaving."

She gasped aloud. Frozen in his arms, she hadn't even a comeback, a face-saving reply. She felt his hands contract under hers, as if he thought she might pull away and run for it.

"Don't panic," he said quietly. "Dodging the issue won't solve it."

"I...didn't realize you could tell," she whispered, her pride in ashes at his feet.

His lean arms contracted, bringing her soft warmth closer to his taut body. "Take it easy. We'll deal with it."

"You don't have to deal with anything," she began huskily. "I'm going to..."

He turned her while she was speaking and his mouth was on hers before she could finish. She fought him for an instant, as he anticipated. But he was slow and very gentle, and she began to melt into him like ice against a flame.

He brought her closer, aware of her instant response when she felt his body harden. He made a rough sound against her mouth and deepened the kiss.

Her fingers caught in the cool flames of his hair, holding on for dear life as his ardor burned high and wild. He kissed her as he'd kissed Nickie at the party, not an inch of space between their bodies, no quarter in the thin lips devouring her open mouth. This time when his tongue penetrated, she didn't pull away. She accepted the intimate contact without a protest, shivering a little as it ignited new fires in her own taut body. The sensation was unlike anything she'd known. She held on tight, moaning, aware somewhere in the back of her mind that his hand was at the base of her spine, rubbing her against him, and that she should say something.

She was incapable of anything except blind response.

She didn't resist even when he eased her back onto her feet and, still kissing her hungrily, slid his hand under her robe against the soft, tight curve of her breast. He felt her heartbeat run away. With a groan, he fought his way under the gown, against the petal-soft warmth of her skin, and cupped her tenderly, dragging his thumb against the small hardness he found. She shivered again. Reeling, he traced the tight nub with his thumb and forefinger, testing its hardness. She sobbed against his mouth. Probably, he thought dizzily, she'd never had such a caress. And he could give her something more; another pleasure that she didn't know yet.

His mouth left hers and found its way down past her collarbone to the softness under his hand. It opened on her body, and he drank in the scented warmth of her while his tongue took the place of his thumb. She gasped and struggled, but he began to suckle her, his arms swallowing her, and she shuddered once and gave in. He felt her body go lax in his arms, so that if he hadn't supported her, she would have fallen. She caressed his nape with trembling hands, gasping a little as he increased the pressure, but clinging, not pushing.

When he thought he might explode from the pleasure it was giving him, he forced his mouth to release her and he stood erect, pulling her up abruptly.

His face was ruddy with high color, his eyes blazing as they met her half-open, dazed ones. She was oblivious to everything except the taste of him. Her lips were swollen. Even her tongue felt swollen. She couldn't say a word.

He searched over her face and then dropped his eyes to her bodice. He moved it out of the way and looked at the small, firm breast he'd been tasting. She looked like a rosebud there, the nipple red from his mouth.

He traced around it lazily and then looked back up at the shocked pleasure in her dark, dark eyes.

"I could have you on the kitchen table, right now," he said in a deep, quiet tone. "And you think you're leaving in two weeks?"

She blinked. It was all so unreal. He'd all but seduced her. His hand was still on her breast and he'd pulled the robe and gown aside. He was looking at her...!

She gasped, horrified, jerking back from him. Her hands grappled with the unruly fabric before she finally got her body covered. She backed away, blushing, glaring at him accusingly.

He didn't move, except to lean back against the kitchen counter and cross his long legs. That action drew her eyes to something she'd felt earlier, and she blushed scarlet before she managed to look away. What had she done? What had she let him do?

"You look outraged," he mused. "I think I like having you blush when I look at you."

"Would you leave, please?" she asked tightly.

"No, I don't think so," he said pleasantly. "Get dressed. Wear jeans and boots. I'm taking you riding."

"I don't want to go anywhere with you!"

"You want to go to bed with me," he corrected, smiling gently. "I can't think of anything I'd enjoy more, but I saddled the horses and left them in the stable before I came over here."

She huddled in her robe, wincing as it rubbed against her body.

"Breast sore?" he asked softly. "I'm sorry. I lost my head a little."

She flushed more and the robe tightened. "Dr. Coltrain…"

"Copper," he reminded her. "Or you can call me Jeb, if you like." He pursed his lips and his eyes were hot and possessive. "You'd really better get dressed, Lou," he murmured. "I'm still pretty hot, and aroused men are devious."

She moved back. "I have things to do…"

"Horseback riding or…?" He moved toward her.

She turned and ran for the bedroom. She couldn't believe what had just happened, and he'd said something about them becoming engaged. She must be losing her mind. Yes, that was it, she'd worried over leaving so much that she was imagining things. The whole thing had probably been a hallucination.

HE'D CLEARED AWAY the breakfast things by the time she washed, dressed, pulled her hair back into a pony-tail with a blue ribbon and came into the kitchen with a rawhide jacket on.

He smiled. "You look like a cowgirl."

She'd felt a bit uneasy about facing him after that torrid interlude, but apparently he wasn't embarrassed. She might as well follow his lead. She managed a smile in return. "Thanks. But I may not quite merit the title. I haven't ridden in a long time."

"You'll be all right. I'll look after you."

He opened the door and let her out, waiting for her to lock it. Then he helped her into the Jaguar and drove her to his ranch.

THE WOODS WERE LOVELY, despite their lack of leaves. The slow, easy rhythm of the horses was relaxing, even if the company wasn't. She was all too aware of Coltrain beside her, tall and elegant even on horseback. With the Stetson pulled low over his eyes, he looked so handsome that he made her toes tingle.

"Enjoying yourself?" he asked companionably.

"Oh, yes," she admitted. "I haven't been riding in a long time."

"I do more of it than I like sometimes," he confessed. "This isn't a big ranch, but I run about fifty head of pedigree cattle. I have two married cowhands who help out."

"Why do you keep cattle?" she asked.

"I don't know. It was always a dream of mine, I guess, from the time I was a boy. My grandfather had one old milk cow and I'd try to ride her." He chuckled. "I fell off a lot."

She smiled. "And your grandmother?"

"Oh, she was a cook of excellent proportions," he replied. "She made cakes that were the talk of the county. When my dad went wrong, it broke her heart, and my grandfather's. I think they took it harder because he lured me into it with him." He shook his head. "When a kid goes bad, everyone blames it on the upbringing. But my grandparents were kind, good people. They were just poor. A lot of people were...still are."

She'd noticed that he had a soft spot for his needy

patients. He made extra time for them, acting as coun-
selor and even helping them get in touch with the proper
government agencies when they needed help. At Christmas, he was the first to pledge a donation to local chari-
ties and contribute to parties for children who wouldn't
otherwise have presents. He was a good man, and she
adored him.

"Do you want children, eventually?" she asked.

"I'd like a family," he said noncommittally. He
glanced at her. "How about you?"

She grimaced. "I don't know. It would be hard for
me to juggle motherhood and medicine. I know plenty
of people do, but it seems like begging from Peter to
pay Paul, you know? Children need a lot of care. I think
plenty of social problems are caused by parents who
can't get enough time off from work to look after their
children. And good day care is a terrible financial head-
ache. Why isn't day care free?" she asked abruptly. "It
should be. If women are going to have to work, companies should provide access to day care for them. I know
of hospitals and some companies that do it for their employees. Why can't every big company?"

"Good question. It would certainly take a burden off
working parents."

"All the same, if I had kids, I'd want to be with them
while they were young. I don't know if I could give up
practice for so long...."

He reined in his horse and caught her bridle, bringing her horse gently around so that they were facing
each other at the side. "That's not the reason. Talk to
me," he said quietly. "What is it?"

She huddled into her jacket. "I hated being a child,"

she muttered. "I hated my father and my mother and my life."

His eyebrows lifted. "Do you think a child would hate me?"

She laughed. "Are you kidding? Children love you. Except that you don't do stitches as nicely as I do," she added.

He smiled ruefully. "Thanks for small favors."

"The secret is the chewing gum I give them afterward."

"Ah, I see. Trade a few stitches for a few cavities."

"It's sugarless gum," she said smugly.

He searched her face with warm eyes. "Touché."

He wheeled his horse and led her off down a pasture path to where the big barn was situated several hundred yards away from the house. He explained the setup, and how he'd modernized his small operation.

"I'm not as up-to-date as a lot of ranchers are, and this is peanut scale," he added. "But I've put a lot of work and time into it, and I'm moderately proud of what I've accomplished. I have a herd sire who's mentioned in some of the bigger cattle magazines."

"I'm impressed. Do I get to see him?"

"Do you want to?"

"You sound surprised. I like animals. When I started out, it was a toss-up between being a doctor and being a vet."

"What swayed you?"

"I'm not really sure. But I've never regretted my choice."

He swung out of the saddle and waited for her to dismount. He tied the horses to the corral rail and led the way into the big barn.

It was surprisingly sanitary. The walkway was paved, the stalls were spacious with metal gates and fresh hay. The cows were sleek and well fed, and the bull he'd mentioned was beautiful even by bovine standards.

"Why, he's gorgeous," she enthused as they stood at the gate and looked at him. He was red-coated, huge, streamlined and apparently docile, because he came up to let Coltrain pet his muzzle.

"How are you, old man?" he murmured affectionately. "Had enough corn, have you?"

"He's a Santa Gertrudis, isn't he?" she asked curiously.

His hand stilled on the bull's nose. "How did you know that?" he asked.

"Ted Regan is one of my patients. He had a breeder's edition of some magazine with him one day, and he left it behind. I got a good idea of coat colors, at least. We have a lot of cattlemen around here," she added. "It never hurts to know a little bit about a good bull."

"Why, Lou," he mused. "I'm impressed."

"That's a first."

He chuckled. His blue eyes twinkled down at her as he propped one big boot on the low rail of the gate. "No, it's not. You impressed me the first week you were here. You've grown on me."

"Good heavens, am I a wart?"

He caught a strand of her hair and wound it around his finger. "You're a wonder," he corrected, searching her eyes. "I didn't realize we had so much in common. Funny, isn't it? We've worked together for a year, but I've found out more about you in the past two weeks than I ever knew."

"That goes for me, too."

She dropped her eyes to his chest, where the faded shirt clung to the hard muscles. She loved the way he stood, the way he walked, the way he looked with that hat tilted rakishly over one eye. She remembered the feel of his warm arms around her and she felt suddenly cold.

Her expressions fascinated him. He watched them change, saw the hunger filter into her face.

She drew a wistful breath and looked up at him with a wan smile.

He frowned. Without understanding why, he held out a lean arm.

She accepted the invitation without question. Her body went against his, pressing close. Her arms went under his and around him, so that her hands could flatten on the muscles of his long back. She closed her eyes and laid her cheek against his chest, and listened to his heart beat.

He was surprised, yet he wasn't. It felt natural to have Lou in his arms. He drew her closer, in a purely nonsexual way, and absently stroked her hair while he watched his bull eat corn out of the trough in his pen.

"Next week is Christmas," he said above her head.

"Yes, I know. What do you do for Christmas? Do you go to friends, or invite people over?"

He laughed gently. "I used to have it with Jane, before she married," he recalled, feeling her stiffen without really thinking much about it. "But last year, since she married, I cooked a TV dinner and watched old movies all day."

She didn't answer for a minute. Despite what she'd heard about Coltrain and Jane Parker in the past year, she hadn't thought that he and Jane had been quite so close. But it seemed that they were. It depressed her more than anything had in recent weeks.

He wasn't thinking about Christmases past. He was thinking about the upcoming one. His hand explored her hair strand by strand. "Where are we going to have Christmas dinner, and who's going to cook it?" he asked matter-of-factly.

That was encouraging, that he wanted to spend Christmas with her. She couldn't refuse, even out of hurt pride. "We could have it at my house," she offered.

"I'll help cook it."

She smiled. "It would be nice to have someone to eat it with," she confessed.

"I'll make sure we're on call Christmas Eve, not Christmas Day," he promised. His arm slid down her back and drew her closer. He was aware of a kind of contentment he'd never experienced before, a belonging that he hadn't known even with Jane. Funny, he thought, until Lou came along, it had never occurred to him that he and Jane couldn't have had a serious relationship even if Todd Burke hadn't married her.

It was a sobering thought. This woman in his arms had come to mean a lot to him, without his realizing it until he'd kissed her for the first time. He laid his cheek against her head with a long sigh. It was like coming home. He'd been searching all his life for something he'd never found. He was closer to it than he'd ever been right now.

Her arms tightened around his lean waist. She could feel the wall of his chest hard against her breasts, the buckle of his belt biting into her. But it still wasn't quite close enough. She moved just a little closer, so that her legs brushed his.

He moved to accommodate her, sliding one boot higher on the fence so that she could fit against him more comfortably. But the movement aroused him and he caught his breath sharply.

"Sorry," she murmured and started to step away.

But his hand stayed her hips. "I can't help that," he said at her temple, secretly delighted at his headlong physical response to her. "But it isn't a threat."

"I didn't want to make you uncomfortable."

He smiled lazily. "I wouldn't call it that." He brushed a kiss across her forehead. "Relax," he whispered. "It's pretty public here, and I'm sure you know as well as I do that making love in a hay barn is highly unsanitary."

She laughed at his humor. "Oh, but this barn is very clean."

"Not that clean," he murmured dryly. "Besides," he added, "it's been a long, dry spell. When I'm not in the market for a companion, I don't walk around prepared for sweet interludes."

She lifted her face and searched his mocking eyes demurely. "A long, dry spell? With Nickie prancing around half-naked to get your attention?"

He didn't laugh, as she expected him to. He traced her pert nose. "I don't have affairs," he said. "And I'm the soul of discretion in my private life. There was a widow in a city I won't name. She and I were good friends, and we supplied each other with something neither of us was comfortable spreading around. She married year before last. Since then, I've concentrated on my work and my cattle. Period."

She was curious. "Can you...well, do it...without love?"

"I was fond of her," he explained. "She was fond of me. We didn't have to be in love."

She moved restlessly.

"It would have to be love, for you, wouldn't it, Lou?" he asked. "Even desperate desire wouldn't be enough." He traced her soft lips with deliberation. "But you and I are an explosive combination. And you do love me."

She laid her forehead at his collarbone. "Yes," she admitted. "I love you. But not enough to be your mistress."

"I know that."

"Then it's hopeless."

He laughed mirthlessly. "Is it? I thought I mentioned that we could get engaged."

"Engaged isn't married," she began.

He put a finger over her lips, and he looked solemn. "I know that. Will you let me finish? We can be engaged until the first of the year, when I can afford to take a little time off for a honeymoon. We could have a New Year's wedding."

CHAPTER EIGHT

"You mean, get married? Us?" she echoed blankly.

He tilted up her chin and searched her dark, troubled eyes. "Sex doesn't trouble you half as much as marriage does, is that it? Marriage means commitment, and to you, that's like imprisonment."

She grimaced. "My parents' marriage was horrible. I don't want to become like my mother."

"So you said." He traced her cheek. "But I'm not like your father. I don't drink. Well," he murmured with a sheepish grin, "maybe just once, and I had justification for that. You were letting Drew hold your hand, when you always jerked back if I touched you at all."

She was surprised. She smiled. "Was *that* why?"

He chuckled. "Yes, that was why."

"Imagine that!"

"Take one day at a time, okay?" he asked. "Let's rock along for a couple of weeks, and spend Christmas together. Then we'll talk about this again."

"All right."

He bent and kissed her softly. She pressed up against him, but he stepped back.

"None of that," he said smartly. "We're going to get to know each other before we let our glands get in the way."

"Glands!"

"Don't you remember glands, Doctor?" He moved toward her threateningly. "Let me explain them to you."

"I think I've got the picture," she said on a laugh. "Keep away, you lecher!"

He laughed, too. He caught her hand and tangled her fingers with his as they walked back to where the horses were tied. He'd never been quite this interested in marriage, even if he'd once had it in the back of his mind when he'd dated Jane. But when he'd had Lou close in his arms, in the barn, he'd wanted it with a maddening desire. It wasn't purely physical, although she certainly attracted him that way. But despite the way she felt about him, he had a feeling that she'd have to be carefully coaxed down the aisle. She was afraid of everything marriage stood for because of her upbringing. Their marriage wouldn't be anything like her parents', but he was going to have to convince her of that first.

THEY MADE ROUNDS together the next morning at the hospital, and as usual, Dana was lying in wait for Coltrain.

But this time, he deliberately linked Lou's hand in his as he smiled at her.

"Good morning," he said politely.

Dana was faintly startled. "Good morning, doctors," she said hesitantly, her eyes on their linked hands.

"Lou and I became engaged yesterday," he said.

Dana's face paled. She drew a stiff breath and managed the semblance of a smile. "Oh, did you? Well, I suppose I should offer my congratulations!" She laughed. "And I had such high hopes that you and I might regain something of the past."

"The past is dead," he said firmly, his blue eyes

steady on her face. "I have no inclination whatsoever to revive it."

Dana laughed uncomfortably. "So I see." She glanced at Lou's left hand. "Quite a sudden engagement, was it?" she added slyly. "No ring yet?"

Lou's hand jerked in his, but he steadied it. "When Lou makes up her mind what sort she wants, I'll buy her one," he said lazily. "I'd better get started. Wait for me in the lounge when you finish, sweet," he told Lou and squeezed her fingers before he let them go.

"I will," she promised. She smiled at Dana carelessly and went down the hall to begin her own rounds.

Dana followed her. "Well, I hope you fare better than I did," she muttered. "He's had the hots for Jane Parker for years. He asked me to marry him because he wanted me and I wouldn't give in, but even so, I couldn't compete with dear Jane," she said bitterly. "Your father was willing, so I indulged in a stupid affair, hoping I might make him jealous. That was the lunatic act of the century!"

"So I heard," Lou said stiffly, glaring at the other woman.

"I guess you did," the older woman said with a grimace. "He hated me for it. There's one man who doesn't move with the times, and he never forgets a wrong you do him." Her eyes softened as she looked at Lou's frozen face. "Your poor mother must have hated me. I know your father did. He was livid that I'd been so careless, and of course, I ruined his chances of staying here. But he didn't do so bad in Austin."

Lou had different memories of that. She couldn't lay it all at Dana's door, however. She paused at her first patient's door. "What do you mean about Jane Parker?" she asked solemnly

"You must have heard by now that she was his first love, his only love, for years. I gave up on him after my fling with your father. I thought it was surely over between them until I came back here. She's married, you know, but she still sees Copper socially." Her eyes glittered. "They say he sits and stares at her like an oil painting when they're anywhere together. You'll find that out for yourself. I should be jealous, but I don't think I am. I feel sorry for you, because you'll always be his second choice, even if he marries you. He may want you, but he'll never stop loving Jane."

She walked away, leaving a depressed, worried Lou behind. Dana's former engagement to Coltrain sounded so much like her own "engagement" with him that it was scary. She knew that he wanted her, but he didn't show any signs of loving her. Did he still love Jane? If he did, she couldn't possibly marry him.

Nickie came up the hall when Lou had finished her rounds and was ready to join Coltrain in the lounge.

"Congratulations," she told Lou with a resigned smile. "I guess I knew I was out of the running when I saw him kiss you in the car park. Good luck. From what I hear, you'll need it." She kept walking.

Lou was dejected. It was in her whole look when she went into the doctors' lounge, where Coltrain had just finished filling out a form at the table near the window. He looked up, frowning.

"What is it?" he asked curtly. "Have Dana and Nickie been giving you a hard time?"

"Not at all," she said. "I'm just a little tired." She

touched her back and winced, to convince him. "Horseback riding takes some getting used to, doesn't it?"

He smiled, glad that he'd mistaken soreness for depression. "Yes, it does. We'll have to do more of it." He picked up the folder. "Ready to go?"

"Yes."

He left the form at the nurses' station, absorbing more congratulations from the nurses, and led Lou out to his Jaguar.

"We'll take some time off this afternoon for lunch and shop for a ring," he said.

"But I don't need…"

"Of course you do," he said. "We can't let people think I'm too miserly to buy you an engagement ring!"

"But what if…?"

"Lou, it's my money," he declared.

She grimaced. Well, if he wanted to be stuck with a diamond ring when she left town, that was his business. The engagement, as far as she was concerned, was nothing more than an attempt to get his life back on an even keel and discourage Nickie and Dana from hounding him.

She couldn't forget what had been said about Jane Parker, Jane Burke now, and she was more worried than ever. She knew how entangled he'd been with Jane, all right, because she'd considered her a rival until the day Jane married Todd Burke. Coltrain's manner even when he spoke to the woman was tender, solicitous, almost reverent.

He'd proposed. But even though he knew Lou loved him, he'd never mentioned feeling anything similar for her. He was playing make-believe. But she wondered what would happen if Jane Burke suddenly became a free woman. It would be a nightmare to live with a man who was ever yearning for someone else, someone he'd loved most of his life. Jane was a habit he apparently couldn't break. She was married. But could that fact stop him from loving her?

"You're very quiet," he remarked.

"I was thinking about Mr. Bailey," she hedged. "He really needs to see a specialist about that asthma. What do you think of referring him to Dr. Jones up in Houston?"

He nodded, diverted. "A sound idea. I'll give you the number."

THEY WORKED IN harmony until the lunch hour. Then, despite her arguments, they drove to a jewelry shop in downtown Jacobsville. As bad luck would have it, Jane Burke was in there, alone, making a purchase.

She was so beautiful, Lou thought miserably. Blond, blue-eyed, with a slender figure that any man would covet.

"Why hello!" Jane said enthusiastically, and hugged Copper as if he was family.

He held her close and kissed her cheek, his smile tender, his face animated. "You look terrific," he said huskily. "How's the back? Still doing those exercises?"

"Oh, yes," she agreed. She held him by the arms and searched his eyes. "You look terrific yourself." She seemed only then to notice that he wasn't alone. She glanced at Lou. "Dr. Blakely, isn't it?" she asked politely, and altered the smile a little. "Nice to see you again."

"What are you doing here?" Coltrain asked her.

"Buying a present for my stepdaughter for Christmas. I thought she might like a nice strand of pearls. Aren't these lovely?" she asked when the clerk had taken them out of the case to show them. "I'll take them," she added, handing him her credit card.

"Is she staying with you and Todd all the time now?"

She nodded. "Her mother and stepfather and the baby are off to Africa to research his next book," she said with a grin. "We're delighted to have her all to ourselves."

"How's Todd?"

Lou heard the strained note in his voice with miserable certainty that Dana had been telling the truth.

"He's as impossible as ever." Jane chuckled. "But we scratch along, me with my horses and my clothing line and he with his computer business. He's away so much these days that I feel deserted." She lifted her eyes to his and grinned. "I don't guess you'd like to come to supper tonight?"

"Sure I would," he said without thinking. Then he made a sound. "I can't. There's a hospital board meeting."

"Oh, well," she muttered. "Another time, then." She glanced at Lou hesitantly. "Are you two out Christmas shopping—together?" she added as if she didn't think that was the case.

Coltrain stuck his hands deep into his pockets. "We're shopping for an engagement ring," he said tersely.

Her eyes widened. "For whom?"

Lou wanted to sink through the floor. She flushed to the roots of her hair and clung to her shoulder bag as if it were a life jacket.

"For Lou," Coltrain said. "We're engaged."

He spoke reluctantly, which only made Lou feel worse.

Jane's shocked expression unfroze Lou's tongue. "It's just for appearances," she said, forcing a smile. "Dana and Nickie have been hounding him."

"Oh, I see!" Jane's face relaxed, but then she frowned. "Isn't that a little dishonest?"

"It was the only way, and it's just until my contract is up, the first of the year," Lou forced herself to say. "I'll be leaving then."

Coltrain glared at her. He wasn't certain what he'd expected, but she made the proposal sound like a hoax. He hadn't asked her to marry him to ward off the other women; he'd truly wanted her to be his wife. Had she misunderstood totally?

Jane was as startled as Coltrain was. She knew that Copper wasn't the sort of man to give an engagement ring lightly, although Lou seemed to think he was. Since Dana's horrible betrayal, Copper had been impervious to women. But even Jane had heard about the hospital Christmas party and the infamous kiss. She'd hoped that Copper had finally found someone to love, although it was surprising that it would be the partner with whom he fought with so enthusiastically. Now, looking at them together, she was confused. Lou looked as if she were being tortured. Copper was taciturn and frozen. And they said it was a sham. Lou didn't love him. She couldn't, and be so lighthearted about it. Copper looked worn.

Jane glared at Lou and put a gentle hand on Coltrain's arm. "This is a stupid idea, Copper. You'll be the butt of every joke in town when Lou leaves, don't you realize it? It could even damage your reputation, hurt your practice," she told Copper intently.

His jaw tautened. "I appreciate your concern," he said gently, even as it surprised him that Jane should turn on Lou, who was more an innocent bystander than Coltrain's worst enemy.

That got through to Lou, too. She moved restlessly, averting her gaze from the diamond rings in the display case. "She's right. It *is* stupid. I can't do this," she said suddenly, her eyes full of torment. "Please, excuse me, I have to go!"

She made it out the door before the tears were visible, cutting down an alley and ducking into a department store. She went straight to the women's rest room and burst into tears, shocking a store clerk into leaving.

In the jewelry store, Coltrain stood like a statue, unspeakably shocked at Lou's rash departure and furious at having her back out just when he'd got it all arranged.

"For God's sake, did you have to do that?" Coltrain asked harshly. He rammed his hands into his pockets. "It's taken me days just to get her to agree on any pretext…!"

Jane realized, too late, what she'd done. She winced. "I didn't know," she said miserably. "It's my fault that she's bolted," Jane said quickly. "Copper, I'm sorry!"

"Not your fault," he said stiffly. "I used Dana and Nickie to accomplish this engagement, but she was reluctant from the beginning." He sighed heavily. "I guess she'll go, now, in spite of everything."

"I don't understand what's going on."

He moved a shoulder impatiently. "She's in love with me," he said roughly, and rammed his hands deeper into his pockets.

"Oh, dear." Jane didn't know what to say. She'd
lashed out at the poor woman, and probably given Lou
a false picture of her relationship with Copper to boot.
They were good friends, almost like brother and sister,
but there had been rumors around Jacobsville for years
that they were secret lovers. Until she married Todd,
that was. Now, she wondered how much Lou had heard
and if she'd believed it. And Jane had brazenly invited
him to supper, ignoring Lou altogether.

She grimaced. "I've done it now, haven't I? I would
have included her in my invitation if I'd had any idea.
I thought she was just tagging along with you on her
lunch hour!"

"I'd better go after her," he said reluctantly.

"It might be best if you didn't," she replied. "She's
hurt. She'll want to be alone for a while, I should think."

"I can't strand her in town." He felt worse than he
could ever remember feeling. "Maybe you're both right,
and this whole thing was a stupid idea."

"If you don't love her, it certainly was," she snapped
at him. "What are you up to? Is it really just to protect
you from a couple of lovesick women? I'm shocked. A
few years ago, you'd have cussed them both to a fare-
thee-well and been done with it."

He didn't reply. His face closed up and his blue eyes
glittered at her. "My reasons are none of your business,"
he said, shutting her out.

Obviously Lou had to mean something to him. Jane
felt even worse. She made a face. "We were very close
once. I thought you could talk to me about anything."

"Anything except Lou," he said shortly.

"Oh." Her eyes were first stunned and then amused.

"You can stop speculating, too," he added irritably, turning away.

"She sounds determined to leave."

"We'll see about that."

Despite Jane's suggestion, he went off toward the department store where Lou had vanished and strode back to the women's rest room. He knew instinctively that she was there. He caught the eye of a female clerk.

"Could you ask Dr. Blakely to come out of there, please?"

"Dr. Blakely?"

"She's so high—" he indicated her height with his hand up to his nose "—blond hair, dark eyes, wearing a beige suit."

"Oh, her! She's a doctor? Really? My goodness, I thought doctors never showed their emotions. She was crying as if her heart would break. Sure, I'll get her for you."

He felt like a dog. He'd made her cry. The thought of Lou, so brave and private a person, with tears in her eyes made him hurt inside. And it had been so unnecessary. If Jane had only kept her pretty mouth shut! She was like family, and she overstepped the bounds sometimes with her comments about how Coltrain should live his life. He'd been more than fond of her once, and he still had a soft spot for her, but it was Lou who was disrupting his whole life.

He leaned against the wall, his legs and arms crossed, and waited. The female clerk reappeared, smiled reassuringly, and went to wait on a customer.

A minute later, a subdued and dignified Lou came out of the small room, her chin up. Her eyes were slightly red, but she didn't look as if she needed any-one's pity.

"I'm ready to go if you are," she said politely.

He searched her face and decided that this wasn't the time for a row. They still had to get lunch and get back to the office.

He turned, leaving her to follow. "I'll stop by one of the hamburger joints and we can get a burger and fries."

"I'll eat mine at the office, if you don't mind," she said wearily. "I'm not in the mood for a crowd."

Neither was he. He didn't argue. He opened the car door and let her in, then he went by the drive-in window of the beef place and they carried lunch back.

Lou went directly into her office and closed the door. She hardly tasted what she was eating. Her heart felt as if it had been burned alive. She knew what Dana meant now. Jane Parker was as much a part of Coltrain's life as his cattle, his practice. No woman, no matter how much she loved him, could ever compete with his love for the former rodeo star.

She'd been living in a fool's paradise, but fortunately there was no harm done. They could say that the so-called "engagement" had been a big joke. Surely Coltrain could get Nickie and Dana out of his hair by simply telling them the truth, that he wasn't interested. God knew, once he got started, he wasn't shy about express-ing his feelings any other time, regardless of who was listening. Which brought to mind the question of why he'd asked her to marry him. He wasn't in love with her. He wanted her. Had that been the reason? Was he getting even with Jane because she'd married and de-serted him? She worried the question until she finished eating. Then her patients kept her occupied for the rest of the day, so that she had no time to think.

JANE HAD WONDERED if she could help undo the damage she'd already done to Copper's life, and at last she came up with a solution. She decided to give a farewell party for Lou. She called Coltrain a few days later to tell him the news.

"Christmas is next week," he said shortly. "And I doubt if she'd come. She only speaks to me when she has to. I can't get near her anymore."

That depressed Jane even more. "Suppose I phone her?" she asked.

"Oh, I know she won't talk to you." He laughed without humor. "We're both in her bad books."

Jane sighed. "Then who can we have talk to her?"

"Try Drew Morris," he said bitterly. "She likes him."

That note in his voice was disturbing. Surely he knew that Drew was still mourning his late wife. If he and Lou were friends, it was nothing more than that, despite any social outings together.

"You think she'd listen to Drew?" she asked.

"Why not?"

"I'll try, then."

"Don't send out any invitations until she gives you an answer," he added. "She's been hurt enough, one way or the other."

"Yes, I know," Jane said gently. "I had no idea, Copper. I really meant well."

"I know that. She doesn't."

"I guess she's heard all the old gossip, too."

He hadn't considered that. "What old gossip?"

"About us," she persisted. "That we had something going until I married Todd."

He smoothed his fingers absently over the receiver. "She might have, at that," he said slowly. "But she must know that—" He stopped dead. She'd have heard plenty from Dana, who had always considered Jane, not her affair with Fielding Blakely, the real reason for their broken engagement. Others in the hospital knew those old rumors, too, and Jane had given Lou the wrong impression of their relationship in the jewelry store.

"I'm right, aren't I?" Jane asked.

"You might be."

"What are you going to do?"

"What can I do?" he asked shortly. "She doesn't really want to marry anyone."

"You said she loves you," she reminded him.

"Yes, and she does. It's the only thing I'm sure of. But she doesn't want to marry me. She's so afraid that she'll become like her mother, blindly accepting faults and abuse without question, all in the name of love."

"Poor girl," she said genuinely. "What a life she must have had."

"I expect it was worse than we'll ever know," he agreed. "Well, call Drew and see if he can get through to her."

"If he can, will you come, too?"

"It would look pretty bad if I didn't, wouldn't it?" he asked dryly. "They'd say we were so antagonistic toward each other that we couldn't even get along for a farewell party. And coming on the heels of our 'engagement,' they'd really have food for thought."

"I'd be painted as the scarlet woman who broke it

up, wouldn't I?" Jane groaned. "Todd would love that! He's still not used to small-town life."

"Maybe Drew can reach her. If he can't, you'll have to cancel it. We can't embarrass her."

"I wouldn't dream of it."

"I know that. Jane, thanks."

"For what?" she asked. "I'm the idiot who got you into this mess in the first place. The least I owe is to try to make amends for what I said to her. I'll let you know what happens."

"Do that."

He went back to work, uncomfortably aware of Lou's calm demeanor. She didn't even look ruffled after all the turmoil. Of course, he remembered that she'd been crying like a lost child in the department store after Jane's faux pas. But that could have been so much more than a broken heart.

She hadn't denied loving him, but could love survive a year of indifference alternating with vicious antagonism, such as he'd given her? Perhaps loving him was a sort of habit that she'd finally been cured of. After all, he'd given her no reason to love him, even to like him. He'd missed most of his chances there. But if Drew could convince her to come to a farewell party, on neutral ground, Coltrain had one last chance to change her mind about him. That was his one hope; the only one he had.

CHAPTER NINE

DREW INVITED LOU to lunch the next day. It was Friday, the week before the office closed for Christmas holidays. Christmas Eve would be on a week from Saturday night, and Jane had changed her mind about dates. She wanted to give the farewell party the following Friday, the day before New Year's Eve. That would, if Lou didn't reconsider her decision, be Lou's last day as Coltrain's partner.

"I'm surprised," Lou told him as they ate quiche at a local restaurant. "You haven't invited me to lunch in a long time. What's on your mind?"

"It could be just on food."

She laughed. "Pull the other one."

"Okay. I'm a delegation of one."

She held her fork poised over the last morsel of quiche on her plate. "From whom?"

"Jane Burke."

She put the fork down, remembering. Her expression hardened. "I have nothing to say to her."

"She knows that. It's why she asked me to talk to you. She got the wrong end of the stick and she's sorry. I'm to make her apologies to you," he added. "But she also wants to do something to make up for what she said to you. She wants to give you a farewell party on the day before New Year's Eve."

She glared at Drew. "I don't want anything to do with any parties given by that woman. I won't go!"

His eyebrows lifted. "Well! You are miffed, aren't you?"

"Accusing me of trying to ruin Jebediah's reputation and destroy his privacy...how dare she! I'm not the one who's being gossiped about in connection with him! And she's married!"

He smiled wickedly. "Lou, you're as red as a beet."

"I'm mad," she said shortly. "That...woman! How dare she!"

"She and Copper are friends. Period. That's all they've ever been. Are you listening?"

"Sure, I'm listening. Now," she added, leaning forward, "tell me he wasn't ever in love with her. Tell me he isn't still in love with her."

He wanted to, but he had no idea of Coltrain's feelings for Jane. He knew that Coltrain had taken her marriage hard, and that he seemed sometimes to talk about her to the exclusion of everyone else. But things had changed in the past few weeks, since the hospital Christmas dance the first week of December.

"You see?" she muttered. "You can't deny it. He may have proposed to me, but it was..."

"Proposed?"

"Didn't you know?" She lifted her coffee cup to her lips and took a sip. "He wanted me to pretend to be engaged to him, just to get Nickie and Dana off his back. Then he decided that we might as well get married for real. He caught me at a weak moment," she added, without details, "and we went to buy an engagement ring. But Jane was there. She was rude to me," she said miserably, "and Jebediah didn't say a word to stop her. In fact, he acted as if I wasn't even there."

"And that was what hurt most, wasn't it?" he queried gently.

"I guess it was. I have no illusions about him, you know," she added with a rueful smile. "He likes kissing me, but he's not in love with me."

"Does he know how you feel?"

She nodded. "I don't hide things well. It would be hard to miss."

He caught her hand and held it gently. "Lou, isn't he worth taking a chance on?" he asked. "You could let Jane throw this party for you, because she badly wants to make amends. Then you could talk to Copper and get him to tell you exactly why he wants to marry you. You might be surprised."

"No, I wouldn't. I know why he wants to marry me," she replied. "But I don't want to get married. I'm crazy about him, that's the truth, but I've seen marriage. I don't want it."

"You haven't seen a good marriage," he emphasized. "Lou, I had one. I had twelve years of almost ethereal happiness. Marriage is what you make of it."

"My mother excused every brutal thing my father did," she said shortly.

"That sort of love isn't love," he said quietly. "It's a form of domination. Don't you know the difference? If she'd loved your father, she'd have stood up to him and tried to help him stop drinking, stop using drugs."

She felt as if her eyes had suddenly been opened. She'd never seen her parents' relationship like that. "But he was terrible to her…"

"Codependence," he said to her. "You must have

studied basic psychology in college. Don't you remember any of it?"

"Yes, but they were my parents!"

"Your parents, anybody, can be part of a dysfunctional family." He smiled at her surprise. "Didn't you know? You grew up in a dysfunctional family, not a normal one. That's why you have such a hard time accepting the idea of marriage." He smoothed her hand with his fingers and smiled. "Lou, I had a normal upbringing. I had a mother and father who doted on me, who supported me and encouraged me. I was loved. When I married, it was a good, solid, happy marriage. They are possible, if you love someone and have things in common, and are willing to compromise."

She studied the wedding ring on Drew's left hand. He still wore it even after being widowed.

"It's possible to be happily married?" she asked, entertaining that possibility for the first time.

"Of course."

"Coltrain doesn't love me," she said.

"Make him."

She laughed. "That's a joke. He hated me from the beginning. I never knew it was because of my father, until I overheard him talking to you. I was surprised later when he was so cool to Dana, because he'd been bitter about her betrayal. But when I found out how close he was to Jane Burke, I guess I gave up entirely. You can't fight a ghost, Drew." She looked up. "And you know it, because no woman will ever be able to come between you and your memories. How would you feel if you found out some woman was crazily in love with you right now?"

He was stunned by the question. "Well, I don't know. I guess I'd feel sorry for her," he admitted.

"Which is probably how Coltrain feels about me, and might even explain why he offered to be engaged to me," she added. "It makes sense, doesn't it?"

"Lou, you don't propose to people out of pity."

"Coltrain might. Or out of revenge, to get back at Jane for marrying someone else. Or to get even with Dana."

"Coltrain isn't that scatty."

"Men are unpredictable when they're in love, aren't they?" she mused. "I wish he loved me, Drew. I'd marry him, with all my doubts and misgivings, in a minute if I thought there was half a chance that he did. But he doesn't. I'd know if he did feel that way. Somehow, I'd know."

He dropped his gaze to their clasped hands. "I'm sorry."

"Me, too. I've been invited to join a practice in Houston. I'm going Monday to speak with them, but they've tentatively accepted me." She lifted her sad face. "I understand that Coltrain is meeting some prospects, too. So I suppose he's finally taken me at my word that I want to leave."

"Don't you know?"

She shrugged. "We don't speak."

"I see." So it was that bad, he thought. Coltrain and Lou had both withdrawn, afraid to take that final step to commitment. She had good reasons, but what were Copper's? he wondered. Did he really feel pity for Lou and now he was sorry he'd proposed? Or was Lou right, and he was still carrying a torch for Jane?

"Jane is a nice woman," he said. "You don't know her, but she isn't the kind of person who enjoys hurting other people. She feels very unhappy about what she said. She wants to make it up to you. Let her. It will be a nice gesture on your part and on hers."

"Dr. Coltrain will come," she muttered.

"He'd better," he said, "or the gossips will say he's glad to be rid of you."

She shook her head. "You can't win for losing."

"That's what I've been trying to tell you. Let Jane give the party. Lou, you'd like her if you got to know her. She's had a hard time of it since the wreck that took her father's life. Just being able to walk again at all is a major milestone for her."

"I remember," she said. And she did, because Coltrain had been out at the ranch every waking minute looking after the woman.

"Will you do it?"

She took a long breath and let it out. "All right."

"Great! I'll call Jane the minute I get home and tell her. You won't regret it. Lou, I wish you'd hold off about that spot in Houston."

She shook her head. "No, I won't do that. I have to get away. A fresh start is what I need most. I'm sure I won't be missed. After all, Dr. Coltrain didn't want me in the first place."

He grimaced, because they both knew her present circumstances were Drew's fault. Saying again that he meant well wouldn't do a bit of good.

"Thanks for lunch," she said, remembering her manners.

"That was my pleasure. You know I'll be going to Maryland to have Christmas with my in-laws, as usual. So Merry Christmas, if I don't see you before I leave."

"You, too, Drew," she said with genuine affection.

IT WASN'T UNTIL the next Thursday afternoon that the office closed early for Christmas holidays—if Friday and Monday, added to the weekend, qualified as holidays—that Coltrain came into Lou's office. Lou had been to Houston and formally applied for a position in the family practitioner group. She'd also been accepted, but she hadn't been able to tell Coltrain until today, because he'd been so tied up with preholiday surgeries and emergencies.

He looked worn-out, she thought. There were new lines in his lean face, and his eyes were bloodshot from lack of sleep. He looked every year of his age.

"You couldn't just tell me, you had to put it in writing?" he asked, holding up the letter she'd written him.

"It's legal this way," she said politely. "I'm very grateful for the start you gave me."

He didn't say anything. He looked at the letter from the Houston medical group. It was written on decal-edge bond, very expensive, and the lettering on the letterhead was embossed.

"I know this group," he said. "They're high-powered city physicians, and they practice supermarket medicine. Do you realize what that means? You'll be expected to spend five minutes or less with every patient. A buzzer will sound to alert you when that time is up. As the most junior partner, you'll get all the dirty jobs, all the odd jobs, and you'll be expected to stay on call on weekends and holidays for the first year. Or until they can get another partner, more junior than you are."

"I know. They told me that." They had. It had depressed her no end.

He folded his arms across his chest and leaned back

against the wall, his stethoscope draped around his neck. "We haven't talked."

"There's nothing to say," she replied, and she smiled kindly. "I notice that Nickie and Dana have become very businesslike, even to me. I'd say you were over the hump."

"I asked you to marry me," he said. "I was under the impression that you'd agreed and that was why we were picking out a ring."

The memory of that afternoon hurt. She lowered her eyes to the clipboard she held against her breasts. "You said it was to get Nickie and Dana off your back."

"You didn't want to get married at all," he reminded her.

"I still don't."

He smiled coldly. "And you're not in love with me?"

She met his gaze levelly. This was no time to back down. "I was infatuated with you," she said bluntly. "Perhaps it was because you were out of reach."

"You wanted me. Explain that."

"I'm human," she told him, blushing a little. "You wanted me, too, so don't look so superior."

"I hear you're coming to Jane's party."

"Drew talked me into it." She smoothed her fingers over the cold clipboard. "You and Jane can't help it," she said. "I understand."

"Damn it! You sound just like her husband!"

She was shocked at the violent whip of his deep voice. He was furious, and it showed.

"Everyone knows you were in love with her," she faltered.

"Yes, I was," he admitted angrily, and for the first time. "But she's married now, Lou."

"I know. I'm sorry," she said gently. "I really am. It must be terrible for you...."

He threw up his hands. "My God!"

"It's not as if you could help it, either of you," she continued sadly.

He just shook his head. "I can't get through to you, can I?" he asked with a bite in his deep voice. "You won't listen."

"There's really nothing to say," she told him. "I hope you've found someone to replace me when I go."

"Yes, I have. He's a recent graduate of Johns Hopkins. He wanted to do some rural practice before he made up his mind where he wanted to settle." He gazed at her wan face. "He starts January 2."

She nodded. "That's when I start, in Houston." She tugged the clipboard closer.

"We could spend Christmas together," he suggested.

She shook her head. She didn't speak. She knew words would choke her.

His shoulders rose and fell. "As you wish," he said quietly. "Have a good Christmas, then."

"Thanks. You, too."

She knew that she sounded choked. She couldn't help herself. She'd burned her bridges. She hadn't meant to. Perhaps she had a death wish. She'd read and studied about people who were basically self-destructive, who destroyed relationships before they could begin, who found ways to sabotage their own success and turn it to failure. Perhaps she'd become such a person, due to her upbringing. Either way, it didn't matter now. She'd given up Coltrain and was leaving Jacobsville. Now all she had to do was survive Jane's little going-away party and get out of town.

Coltrain paused in the doorway, turning his head back toward her. His eyes were narrow, curious, assessing. She didn't look as if the decision she'd made had lifted her spirits any. And the expression on her face wasn't one of triumph or pleasure.

"If Jane hadn't turned up in the jewelry store, would you have gone through with it?" he asked abruptly.

Her hands tightened on the clipboard. "I'll never know."

He leaned against the doorjamb. "You don't want to hear this, but I'm going to say it. Jane and I were briefly more than friends. It was mostly on my side. She loves her husband and wants nothing to do with anyone else. Whatever I felt for her is in the past now."

"I'm glad, for your sake," she said politely.

"Not for yours?" he asked.

She bit her lower lip, worriedly.

He let his blue gaze fall to her mouth. It lingered there so long that her heart began to race, and she couldn't quite breathe properly. His gaze lifted then, to catch hers, and she couldn't break it. Her toes curled inside her sensible shoes, her heart ran wild. She had to fight the urge to go to him, to press close to his lean, fit body and beg him to kiss her blind.

"You think you're over me?" he drawled softly, so that his voice didn't carry. "In a pig's eye, Doctor!"

He pushed away from the door and went on his way, whistling to himself as he went down the corridor to his next patient.

Lou, having given herself away, muttered under her breath and went to read the file on her next patient. But she waited until her hands stopped shaking before she opened the examining room door and went in.

THEY CLOSED UP the office. Coltrain had been called away at the last minute to an emergency at the hospital, which made things easier for Lou. She'd be bound to run into him while she was making her rounds, but that was an occupational hazard, and there would be plenty of other people around. She wouldn't have to worry about being alone with him. Or so she thought.

When she finished her rounds late in the afternoon, she stopped by the nurses' station to make sure they'd been able to contact a new patient's husband, who had been out of town when she was admitted.

"Yes, we found him," the senior nurse said with a smile. "In fact, he's on his way over here right now."

"Thanks," she said.

"No need. It goes with the job," she was assured.

She started back down the hall to find Coltrain coming from the emergency room. He looked like a thundercloud, all bristling bad temper. His red hair flamed under the corridor lights, and his blue eyes were sparking.

He caught Lou's arm, turned and drew her along with him without saying a word. People along the corridor noticed and grinned amusedly.

"What in the world are you doing?" she asked breathlessly.

"I want you to tell a—" he bit off the word he wanted to say "—*gentleman* in the emergency room that I was in the office all morning."

She gaped at him, but he didn't stop or even slow down. He dragged her into a cubicle where a big, angry-looking blond man was sitting on the couch having his hand bandaged.

Coltrain let Lou go and nodded curtly toward the other man. "Well, tell him!" He shot the words at Lou.

She gave him a stunned glance, but after a minute, she turned back to the tall man and said, "Dr. Coltrain was in the office all morning. He couldn't have escaped if he'd wanted to, because we had twice our usual number of patients, anticipating that we'd be out of the office over the holidays."

The blond man relaxed a little, but he was still glaring at Coltrain when there was a small commotion in the corridor and Jane Burke came in the door, harassed and frightened.

"Todd! Cherry said that you'd had an accident and she had to call an ambulance...!" She grabbed the blond man's hand and fought tears. "I thought you were killed!"

"Not hardly," he murmured. He drew her head to his shoulder and held her gently. "Silly woman." He chuckled. "I'm all right. I slammed the car door on my hand. It isn't even broken, just cut and bruised."

Jane looked at Coltrain. "Is that true?"

He nodded, still irritated at Burke.

Jane looked from him to Lou and back to her husband. "Now what's wrong?" she asked heavily.

Todd just glowered. He didn't say anything.

"You and I had been meeting secretly this morning at your house, while he and Cherry were away," Coltrain informed her. "Because the mailman saw a gray Jaguar sitting in your driveway."

"Yes, he did," Jane said shortly. "It belongs to the new divisional manager of the company that makes my signature line of leisure wear. *She* has a gray Jaguar exactly like Copper's."

Burke's hard cheekbones flushed a little.

"That's why you slammed the door on your hand, right?" she muttered, "Because the mailman is our wrangler's sister and he couldn't wait to tell you what your wife was doing behind your back! He'll be lucky if I don't have him for lunch!"

The flush got worse. "Well, I didn't know!" Todd snapped.

Coltrain slammed his clipboard down hard on the examination couch at Burke's hip. "That does it, by God," he began hotly.

He looked threatening and Burke stood up, equally angry.

"Now, Copper," Jane interrupted. "This isn't the place."

Burke didn't agree, but he'd already made a fool of himself once. He wasn't going to try for twice. He glanced at Lou, who looked as miserable as he felt. "They broke up your engagement, I understand," he added. "Pity they didn't just marry each other to begin with!"

Lou studied his glittery eyes for a moment, oblivious to the other two occupants of the cubicle. It was amazing how quickly things fell into place in her mind, and at once. She leaned against the examination couch. "Dr. Coltrain is the most decent man I know," she told Todd Burke. "He isn't the sort to do things in an underhanded way, and he doesn't sneak around. If you trusted your wife, Mr. Burke, you wouldn't listen to old gossip or invented tales. Small towns are hotbeds of rumor, that's normal. But only an idiot believes everything he hears."

Coltrain's eyebrows had arched at the unexpected defense.

"Thanks, Lou," Jane said quietly. "That's more than

I deserve from you, but thank you." She turned back to her husband. "She's absolutely right," Jane told her husband. She was mad, too, and it showed. "I married you because I loved you. I still love you, God knows why! You won't even listen when I tell you the truth. You'd rather cling to old gossip about Copper and me."

Lou blushed scarlet, because she could have been accused of the same thing.

She wouldn't look at Coltrain at all.

"Well, here's something to take your mind off your foul suspicions," Jane continued furiously. "I was going to wait to tell you, but you can hear it now. I'm pregnant! And, no, it isn't Copper's!"

Burke gasped. "Jane!" He exploded, his injured hand forgotten as he moved forward to pull her hungrily into his arms. "Jane, is it true?"

"Yes, it's true," she muttered. "Oh, you idiot! You idiot…!"

He was kissing her, so she had to stop talking. Lou, a little embarrassed, edged out of the cubicle and moved away, only to find Coltrain right beside her as she left the emergency room.

"Maybe that will satisfy him," he said impatiently. "Thank you for the fierce defense," he added. "Hell of a pity that you didn't believe a word you were saying!"

She stuck her hands into her slacks pockets. "I believe she loves her husband," she said quietly. "And I believe that there's nothing going on between the two of you."

"Thanks for nothing."

"Your private life is your own business, Dr. Coltrain, none of mine," she said carelessly. "I'm already a memory."

"By your own damn choice."

The sarcasm cut deep. They walked through the parking lot to the area reserved for physicians and surgeons, and she stopped beside her little Ford.

"Drew loved his wife very much," she said. "He never got over losing her. He still spends holidays with his in-laws because he feels close to her that way, even though she's dead. I asked him how he'd feel if he knew that a woman was in love with him. Know what he said? He said that he'd pity her."

"Do you have a point?" he asked.

"Yes." She turned and looked up at him. "You haven't really gotten over Jane Burke yet. You have nothing to offer anyone else until you do. That's why I wouldn't marry you."

His brows drew together while he searched her face. He didn't say a word. He couldn't.

"She's part of your life," she continued. "A big part of it. You can't let go of the past, even if she can. I understand. Maybe someday you'll come to terms with it. Until you do, it's no good trying to be serious about anyone else."

He jiggled the change in his pockets absently. His broad shoulders rose and fell. "She was just starting into rodeo when I came back here as an intern in the hospital. She fell and they brought her to me. We had an instant rapport. I started going to watch her ride, she went out with me when I was free. She was special. Her father and I became friends as well, and when I bought my ranch, he helped me learn the ropes and start my herd. Jane and I have known each other a long, long time."

"I know that." She studied a button on his dark

jacket. "She's very pretty, and Drew says she has a kind nature."

"Yes."

Her shoulders rose and fell. "I have to go."

He put out a lean hand and caught her shoulder, preventing her from turning away. "I never told her about my father."

She was surprised. She didn't think he had any secrets from Jane. She lifted her eyes and found him staring at her intently, as if he were trying to work out a puzzle.

"Curious, isn't it?" he mused aloud. "There's another curious thing, but I'm not ready to share that just yet."

He moved closer and she wanted to move away, to stop him... No, she didn't. His head bent and his mouth closed on hers, brushing, lightly probing. She yielded without a protest, her arms sliding naturally around his waist, her mouth opening to the insistence of his lips. He kissed her, leaning his body heavily on hers, so that she could feel the metal of the car at her back and his instant, explosive response to her soft warmth.

She made a sound, and he smiled against her lips.

"What?" He bit off the words against her lips.

"It's...very...public," she breathed.

He lifted his head and looked around. The parking lot was dotted with curious onlookers. So was the emergency room ramp.

"Hell," he said irritably, drawing away from her. "Come home with me," he suggested, still breathing roughly.

She shook her head before her willpower gave out. "I can't."

"Coward," he drawled.

She flushed. "All right, I want to," she said fiercely. "But I won't, so there. Damn you! It isn't fair to play on people's weaknesses!"

"Sure it is," he said, correcting her. He grinned at her maddeningly. "Come on, be daring. Take a chance! Risk everything on a draw of the cards. You live like a scientist, every move debated, planned. For once in your life, be reckless!"

"I'm not the reckless sort," she said as she fought to get her breath back. "And you shouldn't be, either." She glanced ruefully toward the emergency room exit, where a tall blond man and a pretty blond woman were standing, watching. "Was it for her benefit?" she added, nodding toward them.

He glanced over her shoulder. "I didn't know they were there," he said genuinely.

She laughed. "Sure." She pulled away from him, unlocked her car, got in and drove off. Her legs were wobbly, but they'd stop shaking eventually. Maybe the rest of her would, too. Coltrain was driving her crazy. She was very glad that she'd be leaving town soon.

CHAPTER TEN

IT DIDN'T HELP that the telephone rang a few minutes after Lou got home.

"Still shaky, are we?" Coltrain drawled.

She fumbled to keep from dropping the receiver. "What do you want?" she faltered.

"An invitation to Christmas dinner, of course," he said. "I don't want to sit in front of the TV all day eating TV dinners."

She was still angry at him for making a public spectacle of them for the second time. The hospital would buzz with the latest bit of gossip for weeks. At least she wouldn't have long to put up with it.

"TV dinners are good for you," she said pointedly.

"Home cooking is better. I'll make the dressing and a fruit salad if you'll do turkey and rolls."

She hesitated. She wanted badly to spend that day with him, but in the long run, it would make things harder.

"Come on," he coaxed in a silky tone. "You know you want to. If you're leaving town after the first, it will be one of the last times we spend together. What have you got to lose?"

My self-respect, my honor, my virtue, my pride, she thought. But aloud, she said, "I suppose it wouldn't hurt."

He chuckled. "No, it wouldn't. I'll see you at eleven on Christmas morning."

He hung up before she could change her mind. "I don't want to," she told the telephone. "This is a terrible mistake, and I'm sure that I'll regret it for the rest of my life."

After a minute, she realized that she was talking to a piece of equipment. She shook her head sadly. Coltrain was driving her out of her mind.

SHE WENT TO the store early on Christmas Eve and bought a turkey. The girl at the check-out stand was one of her patients. She grinned as she totaled the price of the turkey, the bottle of wine and the other groceries Lou had bought to cook Christmas dinner.

"Expecting company, Doctor?" she teased.

Lou flushed, aware that the woman behind her was one of Coltrain's patients. "No. No. I'm going to cook the turkey and freeze what I don't eat."

"Oh." The girl sounded disappointed.

"Going to drink all that wine alone, too?" the woman behind her asked wickedly. "And you a doctor!"

Lou handed over the amount the cashier asked for. "I'm not on duty on Christmas Day," she said irritably. "Besides, I cook with wine!"

"You won't cook with that," the cashier noted. She held up the bottle and pointed to the bottom of the label. It stated, quite clearly, Nonalcoholic Wine.

Lou had grabbed the bottle from the wrong aisle. But it worked to her advantage. She grinned at the woman behind her, who looked embarrassed.

The clerk packaged up her purchases and Lou pushed

them out to her car. At least she'd gotten around that ticky little episode.

Back home, she put the turkey on to bake and made rolls from scratch. Nonalcoholic wine wasn't necessarily a bad thing, she told herself. She could serve it at dinner without having to worry about losing her wits with Coltrain.

The weather was sunny and nice, and the same was predicted for the following day. A white Christmas was out of the question, of course, but she wondered what it would be like to have snow on the ground.

She turned on the television that night, when the cooking was done and everything was put into the refrigerator for the next day. Curled up in her favorite armchair in old jeans, a sweatshirt and in her sock feet, she was relaxing after her housecleaning and cooking when she heard a car drive up.

It was eight o'clock and she wasn't on call. She frowned as she went to the front door. A gray Jaguar was sitting in the driveway and as she looked, a tall, redheaded man in jeans and a sweatshirt and boots got out of the car carrying a big box.

"Open the door," he called as he mounted the steps.

"What's that?" she asked curiously.

"Food and presents."

She was surprised. She hadn't expected him tonight and she fumbled and faltered as she let him in and closed the door again.

He unloaded the box in the kitchen. "Salad." He indicated a covered plastic bowl. "Dressing." He indicated a foil-covered pan. "And a chocolate pound cake. No, I didn't make it," he added when she opened her mouth.

"I bought it. I can't bake a cake. Is there room in the fridge for this?"

"You could have called to ask before you brought it," she reminded him.

He grinned. "If I'd phoned, you'd have listened to the answering machine and when you knew it was me, you'd have pretended not to be home."

She flushed. He was right. It was disconcerting to have someone so perceptive second-guessing her every move. "Yes, there's room."

She opened the refrigerator door and helped him fit his food in.

He went back to the big box and pulled out two packages. "One for me to give you—" he held up one "—and one for you to give me."

She glared at him. "I got you a present," she muttered.

His eyebrows shot up. "You did?"

Her lower lip pulled down. "Just because I didn't plan to spend Christmas with you didn't mean I was low enough not to get you something."

"You didn't give it to me at the office party," he recalled.

She flushed. "You didn't give me anything at the office party, either."

He smiled. "I was saving it for tomorrow."

"So was I," she returned.

"Can I put these under the tree?"

She shrugged. "Sure."

Curious, she followed him into the living room. The tree was live and huge; it covered the whole corner and reached almost to the nine-foot ceiling. It was full of lights and decorations and under it a big metal electric train sat on its wide tracks waiting for power to move it.

"I didn't notice that when I was here before," he said, delighted by the train. He stooped to look at it more closely. "This is an American Flyer by Lionel!" he exclaimed. "You've had this for a while, haven't you?"

"It's an antique," she recalled. "My mother got it for me." She smiled. "I love trains. I have two more sets and about a mile of track in a box in the closet, but it seemed sort of pointless to set all those trains up with just me to run them."

He looked up at her with sparkling eyes. "Which closet are they in?" he asked in a conspiratorial tone.

"The hall closet." Her eyes brightened. "You like trains?"

"Do I like trains? I have HO scale, N scale, G scale and three sets of new Lionel O scale trains at home."

She gasped. "Oh, my goodness!"

"That's what I say. Come on!"

He led her to the hall closet, opened it, found the boxes and started handing them out to her.

Like two children, they sat on the floor putting tracks together with switches and accessories for the next two hours. Lou made coffee and they had it on the floor while they made connections and set up the low wooden scale buildings that Lou had bought to go with the sets.

When they finished, she turned on the power. The wooden buildings were lit. So were the engines and the cabooses and several passenger cars.

"I love to sit and watch them run in the dark," she said breathlessly as he turned on the switch box and the trains began to move. "It's like watching over a small village with the people all snug in their houses."

"I know what you mean." He sprawled, chest down, on the floor beside her to watch the trains chug and whistle and run around the various tracks. "God, this is great! I had no idea you liked trains!"

"Same here," she said, chuckling. "I always felt guilty about having them, in a way. Somewhere out there, there must be dozens of little kids who would do anything for just one train and a small track to run it on. And here I've got all this and I never play with it."

"I know how it is. I don't even have a niece or nephew to share mine with."

"When did you get your first train?"

"When I was eight. My granddad bought it for me so he could play with it," he added with a grin. "He couldn't afford a big set, of course, but I didn't care. I never had so much fun." His face hardened at the memories. "When Dad took me to Houston, I missed the train almost as much as I missed my granddad and grandmother. It was a long time before I got back there." He shrugged. "The train still worked by then, though, and it was more fun when the threat of my father was gone."

She rolled onto her side, peering at him in the dim light from the tree and the small village. "You said that you never told Jane about your father."

"I didn't," he replied. "It was something I was deeply ashamed of for a long time."

"Children do what they're told, whether it's right or wrong," she reminded him. "You can't be held responsible for everything."

"I knew it was wrong," he agreed. "But my father was a brutal man, and when I was a young boy, I was afraid of him." His head turned. He smiled at her. "You'd understand that."

"Yes."

He rested his chin on his hands and watched the trains wistfully. "I took my medicine—juvenile hall and years of probation. But people helped me to change. I wanted to pass that on, to give back some of the care that had been given to me. That's why I went into medicine. I saw it as an opportunity to help people."

"And you have," she said. Her eyes traced the length of his fit, hard-muscled body lovingly. He was so different away from the office. She'd never known him like this, and so soon, it would all be over. She'd go away. She wouldn't see him again. Her sad eyes went back to the trains. The sound of them was like a lullaby, comforting, delightful to the ears.

"We need railroad caps and those wooden whistles that sound like old steam engines," he remarked.

She smiled. "And railroad gloves and crossing guards and flashing guard lights."

"If there was a hobby shop nearby, we could go and get them. But everything would be closed up on Christmas Eve, anyway."

"I guess so."

He pursed his lips, without looking at her. "If you stayed, after the New Year, we could pool our layouts and have one big one. We could custom-design our own buildings and bridges, and we could go in together and buy one of those big transformer outfits that runs dozens of accessories."

She was thinking more of spending that kind of time with Coltrain than running model engines, but it sounded delightful all the same. She sighed wistfully.

I would have enjoyed that," she murmured. "But I've signed a new contract. I have to go."

"Contracts can be broken," he said. "There's always an escape clause if you look hard enough."

Her hips shifted on the rug they were lying on. "Too many people are gossiping about us already," she said. "Even at the grocery store, the clerk noticed that I bought a turkey and wine and the lady behind me said I couldn't possibly be going to drink it alone."

"You bought wine?" he mused.

"Nonalcoholic wine," she said, correcting him.

He chuckled. "On purpose?"

"Not really. I picked up the wrong bottle. But it was just as well. The lady behind me was making snide comments about it." She sighed. "It rubbed me the wrong way. She wouldn't have known that my father was an alcoholic."

"How did he manage to keep his job?"

"He had willing young assistants who covered for him. And finally, the hospital board forced him into early retirement. He *had* been a brilliant surgeon," she reminded him. "It isn't easy to destroy a career like that."

"It would have been better than letting him risk other people's lives."

"But he didn't," she replied. "Someone was always there to bail him out."

"Lucky, wasn't he, not to have been hit with a multi-million-dollar malpractice suit."

He reached out and threw the automatic switches to change the trains to another set of tracks. "Nice," he commented.

"Yes, isn't it? I love trains. If I had more leisure time,

I'd do this every day. I'm glad we're not on call th.
weekend. How did you manage it?"

"Threats and bribery," he drawled. "We both worked
last Christmas holidays, remember?"

"I guess we did. At each other's throats," she recalled demurely.

"Oh, that was necessary," he returned, rolling lazily
onto his side and propping on an elbow. "If I hadn't
snapped at you constantly, I'd have been laying you
down on examination couches every other day."

"Wh...what?" she stammered.

He reached out and brushed back a long strand of
blond hair from her face. "You backed away every time
I came close to you," he said quietly. "It was all that
saved you. I've wanted you for a long, long time, Dr.
Blakely, and I've fought it like a madman."

"You were in love with Jane Parker," she said.

"Not for a long time," he said. He traced her cheek
lightly. "The way I felt about her was a habit. It was one
I broke when she married Todd Burke. Although, like
you, he seems to think Jane and I were an item even
after they married. He's taken a lot of convincing. So
have you."

She moved uncomfortably. "Everyone talked about
you and Jane, not just me."

"I know. Small communities have their good points
and their bad points." His finger had reached her mouth.
He was exploring it blatantly.

"Could you...not do that, please?" she asked unsteadily.

"Why? You like it. So do I." He moved closer, easing
one long, hard-muscled leg over hers to stay her as he

...ifted so that she lay on her back, looking up at him in the dim light.

"I can feel your heart beating right through your rib cage," he remarked with his mouth poised just above hers. "I can hear your breath fluttering." His hand slid blatantly right down over her breast, pausing there to tease its tip into a hard rise. "Feel that?" he murmured, bending. "Your body likes me."

She opened her mouth, but no words escaped the sudden hard, warm pressure of his lips. She stiffened, but only for a few seconds. It was Christmas Eve and she loved him. There was no defense; none at all.

He seemed to know that, because he wasn't insistent or demanding. He lay, just kissing her, his lips tender as they moved against hers, his hand still gently caressing her body.

"We both know," he whispered, "why your body makes every response it does to the stimuli of my touch. But what no one really understands is why we both enjoy it so much."

"Cause...and effect?" she suggested, gasping when his hand found its way under the sweatshirt and the lacy bra she was wearing to her soft flesh.

He shook his head. "I don't think so. Reach behind you and unfasten this," he added gently, tugging on the elastic band.

She did as he asked, feeling brazen.

"That's better." He traced over her slowly, his eyes on her face while he explored every inch of her above the waist. "Can you give this up?" he asked seriously.

"Wh...what?"

"Can you give it up?" he replied. "You aren't responsive to other men, or you wouldn't still be in your present pristine state. You allow me liberties that I'm certain you've never permitted any other man." He cupped her blatantly and caressed her. She arched, shivering. "You see?" he asked quietly. "You love my touch. I can give you something that you've apparently never experienced. Do you think you can find it with someone else, Lou?"

She felt his mouth cover hers. She didn't have enough breath to answer him, although the answer was certainly in the negative. She couldn't bear the thought of letting someone else be this intimate with her. She looped her arms around his neck and only sighed jerkily when he moved, easing his length against her, his legs between both of hers, so that when his hips pressed down again, she could feel every hardening line of his body.

"Jebediah," she moaned, and she wasn't certain if she was protesting or pleading.

His mouth found her closed eyelids and tasted the helpless tears of pleasure that rained from them. His hips shifted and she jerked at the surge of pleasure.

He felt it, too, like a throbbing ache. "We're good together," he whispered. "Even like this. Can you imagine how it would feel to lie naked under me like this?"

She cried out, burying her face in his neck.

His lips traced her eyelashes, his tongue tasted them. But his body lay very still over hers, not moving, not insisting. Her nails dug into his shoulders as she felt her control slipping away.

But he still had his own control. He soothed her, every soft kiss undemanding and tender. But he didn't move away.

"A year," he whispered. "And we knew nothing about each other, nothing at all." He nibbled her lips, smiling hen they trembled. "Trains and old movies, opera and cooking and horseback riding. We have more in common than I ever dreamed."

She had to force her body to lie still. She wanted to wrap her legs tight around him and kiss him until she stopped aching.

He seemed to know it, because his hips moved in a sensual caress that made her hands clench at his shoulders. "No fear of the unknown?" he whispered wickedly. "No virginal terror?"

"I'm a doctor." She choked out the words.

"So am I."

"I mean, I know…what to expect."

He chuckled. "No, you don't. You only know the mechanics of it. You don't know that you're going to crave almost more than I can give you, or that at the last minute you're going to sob like a hurt child."

She was too far gone to be embarrassed. "I don't have anything," she said miserably.

"Anything…?" He probed gently.

"To use."

"Oh. That." He chuckled and kissed her again, so tenderly that she felt cherished. "You won't need it tonight. I don't think babies should be born out of wedlock. Do you?"

She wasn't thinking. "Well, no. What does that have to do…with this?"

"Lou!"

She felt her cheeks burn. "Oh! You mean…!"

He laughed outrageously. "You've really gone off the deep end, haven't you?" he teased. "When people make love, the woman might get pregnant," he explained in a whisper. "Didn't you listen to the biology lectures?"

She hit him. "Of course I did! I wasn't thinking. Jeb!"

He was closer than he'd ever been and she was shivering, lost, helpless as she felt him in a burning, aching intimacy that only made it all worse.

He pressed her close and then rolled away, while he could. "God, we're explosive!" he said huskily, lying very still on his belly. "You're going to have to marry me soon, Lou. Very soon."

She was sitting up, holding her knees to her chest, trying to breathe. It had never been that bad. She said so, without realizing that she'd spoken aloud.

"It will get worse, too," he said heavily. "I want you. I've never wanted you so much."

"But, Jane…"

He was laughing, very softly. He wasn't angry anymore. He rolled over and sat up beside her. He turned her face up to his. "I broke it off with Jane," he said gently. "Do you want to know why, now?"

"You…you did?"

He nodded.

"You never said that you ended it."

"There was no reason to. You wouldn't let me close enough to find out if we had anything going for us, and it didn't seem to matter what I said, you wanted to believe that I was out of my mind over Jane."

"Everyone said you were," she muttered.

He lifted an eyebrow. "I'm not everyone."

"I know." She reached out hesitantly and touched him. It was earthshaking, that simple act. She touched his hair and his face and then his lean, hard mouth. A funny smile drew up her lips.

"Don't stop there," he murmured, drawing her free and down to his sweatshirt.

Her heart jumped. She looked at him uncertainly.

"I won't let you seduce me," he mused. "Does that make you feel more confident?"

"It was pretty bad a few minutes ago," she said seriously. "I don't want... Well, to hurt you."

"This won't," he said. "Trust me."

"I suppose I must," she admitted. "Or I'd have left months ago for another job."

"That makes sense."

He guided her hand under the thick, white fabric and drew it up until her fingers settled in the thick, curling hair that covered his chest. But it wasn't enough. She wanted to look...

There was just enough light so that he could see what she wanted in her expression. With a faint smile, he pulled the sweatshirt off and tossed it to one side.

She stared. He was beautiful like that, she thought dizzily, with broad shoulders and muscular arms. His chest was covered by a thick, wide wedge of reddish-gold hair that ran down to the buckle of his belt.

He reached for her, lifting her over him so that they were sitting face-to-face, joined where their bodies forked. She shivered at the stark intimacy, because she could feel every muscle, almost every cell of him.

"It gets better," he said softly. He reached down and found the hem of her own sweatshirt. Seconds later, that and her bra joined his sweatshirt on the floor. He looked down at her, savoring the hard peaks that rose like rubies from the whiteness of her breasts. Then he drew her to him and enveloped her against him, so that they were skin against skin. And he shivered, too, this time.

Her hands smoothed over his back, savoring his warm muscles. She searched for his mouth and for the first time, she kissed him. But even though it was sensual, and she could feel him wanting her, there was tenderness between them, not lust.

He groaned as his body surged against her, and then he laughed at the sudden heat of it.

"Jeb?" she whispered at his lips.

"It's all right," he said. "We won't go all the way. Kiss me again."

She did, clinging, and the world rocked around them.

"I love you," she murmured brokenly. "So much!"

His mouth bit into hers hungrily, his arms contracted. For a few seconds, it was as if electricity fused them together. Finally he was able to lift his lips, and his hands caught her hips to keep them still.

"Sorry," she said demurely.

"Oh, I like it," he replied ruefully. "But we're getting in a bit over our heads."

He lifted her away and stood up, pulling her with him. They looked at each other for a long moment before he handed her things to her and pulled his sweatshirt back on.

He watched the trains go around while she replaced her disheveled clothing. Then, with his hands in his pockets, he glanced down at her.

"That's why I broke up with Jane," he said matter-of-factly.

She was jealous, angry. "Because she wouldn't go all the way with you?"

He chuckled. "No. Because I didn't want her sexually."

She watched the trains and counted the times they

crossed the joined tracks. Her mind must not be working. "What did you say?" she asked politely, turning to him.

"I said I was never able to want Jane sexually," he said simply. "To put it simply, she couldn't arouse me."

CHAPTER ELEVEN

"A WOMAN CAN arouse any man if she tries hard enough," she said pointedly.

"Maybe so," he said, smiling, "but Jane just never interested me like that. It was too big a part of marriage to take a chance on, so I gradually stopped seeing her. Burke came along, and before any of us knew it, she was married. But I was her security blanket after the accident, and it was hard for her to let go. You remember how she depended on me."

She nodded. Even at the time, it had hurt.

"But apparently she and her husband have more than a platonic relationship, if their forthcoming happy event is any indication," he said, chuckling. "And I'm delighted for them."

"I never dreamed that it was like that for you, with her," she said, dazed. "I mean, you and I...!"

"Yes, indeed, you and I," he agreed, nodding. "I touch you and it's like a shot of lightning in my veins. I get drunk on you."

"So do I, on you," she confessed. "But there's a difference, isn't there? I mean, you just want me."

"Do I?" he asked gently. "Do I really just want you? Could lust be as tender as this? Could simple desire explain the way we are together?"

"I love you," she said slowly.

"Yes," he said, his eyes glittering at her. "And I love you, Lou," he added quietly.

Dreams came true. She hadn't known. Her eyes were full of wonder as she looked at him and saw them in his own eyes. It was Christmas, a time of miracles, and here was one.

He didn't speak. He just looked at her. After a minute, he picked up the two parcels he'd put under the tree and handed them to her.

"But it's not Christmas," she protested.

"Yes, it is. Open them."

She only hesitated for a minute, because the curiosity was too great. She opened the smallest one and inside was a gray jeweler's box. With a quick glance at him, she opened it, to find half a key chain inside. She felt her heart race like a watch. It was half of a heart, in pure gold.

"Now the other one," he said, taking the key chain while she fumbled the paper off the second present.

Inside that box was the other half of the heart.

"Now put them together," he instructed.

She did, her eyes magnetized to the inscription. It was in French: *plus que hier, moins que demain.*

"Can you read it?" he asked softly.

"It says—" she had to stop and clear her throat "—more than yesterday, less than tomorrow."

"Which is how much I love you," he said. "I meant to ask you again tomorrow morning to marry me," he said. "But this is as good a time as any for you to say yes. I know you're afraid of marriage. But I love you and you love me. We've got enough in common to keep us together even after all the passion burns out, if it ever does. We'll work out something about your job and children. I'm not your father and you're not your mother. Take a chance, Lou. Believe me, there's very little risk that we won't make it together."

She hadn't spoken. She had both halves of the key chain in her hands and she was looking at them, amazed that he would have picked something so sentimental and romantic for a Christmas gift. He hadn't known if he could get her to stay or not, but he would have shown her his heart all the same. It touched her as a more expensive present wouldn't have.

"When did you get them?" she asked through a dry throat.

"After you left the jeweler's," he said surprisingly. "I believe in miracles," he added gently. "I see incredible things every day. I'm hoping for another one, right now."

She raised her eyes. Even in the dim light, he could see the sparkle of tears, the hope, the pleasure, the disbelief in her face.

"Yes?" he asked softly.

She couldn't manage the word. She nodded, and the next instant, she was in his arms, against him, close and safe and warm while his mouth ravished her lips.

It was a long time before he had enough to satisfy him, even momentarily. He wrapped her up tightly and rocked her in his arms, barely aware of the train chugging along at their feet. His arms were faintly unsteady and his voice, when he laughed, was husky and deep.

"My God, I thought I was going to lose you." He ground out the words. "I didn't know what to do, what to say, to keep you here."

"All you ever had to say was that you loved me," she whispered. "I would have taken any risk for it."

His arms tightened. "Didn't you know, you blind bat?"

"No, I didn't! I don't read minds, and you never said—!"

His mouth covered hers again, stopping the words. He laughed against her breath, anticipating arguments over the years that would be dealt with in exactly this way, as she gave in to him generously, headlong in her response, clinging as if she might die without his mouth on hers.

"No long engagement," he groaned against her mouth. "I can't stand it!"

"Neither can I," she admitted. "Next week?"

"Next week!" He kissed her again. "And I'm not going home tonight."

She laid her cheek against his chest, worried.

He smoothed her hair. "We won't make love," he assured her. "But you'll sleep in my arms. I can't bear to be parted from you again."

"Oh, Jeb," she whispered huskily. "That's the sweetest thing to say!"

"Don't you feel it, too?" he asked knowingly.

"Yes. I don't want to leave you, either."

He chuckled with the newness of belonging to someone. It was going to be, he decided, the best marriage of all time. He looked down into her eyes and saw years and years of happiness ahead of them. He said so. She didn't answer him. She reached up, and her lips said it for her.

THE GOING-AWAY PARTY that Jane Burke threw for Lou became a congratulatory party, because it fell on the day after Coltrain and Lou were married.

They almost stayed at home, so wrapped up in the ecstasy of their first lovemaking that they wouldn't even get out of bed the next morning.

That morning, he lay looking at his new bride with wonder and unbounded delight. There were tears in her eyes, because it had been painful for her at first. But the love in them made him smile.

"It won't be like that again," he assured her.

"I know." She looked at him blatantly, with pride in his fit, muscular body, in his manhood. She lifted her eyes back up. "I was afraid…"

He traced her mouth, his eyes solemn. "It will be easier the next time," he said tenderly. "It will get better every time we love each other."

"I know. I'm not afraid anymore." She touched his hard mouth and smiled. "You were apprehensive, too, weren't you?"

"At first," he had to admit.

"I thought you were never going to start," she said on a sigh. "I know why you took so long, so that I'd be ready when it happened, but I wondered if you were planning on a night of torture."

He chuckled. "You weren't the only one who suffered." He kissed her tenderly. "It hurt me, to have to hurt you, did you know? I wanted to stop, but it was too late. I was in over my head before I knew it. I couldn't even slow down."

"Oh, I never noticed," she told him, delighted. "You made me crazy."

"That goes double for me."

"I thought I knew everything," she mused. "I'm a doctor, after all. But theory and practice are very different."

"Yes. Later, when you're in fine form again, I'll show you some more ways to put theory into practice," he drawled.

She laughed and pummeled him.

They were early for Jane's get-together, and the way they clung to each other would have been more than enough to prove that they were in love, without the matching Victorian wedding bands they'd chosen.

"You look like two halves of a whole," Jane said, looking from Lou's radiant face to Copper's.

"We know," he said ruefully. "They rode us high at the hospital when we made rounds earlier."

"Rounds!" Todd exclaimed. "On your honeymoon?"

"We're doctors," Lou reminded him, grinning. "It goes with the job description. I'll probably be trying to examine patients on the way into the delivery room eventually."

Jane clung to her husband's hand and sighed. "I can't wait for that to happen. Cherry's over the moon, too. She'll be such a good older sister. She works so hard at school. She's studying to be a surgeon, you know," she added.

"I wouldn't know," Copper muttered, "having already had four letters from her begging for an hour of my time to go over what she needs to study most during her last few years in school."

Jane chuckled. "That's my fault. I encouraged her to talk to you."

"It's all right," he said, cuddling Lou closer. "I'll make time for her."

"I see that everything finally worked out for you two," Todd said a little sheepishly. "Sorry about the last time we met."

"Oh, you weren't the only wild-eyed lunatic around, Mr. Burke," Lou said reminiscently. "I did my share of conclusion jumping and very nearly ruined my life because of it." She looked up at Coltrain adoringly. "I'm glad doctors are persistent."

"Yes." Coltrain chuckled. "So am I. There were times when I despaired. But Lionel saved us."

They frowned. "What?"

"Electric trains," Coltrain replied. "Don't you people know anything?"

"Not about trains. Those are kids' toys, for God's sake," Burke said.

"No, they are not," Lou said. "They're adult toys. People buy them for their children so they'll have an excuse to play with them. Not having children, we have no excuses."

"That's why we want to start a family right away," Coltrain said with a wicked glance at Lou. "So that we have excuses. You should see her layout," he added admiringly. "My God, it's bigger than mine!"

Todd and Jane tried not to look at each other, failed and burst into outrageous laughter.

Coltrain glared at them. "Obviously," he told his new wife, "some people have no class, no breeding and no respect for the institution of marriage."

"What are you two laughing at?" Drew asked curiously, having returned to town just in time for the party, if not the wedding.

Jane bit her lower lip before she spoke. "Hers is bigger than his." She choked.

"Oh, for God's sake, come and dance!" Coltrain told

Lou, shaking his head as he dragged her away. The others, behind them, were still howling.

Coltrain pulled Lou close and smiled against her hair as they moved to the slow beat of the music. There was a live band. Jane had pulled out all the stops, even if it wasn't going to be a goodbye party.

"Nice band," Dana remarked from beside them. "Congratulations, by the way," she added.

"Thanks," they echoed.

"Nickie didn't come," she added, tongue-in-cheek. "I believe she's just accepted a job in a Victoria hospital as a nurse trainee."

"Good for her," Coltrain said.

Dana chuckled. "Sure. See you."

She wandered away toward one of the hospital staff.

"She's a good loser, at least," Lou said drowsily.

"I wouldn't have been," he mused.

"You've got a new partner coming," she remembered suddenly, having overlooked it in the frantic pace of the past few days.

"Actually," he replied, "I don't know any doctors from Johns Hopkins who would want to come to Jacobsville to practice in a small partnership. The minute I do, of course, I'll hire him on the...oof!"

She'd stepped on his toe, hard.

"Well, I had to say something," he replied, wincing as he stood on his foot. "You were holding all the aces. A man has his pride."

"You could have said you loved me," she said pointedly.

"I did. I do." He smiled slowly. "In a few hours, I'll take you home and prove it and prove it and prove it."

She flushed and pressed closer into his arms. "What a delicious idea."

"I thought so, too. Dance. At least while we're dancing I can hold you in public."

"So you can!"

Drew waltzed by with a partner. "Why don't you two go home?" he asked.

They laughed. "Time enough for private celebrations."

"I hope you have enough champagne," Drew said dryly, and danced on.

As IT HAPPENED, they had a magnum of champagne between them before Coltrain coaxed his wife back into bed and made up for her first time in ways that left her gasping and trembling in the aftermath.

"That," she gasped, "wasn't in any medical book I ever read!"

"Darlin', you've been reading the wrong books," he whispered, biting her lower lip softly. "And don't go to sleep. I haven't finished yet."

"What?"

He laughed at her expression. "Did you think that was *all?*"

Her eyes widened as he moved over her and slid between her long legs. "But, it hasn't been five minutes, you can't, you *can't...!*"

He not only could. He did.

Two MONTHS LATER, on Valentine Day, Copper Coltrain gave his bride of six weeks a ruby necklace in the shape of a heart. She gave him the results of the test she'd had the day before. He told her later that the "valentine" she'd given him was the best one he'd ever had.

Nine months later, Lou's little valentine was delivered in Jacobsville's hospital; and he was christened Joshua Jebediah Coltrain.

* * * * *

Cort Grier was disillusioned with life. He owned a huge
Santa Gertrudis breeding stud ranch in West Texas. He
was thirty-three now, in his prime, and he wanted to have
a family. His father had remarried and moved to Vermont.
His brothers, except for the youngest, were all married with
families. He wanted one of his own. But every woman he
thought might be the one turned out to be after his money.
The last one, a singer, had laughed when he mentioned
children. She was in her prime, she told him, and she had a
career as a rising star. No way was she giving that up to live
on some smelly ranch in Texas and start having babies. She
wasn't certain that she was ever going to want a child.

And so it went. Women had been a permissible pleasure
for many years, and while he was no playboy, he'd had his
share of beautiful, cultured lovers. The problem was that
after a time, they all looked alike, felt alike, sounded alike.
Perhaps he was jaded. Certainly, age hadn't done much for
his basically cynical nature. He found more pleasure these
days in running the cattle ranch than he did in squiring
debutantes around El Paso.

The ranch was a bone of contention with prospective
brides. Every one of them seemed enthused about his vast

herds of Santa Gertrudis cattle, until they actually saw the ranch and realized that cattle were dusty and smelly. In fact, so were the cowboys who worked with them. One date had actually passed out when she watched one of the hands help pull a calf.

None of his dates had liked the idea of living so far from the city, especially around smelly cattle and hay and the noise of ranch equipment. Park Avenue in New York would have suited them very well. Perhaps a few diamonds from Tiffany's and an ensemble from one of the designers who showed their wares during Fashion Week. But cattle? No, they said. Never.

Cort had never liked the girl-next-door sort of woman. In fact, there'd been no girls next door when he was younger. Most of the ranchers around where he lived had sons. Lots of sons. Not one female in the bunch.

The point was, he reminded himself, that the kind of woman who'd like ranch living would most likely be a woman who'd grown up on a ranch. Someone who liked the outdoors and animals and didn't mind the drawbacks. He probably shouldn't have been looking for a bride in the high-rent districts of big cities. He should have been looking closer to home. If there had been anyone closer to home to look at.

He'd had a brief encounter with a pretty young woman in Georgia during a visit with Connor Sinclair, a multimillionaire who had a lake house there. The woman's name had been Emma, and her zany sense of humor had interested him at once. It was one of the few times he'd been paying attention to what a woman said instead of how she looked. Emma was Connor's personal assistant, but there was more than business there or he missed his guess. Connor had separated Cort from Emma with surgical precision and made sure there were no more opportunities for him to get to know her.

Not too many months later, he heard from his brother Cash Grier, who was a police chief in East Texas, that Connor had married Emma and they had a son. He'd actually thought about going back to northern Georgia and courting her, despite her testy boss. That was no longer possible. He balanced Emma against the girls with diamonds in their eyes and greedy hands who'd filed through his life. He'd felt suddenly empty. Alone. The ranch had always been the core of his existence, but it was no longer enough. He was in a rut. He needed to get out.

So Cort had decided that he needed a holiday. He'd called a fourth cousin in Catelow, Wyoming—Bart Riddle—and invited himself to help work around the ranch incognito. He explained the situation to his cousin, who told him to come on up. If he wanted to ruin his health digging post holes and chasing cattle, welcome.

He also had another cousin in Carne County, Wyoming— Cody Banks, who was the local sheriff—but Banks lived in town and didn't own a ranch. Cort wanted to get his hands busy. But he had plans to visit with Cody while he was in town.

Bart met him at the airport, an amused smile in his dark eyes as they shook hands. "You own one of the biggest ranches in Texas and you want to come up here and be a cowboy?" Bart asked.

"It's like this," Cort explained on the way out of the airport. "I'm tired of being a walking, talking dollar sign to women."

Don't miss
Wyoming Heart *by Diana Palmer,*
available November 2019 wherever
Harlequin® books and ebooks are sold.

Harlequin.com